CYNTHIA HAS A SECRET

CYNTHIA HAS A SECRET

P.D. WORKMAN

ISBN: 9781988390000 (IS Hardcover)

ISBN: 9781926500348 (IS Paperback)

ISBN: 9781926500164 (KDP Paperback)

ISBN: 9781926500171 (Kindle)

ISBN: 9781926500188 (ePub)

pdworkman

YOUNG ADULT FICTION:

Between the Cracks:

Ruby

June and Justin

Michelle

Chloe

Ronnie

June, Into the Light

Tamara's Teardrops:

Tattooed Teardrops

Two Teardrops

Tortured Teardrops

Vanishing Teardrops

Medical Kidnap Files:

Mito

EDS

Proxy

Toxo

Pain

Breaking the Pattern:

Deviation

Diversion

By-Pass

Stand Alone YA novels

Stand Alone

Don't Forget Steven

Those Who Believe

Cynthia has a Secret

Questing for a Dream

Darkness before the Dream (prequel story)

Once Brothers

Intersexion

Making Her Mark

Endless Change

Gem, Himself, Alone

MYSTERY/SUSPENSE:

Parks Pat Mysteries

Out with the Sunset

Long Climb to the Top

Dark Water Under the Bridge

Immersed in the View (Coming Soon)

Skimming Over the Lake (Coming Soon)

Hazard of the Hills (Coming Soon)

Stand Alone Suspense Novels

Looking Over Your Shoulder

Lion Within

Pursued by the Past

In the Tick of Time

Loose the Dogs

AND MORE AT PDWORKMAN.COM

To those with secrets of their own.

ONE

Carmina could see the flashing lights before she got up to their property. She could tell they were close, and was curious as to what the neighbors had been doing that the police were there. Julius, her dad, was always suspicious of what their neighbors were up to, so it came as no surprise to Carmina that they were in trouble.

But as she got closer, she realized the emergency vehicles were not, in fact, in the neighbor's long driveway. They were at hers. She slowed her walk, and then stopped.

Her first thought was that someone was hurt. Maybe her mother had slipped on the stairs or cut herself. She always overreacted when she got hurt, and thought she needed stitches or a cast or something. But the flashing lights were not an ambulance, they were police cars. Not just regular police cars. They were unmarked black cars. Feds.

Carmina hid behind one of the big trees, and watched, acid burning in her stomach and chest. Black-suited men went in and out of the house. Two of them came out with her father between them, his hands cuffed behind his back. They put him in one of the waiting black cars. Then a few minutes later, a couple more came out with her mother. Esther Knight's long, blond hair blew back slightly in the breeze. Even at a distance, Carmina couldn't help but admire and envy her mother's beauty. Her own hair was quite dark. Her skin was darker and her facial features rounder and not so finely shaped. Esther always looked impeccably groomed, her make-up perfect, her hair shining, even when she was painting first thing in the morning, trying to catch the early morning light.

Esther was upset. She was trying to pull away from the two agents holding onto her. Esther hated people in her personal space. She didn't like her routine to be broken. Carmina swallowed, wishing she could just brush off the feeling of dread. Sometimes she awoke early in the morning with an inexplicable feeling of impending doom, and she would tell herself how silly she was being. She had no reason to be worried. Carmina had a good life, and nothing horrible was going to happen to her. But this time, watching her parents being escorted out of their home into the waiting vehicles, she couldn't think of what to tell herself.

Maybe it was all a mistake. Maybe it was just some kind of clerical error. Or mistaken identity. Her father had often warned her how easy it was for someone to steal your identity, to do things in your name and mess up your credit and your reputation. That had to be what had happened. It was either a mistake or someone had stolen her parents' identities. They would take Julius and Esther Knight down to the police station, or whatever building these agents worked out of, and they would sit down and talk, and they would figure out that this was all just a mistake. It was all a big mistake.

A wave of dizziness passed over Carmina, and she turned away from the scene for a moment, leaning her back against the tree and closing her eyes. She took a deep breath. Calm. She had to stay calm. Think. What would her father tell her to do? They had handcuffed him and put him in a car, caged him. He couldn't explain it to her this time, couldn't tell her what to do. She had to think about all he had taught her and figure it out herself.

She looked back around the tree toward the house. With both of her parents in separate cars, the feds were apparently wasting no time moving the process along. With at least half a dozen agents still in the house, the two cars pulled away from the house and headed back down the long, winding driveway toward Carmina. She stayed hidden behind the tree the best she could and watched them go past her. She knew she should not peek out to watch them drive by. But she had to see. She had to know everything she could about what was happening to her family.

The black car with Esther in it drove by first. The red and blue lights were flashing. There was one agent driving and another in the passenger seat. Esther's head was bowed. Carmina wasn't close enough to see tears, but she was sure they were there. Running down Esther's beautiful face. They wouldn't smudge her waterproof make-up. That would stay perfect, like always. Esther didn't look out the window. Didn't see her daughter hiding behind the tree, wondering what was going on and what she should do.

The car with Julius in it followed close behind. His head was not bowed like her mother's but up, swiveling this way and that, taking everything in, his dark eyes glaring out from underneath bushy black brows, collecting a hundred bits of information about his environment in case there was somehow the opportunity for escape. Julius' head stopped moving momentarily as the car drove past the tree. He didn't make any sign he had seen her, adding this new piece of information to everything else. He did nothing that would attract the agents' attention to Carmina. Didn't try to mouth a message or make any kind of gesture to her. He just watched her for the few seconds the car took to pass by the tree, then his head started to swivel again.

Carmina waited until the cars had pulled out of the long lane, through the tall gates, disappearing out of her sight onto the residential street. She looked toward the house to make sure no one would see her, and then started to work her way back down the driveway the way she had come, this time sticking close to the trees, hiding behind them or in their shadows. She knew what she had to do. Knew what her father would say to her. He wouldn't want her sticking around to get arrested herself. He wouldn't want her to be in danger. She had to disappear before they started looking for her. They might already be on her trail.

NEIL CROWTHER STOPPED outside the house to look down the long driveway to make sure Julius and Esther Knight were out of the way. He wouldn't be the one doing the initial interrogations, he had to stay around the house and supervise the search and seizure of anything incriminating. He had to make sure everything was done by the book and that the chain of evidence was preserved and it could all be used in court when the time came.

The foliage around the lane was lush and thick. It was a beautiful place. There were few people who would turn down living in a mansion like Knight House. It was luxurious and impeccably cared for. It was Neil's job to discover all of its secrets. Judging by all of the work that had gone into the investigation up until now, Neil suspected it would be a long process. There were lots of secrets in Knight House.

Other agents had started the process of boxing up Julius' office files, and were loading them into the trunks of the waiting vehicles. Neil had ordered a van as well, after taking a look at the man's office. They weren't just talking about a few file drawers on a desk. Julius had several banks of lateral files, all carefully catalogued and labelled. It was going to take weeks of work to go through them all.

They would need a second van just for Esther's canvases. The Knights didn't store all of them at Knight House; most of them would be at the galleries. But there were still plenty of them in her studio. Neil recognized copies of some of the more famous paintings, but most of them were too obscure for him to know. He was no art major. For the more part, the best he could do was discern which of the paintings were Esther Knight originals, and which were copies of someone else's work. Esther's original work was light and airy, lots of soft colors, wind and water, fantastic beasts, and elves with her daughter's features. Her copies ran the full gamut of art history. She seemed equally able to reproduce a renaissance piece, a surrealist, and a modern work. It would take an expert to tell the reproductions from the originals, and Neil was not an art expert.

Mike put down a stack of boxes and wiped his forehead with the back of his arm. "What about the girl's room?"

"Huh? Oh, yeah. Well, run through it carefully, but be respectful. Leave things where they are, unless something is obviously suspicious."

"Her computer?"

"Better take that."

"There's artwork in her room too."

"Take it. Make sure it's labeled as coming from her room rather than the studio."

Mike nodded. "Okay. Is someone going to go over to the school to pick her up?"

Neil looked at his watch. "Mandy. But she doesn't get out until three-thirty, so we've still got a few hours."

"Poor kid. This is going to devastate her."

Neil felt a pang of guilt. But they couldn't let criminals operate just because they had kids. It wasn't Neil's fault the Knight family was being ripped apart. That was the parents' fault. Their choices had led to this. At least he didn't have to rip screaming toddlers from their mother's arms. The teen was old enough to understand what was going on. Old enough she would only have a few years in foster care or with relatives before she could get out on her own.

"She'll be all right," he told Mike. "Kids are tougher than you think."

Mike shrugged and nodded, heading back into the house to continue with the work of removing all of the evidence. Neil waited until Mike was inside again before popping a Pepto pill in his mouth, chewing it well before swallowing, and waiting for it to take effect.

ONCE CARMINA WAS AWAY from the house, she stopped to sort things out. She was on her own. She couldn't rely on anyone else, she was going to have to get along on her own. All those times she had secretly thought her parents were smothering her, and she just wanted some freedom and independence? Well, that time had come. And now she wasn't so sure she was ready for it.

She sat down on a big rock, under a tree with a wide, green, rustling canopy. There was a little stream at her feet. Just deep enough to hide a few fish or to get her shorts wet if she decided to wade through it. If she'd been wearing shorts. Carmina unzipped her backpack, and slowly reviewed the contents.

Schoolbooks were out. She wasn't going to need those anymore. Although the text on graphic design… she still kind of wanted to hold onto that one. Carmina opened it up. Her name was neatly inked in her mother's manuscript printing on the first page. Carmina tore it out. She figured if she ripped it off quickly, like a bandaid, it wouldn't hurt so much. She hated to deface a book. And that one was a particular favorite. But she couldn't keep anything that would identify her. She put the discarded books and page in a neat pile at her feet.

Her lunch was still in her bag. She had felt sick at lunchtime. That was one less meal to worry about scrounging now that she was on her own. She set it to the side. Pushing around other items, she dug to the bottom of her bag to pull out her emergency kit.

Julius had always insisted they keep emergency kits with them at all times. In the car, in Carmina's school backpack, in Esther's purse. Julius had small kits that fit in his suit pockets. Carmina clutched it to her, hearing his often-repeated words.

You never know when and where you will be when an emergency happens. That's why you have to be prepared. Always.

She slowly unzipped the top of the little daypack. Nothing fell or sprang out. Everything was neatly arranged. Silver space-age blanket to capture body heat. Granola bars, gum, and bouillon cubes. Rope, string, and a multi-tool. Safety pins. A minuscule first aid kit. She didn't take anything out, not wanting to risk losing anything or not being able to fit it all back in properly. She zipped it back up and put it back in her backpack. There was another package right at the bottom of the backpack. Carmina pulled out the money belt. Taking a quick look around to make sure she was still alone and unobserved, she pulled up her shirt and buckled it on, pressing it to lay flat and snugging it into place. She didn't open it to see how much cash was there.

Her wallet contained her social, which she had never been able to memorize, her learner's license, her school ID, and her credit card. It would have to go as well. She re-opened the emergency kit to remove the multi-tool, and opened it into a big pair of sturdy scissors. She cut the cards into small pieces and buried them and the wallet under a nearby log.

Carmina looked at her phone for a long moment. If only she could call someone and tell them what was going on. But she couldn't involve anyone else. Couldn't trust anyone else. And who did she really have that she would tell anyway? It wasn't like she was popular or even had a best buddy. Her best friend was her mother, and since Esther was so reclusive, they didn't have a larger circle of friends who went out together for movies or tea or shopping. It was just Carmina and Esther. And Julius. And Esther and Julius couldn't communicate with her now.

Carmina tossed the phone into the stream. It made a little sploosh sound, and disappeared.

Now she was really on her own.

NEIL LOOKED AT HIS WATCH. They were on their fourth van, and there was no sign they were going to be finished clearing out Julius Knight's file drawers any time soon. His boss, Mandy Foss, a diminutive, tough-as-nails black woman, was getting out of her car and coming up to the mansion, and she would be looking for some kind of ETA until they would be finished with the house.

"We're working as fast as we can," Neil said, getting to his feet.

He had only been sitting down on the grand stairway leading to the front door for a minute. The rest of the day he had been on his feet, and he was really feeling it. He eased his legs and feet stiffly.

"I'm not here to hurry you along," Mandy assured him. "It's more important to be thorough and get it done right, than to be fast. Let's get all we can."

Neil nodded his agreement. "Right. So… what's up?"

She didn't need to be checking up on him in the middle of an investigation. They had planned everything out properly, and she knew all of what was going on without coming into the middle of it personally.

Mandy looked at him. She swept one hand through her corn-rows, and pursed her full lips. She looked tired around the eyes. Like maybe she'd been up all night before the bust, going through the files and making sure everything was in order.

"We have a problem."

Neil's heart sped up immediately, and he had to remind himself that 'a problem' when you were on reduced duties was not the same as a problem when you were out in the field chasing down the bad guys. Taking down white-collar criminals like Julius and Esther Knight did not generally involve gunplay or high-speed chases. It was the first time Neil had even been out of the bull pen in weeks.

"What is it?" he asked.

"It's the girl."

Neil tried to recall what details he knew about Julius and Esther's daughter, who had only been incidental to the investigation. "Carmen?"

"Carmina," Mandy corrected.

"Carmina. What's the problem? I thought you were going to pick her up from the school."

"That's the problem. She's not there."

Neil frowned at her. "Where is she? Truant?"

"Apparently, she wasn't feeling well, and left the school early this afternoon."

Neil looked at the government vehicles intruding in the driveway in front of the mansion. He looked down the long lane leading up to the house. At the still-wild woods alongside the road. He started to work through possibilities in his mind.

"She might be skipping, out with friends."

"The school doesn't think so."

"Of course they don't, that would suggest a problem with their attendance monitoring. Why don't they think so?"

"Apparently she doesn't really have a group of friends she hangs out with. I'll leave you to follow up with them on details. But in the meantime… she's not there, and she's not here."

"We'd better get a missing persons alert out."

"I agree."

Neil looked down the driveway again, and sighed. "I think I'd better pull the guys off of clearing out files, and start a search. She's probably just out with a friend, but if she came here and saw intruders… she might be scared."

Mandy agreed. "The files will wait. We don't want a kid out there alone once it starts to get dark."

TWO

Leaving the other agents to search the grounds of Knight House and the nearby neighborhood, Neil looked up the details of the school and headed over.

Carmina's private school was conveniently close. Although she normally took a bus to and from school, it was close enough to walk, if you didn't mind a little effort. His stomach tight and slightly nauseated, Neil walked through the echoing, empty hallways to the school office and showed his badge.

"Agent Neil Crowther. I'm here to see Principal Norton."

The receptionist's eyes were big. She nodded agreement. "I'll get her for you right away!"

Neil looked at the 'principal' name plate on the nearby door, remembering the mnemonic he'd learned when he was in school, to help remember that the principal of the school was -pal and not -ple. The principal is your pal. He wondered if there was any pupil who had ever considered the school principal as his pal. Neil certainly hadn't, and he'd been a pretty good student. Not a trouble-maker. But still troubled.

"Agent Crowther. Come on in."

The principal was pretty, quite a bit shorter than Neil, maybe part Hispanic or Indian, with a natural tan that made her glow. She was dressed in a conservative blazer and skirt, but it ended up looking trendy on her.

Like she was a model. She led him into her office and motioned to the chair.

"I'm Augusta Norton. Please have a seat."

"Thanks." Neil sat down, and flexed his feet, trying to loosen up the stiff muscles and tendons. He rubbed his knees, and looked at Principal Norton.

"So, tell me what you know about Carmina," Neil suggested. "When she left, where she might have gone, who she might hang out with?"

"She left shortly after lunch. She said she wasn't feeling very well and needed to go home."

"And a student doesn't need any permission or supervision, they can just take off?"

"Well… yes… it's not a prison, Mr. Crowther. Kids do come and go. Sometimes they have appointments, or a spare period, or… they aren't feeling well."

"But she did tell someone she wasn't feeling well and was going home?"

"Yes. Carmina is good about letting us know if she is going home. Some kids just leave, but she checks in with the nurse or the office before she leaves."

Neil made note of this in his notepad and looked back at the principal. He didn't say anything at first. Silence was often more important than questions in getting information from people. The principal looked uncomfortable. Guilty.

She sighed deeply. "I don't like to speak unkindly of Carmina. She's a lovely girl…"

Neil nodded. "Yes…?"

"She often goes home with… stomach problems… but we really couldn't challenge her on it, suggest she might be malingering just a little… her parents said she had some medical problems, and if she said she wasn't feeling well, she should be allowed to go home."

Neil nodded, and tipped his chair back slightly onto two legs. "And you think maybe she was taking advantage of it a little?"

"I've seen that girl eat, Mr. Crowther. There's nothing wrong with her stomach. And there were never any notes from doctors or even from home saying she'd been unwell. I think…" Principal Norton tapped her pen on the table in front of her. "I think she might have been just a little bit spoiled. Only child, wealthy parents, they imagine the worst whenever she overeats or has a bit of a bug…" She shrugged expressively. "Like I said… I don't like to say anything negative about Carmina. I think she's a good girl. She has never been any trouble. I just think… well…"

"That she might be a bit spoiled," Neil summed up.

"Yes. It's not a huge character flaw or anything. Just… she's very close to her mom."

Neil nodded, writing a few more words in his notepad. "Thank you for filling me in on that. So she left a little after lunch. Not feeling well."

"So she said," Principal Norton inserted.

"So she said," Neil repeated, frowning. "And she was given permission to go home."

"Of course."

"Did anyone offer to drive her?"

"Well… no. We don't do that. That would attract liability…"

"But letting her walk home when she's sick, no liability there."

The principal looked as if she'd never thought of that before. She frowned. "If she was really sick, she could have stayed in the nurse's office. She was well enough to walk home, just like always."

"But you don't know if there might have been something more wrong this time. She could have collapsed on the way home… gotten disoriented… anything, really."

"Well… I suppose," Norton clearly didn't like this idea. "I told you, though, she went home by herself because she was sick all the time. It wasn't anything new. Why would she collapse?"

"I don't know. But she didn't make it home, did she?"

The principal sat there, frowning.

"You don't think she could be off with a friend?" Neil asked.

"No," Norton said flatly. She shook her head. "She's not with a friend."

Neil waited again, letting the silence draw out. He flexed his foot and pressed on the heels, wishing he could take his shoes off and stretch and massage them properly.

"Carmina's a bit of an odd ball. She doesn't share many interests with other students. She keeps to herself. Maybe if her parents got her into some after-school activities, clubs… she doesn't have anyone she really hangs around with. And no one else was conspicuously absent this afternoon."

"That you noticed."

"We do take attendance every class. I don't see anyone who was absent the last class or two that Carmina would have anything to do with. No one in her social group."

"Maybe she has a boyfriend…?"

"Carmina? Oh, no! I've never seen her so much as look at a boy, much less hold hands or talk in the hallway with one. She's not… that mature yet."

"Her friends may tell a different story."

The principal gave a little shrug.

"Is there anything else we should know?" Neil asked. "What do you think happened?"

"I don't know… I hope she didn't get hurt, or kidnapped or something. She's such a nice girl. Her father is very wealthy. Maybe she just… I don't know… changed her mind and decided to go to the zoo or something."

"The zoo. Well, I hope it was nothing serious, and she'll show up at home any minute now. But I am concerned."

Norton nodded. "Can I ask… how you are involved…? It doesn't seem like a child being truant from school for an afternoon… it doesn't really warrant a missing persons report. Yet."

Neil didn't enlighten her. The news was bound to break by the morning papers, but he wouldn't be the one to spread any details around. He especially didn't want Carmina to hear what was going on through the grapevine and run away.

"Thank you for your help, Ms. Norton. I'll leave my card with you, in case anything should occur to you, or you happen to hear something. And I'll need the names of any of Carmina's classmates who you think might be helpful…"

CARMINA CAME out of the woods on the other side, where there was a public park. She watched people jogging and riding bikes, walking dogs, playing games with their kids, and eating picnic lunches. It was a warm, sunny day and it seemed like everyone was out.

Carmina felt at loose ends. How was she supposed to live now? She felt hopeless and helpless. Her mother would normally be putting dinner on the table now, asking Carmina questions about how school was today. Talking about her latest challenges in her painting, what projects she was thinking of doing. Julius would sit and listen. Maybe pull out his notebook to jot down a reminder for himself. She'd asked him once what all of the codes in his notebook meant, but he just shook his head, his thin mouth going thinner and pointing down.

"Sometimes you need to keep records, write things down," he explained. "But you should never write it down in a way someone else can understand it."

Carmina stared down at his open notepad. She tried reading it backwards to see if it made sense that way. But it still looked like a cypher. Even her mother couldn't read it. Julius was the only one.

"I had graphic design this morning," Carmina whispered to herself, as if she was at the table, telling her mother about the day, like she should be. "Mr. Burpeau liked my project proposal. He says I should focus on social change. What do you think?"

Nobody could hear her whispering. She couldn't even hear it herself with the noise of the park around her. She didn't want someone thinking she was a crazy person, and trying to take her to the hospital or worse. But it was comforting, something to connect her back to her family. Being away from them made her feel invisible. Nonexistent.

What would her mother say? Social change wasn't something at the top of her to-do list. As far as Mr. Burpeau was concerned, social change was the highest and noblest calling. The reason you did anything. But for Esther, the highest and noblest calling was art. Art for its own sake. You didn't draw or paint or design to influence someone's course in life, their decisions. You painted to give them beauty, or balance, or color. For Esther, true art was always art, not a vehicle for social change or influence.

There was a big group in the park having a celebration. Maybe a birthday party. There were lots of kids and a few dogs. Adults frying up burgers and hot dogs on hibachis, there was cut watermelon and half a dozen different kinds of desserts.

Carmina hadn't felt well at lunchtime, but the savory smell of the hot dogs cooking was making her stomach rumble. She had enough food for at least two meals. She could eat her school lunch for supper, and she had granola bars and other food in her emergency kit. After that, she'd have to start buying or scrounging for food. Or, she could try to stretch the food she already had out yet further. Carmina passed by one of the picnic tables at the edge of the party. Some child had left a half-eaten hot dog behind while he went to play with the dogs or frisbees, or maybe to swing on the swings. Carmina took a quick glance around, and picked up the paper plate. She walked away, turning her back on the group, and ate the hot dog in three bites on the way to the garbage can, where she disposed of the plate. She wandered around the park, aiming to walk by the tables on the other side, and maybe swipe a slice of watermelon and a brownie for dessert.

"Hey!"

Carmina looked up quickly at a dark-haired woman who called out. She took a step backward, getting ready to run.

"Do you want some?" the woman questioned, with a smile and raised eyebrows. "There's lots here, if you're hungry."

Carmina looked at the spread, and back at the woman, suspicious. "I shouldn't…"

"Why not? It's here. Half of it is just going to end up in the garbage. If you're hungry, have some."

"I'm going home for supper," Carmina said. "My mom wouldn't like me to spoil my appetite."

"Oh. Well, whatever. Most teenagers I know could put away one supper and still go home and eat another."

She looked away from Carmina to put a few bits on a plate for a whining toddler. Carmina watched her, wondering if it was safe. She should take food while she had the opportunity, as long as they wouldn't report her or call the police. She didn't look like a homeless person or a con of some kind. Just a kid walking through the park. The woman had no way of knowing Carmina had lost her family and her home. She was just being nice.

"Help yourself," the woman said, giving her one more smile and raising an eyebrow in invitation.

Carmina decided she'd better take the chance while she could. It was likely the last time the woman was going to offer. "Um, okay. If you really don't mind."

"No, not at all. We've got way too much. You know how it is at these family reunions. Everybody brings something, or two, or three, and nobody wants to take it all home to put in their fridges. Or they have to drive a long way to get home. So it all just ends up going to waste."

Carmina grabbed a plate and started to load it up. "Well, that's very nice of you," she said.

Not that she knew anything about family reunions. Her family consisted of three people. She'd met her mother's parents once or twice, but they were distant, uninterested people, not like the grandmas and grandpas you saw on TV, if you watched that kind of thing. Her father's parents were dead. She didn't remember ever meeting them. The idea of all of these people belonging to just one family was mind-boggling.

"Thanks," she told the woman.

"Thank you, for helping us to get rid of some of it!"

Carmina walked briskly to the other side of the park, and she sat down on an unoccupied bench and scarfed the treats down, out of sight of the woman and her family reunion. Her stomach full and satisfied, she threw out the second plate, and walked on. Her chest burned a little, letting her know she'd filled her stomach too full. Esther would have gotten after her for eating so much so fast. But she had to eat while she could. That's what Julius would have said.

NEIL WALKED BACK to his desk to put down his paperwork and to kick off his shoes, which were driving him crazy. Agnes gave him a little wave and a smile, and he went over to her desk.

"Do you have a few minutes?"

"For you? Always," she smiled tentatively, and pulled her long brown hair back behind her head, forming a ponytail for a moment, and then letting it go to spill down her back. A few loose strands still fell around her face, refusing to be corralled.

"I've got a couple of school kids I need to come in to answer some questions. I don't have time to go to their houses, so I need their parents to bring them in here. Okay?"

Agnes pursed her lips and didn't look too excited by this. She preferred tracking people down by computer, stalking them online, and giving him all of the details to chase them down in person. Talking to them on the phone was very low on her list of preferred jobs.

"Sorry," Neil told her, shaking his head. "I really need you to talk to them. Get them in for me, okay?"

"Sure, boss," she agreed.

But her smile was gone as she looked at the names on the note and prepared to do as he had asked. Neil gave another little shrug, and headed down the hall to the elevators. The Knights were on the fourth floor, and it was time for him to get down to business and find out what he could from them.

Esther Knight was probably his best bet. He suspected from his investigation that Julius would be a hard nut to crack. Neil stood and looked at Esther through the observation mirror for a couple of minutes before going in. He always thought of 'Esther' as a name for a dark-haired woman. Black locks curled around her face. But Esther Knight was a beautiful blonde. Long, golden hair streamed around her face, falling into place every time she moved like it had been designed by a Hollywood director. It was darker toward the roots, but seemed to be natural, not bleached. She had a beautiful, finely featured face. But right now she was very upset. They had tried several different interrogators, but no one seemed to be able to connect with her to get any information out of her. She just continued to moan and put her face in her hands and beg them to let her go home.

Neil grimaced and went in to see her.

Esther looked at him as he entered, and was perhaps hopeful at seeing a face she hadn't already dealt with before. "Are you in charge?" she questioned. "Can you tell them to let me go home?"

"I'm afraid you're not going to be going home, Esther," Neil said as gently as he could, and he sat down across from her. "But right now, I need you to focus on your daughter."

"Carmina?" Esther looked puzzled. "Did you arrest her too? Where is she?"

"We didn't arrest her."

"Is she at home? She must be scared, being alone. Carmina never likes to be alone."

"Carmina didn't come home from school today."

Esther pulled her hands back from her face and drummed her fingers restlessly on the table.

"I missed the afternoon sun today," she said. "I can't get the Van Gough completed without the afternoon sun."

Neil stared at her. He waited for her to look at him again. She glanced at his face, and her eyes slid away.

"Carmina didn't come home from school," Neil repeated. "She never went home. Had she arranged to go to a friend's house or something? Do you know where she intended to go?"

"No," Esther shook her head. "Carmina always comes home. She doesn't go to friends' houses. She comes home, and after I'm done my afternoon project, I make some supper, and we talk." She drummed her fingers again and shook her head. "But I didn't get the afternoon light today."

Neil had thought at first that the third floor studio was pretentious; all of those big windows, looking out in every direction. It seemed like it was just show. But each window caught the best light at a different time of day, and there was a different project at each one, or several projects, and Esther rotated through them throughout the day.

"Mrs. Knight."

She rubbed her temples, not looking at him.

"Mrs. Knight, can you focus on me, here? This is important."

She looked at his face, frown lines above her nose.

"Carmina is missing. Can you think of where she might go, if she didn't go home?"

"No. She always goes home."

"Please think about it."

She didn't say anything. Neil waited. "You should ask Julius," Esther said finally.

"You don't have any idea where your daughter might have gone?"

"She will come home," Esther insisted.

"She didn't come home. She is missing. We need to find her."

"Do you think you could get me some paper?" Esther suggested. "And some pencils? I need to do something with my hands."

"We'll see," Neil said.

She grimaced, and covered her face with her hands again. "I can't focus on anything."

"If I give you something to draw with, can you tell me where Carmina might have gone?"

She started to rock back and forth slightly, moaning.

"Mrs. Knight?"

She didn't look at him again. Neil pushed himself away from the desk. He walked out of the interrogation room and made sure the door shut securely behind him. He went down the hall to Julius Knight's interrogation room. Judging by Julius' growled responses, Mandy was not getting very far with establishing a relationship. He opened the door and raised his brows at her. She stood up and walked out, pulling the door shut behind her and leaning against it.

"Nice to see you, Agent Crowther." She rubbed her forehead in a gesture of fatigue. "How are things progressing?"

"Not well, as far as getting Carmina back. I'd like to ask Julius some questions."

"He's not very cooperative."

"I'm hoping he'll be more cooperative where his daughter's safety is concerned."

She nodded. "Sure. Have at him. I'd really like to be able to say, at the end of the day, that the girl is safe."

"Right. Could you do me a favor while I'm talking to him?"

"What do you need?"

"Mrs. Knight needs paper and pencils."

Mandy frowned at him. "Is she going to sign a statement?"

"No… I'm still getting a feeling for her… but I think she can help us more with a pencil in her hand."

"Okay. As long as she promises not to use them as weapons."

Neil went into the interrogation room. Julius looked at him and scowled. His black, bushy brows drew closer together. "You were at my house this morning," he accused.

Neil nodded and sat down. "My name is Agent Neil Crowther."

Julius folded his arms across his chest. A signal he would not be cooperative.

"Mr. Knight, I'm not here to discuss the charges with you at this time. We have a more immediate problem."

"I don't care about your problem."

"I think you do. We're trying to find your daughter."

"You leave my daughter alone!"

It was not the reaction Neil has expected. He blinked. "I don't think you understand. Carmina did not come home from school today. We don't know where she is. Unless you know where she went, she could be in danger."

"*You* don't understand," Julius countered. "I don't want you anywhere near my daughter."

Neil studied Julius' eyes, trying to figure him out. He had never seen any parents respond the way Mr. and Mrs. Knight had to Carmina's disappearance. "Does that mean you know where Carmina is? Do you know if she's safe?"

Julius shook his head. "No, I don't know where she is. But she is a smart girl. She's okay."

"Well, let's keep her that way. Where do you think she would go? Do you think she's running scared or that she's somewhere with a friend?"

The man just glared at him and said nothing.

"Your wife says she doesn't think Carmina would be with a friend. The school seems to think the same."

"She doesn't go out with friends."

"So your daughter is on the run, out there all by herself, and you don't care? We need to get to her. Keep her safe."

Julius set his jaw. "I think we're done here. You can just stay away from my daughter. Leave her alone."

Neil shook his head in disbelief. But sensing Julius had no intention of continuing this line of discussion, he abandoned the attempt and switched direction.

"Tell me about your wife," he suggested. "She seems… a little anxious. Is she on any kind of medication…?"

Julius considered this new question. He had big bags under his eyes, which made it look like he hadn't slept for a long time. He looked as if he was chronically short of sleep and on edge. "Esther is an artist," he said. "Artists are often… eccentric. Unconventional."

Neil nodded encouragingly.

"She's an artist," Julius repeated, with a heavy shrug.

"Is she on any medication? Under a doctor's care?"

The question only needed a simple yes or no, but Julius apparently needed to think about it. Eventually, he shook his head. "No, she is not."

Neil studied Julius, evaluating him, trying to get inside of his head. He knew a lot about the man as a result of his months-long investigation, but he still had difficulty figuring out what made Julius Knight tick. By all indications, he was a brilliant businessman, but as far as understanding his personality, he was almost as hard to pin down as his reclusive wife.

Julius stared back at him with hard eyes. Maybe he was evaluating Neil as well; this enemy who had remained unseen over the past few months, uncovering his secrets, stalking him from the shadows.

"I get the feeling you're a little unconventional yourself," Neil said.

Julius gave him a grim smile that reminded Neil of a shark.

WHEN NEIL LEFT the interrogation room, Mandy met him in the hall. She shook her head, sending her corn-rows bouncing. "Unconventional is right," she agreed. "Both of them."

Neil had to agree. "They're certainly challenging all of my faculties."

"Have you heard what your crew has turned up at the mansion since you left?"

Neil raised his brows. "Did they find the girl?"

"No. And we've got another team on that search, so your guys are back to clearing out the evidence."

"Okay. So what did they find?"

"They have finished loading the files. So they started a more intensive search of the rest of the house, checking for safes or other hiding places."

"They found one?"

She raised her eyebrows and shook her head. "The whole house is honeycombed with hiding places! They've turned up safes, a couple of panic rooms, hoarded food supplies and survivalist gear… this guy is a real nut. Conspiracy theories, the whole nine yards."

Neil let that sink in for a moment. It gradually began to make sense. The coded files. The lack of public information about Julius. The lack of social structure around Esther and Carmina. Julius thought there was a conspiracy against him. He was protecting them all.

"I'm going to have to think about that," he told Mandy. "This is getting complicated."

"Welcome to my world."

"And no progress at all on the search for the girl?"

"Not yet. We're going to have to call it off for the night. You miss things in the dark."

"Yeah. I just hope… there was an escape plan. That they had arranged for her to go to someone if something ever happened to them. Even though it may be harder to track her down if she had someone she could rely on for help… I just hope she's safe, and not all by herself out there."

"Mom's not any help?"

"I'll try again. Did she get some pencils?"

Mandy nodded. "She's drawing away."

Neil took a step toward the other interrogation room, and Mandy put a restraining hand on his arm. He stopped and looked at her. "You're pretty sure Carmina has run? You don't think there was an accident, or a kidnapping…?"

"Looking at the timeline… if she left the school when they say she did, then she probably walked right into the operation at the house. And if she buys into daddy's conspiracy theories, even a little, she's not going to wait around and ask questions."

"No, you're right. And for a kidnapping to just happen to happen to her on the way home, it's too much of a coincidence. It's far more likely she ran."

Neil agreed.

"Okay. Good luck with Mom."

Neil took a deep breath before going back into Esther's interrogation room. He could see through the narrow window that she was bent over the papers she had been provided with, deep in concentration. He walked in and looked down at the drawing she was working on.

In the short time since she had been given drawing materials, she had sketched a likeness of Carmina. A bit younger than real life, perhaps. With fairy ears and a jeweled tiara. Neil stood looking over Esther's shoulder. In the picture, Carmina was in a forest, enveloped in the lush leaves of the trees and flowers. There were other animals hiding in the foliage. A deer. A chipmunk. And in the corner, a lean, dark wolf.

"Did you know you're not wearing any shoes?" Esther questioned, without looking up.

"Uh, no. I'm not. How did you know? You didn't even look."

"Everybody else clatters when they walk."

"Well, I hope I didn't startle you, coming in too quietly."

She glanced up at him briefly. "You didn't."

Her face was much more relaxed now. Art was definitely her drug of choice. Neil sat down at the table, looking at the picture. "That's Carmina?"

"Yes."

"Does Carmina like the woods?"

"She's a wood elf. Of course she does."

"But I mean in real life. When she's a girl, not an elf."

"Well…" Esther trailed off. "She likes me to draw her in the woods."

"She doesn't actually like being in the woods in real life?"

"Yes… but she has school, and her projects. She doesn't spend a lot of time outside."

"Sure. That's how kids are these days, isn't it? Too much screen time. Does she have a favorite place to go in the woods, when she gets out? Does she have a tree house on the estate, or a favorite duck pond in the park, or something?"

"I don't know. I don't go out a lot."

Neil watched her darken the shading on the wolf.

"Did you tell me she's missing?" Esther questioned, looking up from her drawing again, her eyebrows squeezing toward each other.

"Yes. And it's dark out. We need to find her to keep her safe."

She went back to shading the wolf.

"Is the wolf dangerous?" Neil asked.

"Oh, yes."

"We don't know what kind of dangers Carmina might be facing out there for real. We need to know where to find her."

"Julius didn't know?" It was finally starting to sound like a real conversation.

"No. He said not. But he doesn't know her like you do, does he?"

Esther stopped for a moment, then started to touch up the jewels in elf Carmina's tiara. "I always wanted a little girl. Carmina was a dream come true."

"I bet you do a lot of things with her."

"She's taking design in school."

"Do you draw together?"

"Of course. I've taught her since she was very small, coloring with crayons."

"What does she like to draw?"

"She's good at faces. Capturing a likeness. She doesn't do much fantasy. She does things that are more… commercial."

"You capture a good likeness too," Neil said, looking at the elf.

Esther cocked her head, looking at it critically. "It's technically perfect. But it doesn't have as much… emotional appeal."

"You said Carmina does work that is more commercial. Does that mean she is selling her work?"

He watched Esther painstakingly add individual leaves and blades of grass.

"Ad copy, freelance work on spec, community murals. Very… commercial."

"I take it you don't approve. But don't you sell your work? Don't your *copies* bring in quite a bit of money?"

"Julius takes care of that," Esther said, waving her free hand. "But they are not to sell something else. They are for people who enjoy great works of art, who want them in their own home."

"Oh, I see. Advertisements sell a product that is not the art. The art is just the medium."

She lifted her head and looked at him, raising one eyebrow. "Yes," she agreed.

Neil watched her drawing, pondering over what he knew about the family so far. "Do you have any friends or family Carmina might go to for help?"

"I have parents, but she wouldn't go there. She wouldn't go to anyone for help. Julius says…" She trailed off. She shaded the area around the wolf, making it look as though it was exuding darkness.

"What does Julius say?" Neil asked finally, breaking the silence.

She shook her head.

"What would he tell Carmina to do, if he was with her now? He wouldn't tell her to go to someone?"

"No."

"What would he tell her?"

"You should go ask him."

"Would he tell her to go to a certain place? Would he make a plan to meet her in a safe place?"

"No. I don't think so."

"How would he keep her safe, then? He loves Carmina, doesn't he? How would he keep her safe from harm?"

She didn't answer and didn't look at him. Neil touched the wolf in appeal. "You can see the danger she's in. How are we going to help her?"

"Don't touch the paper!" Esther shouted, pulling it away from him. "The oils from your fingers will ruin the picture! Never touch it!"

Her face had changed from peaceful calm as she worked on the picture to anger. Neil's heart sped up in spite of the fact that she was not a physical threat to him. Her reaction was so unexpected he was taken aback, ashamed at what he had done.

"I'm sorry. I'm sorry, I didn't mean to damage your picture. I didn't realize."

"You must never touch. Never."

"Okay. I understand."

She glared at him once more, then started to work on it again, positioning the paper and herself so her body was between Neil and the picture. Neil watched her, waiting as her body started to relax again, and she was lost in her work.

"Where do you think Carmina will sleep tonight?"

It was a long time before she responded, but Neil was starting to get a feel for her rhythm, and waited patiently for her answer.

"You should check her bed," Esther said guilelessly. "Or maybe she is in one of the safe rooms."

Neil sighed. He leaned back in the chair and closed his eyes, rubbing the bridge of his nose.

❧

CARMINA HAD BEEN WALKING for a long time. She knew she had to find somewhere to settle for the night. Tonight would be her first night on the streets. But certainly not her last. She needed to find somewhere safe.

"There's safety in numbers," Julius had told her many times in the past. "If you don't want to be seen, don't be alone."

And especially a young girl. People would notice her, would target her if she was off on her own. But she wasn't really sure where homeless people congregated. She had heard they slept under bridges. But what bridges? Where? She had mainly stayed on the green belt throughout the afternoon and evening, and she had seen some homeless people, but they were all alone, not together for protection. Carmina sighed, and headed toward the river. There were plenty of river-walk pathways, and she kept her eyes peeled, looking for bridges or other areas that might be promising. They seemed to be few and far between.

Eventually, she stopped. She had found a bridge that seemed promising, lots of space underneath, it was well-sheltered in case it started to rain. But there was no one else there.

Her feet hurt from walking. Her stomach hurt. Carmina wasn't just tired after the long day, she was exhausted. She couldn't go much further, and it was probably a couple of miles until the next bridge, which would likely be just as deserted as this one. She couldn't make it that far, especially now that her stomach was cramping up. She needed to lie down. She needed to make a decision where to settle for the night.

Carmina put down her backpack, and surveyed the space. It was roomy. Quiet. Dry. The multipurpose biking and jogging trail ran under the bridge, so there would be traffic through there, even if no one else was sleeping there. She decided she should sleep as high up as possible. There was a gentle slope that went all the way up to the underside of the bridge, and if she slept up there, above the heads of people who used the multipurpose pathway, she would not be as noticeable. Most of them would probably never look high enough to see her.

There were signs other people had camped there in the past, so maybe it wasn't such a bad choice. Carmina cleared a small space of garbage and rocks, and retrieved the space blanket from her emergency kit. It wasn't comfortable. It crinkled, it was too shiny to be inconspicuous, and it didn't feel warm. She knew it would help her to preserve her body heat, but she was going to have to find a good blanket the next day. It was going to be a restless night.

She put her backpack under her head and curled up on her side, rubbing her stomach and hoping the cramps would not last for long. As darkness started to fall, she opened her backpack and pulled out Cynthia. The rag doll was old and a little worn, but she was Carmina's only comfort item. She was careful not to let anyone at school see Cynthia in her backpack, but she carried the doll everywhere she went. She knew she was way too old to be dragging her dolly around with her, but she felt she had to. It was like her dad's emergency kits. She never knew what was going to happen. She had to be prepared. And she had been right, because now she needed Cynthia more than ever.

Clutching the rag doll in her arm, Carmina closed her eyes and tried to sleep.

THREE

Back at his desk, Neil slid his feet back into his shoes without untying the laces. He dialed Mattias Bishop, who was heading up the crew at the mansion in Neil's absence. The phone rang a number of times before Bishop answered it.

"Sorry, boss," he said without greeting. "I was under a floor."

"*Under* a floor?"

"You wouldn't believe this place. It's like swiss cheese. I'd like to find one wall that wasn't false!"

"I have a question for you. And it's a little crazy, though…"

"Well, this is a crazy case. So, shoot."

"Carmina. There's no way she's actually in the house, is there?"

Bishop was silent for a very long time. Neil looked at his display a couple of times to make sure the call was still connected. But he didn't prompt Bishop further or try to fill the silence with his own thoughts. He just gave Bishop time to consider it.

"I couldn't definitively say no, boss. I'm not confident we've found all of the secret rooms and cubbies, and some of them have passages connecting them, so she could get from one part of the house to another without being seen, unless someone happened to be guarding the passage at the time. Which no one is. But I certainly don't get the feeling that there's anyone here besides us. And she would have had to get into the house without us seeing her, and there's been people in and out the doors all day."

"None of those secret passages lead outside? Into the woods or an outbuilding somewhere?"

Bishop made a choking noise. "Not that we've found. Yet. But we haven't been looking for one, we've only been looking for what's inside the house."

"Well, if you'd do me a favor…"

"Sure."

"Check her room before you lock up for the night. Make sure she's not in her bed, and maybe mark things somehow, so you know if anything is moved while you're gone."

"Check her bed?" Bishop repeated.

"I know. Just do it. A favor for your crazy boss in the middle of a crazy case."

"Will do," Bishop agreed. "And come to think about it… it may not be as crazy as all that."

"Thanks. You guys going home soon?"

"Yeah. I think another half hour. We need to get some sleep, and start fresh in the morning to see if we've missed anything."

WHEN NEIL HUNG up from the call with Bishop, his phone started to ring. He glanced at the call display, and turned to look at Agnes as he picked it up.

"You could come over here," he pointed out.

Her voice came to him through the receiver. "Then I'd have to take my headset off."

"What have you got?"

"The school kids you wanted to talk to about Carmina."

"Oh, yeah. How did you make out?"

"They're both here, whenever you can take them."

She gestured to the visitor area, where several adults and a couple of teenagers were sitting, playing with their phones or leafing through magazines.

"Great job, Agnes. Thanks for that. I'll take them now. You should be heading home before long."

"Yeah, I've just got a couple more things to clean up, and then I will."

"Hopefully you'll be gone before I'm finished with these kids. I'll see you in the morning."

"Are you coming in here, or going over to the Knight House?"

"I'll probably stop at Knight House first. Then I've got to start reviewing reports."

"Okay. See you."

Neil put down the receiver, and went over to the waiting room. "Sorry to keep you folks waiting. I hope you haven't been here too long."

One of the mothers looked crabby. "I don't quite understand what this is all about. You think my daughter knows something about this Knight girl's disappearance?"

"No, no. Nothing like that." He bent down to shake her hand and motioned her daughter to stand. He figured he'd better take the angry one first. The other mother and father looked fine with sitting there a while longer. "I'm Agent Neil Crowther. We don't think your daughter…"

"Ange," the girl supplied, chewing on a wad of gum. Short for Angela or Angie, he assumed.

"We don't think Ange knows anything about what has happened to Carmina, but she knows Carmina, and she might be able to give us some insight into what Carmina might have been thinking, somewhere she might have gone, if she thought she was in trouble or in danger."

"I don't really know Carmina," Ange said. "Not real well. I don't know where she would go."

"Well, if you could just come with me for a few minutes, we'll have a little chat, and then you can get back home again. I'm sorry again for keeping you waiting." He directed the last comment at the mother. She shrugged impatiently, and did not insist she would have to come with Ange and supervise the interrogation, as Neil had expected she would. Neil nodded and escorted Ange to an unused room.

"Can I get you a coffee or soda or anything, Ange?"

"Coffee," Ange said fervently. "I could really use a coffee!"

"You're not the only one. If you'll just have a seat, I'll just pop next door and grab us one."

Ange settled herself into a seat, and Neil made a fresh pot of coffee in the nearby kitchen. He took a sip himself before taking them back to the interrogation room, even though he knew it was still too hot to drink. He really needed the caffeine to keep going.

"Here you go." Neil sat down and stretched out his legs, pausing for a moment to untie and retie his shoe, to cover up for the fact that he was rubbing his calves and Achilles tendons. "We'll just jump right into things. How long have you known Carmina?"

"I think we've gone to school together right from the start," Ange said slowly. "Like, kindergarten or grade one. Like I said, though, we're not best friends or anything."

"Is there anyone you can think of who does know her really well?"

Ange was silent for a moment, considering. Then she sat back, rolling her eyes and shaking her head. "No, I guess not. Carmina's sort of… a loner. She's different, you know? Always has been."

"What was so different about her when she was in kindergarten?"

Neil could tell from her eyes that she was thinking back, trying to remember clearly. "She was a real mama's girl back then. Really whiny and clingy and didn't want her mom to go. Her mom let her bring her teddy bear to kindergarten, to comfort her, so she would stay without crying. So everyone kind of thought of her as a *baby*, you know?"

Neil nodded.

"And she wasn't potty trained in kindergarten," Ange said, her nostrils flaring. "I remember that. She still wore a diaper. You weren't supposed to know, she had pull-ups or whatever, but everyone knew."

"That wouldn't make her very popular."

"Exactly. No one wanted to be friends with the stinky baby girl."

"And that reputation really sticks with a kid."

"Yeah. Her parents have always made her out to be this frail little girl, you know. She's too sickly to participate in phys ed or after-school sports. She has to go to the nurse's office to rest, or go home if she's not feeling well. Like the rest of us wouldn't like to go home halfway through the day too."

"How were her marks with all of those absences? Did she keep up with the work?"

"Oh, yeah. I think she's pretty smart. Book smart, you know. Not social smart. And if her parents say she was sick, then she's allowed to hand stuff in late and not get docked for it."

"So you see her as sort of privileged."

"Yeah. She gets special treatment everyone else doesn't get. Just because of her parents."

Ange took a long sip of the coffee. Then continued to chew on her gum. Neil looked away.

"But you're sort of friends with her now?"

"Well… friendly. I don't sit with her at lunch or anything." Ange paused. "Nobody sits with her at lunch," she said apologetically. "But, we were assigned locker partners a couple of years, and are always in the same homeroom and everything. Her name comes after mine on the roll call, so we always come together on seating charts. I guess… she's grown up a lot. She's not quite as weird as she used to be. So we talk, if there's nothing else to do."

"What do you know about her parents?"

"Her mom is, like, this brilliant artist. Carmina wants to be just like her. Her dad is a big businessman. Super rich. They're both kind of weird, so I guess Carmina didn't have much chance of turning out normal."

"How are they weird?"

Ange ran her finger around the rim of her coffee mug. "I dunno. They don't do any of the things the other parents do. No after-school stuff, or community involvement or anything. They don't talk to the other parents. And when they do come for school stuff, they just… seem… weird."

"What kind of things do you and Carmina talk about?"

"I dunno. Just schoolwork, mostly."

"Does she ever talk about her family? Or her plans for the future?"

"Mmm… no, not really."

"She doesn't have a boyfriend?"

Ange laughed, and clapped her hand over her mouth to avoid losing her gum. "A boyfriend? Carmina? I don't think she even knows boys exist!"

"No boyfriend, then. Does she have anyone at school who she might confide in? It doesn't have to be a student. It might be some kind of mentor or teacher."

"I don't think so. She's really big on her graphic design class. That's Mr. Burpeau. I don't know if she'd confide in him, though."

Neil nodded, and wrote it down. "Has she ever talked about somewhere she'd like to travel to?"

"Travel? No, not that I remember."

"What she wants to do when she graduates?"

"Graphic design." Ange shrugged. "I don't really know what that means. It's art, anyway, just like her mom."

"Was her mom happy about that?"

"I guess. Why wouldn't she be?"

Neil doodled in his notepad for a moment, trying to look like he was writing down something important while he thought things through. "Is there anything else you think I should know?"

Ange swirled the coffee that remained in her mug. "Um, no. I wish I could help you, but I don't really get what's going on, and I don't know where she would go or anything."

"Well, if you think of something…" Neil pulled a business card out of his shirt pocket and handed it to her. "Call me anytime, day or night. Even if you're not sure it's important. I'd rather waste a few hours than miss the opportunity to track Carmina down."

"Okay." Ange played with the card. "Carmina's nice enough. I hope nothing happened to her."

THE OTHER GIRL'S name was Miranda. She showed less confidence than Ange, shooting Neil frequent anxious looks. She was tentative about picking a chair, and didn't want any coffee. Neil refilled his. When he sat down, Miranda looked at the coffee.

"Actually," she licked her lips, "could I get a glass of water?"

"Of course."

Neil eased himself to his feet again and went to the kitchen to get her water from the cooler. He returned and handed it to her. "There you go."

"Thanks."

He gave her a minute to take a couple swallows of water. "So Miranda, how long have you known Carmina?"

"Just a couple of years." Without prompting, she provided further details. "We're in design together. And art history."

"I understand she's a pretty good artist."

"Brilliant," Miranda agreed. "Really, she's the best one in the class. Burpeau is in love with her. Thinks she's destined for great things."

"What did she think of him?"

"He's a good teacher."

"She liked him?"

"Sure."

"Do you think she would go to him if she was in trouble?"

Miranda pursed her lips, shaking her head slightly. "Carmina's pretty private. I don't think she'd ever go to a teacher…"

"Can you think of anyone she would go to?"

"No."

"Has she contacted you?"

"No way. I haven't heard a thing from her."

Neil waited, giving her time to think about it. To give him some unconscious signal if she was lying. But he didn't think she was.

"Okay. So do you guys talk to each other during class?"

"Sure. There's not a lot of lecturing. Most of the time we're just working on our projects and can talk."

"So what do you talk about?"

"Mostly art. But sometimes other things… Like I said, Carmina's pretty private… so she didn't really share personal stuff."

"She wanted to become a graphic designer?"

"Yes."

"And her family was happy with that? They didn't expect her to become… an accountant or a doctor or something?"

Miranda smiled. "No. Her mom is an artist. They were happy with it."

"What are her parents like?"

"They seem nice. I don't know. I've only seen them at our art shows. They always come to our shows."

"Have you talked to them?"

"Umm… not her dad. Her mom a little bit."

"What did you talk about?"

"She asked me some stuff about my project. That's all, really."

"Did Carmina ever talk to you about the future? What else she wanted to do with her life?"

"No… just being a designer." She gave a helpless shrug. "Sorry. I wish I could help you more."

❧

IT WAS A LONG NIGHT, and Carmina got up in the morning feeling like she hadn't gotten a wink of sleep. She was cold and uncomfortable. The ground was so hard it made her bones ache. She had tossed and turned. She had forced herself to lay still. Whenever she closed her eyes, something else disturbed her. Someone going down the pathway. Nearby traffic. The calls of night birds. She just wanted to turn it all off and go to sleep. In the morning, as the sky started to pink up, she folded the silver blanket carefully and put it back in her emergency kit. She took out a granola bar to eat for breakfast. And she put Cynthia back away.

"You have Cynthia with you," she murmured. That's what Esther would have told her. "Even if Mom and Dad aren't here, you're not alone as long as Cynthia is here. You don't have to be alone."

She said the words aloud because she wanted to hear them. She wanted them to be true. Cynthia had seen her through many years of loneliness. Had kept her from being alone when she was at school, or sitting in her room at home. Or on the road between the two. Without her parents, she always felt like she was just going to float away into the air. They were her anchors, her stabilizers. Without them, she felt like she might just fade away or float into the sky and disappear.

Carmina started walking down the trail, toward the next bridge. She checked her directions. She was walking toward downtown, and surely that was where most of the homeless would congregate. She would find where there was a group she could camouflage herself in. Then she would be safer, harder for anyone who was looking for her to find.

NEIL HAD BEEN unable to sleep. He had stayed at the office late. And once he got back home to his apartment, he had stayed up watching TV until long after he should have been asleep. But he knew he wouldn't sleep. Especially with an active case pressing on his brain. If Carmina wasn't missing, this would be his time to celebrate. An arrest had been made, they had pulled a ton of evidence out of the house, and all was well with the world. But it wasn't. All wasn't well with Carmina. She was still out there, somewhere. A naive, spoiled child who had probably never even slept away from home.

He still hoped she might be with someone. There must be someone she could trust.

Once the sky started to get light, he got out of bed, showered and dressed, and poured himself a big travel mug full of coffee to help wake himself up. His stomach was aching, and he knew he should have something other than coffee, but he wasn't a morning eater. Food in the morning just made him queasy. So instead, he popped a couple of antacids and started off.

The Knight House property was majestic in the early morning sunlight. Dew glistened on the leaves and grass. He could almost see the fairies that Esther drew dancing in the woods and peeping at him through the branches. It was stunning.

It looked at first like he was the first one there. There was no one guarding the doors, checking any cars that came down the lane. But there were a number of cars parked beside the house, almost out of view of the driveway. Looking over them, Neil decided they were the search crew, out early to take advantage of the first light. Taking his coffee with him, he walked into the trees, and looked for the searchers.

"Hello? Anyone here?"

After a few calls, he unexpectedly stumbled upon Fisher, the agent heading up the search team. "Hey, Crowther. Didn't expect to see you out so early. How late did you work last night?"

Neil shrugged. "It's an active investigation. You have to run down leads for as long as you can."

Fisher accepted this non-answer. "We're continuing a grid search," he said without Neil asking for a progress report. "If she's out here, we'll find her. But it's a big area, and once you get off of the Knight property, you're on municipal parkland, and it goes for miles… she could walk for a long time and never be seen by anyone."

"Yeah," Neil agreed. "And I haven't even been able to find out whether she is more likely to hide in the woods or to hit the street."

"I'm guessing from her bedroom that she's a loner," Fisher said.

"That's the sense I've gotten."

"So I'd guess the woods before the streets. Fewer people. She doesn't have to talk with them, interact."

"Right. But she's a lot safer if she'll talk to people than to stay on her own. A young, naive kid like that, out on her own? I hate to think of how much danger she could be in."

"If she's stayed on her own property, she should be safe. Not a lot of people are going to be walking through there, let alone taking advantage of her."

Fisher's phone rang. He pushed a button and held it to her ear. "Fisher," he greeted. He listened for a minute, his eyes flicking around at their surroundings. "I'll be right there." He hung up and looked at Neil. "They've found something. You want to come?"

"Does 'something' mean a body?"

"No."

"Well, let's see, then."

Neil followed Fisher through the trees. He wasn't sure where they were going, but Fisher seemed to have an unerring sense of direction, and led him through the trees like a bloodhound. Maybe that's what they were missing. They needed a bloodhound. It would just smell Carmina out and take them to her. Fisher led him to a clearing beside a stream. It had the same pristine beauty as the rest of the woods they had walked through, but it was now teeming with agents poking through trees and bushes, and placing yellow evidence numbers on the ground. Neil and Fisher walked toward the largest grouping of agents, and looked down at the neat stack of school books tagged with the number one.

"Damn!"

One of the agents looked up. "We found her trail. That's a good thing."

"She's not planning on being able to go back to school."

They all looked down at the pile.

"I was hoping she would run to someone at school. But she's already distanced herself. She doesn't intend to go back."

A man in hip waders in the middle of the stream gave a shout, and everyone looked up. He held something small and rectangular in his hand, water streaming down from it.

"I guess that's why we couldn't track her phone," Neil observed.

"She knew it could be tracked," Fisher said.

"Yeah, I'm sure she did." Neil sat down on the big rock by the books, and stared at the stream. "So where is she going? Is she staying in the woods? In the city? Hitchhiking out of here? Where would she go?"

"We haven't found her wallet. There's still the possibility we will at least get a hit on her credit card."

"No." Neil shook his head. "Julius would have told her never to use a credit card."

"She's not in contact with him."

"No, but a guy as paranoid as that? He's run her through scenarios in the past. He's given her instruction. This isn't unplanned behavior."

"We've got something buried here," one of the agents called.

The woman went down on her knees and scraped at the loose dirt under the edge of a log with her hands. Everyone stopped what they were doing to see what she found. Obviously, it wasn't going to be a body. The area of disturbed earth was far too small. She evacuated the hole, and they all stared numbly at the wallet and cut-up plastic cards.

"I told you," Neil said. "She knows what she's doing. She's been taught what to do. That's why Julius is not concerned about helping us find her. He knows he's taught her how to survive on her own. He always figured this would happen, sooner or later."

FOUR

Carmina found the next bridge, but this time instead of staying on the greenway, she decided to take the bridge across to downtown. There would be more people there. A better place to hide. And she could always come back across the bridge to the park lands later. She saw individual homeless people. Old men and women. Panhandling or rummaging through garbages. But she was too shy to approach them. Especially when they weren't part of a group. She knew there had to be more people that she wasn't seeing. The hidden homeless. Families living in cars. Moms and dads already gone to work. Kids sent to school early to catch the school's free breakfast program. Teenagers, kids Carmina's age, who had been kicked out of their homes for doing drugs or coming out. The old bag ladies and panhandlers were visible, but they were the minority.

Mr. Burpeau had suggested she target homelessness or poverty as part of her next design project. Carmina had found it strange, at the time. Did he tell her to study poverty because her family was wealthy? Homelessness because she lived in a big house? He didn't really know her. He didn't know if she was the kind of person who would just turn a blind eye to people in need. Carmina had spent the rest of her art period in the library, doing research on the computers and browsing through some slim photoessay books. Others had tried to raise awareness of homelessness with art projects. They made it to the newspapers, but Carmina wondered how effective they really were. Did they make a difference for the people who were homeless? Or only to the artist's portfolio? None of the artists had actually been homeless, like Carmina now was. Maybe that would make a difference.

Carmina stopped and rested for a minute, looking around. Her stomach was rumbling. The granola bar hadn't been nearly enough to satisfy her hunger. There were still more, and she hadn't yet eaten her lunch from the day before. She walked down to the bus stop and sat on the bench, digging into her backpack. Her lunch consisted of one of those commercial boxes of crackers, cheese, and lunch meats. It could probably last weeks before she had to worry about it going bad, but she was hungry now. She also had a juice box and an apple. She opened the box of crackers and cheese, and made little sandwiches and canapés, pretending it was their traditional New Year's snack. Esther always had different kinds of crackers and cheese for New Year's Eve. And some sodas and virgin drinks.

"That's not very good for you." A young woman sat down next to Carmina. She had close-cropped hair, bleach blond with pink tips, and lots of earrings and piercings. She had garish blue eyeshadow and red, red lips.

"It tastes good," Carmina countered.

"You should make sure you eat good, healthy food. Don't waste your money on that kind of processed crap."

Carmina nodded. There was no point in arguing with busybodies.

"And those things are so high in sodium. You'd be shocked."

"I know they are," Carmina agreed. She was familiar with the sodium levels of all of the foods she ate. Julius wasn't allowed to eat things with high sodium, but Carmina was.

"I'm Reenie," the girl offered, holding out her hand to Carmina.

Carmina hesitated, studying Reenie's eyes before finally taking her hand and giving it a brief, firm shake. "Hi."

Reenie laughed. "You're pretty stingy with your name, there."

Carmina still didn't offer it. It wasn't something she had thought through yet. She was going to have to give people a name. But she couldn't use Carmina. Not when the feds might be looking for her.

"You get kicked out?" Reenie questioned sympathetically.

Carmina frowned at her. "No." She looked down the street. "I'm just waiting for the bus."

"This bus stop has been closed for months."

"Oh… it was still on Google Maps," Carmina tried.

Reenie's eyes were piercing. Carmina looked away from her and focused on her crackers.

"You can't always trust those directions," Reenie said. "So… you don't need any help?"

Carmina swallowed a big lump of dry crackers, and quickly washed it down with a sip from her juice box. "What kind of help?"

"I don't know. Soup kitchens, shelters, outreach programs."

Carmina looked down at her backpack. She was dressed for school, carrying her school book bag, and hadn't had time to get dirty and smelly. So how did Reenie know?

"You want to know where to go for breakfast?" Reenie prompted further. "You keep eating crap like that, and you're going to be sick. Not to mention it's a waste of your money. You need to save whatever you can get for other things."

"Yeah, I guess."

"Yeah, that's what I thought. Come with me, I'll show you where to go."

Carmina got up. Reenie looked at her backpack. "Is that all you've got?"

Carmina nodded. Reenie didn't make any further comment. She led Carmina down the street at a brisk pace, occasionally pointing out important landmarks.

"If you come over here at lunchtime," she pointed to a park with a fountain, "the mobile kitchen hands out sandwiches. It's not a hot meal, and they run out pretty fast, but it's food in your belly if you can get there in time."

"Okay."

"Don't sleep there, though. Cops will roust you."

"Okay."

"Where did you sleep last night?"

Carmina didn't answer.

"There's shelters. I can show you where. They're safe. But you gotta get there early. Like in the afternoon. Before people start getting off work or school."

"Uh-huh."

The list went on. Carmina tried to focus on all of the details, but it was too much. Food, shelters, needles, condoms, day labor, meetings, cops… she couldn't keep track of it all.

Eventually, they made it to the soup kitchen. Carmina could tell they were too late. Mostly people were standing outside, visiting with each other, exchanging the latest news and gossip. When Carmina and Reenie walked into the hall, kitchen staff were clearing up.

"Wait, let us grab a couple of plates," Reenie called out. "There anything left?"

A big man with a red doo-rag around his head looked up and scowled.

"Reenie. You're late. Out picking up stragglers again?" His eyes moved to Carmina. Carmina kept her eyes down, not wanting to be in trouble for showing up so late.

"Yeah, she's pretty green. I couldn't just leave her!"

The man put a couple of clean plates on the counter. "I'm Bern. Nice to meet you. Normally, you have to be here before eight."

"Okay."

There was a moment of silence while Reenie and Bern looked at each other, silently communicating something Carmina didn't quite get.

"Come on," Reenie invited. "The eggs are bad enough, without waiting until they get cold."

"Bad?" Bern repeated, his voice high. "You watch your mouth, Reenie."

"I do. That's the trouble." She laughed.

Reenie quickly dished up some eggs, sausages, and hash browns that remained in the bottoms of the chafing dishes. Carmina followed suit. The staff was already putting up the chairs and tables, so Reenie and Carmina ate standing up, gobbling it down quickly.

"So, what's your handle?" Bern asked.

Carmina looked at him. "What?" she questioned through a mouthful of scrambled eggs.

"Your name. What do you go by?"

"Oh." Carmina looked over at Reenie, her face getting hot. "I… don't know yet."

"You don't know your name?"

"She doesn't want to use her real name," Reenie said. "Which is pretty smart, if you don't want someone to track you down. You'll pick up a street name anyway. No one would call you by your given name for long."

"Like Reenie?" Carmina asked.

"Sabrina," she explained.

"Oh."

"So, what's your story?" Bern persisted. "You run away? Get kicked out?"

Carmina took another bite and chewed it in silence.

"Mystery girl," Bern observed.

"Leave her be," Reenie said. "She's still getting her legs under her."

"She's pretty careful."

Reenie nodded. "Gotta be careful if you want to stay safe."

Carmina speared a sausage with her fork and took bites of it. Esther would be mortified by her manners. She usually was.

"You're really packing it away," Reenie said. "How long since you had a good meal?"

Carmina put the last bite of the sausage in her mouth and raised her eyebrows, shrugging.

NEIL NODDED at Agnes as he approached his desk. He sat down, glad to get off of his feet, then decided he wanted a coffee, but was too lazy to get up and get it. Agnes came over with a stack of papers.

"Most of these are just reports for you to review and sign," she said. "Everyone's summaries of yesterday's arrest and all. You need to get your notes in too. They want to be able to start serious interrogations on the Knights today. Are you up to it?"

Neil looked up at her, startled. Her brown hair hung around her face, looking slightly tousled. "Sure, of course. Why wouldn't I be?"

"You look like hell."

Neil rubbed his eyes and then his temples, as if he could erase whatever it was she saw in his face. "I'm fine. Just didn't sleep very well."

"Have you had anything to eat?"

"No… but I'll get around to it."

"When?" she looked at her watch pointedly. "Noon? I'll make a muffin run. What kind do you want?"

"I don't know…"

"You know you need to eat. Especially since…" she trailed off.

Neil folded his arms across his chest and looked at her challengingly. "Are you channeling my mother?"

She swallowed. "No. I'm sorry, I just want you to take care of yourself. Men can be so… stupid about their health."

"I know how to take care of myself. I know how many calories I need to eat in a day. What sodium intake I need to maintain. All of that."

"Your doctor won't be happy when he sees you. You haven't put on any weight. If anything, you've lost."

He'd been avoiding weighing himself, but he knew it was true. His clothing kept getting roomier. His face bonier. Even his skin was getting looser, sagging in places.

Agnes stared him down. "So what kind of donut do you want?"

"It's donuts now?"

"You know it was never going to be muffins," Agnes laughed. "So? Boston Cream? A couple of them?"

"Boston Cream. Whatever looks good." He knew he'd regret the sweets, but not much appealed to him. "And some good coffee?"

She nodded. "Sure."

NEIL WATCHED Esther before going into the room. She had again been given paper and pencils, and was busy drawing. The whole situation was like a puzzle. One with a lot of pieces, and some of them seemed to be missing. He liked solving puzzles, but this one was giving him some unexpected challenges. The puzzle was usually solved when an arrest was made, but this one continued to test him.

Taking a deep breath, he went into the room. Esther remained focused on her picture, not looking up at him. Neil took a look at her latest creation. Carmina again. He didn't think she was a fairy in this one, but she didn't quite look human either. She was ethereal. She stood by a fountain, eyes closed, with the mist blowing in her face. Droplets beaded on her hair. There were a few creatures in the picture. A fat goldfish in the fountain. A bird flying overhead, catching the sun.

"I liked it better when you didn't wear shoes."

Neil chuckled. "Well, you're the only one. My boss gets on my case about it. Others complain about the smell. If you're going to buck social conventions, people are going to complain."

She glanced sideways at him. "Yes."

Neil sat down around the corner of the table from her, watching her slim, sure hands as she manipulated the pencil, bringing the picture to life. "You really are talented. I can't believe the way you can make it so... real and fantastic at the same time."

"I've always been able to draw."

"It's amazing. She's not a wood elf in this one."

"No."

"Because she doesn't have pointed ears, right? But it's almost like she's part of the mist in the fountain."

Esther nodded. "She's a naiad. A water nymph."

"Ah. No wolf today?"

She looked at the picture for a moment as if she wasn't sure. "No. Not today."

"Where do you think Carmina really is today?" Neil studied the setting in the picture. "In a park, maybe?"

"I don't know. It's just a picture."

"Is it? I think your pictures tell me more than your words do."

She didn't seem to take any offense at this. "I like pictures better than words. I think they are more honest. As long as they are not illusions."

"So..." he knew he was supposed to be interviewing them about the charges today. Fisher and his team would work on tracking Carmina down. But Neil couldn't let go the opportunity to explore it further. "What kind of place would Carmina choose to live in? The forest? The city? With a friend? Where would she go, if she could choose wherever she wanted?"

"Water nymphs in the water. Wood elves in the woods."

"And little girls? Where?"

"In real life?" she said faintly.

"In real life."

"She belongs in our home. That's where she should be. That's where she would choose."

"But what if she couldn't? What would she choose next?"

Esther suddenly looked up from her picture. "Does she have Cynthia with her?"

Neil tried to close his mouth and come up with the words to answer her. Cynthia? A friend? Employee? Nanny? "Carmina isn't with anyone, that we know of. Do you think she would go to Cynthia?"

"She would take Cynthia with her," Esther said with a small smile. "She did, didn't she?"

"Who is Cynthia?"

"Cynthia is her doll. Her comfort object. She's had Cynthia since she was a little girl. Takes her everywhere."

"Oh. Would she have taken Cynthia to school? She was on her way home from school when she disappeared."

"Oh, yes. She always had Cynthia in her bag."

"Then I guess she has Cynthia with her. Didn't kids tease her about carrying around a doll?"

"When she was younger. Carmina keeps her hidden now. Out of sight."

"I see. Do you think… you could draw Cynthia for me?"

Esther looked at him for a moment, then grabbed a blank piece of paper, and started to sketch. Neil watched the rough lines quickly come together to form a rag doll. The little girl wore a simple dress and had smiley eyes. Esther smiled affectionately, looking at it, then handed it to Neil.

"You can keep it."

"Thank you."

She went back to working on the water nymph. "You want something else."

"Yes, I do."

"Tell me what."

"I want you to tell me about your artwork. Not the pictures of Carmina, or anything original…"

"The reproductions?"

"Yes. Tell me about the reproductions."

"I am very good at making copies. Any style. Mixing colors, brushwork, everything. I use old materials, or only materials that were around at the time the original work was painted. That makes it more authentic."

"Sure."

"A lot of people want reproductions of famous or expensive paintings in their houses. They can't get the originals, of course. So they get reproductions."

"And you provide them."

"Yes."

Acid burned in Neil's chest, and he swallowed, trying to calm it. He took a drink of his coffee, though he knew it would only make it worse.

"And that's how you justify forgery? People want reproductions, so you provide them?"

"Forgery?"

Esther looked at him, frowning. She looked back down at her paper. "It's only forgery if you try to pass it off as the original. Do you know how many students paint the Mona Lisa every year to learn daVinci's style? Thousands. But they're not forgeries. Just clumsy copies."

"And yours aren't quite so clumsy."

"Mine are technically perfect," Esther said, her voice expressionless and flat. She wasn't arguing, and she wasn't bragging. She was just stating a fact. "But I don't try to pass them off as originals."

"You and your husband are selling them as originals."

She waved a hand at him. "Julius does the selling. I just paint."

Neil sat back and stared at her. It simply wasn't possible she didn't know her husband was passing her reproductions off as the real thing. They lived in the same house. Worked together hand-in-glove. Without her, there were no paintings to sell. And without Julius…?

"Julius sells them as originals."

A shadow cross her face, and was quickly gone. "No, not as originals. That would be wrong."

"That's why you've been arrested. Don't you understand that?"

"Then you will let me go. Because I am innocent." She straightened her papers as if getting ready to leave. "So I can go home. And Carmina can come back."

"Do you know what provenance is?"

"I am an artist. Of course I know what provenance is. Provenance is the origin of the work of art and the chronology of its ownership. Being able to show what hands it has passed through to get where it is now."

"What is the provenance of your reproductions?"

"That's silly. My reproductions start with me. There are no other owners."

"And yet, Julius is selling them with very impressive provenance. Would you like to see?"

She started working again on the water nymph, perhaps realizing she wasn't going to go home any time soon. "That's ridiculous."

"I'll show you."

Neil left the room, and in the evidence locker, flipped through one of the boxes to find a detailed provenance that had already been packaged and catalogued. He signed it out, and returned to the interrogation room. Esther looked as if she had not stirred during his absence. Neil walked in and began to lay each individually bagged document out on the table, in chronological order, with the typed and certified summary in the final position. There were handwritten letters, typed documents, certificates, auction catalogs, and newspaper articles. He glanced over at Esther. She had stopped drawing, and was watching him with a slight frown.

"Come take a look," Neil invited.

She got up from her seat and stood beside him, her eyes flitting rapidly from one page to another. Neil pointed to the photograph attached to the certification. "You recognize this painting."

"Of course. That is a Rodin."

"That is a Knight," Neil corrected.

"Yes," she agreed, smiling. "An Esther Knight reproduction of a Rodin."

"Now look at the provenance."

She picked up the first document and read it through, frown lines appearing between her eyebrows. She started to put it down, then kept it in her hand and grabbed the next document, looking at it and shaking her head slowly. She picked up another, her movements jerky now, almost frantic. She shook her head.

"Where did this come from? These are not the provenance of the original Rodin. And my work… has no provenance."

She picked up another document, and another, not stopping to read them anymore, just looking at them as if she couldn't believe her eyes. She was starting to crush the pages, careless in her distress. Neil tried to tug them out of her hands.

"Put them down on the table, before they get damaged. Just look at them. You can see what he's done."

"What does it matter if they get damaged?" Esther asked, her voice shrill. "They are garbage! They are trash! Worthless!" She intentionally crumpled one up and flung it.

"It's still evidence. Just put them down."

She dropped them onto the table, and nearly collapsed, catching herself on the table with both hands. Neil grabbed her and guided her back into her chair to sit down. She cradled her face in her hands, and rocked.

"No. No, he wouldn't do that!"

"Then who did? Did you forge these letters too?"

"No! No, I would never… I couldn't…"

"You're trying to tell me you had no idea Julius was selling your reproductions as originals."

Neil's tone was sarcastic, but he believed her performance. He saw in Esther a woman without guile, without any pretense or attempt at deceit. Her distress over the forged provenance felt genuine.

"No. No, this can't be!"

"Where do you think all the money came from? You think people pay that much for reproductions?"

"Yes."

"You forged the paintings, and Julius forged the provenance. And the two of you raked in the cash."

"I never had anything to do with the sales. Ask Julius. He'll tell you. I painted reproductions. Not forgeries!"

"It all comes out the same."

"No. No, I would never do that." She rocked back and forth, holding her face and sobbing.

∽

CARMINA SAID GOOD-BYE TO REENIE, thanking her politely for all of her help and advice. Her mind was still whirling with all of the new information. She needed to be alone now, to work it all through and to figure out the best course of action. She wandered the streets, trying to burn them into her memory, to remember every bit of information Reenie had told her. She was afraid she wasn't going to be able to remember half of it.

She saw the park with the fountain Reenie had said the mobile kitchen would come to at lunchtime, and glanced at her shadow. It was small and almost completely below her now. The sun almost at its zenith. So she stopped and sat on one of the park benches and stared at the fountain, trying to relax.

There were other people starting to gather. While there were a few who looked homeless, dirty and grubby, most looked like regular people. There were some parents with young children and she watched the kids play, wondering if they were there waiting for the sandwiches too. They were neatly dressed and happy, enjoying playing around the fountain. A couple of boys started splashing each other, until their mom ran in to separate them.

Eventually, a white van pulled up. People started to close in on it immediately, and Carmina's heart raced, wondering if she was going to be able to get in quickly enough to get a sandwich before they were all gone. She got up and hurried closer. She could have pushed her way in front of one of the families, but she didn't want to take food out of the little ones' mouths. So she waited behind them.

One of the workers reached toward her with a plastic-wrapped sandwich, and Carmina grabbed it. "Thank you!"

She was pushed out of the way by others reaching for the last remaining sandwiches, and moved away from the crowd.

"You get one?"

Carmina turned to look at a boy a little older than her. He had a dark gray hoodie that was too warm for the weather. He had a prominent nose and jawline, and though he was smiling at her, he didn't look happy.

"Yeah, thanks," she said, moving away from him.

"Sometimes there aren't enough to go around," he said, following her.

"I got one," Carmina said, holding it up and trying to move more quickly away from him.

"You don't need to run away," he laughed. "I'm just making sure you're taken care of…"

"Go away," Carmina objected. "Leave me alone."

"Hey…" He reached out to try to stop her.

"Leave me alone!" Carmina shouted, giving him a shove.

They were attracting attention. The boy fell back, not wanting to pursue her any further with everyone watching. Carmina glared at him. She wanted to run away, to hide, but that was the worst thing she could do. If she went somewhere alone, by herself, she made herself vulnerable to attack. So instead she moved back toward the van. The workers who were no longer handing out sandwiches, but were preparing to leave, looked at her.

"Are you okay?"

"That guy is bugging me."

They looked at the boy and back at Carmina. "Toto is harmless," one of them said. "He's not going to hurt you."

"Toto?" Carmina looked back at the boy. "But he won't leave me alone."

"Toto!" one of them called out to him.

"What?" Toto spread his hands as if he didn't understand what was going on.

"Leave the girl alone."

"I am!"

"You want someone to call the cops on you?"

"I'll leave her alone. I was just making sure she got something to eat."

"Go on, get out of here."

Scowling, the boy marched off. Carmina watched him disappear around a corner down the street. She breathed out. "Thanks."

"You really don't have to worry about Toto, though. He probably was just looking out for a pretty girl. I've never known him to cause any real trouble."

Carmina shrugged at this. There was always a first time. And they were only around for a few minutes every day, they wouldn't know much about what went on. Carmina scanned the crowd. Now that the show was over, people were munching on their sandwiches and going back to their own conversations.

"There was a camping store somewhere around here," she said to the van men. "I can't remember which way."

"Sure. Go for two blocks down this street," he pointed, "then take a right, and it's about… another three. On the right-hand side of the street. You can't miss it."

"Thanks."

"Don't steal there. They donate blankets and other stuff to the shelters. If you're in a pinch, sometimes they'll give you what you need for free. Don't steal from them."

Carmina swallowed and nodded. "Yeah. Okay."

NEIL WAS BACK at his desk, carefully smoothing out the crumpled provenance papers before returning them to the evidence locker.

"Well, well, well, if it isn't Neil Crowther, investigator extraordinaire!"

Neil looked up at the familiar voice. "Sandler! What brings you down here?"

They shook hands and gave each other a half-hug, slapping hands on each other's backs. "How's it been going?" Sandler questioned.

Kyle Sandler was shorter than Neil, with wavy, sandy-colored hair, always artfully mussed. He had a mobile face that changed quickly from mischievous and good-humored to bitter disappointment. Neil couldn't erase from his memory the look on Sandler's face when Neil had been lying on the pavement, fighting for breath, and Sandler had held tightly to his hand, encouraging him, while they waited for the ambulance. His other hand had been pressed to Neil's belly, putting pressure on a gaping wound he had no hope of stopping from bleeding. Sandler had looked strangely old and unfamiliar, the boyish look gone from his eyes as he strove to keep his partner's body and soul together.

Now Sandler looked his usual self. Good-humored and roguish, but with a hint of extra reserve, something held back.

"Man, you're looking good," Neil told him.

Sandler patted him on the arm and let go of the handshake. "More than I can say for you, partner."

"He's not eating properly," Agnes interposed, putting another stack of papers on Neil's desk. "And I don't think he's sleeping too well either."

Neil's stomach clenched at her mothering him in front of Sandler. "When they remove half of your guts, there tend to be some unpleasant side effects," he said dryly. "Eating loses a lot of its appeal."

"Always thought you were gutless," Sandler joked.

His face was unusually pale, and Neil wondered if he wasn't feeling quite up to par either. They hadn't seen much of each other since the shooting. And when they did, there was a strained awkwardness between them.

"Agnes, meet Kyle Sandler, my old partner and—" he had been about to say 'the man who shot me,' and decided at the last minute that might sound bitter, "the best friend a guy could have."

Sandler gave him a frozen-looking smile.

"You were there when he got shot?" Agnes asked, her eyes alight with interest.

"Sure was. We almost lost this guy." Sandler slapped Neil on the shoulder, smiling broadly.

"Wow." Agnes shook her head. "That must have been terrifying. Do you remember it?" she asked Neil. "I know a lot of people don't remember when they were in an accident or got shot. It gets erased from their memory. The trauma."

Neil breathed in, held it for a moment, and breathed back out. His heart was pounding wildly, remembering all too many details of that day.

"I'll bet you were a great field agent," Agnes said apologetically, when he didn't answer.

"Don't let him fool you," Sandler said, laughing. "The reason he's tied to a desk isn't because he got shot. He could be out there chasing down baddies again, if it wasn't for his feet."

Agnes looked doubtful. Neil felt a wave of heat go over his face and hoped he wasn't as red as he felt.

"What happened to your feet?" Agnes asked with a frown, tucking a loose lock of hair back behind her ear.

Neil cleared his throat. "Nothing *happened* to them. I have plantar fasciitis. A lot of people who are on their feet too much get it. But once it heals up…" he trailed off.

His doctor had talked to him about cortisone shots. About surgery. The physical therapy and various splints and sleeves were not helping. It was unusual to get it in both feet, his doctor said, as if Neil had won the lottery or something. There was no guarantee surgery would fix it. And cortisone was only a temporary fix. The pain would almost certainly come back.

Neil's therapist, the man he'd been assigned to in order to work through the trauma of the shooting, had speculated whether Neil's PF was a physical manifestation of his reluctance to return to the field, where he'd been hurt. He didn't have any idea how many foot cops ended up with bad feet. Neil wasn't a special case.

But, maybe it *would* go away after he had worked through all of the emotions the shooting had left him with. He held onto that hope. That once he was ready emotionally to go back to his old life, his body would follow suit.

"I never knew that," Agnes said. "I just assumed it was because of the… accident."

Neil looked at the piles of paper on his desk. "I'd better get back to work," he said. "We're in the middle of a big case. Just made arrests yesterday…"

"I saw it in the paper," Sandler agreed. "Well, I'm sure you're good at it. You always were top-notch at the investigative work."

"Yeah. We should do lunch or go for a beer sometime…"

Sandler looked at him, eyes narrow. "Are you allowed to drink, with your…"

"Well, I'm not supposed to, but I could get a Coke or something."

Sandler shrugged. "Yeah, we'll have to set it up sometime," he agreed.

If he'd really wanted to do it, he would have suggested a time. Even a late lunch after whatever appointment he was headed to now. But he didn't want to. It was no longer comfortable for them to see each other socially.

Neil forced a smile and said good-bye. He watched Sandler walk toward the elevator bank.

FIVE

An older woman answered the door. She may have had golden blond hair like Esther's once, but it was now white. She looked Neil over. "Yes? Can I help you?"

"My name is Agent Neil Crowther, ma'am. Are you Esther Knight's mother?"

"I was once."

Neil was taken aback. "You were once...? Could I come in for a minute?"

The frown lines around her mouth deepened, and he thought she was going to tell him no. But after a minute she stepped back and motioned him in. Neil entered the house. It was an older model, small home, similar to the one Neil's grandmother had lived in. It could have used some better lighting. She led him into the living room, and Neil selected a cushioned chair facing the couch where she sat down. They were joined by a white-haired man, slightly shorter than his wife.

"Raymond Raynor," he introduced himself, stepping forward and shaking Neil's hand vigorously. "And this is my wife, Irene. What is this about, then?"

"I'm the lead investigator in the forgery case against Julius and Esther Knight."

Raymond sat down next to his wife, his face twisting bitterly. "We've been fielding all kinds of calls from the media about Esther. And from friends as well. I'll tell you what we told them. Esther is not a part of our lives anymore. We have not had any contact with her."

"In how long?"

They looked at each other.

"Twenty years?" Raymond suggested, shrugging. "Not since she hooked up with that man."

"Oh. So you've never even met her daughter, Carmina?"

They exchanged another look, and Raymond made a face.

"We've met her," Irene admitted after a long pause. "I think… three times. But we're not in regular contact with them."

Neil leaned forward on his knees. He rubbed his chin. "I take it you disapprove of Julius?"

"Yes. We told Esther not to get mixed up with that man."

"What was it about Julius you objected to?"

"He was not an appropriate match for Esther," Irene tried to explain. "She is a very… special kind of girl. He was… worldly… we knew he would corrupt her."

"You were aware he was a forger?"

"No." Irene was shocked. "We didn't know anything of the kind. Just that he was the type of person who would turn her away from the way she had been brought up, from her innocence."

"Was Esther…" Neil looked for an inoffensive word. "Was she identified… as having special needs?"

"We fought her whole school career against people who wanted to diagnose her with one thing or another," Raymond growled. "There was always someone who thought she should be coded with some delay or disability. We had to push to get her the opportunities she deserved. She was a good girl with a special talent."

"Her art, you mean?"

"She could have been famous for her work. She was a brilliant artist, right from the time she was a toddler. But that man crushed her talent. He didn't encourage any of her original work, her real voice."

Neil nodded his understanding. "It looks like they kept most of her original work instead of selling it."

"Was there a lot?" Irene questioned, showing real interest for the first time.

"Yes. Quite a lot. Carmina seems to be one of her favorite subjects."

Irene gave a slight nod. Neil waited for more.

"She sometimes sent me pictures," Irene said. She got up from her seat and went over to the bookcase, where she pulled out an oversized album. She handed it to Neil. He opened it up. There were a number of pictures contained in the protective pages. Some pencil sketches, some pastel or watercolor. As Irene had indicated, many of them were of Carmina. Mostly in fantasy settings. Neil flipped through them.

"So she sent pictures to you. Did you respond? Send her letters?"

"No."

"Why not? It seems like she was making an effort to keep in contact."

"We told her if she stayed with that man, we couldn't have anything more to do with her. She never seemed to understand that."

Neil pondered on this. "I came here in the hopes Carmina would have had some kind of contact with you… or that you would be interested in taking her in, when we found her."

They both shook their heads.

"I could never take in that man's child," Irene declared. "Never."

"And she hasn't contacted us," Raymond added.

"I see." Neil dug into his pocket for a business card. "Well, if she did happen to make some kind of contact, would you please call me? We're trying to make sure she is safe."

Raymond took the card from him and looked down at it. "I'm sure she wouldn't call us. We've never encouraged any kind of contact."

CARMINA WAS BETTER PREPARED for the night this time. She had picked up a few essential items at the camping store, choosing very carefully what she should spend her limited cash on. She had a hot meal under her belt from the soup kitchen. And she knew now where the other homeless tended to congregate at night, where she was more likely to be able to sleep safely.

But she still felt incredibly anxious. She stood out too much. People knew she was new on the streets, and paid attention to her. It was strange, feeling both non-existent and too visible at the same time. Like she was caught in some kind of Twilight Zone episode. She unrolled her new sleeping bag—she'd splurged on one that squished down to a very small package and clipped to the outside of her backpack—and she slid inside. There were other people moving around, talking, laughing around a fire burning in a barrel. She wasn't sure if she would be able to sleep with all of the activity going on. But there wasn't anything else to do.

"What did you paint today?" she whispered to Esther, a question she regularly asked at the end of the day. But Esther wouldn't have painted anything today. She had been arrested and taken away. Carmina worried about her mother. Esther wouldn't do well in prison. Surely the authorities would realize she was innocent, that she couldn't be guilty of anything. They wouldn't dare to torture the beautiful blonde, would they? She would catch some guard's eye and he would protect her.

She didn't worry so much about her father. Julius would know how to handle himself. He always knew what to do. He was tough. Not like Esther.

"I didn't draw today either," Carmina whispered. Just thinking about it made her fingers itch. She didn't have a lot of supplies with her, but she had a few pens and pencils, and two sketch pads. Tomorrow she would spend some time drawing. It wouldn't be like today, when her whole focus had to be on survival. She'd be able to relax a bit more.

"Hey, pretty girl."

Carmina opened her eyes, startled. She saw the boy who had bothered her earlier. Toto, they had called him.

Before she could yell at him, he jumped into a speech. "I'm sorry if I scared you at lunch. I didn't mean to. I just wanted to make sure you got a sandwich and didn't go hungry."

"Did you follow me here?" Carmina glanced around, measuring how close they were to help. While she had tried not to lay down too close to anyone else, there were plenty of people within earshot if she called out.

"No, no I didn't follow you. I just saw you when I got here. Lots of people sleep around here, when we can. I'm not some creepy stalker, honest."

Which was exactly what a creepy stalker would say. Carmina watched him with suspicion.

"That's a nice sleeping bag," he said.

"Yeah."

"It looks brand new. Did you just get it?"

Carmina scowled at him, not answering. Why was he being such a busy-body? Was he a spy? An undercover agent? Or just a guy on the make?

"Come on. We can be friends, can't we? What's your name?"

Carmina rolled over to face away from him, and pulled the sleeping back up close to her face. Her backpack was under her head like a pillow. Not because it was comfortable, but because she wanted to hold onto it to keep it safe.

"Aw, come on," Toto tried once more.

She ignored him, and eventually, he sighed loudly and left her alone.

NEIL LOOKED at the pile of reports. He was only halfway through them, and knew he needed to finish reviewing them. He needed to have a full understanding of the case and where everyone was on it. He needed to be aware of all of the moving parts, to make sure they worked together as effi-ciently as possible. But he was getting report fatigue. He was skimming without really taking anything in. It would not do to sign off on something, only to realize later it contained something important that he hadn't really picked up on.

He stood up and stretched, arching his back and rubbing his aching abdominals. They said all of his stomach muscles had knit back together properly, but they felt different than they used to. He didn't feel as strong. Maybe it was just his mental perception; he had come to realize how fragile the human body really is. How fragile the hold on life is. Or maybe it just needed more time to heal and recover.

"I'm going for coffee," he told Agnes.

She sometimes wore glasses for computer work, when her eyes started to get fatigued, and she lowered them now, looking at him over the rims. "Just coffee?" she questioned.

"I may do a couple of other things while I'm out."

"What should I say if Mandy comes by?"

Neil shrugged. "Tell her I went out for coffee."

"Okaaay…"

He gave her a nod, and left. At first, he was just going to drive down to the little coffee shop where they sometimes picked up real coffee when the office stuff got too vile. Or muffins and donuts on those days when he wasn't eating well. But once he got in the car, he just kept going, driving back toward the Knight House. As he thought things over, he called the computer lab.

"We haven't really made any progress on the computers yet," Germain said immediately when Neil got through and identified himself.

"Backlogged?"

"No… but they have very good security. They're going to be just about impossible to hack, and if we do the wrong thing, they might do an automatic wipe. Then everything will be gone."

"But still recorded on the hard drive somewhere, right?"

"Well, if you're lucky and it doesn't do some kind of overwrite. But even if you're lucky… it looks like the contents are encrypted. You'd still need the password to read it."

Neil groaned. "That would make sense. All of his hard copies and hand-written notes are in code. He's pretty paranoid."

"Yeah. I don't know if we can recover anything."

"What about the daughter's? Same story?"

"Yeah. He probably set it up for her. Her diary is safe from all prying eyes."

"Okay."

"Where are you? You sound like you're inside a garbage can."

Neil pulled into a nearby parking lot, and picked up the phone, disabling the hands-free. He looked at the building in front of him. "I'm… I guess I'm at the school."

"I thought you were done questioning her friends."

Neil opened the door and stretched his legs, flexing his feet, before he got out. "Yeah, I am. But I still want to talk to one of her teachers."

"All right. I'll let you know if we find anything. But don't hold your breath. This is pretty sophisticated stuff."

"Thanks."

Neil hung up, and continued across the parking lot and into the school. At the office, he asked for Mr. Burpeau and was directed to his classroom. Walking through the halls, he felt a familiar sense of anxiety and dread. School had not been a good place for him as a kid. Not a safe place. He took a deep breath and pressed on. He wasn't a kid anymore. He was a grown man. With a gun. There was no reason he needed to feel threatened at a school. He was just here to question a witness.

In the art room, a stereo played while students worked on their projects and chatted with each other. Neil had to look for the teacher, who didn't lecture from the front of the room, but wandered around from one work-table to another, dealing with the students one-on-one. Neil finally spotted the short, balding man in a polo shirt and khakis, talking to a girl on the far side of the room, looking at a huge painting of an orchid in mauve and pink. The girl noticed him before Mr. Burpeau did.

"Mr. B…"

"What? Oh, we have a visitor."

"Could I talk to you alone for a few minutes?" Neil questioned, showing his badge. "Maybe now isn't a good time…"

Burpeau shrugged. "No problem. They're used to working independent-ly," he said. "Good work, Rachel. Just work on the depth."

The girl nodded and picked up a paintbrush. Burpeau motioned Neil to the door ahead of him, and when they were out in the hallway, led him to a tiny, closet-sized office across the hall.

"I heard about Carmina's parents," he said, sitting down. Neil sat in the visitor chair. "How very strange."

"Did you know them well?" Neil asked hopefully.

"No. Really only saw them a couple of times a year at art shows. Of course, I knew their reputations… I really can't reconcile that to what's being printed in the paper. Is it really true, that they've been selling forgeries?"

Neil nodded. "Afraid so."

"How very strange."

Neil let the silence grow in the tiny room for a few moments before broaching the topic of his inquiry.

"I assume you've also heard Carmina is missing."

Burpeau's face darkened. He shook his head, looking down at the top of his desk. "I was hoping that part was just gossip."

"No. She is missing, and I am quite concerned. I think it is imperative we find her as quickly as possible. Before she gets hurt."

"She has a brilliantly creative mind, that girl. Some of the stuff she produces… well, it's top notch. She's going to be a big name, someday."

"If she can get on the right track toward success. That's not going to happen if she's on the run or sleeping on the streets."

Burpeau considered this and nodded. He picked up a pencil and started to sketch on his blotter.

"Did you ever talk to Carmina about her family?" Neil asked.

"No… only as it pertained to her art. Art shows, opportunities to meet people in the business, things she could learn from her parents, that kind of thing. We didn't really talk about… personalities."

"Was she close to her parents?"

"Very close to her mother. Her father, I'm not sure. But she and her mother were more like sisters or best friends. They spent a lot of time together."

"Did she ever talk about other friends or family?"

"No, not that I can remember."

Neil tipped back his chair slightly. "Did she talk about her future? What she would like to be? Where she would like to go?"

"Sure. She very much wanted to be an artist like her mother. She had quite a knack for graphic design. I figured with her father's help, she could make some real connections, commercialize her work pretty quickly."

"Yes," Neil agreed dryly.

"Well… we didn't know about the forgeries at the time. Just that he was an art dealer, and sold her mother's work."

"You don't think Carmina knew her mother was passing off her own work as originals?"

"Oh, no!" Burpeau's voice was shocked. "Certainly not. She was quite proud of her mother and how talented she was. The suggestion of forgery never came up."

"Did you have class discussions on forgery in general?"

Burpeau considered this, his lips pressed tightly together. Neil leaned forward. "It's not a trick question, Mr. Burpeau. You teach art. Did you discuss forgery?"

"Yes. Of course. We talked about art and its commercialization. Forgery came up. Honesty in the profession. Provenance. Public domain and copying the work of others. All of that."

"Did Carmina participate in these discussions?"

"Carmina participated fully in her classes."

"So she did participate in the discussions about forgery?"

"I… imagine so. I don't remember any particulars."

Neil let him think for a moment. Burpeau shook his head again in response.

"Did Carmina ever seem upset by these discussions?"

"Not that I recall…" His brows twitched slightly. He looked upward, with a slight frown.

"Or did she?" Neil prompted.

"Well… there was one day… but I'm sure it was nothing."

"Why don't you let me be the judge of that?"

"Carmina was rarely absent from her art classes. But there was one, and I think we were discussing forgery… and she had to go home, sick…"

Neil raised his eyebrows.

"I'm sure they've told you, she had some medical issues," Burpeau was quick to add. "It wasn't unusual for her to have to go home, if her stomach was acting up."

"But it was unusual for her to miss art."

"Yes."

"And especially to leave in the middle of class."

"Well… yes… that's why it stands out in my mind. But I'm sure it was nothing. Just one of those days when she wasn't feeling well."

Neil nodded. He thought about the case. About dealing with Esther.

"What was Carmina working on right now?"

"Oh." Burpeau sat up a little straighter, looking eager. "She actually just submitted a new project proposal. She was considering some sort of public art installation. Maybe a sculpture or a mural. Something with visibility."

"Like…?"

"I talked to her about social change. Maybe looking at an important issue like homelessness, poverty, or addiction. Trying to make a difference in the world."

"What did she think about that?"

"It was a new idea for her… I mean, we've talked about it in class, but she hadn't really considered her message, what she wanted to say."

"Do you have any of her work here? A portfolio?"

"Sure. Back in the classroom."

Neil got to his feet, and Burpeau followed. There was surprisingly little horseplay going on in the unsupervised class. Generally, the students were continuing to work independently on their projects just as they had been when Burpeau was in the room. A few glanced up and went back to their own canvases or stopped talking, but in general, all remained quiet.

Burpeau went over to a vertical filing system, and looked down the slots to locate the one that held Carmina's portfolio. He laid it out on an unoccupied table and unzipped it.

If Neil had been expecting high-school level work, he would have been shocked. But he had been told repeatedly Carmina was very good, and that she had been trained by Esther from the time she was little. Even so, he couldn't help but be impressed by the quality of her work. He slowly paged through canvas-board paintings, sketches, photos, and computer-generated images.

"She has a broad range of skills," he said. "I don't see a lot of stuff all in one genre."

"She is very diverse," Burpeau agreed.

"Has she done any portraits of her parents?"

Burpeau considered. "No, not this year, I don't think. Maybe before that."

"Did she want to go to school? College or university, I mean?"

"She planned to, yes."

Neil pulled a business card from his pocket. "Will you call me if she contacts you? She may eventually need to touch base with someone, and I think you are a highly likely candidate."

Burpeau took it from him slowly. "You really think she would call me?" he asked.

"There aren't a lot of other people in her life. You are a mentor for her, so… maybe."

"All right. I'll let you know if she calls."

CARMINA AWOKE GROGGILY. Her eyes were still heavy and she had a headache. The ground was hard. She hadn't splurged on any kind of mattress pad at the camping store, and her hips and other bones hurt from lying on the ground again. The sky was just starting to get light, and there were people moving around. She clutched at her backpack, and realized it was gone.

Carmina sat up abruptly and looked for it, panicking. A few feet away from her, Toto sat cross-legged with her backpack in his lap, holding Cynthia in his hands. Carmina was out of her sleeping bag without even being sure how she had crawled out of it, and launched herself at the boy, snatching her bag and the doll from him.

"That's my stuff! What are you doing with my stuff?" she screamed.

She hit him across the face with her closed fist and then shoved him over. She stuffed Cynthia back into the backpack, and went over to her sleeping bag. She sat down and hugged the backpack to herself, glaring at Toto.

There was laughter and whispers from some of the others who had camped out there. "Go, girl," one of them called out, to more laughter.

Toto righted himself, looking at her with wide eyes.

"Stay away from me, and stay away from my stuff," Carmina told him.

"I was just—seeing what you had—seeing if you needed anything."

"Stay the hell away from my stuff!"

"Okay, okay, I'm sorry. I shouldn't have done that."

"No," she agreed, squeezing the bag to her.

"You carry a doll?" he asked. "Who does that?"

"That's Cynthia."

"Cynthia?" He patted his pockets to find a cigarette, and lit it.

"Yeah."

"What's so special about Cynthia?"

Carmina closed her eyes. What was so special about Cynthia? She had carried the doll with her every day for as long as she could remember. Through separations from her parents, nightmares, late-night stomachaches, and long, lonely days at the mansion without any friends. She slid her hand inside the backpack and touched Cynthia's yarn hair.

"Cynthia has a secret," she said.

"What do you mean?"

She didn't explain. One of the men walked over to them. A black man, with graying hair, in a long overcoat. "You don't look like you need any help in handling this boy," he said. "But I thought I'd ask."

Carmina looked at him, and then over at Toto again. "I thought there'd be some kind of rule," she said. "That you don't touch other people's stuff."

The black man looked at Toto. "If you're gonna get into other people's things, you deserve what you get."

Toto made a little shrug with his hands. "I was just trying to help."

"Your sticky fingers will get you in trouble."

Toto cut a glance toward Carmina, getting pink. "I wasn't stealing."

"You watch him," the man warned Carmina. "He gets… impulses sometimes. Does stupid things."

"Next time he gets an impulse like that, I'm going to break his nose."

Toto blew out a stream of smoke and grinned. "Fair 'nough."

The man nodded, and walked away again. Carmina put her backpack down and started to roll her sleeping bag up. She kept it taut and rolled it up tightly so it would fit back in the little sack that attached to her backpack.

"I'm sorry," Toto said.

She said nothing.

"I won't touch your things again."

"Darn right you won't." Carmina looked at the brightening sky. "Is it too early for breakfast?" she questioned.

"Yeah. Too soon for the kitchen, anyway. If you've got cash, McDonalds and some of the coffee shops are open." He looked at her with glittering eyes. Carmina took care not to make any movement or look toward her concealed money belt.

"You didn't find the millions in my backpack?"

He smiled, getting red again. "Well, in my defense, I didn't have it in my possession for very long. Didn't get a chance to see much other than the doll. Tracy."

"Cynthia."

"Whatever. She didn't look like anything special."

After attaching her sleeping bag to the backpack, Carmina sat down and reached into the backpack. Pushing Cynthia gently to the side, she slid out a sketch pad and pencil case.

"A doll *and* crayons?" Toto questioned. "What are you, five?"

She ignored him and leaned against one of the bridge's supporting pillars, balancing the sketch pad on her knees, and started to draw. She just let her mind wander and drew shapes and patterns at random to start with. Toto moved closer to her, his movements tentative, as if he was afraid she might blow up at him. He watched her constructing a spiral out of rectangular shapes.

"Fibonacci!" he exclaimed.

Carmina was startled. She looked at him. "Fibonacci? How do you know about Fibonacci?"

"It's a mathematical progression that's repeated over and over in nature," Toto said. "It's beautiful!"

"The picture?" She looked at it.

"The sequence! Zero, one, one, two, three, five, eight, thirteen..." His face lit up, glowing from some inward source.

Carmina looked at him and smiled for the first time. She looked past the grungy hoodie and lit cigarette and saw the passion stirring. "You like art?" she questioned.

"Art? I suppose. But the Fibonacci spiral... it's more than art. It's... like drinking pure water. Genius. Nature and numbers..."

Carmina darkened a few lines, adding depth. "You like math."

He nodded. "Yeah, I know, it's weird," he admitted. "I'm not the kind of geeky guy you'd expect."

Carmina glanced at his face. "You don't have to look or act a certain way to like math. Everyone should be able to pursue whatever passion they have."

"Yeah?" He looked pleased. He scooted up beside her, leaning against the same pillar. "Most girls don't like geeks."

"I didn't say I liked you."

He laughed. "Okay. You didn't. But you like people the way they are. That's very... enlightened of you."

Carmina flipped the page in her sketch pad. She wanted to draw her parents. She missed her mother desperately. But she knew she couldn't draw anything that would identify her. She was a blank, a cipher. No name, no identity, no parents. She started drawing Toto instead.

He looked startled when he realized she was drawing him. "Hey, you're good."

"Uh-huh."

"Where did you learn to do that?"

"Just practice."

He watched it take shape under her pencil. "I didn't used to like math," he confided. "I used to be... more of a jock. Sports, and drinking, and girls... I was good at all that, thought I was something special." He pushed the hood of his hoodie back off of his head, and rubbed at the short, bristly hair. Carmina noticed twisting tracks through his scalp where the hair did not grow. Toto ran his finger along one of them, and Carmina saw they were thick scars.

"What happened?"

"I got beat up. Messing around with another guy's girl because you're drunk… it's not such a good idea."

"No."

"Alcohol messes with your judgment. I didn't think I could get caught. He and his buddies… tried to explain to me what a mistake I had made…"

Carmina shuddered at the thought of such violence. All of those scars… he'd obviously been lucky to make it out alive.

"After that… when I woke up in the hospital… everything was different. The world looked different. I could *see* the math. It all made sense to me."

Carmina squinted at him. "You woke up with new abilities?"

"More than abilities. The whole way I see the world is different. And yes… I can do really advanced math now. I haven't found anything I can't at least comprehend. One of the professors at the university, he's letting me sit in on classes, even though I can't pay for them or get a degree or anything. I just love to go… and experience the math."

"Like going to a concert or art museum."

"Yeah, exactly! It's more beautiful than anything you've ever seen."

He stared off into the distance, reliving it. For a while, Carmina just drew, trying to capture his essence.

"Do you have any problems, since getting hurt?" she asked. She'd had some experience of her own with savants.

Toto came back to earth. "I had to relearn everything. Walking, eating, talking. And now… well, I'm not a jock anymore. All that stuff I used to be able to do so well…? It's all gone. I remember being able to sink a basket from half-court. It wasn't even hard. I could do it every time. But now… now, I guess I should be happy I can walk and talk."

"You're lucky you didn't die, or end up in a coma or something."

"I suppose. Sometimes I think that would be better. Or if I couldn't remember the way it used to be, so I didn't know what I was missing. I don't like being a different person than I was."

"It sucks. When things change."

"I get headaches sometimes. Really bad. Don't get along with people like I used to."

Carmina felt a little bit bad about getting mad at him. Maybe he couldn't help acting creepy around her. Maybe he was just trying to help, in his way, but was awkward about it. Carmina knew plenty about social disabilities. People didn't always understand how hard proper social behavior could be for others.

"Is that why you're here?" she asked. "And not with your family anymore?"

"Maybe. I guess."

"I'm sorry."

He put his arm around her. "We're just one big, happy family out here."

"Uh—no." Carmina squirmed out of his grasp. She stood up, and tore the sketch off. "Here. You can keep that."

Toto studied it. "Thanks. Can I have the one of the spiral too?"

It figured he would like the mathematical one better than the picture of his face. Carmina tore that one off too.

"Are you going to sign them?"

Carmina took them back from him and hesitated. She couldn't use her usual signature. She couldn't use her name, and still didn't know what name she was going to go by on the streets. She wondered about using just her initials. CK. Even that seemed too close, it made her feel too exposed. She scribbled in the corner of each sketch, and handed them back to Toto. He looked at the signature.

"KC?"

"Yeah."

"Well, nice to meet you, KC. They call me Toto."

He stuck out his hand to shake. Carmina held back, and just gave him a brief wave. "Yeah. Hi."

SIX

Neil woke up, and for a few minutes, just sat there, getting his bearings. He was in his car. His phone was buzzing. He pulled it out of his pocket and looked at the text from Agnes.

Mandy wants to know if you need Esther again today.

Blinking, Neil thought about it. He texted back.

Yes. Need her one more day.

He waited a few minutes to see if there would be any further reply, and when there wasn't, put the phone back away. He opened the car door and stretched his legs out the side, then stood up, stretching and rubbing the sore spots. His intestines spasmed with the abrupt change in position, and Neil just about doubled over with the sudden, acute pain. He leaned against the car, breathing, waiting for them to ease. Eventually, he managed to straighten up again, and he walked down the street, hoping the regular movement would calm the cramps so he could continue to function. He didn't need a sick day right in the middle of this investigation. Missing kids had to be a high priority, and he had to get the leads early, while they were still hot. Carmina may have left of her own volition, but that didn't mean she knew how to take care of herself, and they needed to know she was okay.

Neil breathed slowly through the pain, trying to focus his concentration on the rest of his body functions. His guts would settle down, given time.

There were other things that were more important. His phone buzzed again, and he looked at it.

In soon? Mandy looking for signed reports.

Yes. On my way.

Taking a few more deep breaths, he went back to his car and climbed in. As he reached for the key, he realized he was still wearing yesterday's clothes, and he'd better change before going in looking wrinkled and smelling funky. For a moment, he flashed on Carmina, curled up in a ball in some hiding place, three days into her own sleepless, nightmarish journey. He removed the keys from the ignition and walked up the sidewalk to his townhouse. His body was obviously exhausted, falling asleep before even getting out of his car. Since he'd already told Agnes he was on his way, he didn't stop to shower, but quickly changed clothes and shaved, and headed in.

At the office, Agnes gave him a warning look as he walked by her desk, but didn't say anything. Neil glanced around for Mandy. She had perhaps been and gone, since he didn't see her. He sat down and started scribbling signatures on the reports.

"You've read those, right?"

Neil startled, drawing a jagged line across one of the signature pages, and looked up at Mandy, who had apparently materialized out of thin air.

"Sheesh, boss. You want to put some bells on your shoes, or something?"

"Maybe I should do like you, and walk around without any shoes at all."

"Our witness finds it endearing."

He wasn't sure endearing was the word Esther would have used to describe his quiet stocking feet, but she had expressed a preference for it, at least. Neil stuck his feet out where Mandy could see them.

"Besides, I have shoes on now."

"For however long that will last. Any progress with Mr. and Mrs. Knight?"

"I haven't talked with Julius lately. He's pretty tough to crack. Hard to establish trust with someone so paranoid. But Esther… I feel like I'm making progress there."

"How much does she know about the details of the sales?"

Neil grimaced. "Well, to be honest, I don't think she knows anything about it at all. I think Julius just kept her painting, and took care of the rest of the business by himself."

"You're saying she didn't know anything about the business side."

"No… she seemed pretty shocked when I showed her the forged provenance of one of her reproductions. I don't think it was put on. I think she was honestly stunned."

"According to the prison authorities… she's been quite difficult since we sent her back yesterday."

"Difficult how?"

"Ignoring what she's told to do, completely disregarding any of the rules or routines they're expected to follow… crying and refusing all communication…"

Neil sighed. "Well… I'll see if I can get anywhere with her. She was pretty upset. Maybe now that she's had a chance to sleep on it…"

"Hopefully *someone* is getting some sleep." She looked up into his face.

Neil rubbed his eyes, as if he could erase the bags there. "I did sleep last night," he said. Though he didn't tell her he'd fallen asleep in his car. Lucky the local cops hadn't found him there and busted him for vagrancy.

"Good… because you really can't stay sharp, if you don't get the rest you need."

"I'm doing my best."

Her expression softened. "I know you are, Agent Crowther. And if you asked for any help, you know I'd give it in a heartbeat. But you have to ask."

She held his gaze for a moment. Neil looked back down at the reports, his eyes burning. "I'm fine," he said. "Entirely fit for duty. Ready, willing, and eager to put this case to bed. And find the girl in the process."

"Okay. Well, keep me in the loop. Have we extended the search to the street population? We have to get her picture out there as quickly as we can."

"Yeah. Fisher is looking after that. I may take a few flyers around later on today. He's got the resources to handle it," he hurried on, heading off any objections, "but I'd like to keep a hand in. I probably have the best understanding of what's going on in her head. What she might do or where she might go."

Mandy nodded. "Okay. If you're done with those," she motioned to the reports, "I'll take them now."

He handed her the ones he had signed, and looked at the rest. "I just have a few more to go through. I'll do that before I talk to Mrs. Knight."

HE TOOK his shoes off before going in to see Esther. Not so much because they were bothering him, but because he wanted her to see he remembered what she had said and respected her. If she had gotten oppositional, she needed to see he was doing his best to help and work together with her.

As usual, he checked on her through the observation window before going in. She sat in the chair, with her arms and head on the table. There were no drawing tools in sight. He backtracked to the copy room and picked up a small sheaf of copy paper and a handful of pens and pencils. When he got to the door of the interrogation room, there was a guard stationed there.

"Wait a minute," the guard said, holding out his hand. "You can't give those to her."

Neil looked at the young man. "What?"

"Administration is concerned she may be a danger to herself or to others. As such, she is not allowed to be in possession of anything that might be used as a weapon."

"Pens and pencils? Paper?"

"They're sharp."

"Seriously?"

The guard looked at him, frowning. Neil waited, and held up the pencils.

"I'll tell you what. You can take one pencil. As long as it is not sharp. You give it to her while you're in there, and you take it back away when you come out. And if you get attacked with it… that's your own fault."

"I promise not to claim compensation," Neil said dryly.

He examined the pencils he had grabbed, picked one out. "How's that one? Nice and dull. Short and stubby. I can't think of anything less like a weapon."

"Okay. Just that one."

Neil was allowed to enter. Esther's head was bowed and she didn't move as he approached. He cleared his throat, not wanting to startle her. He took his usual chair, and put the paper and the pencil down on the table.

"Esther."

She didn't move.

"Mrs. Knight."

Neil hesitantly touched her shoulder to get her attention. She pulled away from him.

"I brought you paper, Mrs. Knight. And a pencil."

She took a long breath, and raised her head. She looked somberly at the paper, and then back at him. Neil sat, waiting. Esther looked at the paper and did not pick up the pencil.

"Come on. I know it helps you to calm down and focus. So why don't you give it a try?"

She still didn't make a move to pick them up.

"What's wrong? The prison said you have been having a hard time. The guard at the door says you're on watch. What's up?"

She stared straight ahead of her, unmoving.

"Mrs. Knight. I want to help Carmina. I want to find her and make sure she's safe. I need your help."

She looked at him now, and reached tentatively for the pencil. He nodded.

"Please. Even if you can't tell me anything new, your pictures help me get the juices flowing. I'm going to go downtown today with her photo and see if anyone has seen her."

Esther slowly picked up the pencil, pulled the stack of paper towards her, and closed her eyes. Neil waited for inspiration to strike her. After a couple of minutes of thought, Esther bent over the page and started to sketch out a new scene. Neil watched it take shape. Carmina was somewhere dark. Her face was shadowed. Around her was a dark forest. There were animal shapes, bright eyes.

"The wolf is back," Neil observed.

She glanced at him, her eyes lingering for just a moment, and then she looked back down at what she was doing.

"What is she today?"

Not an elf, Neil didn't think. Not a naiad. Something darker, more feral. Her eyes were angular and pointed. Like a wolf's. He thought about what that might mean. She was changing? She was becoming affected by the dark world she had joined? Did Esther fear Carmina would become something else, too wild to ever come back to the family? Or was it just a reflection of Esther's own dark, despairing mood.

"Is she a wolf?" Neil questioned. "Or a wolf-girl? A werewolf?"

Esther continued to draw without a word.

"Do you think she's downtown?" Neil asked after a while. "Is that where you think she would go?"

Neil drummed his fingers on the table, impatient and trying to sort the situation out.

"Mrs. Knight. Esther. Are you upset with me for showing you the forged provenance yesterday? Is that what this is about?"

But Mandy had said she had been a problem at the prison, too. So this wasn't just a problem with him. She was uncommunicative and didn't follow the rules at the prison. She'd moved from being difficult to hold a conversation with him to not speaking at all.

"I don't know what to do, Esther. Do you want to write notes? Play Charades?" He looked at the sketch. "Pictionary?"

She flashed him a sudden look of amusement. It broke through the dark clouds of her expression for an instant, and then disappeared again. Neil closed his eyes and breathed. It was time for him to have something to eat, but he ignored his groaning belly and focused on her picture. Even with his eyes closed, he could still see the elements. He tried to talk them through.

"She's in a dark place. You're worried about her. There are dangers nearby. She is… changing into something. She's feral. Maybe even dangerous herself." He opened his eyes and studied the curves of Carmina's face. The way her hair fell. The other animals were closing in around her. Very close. "She's… becoming part of their community. They're taking her away. The wolf is… her father." He blinked at Esther. "Is the wolf Julius? And that's why she's part wolf too? You blame him for taking her away, putting her in this danger?"

Esther didn't answer, but for a moment her hand slackened, and she stopped drawing. Then she began again, as if nothing had happened.

"Is there anyone to save her?" Neil questioned, looking at the other shadowy animals in the picture. "Are any of these animals friendly? Are any of them me?"

He watched her shade in some blocky shapes in the background. Tall buildings. Downtown. He was silent, watching her pencil. The dull pencil managed to produce remarkably variable lines.

"Do you want to tell me about Julius?" He looked at Esther's face, but she didn't meet his eyes. Her expression was blank. No affect. "Do you want to tell me how Julius got you involved in this mess? How he ran the art business? What he told you and told Carmina?"

She sat there for a minute, as if trying to read her own mind. Then finally, she shook her head, an infinitesimal movement.

"You know I want to help you, right? I want to help Carmina. The more you can tell me, the better I can do that."

He took a business card out of his pocket, and put it down on the table between them.

"That's my card. If you want to see me, give them my card. I'm not going to have you brought in here every day. When you're ready to see me, you let someone know."

She worked on the picture for a little while longer, then firmly laid the pencil down on the table. She picked up Neil's business card. Picking up the pencil so it could not be used as a dangerous weapon, Neil left the room.

~

"TIME TO EAT," Toto announced.

Carmina looked at the sky. "How do you know?"

"It will take about twenty-one minutes to get to the kitchen. If you want to get in when it opens—and you do—then you have to be there early. If we leave now…"

"How do you know what time it is?"

He smiled. "The angle of the sun. The length of the shadows."

"It's all math, huh?"

He nodded. They both lifted up their backpacks. Toto's bulky bedroll was attached to his.

"Can you imagine waking up tomorrow, and being able to speak a different language? Or seeing a new color you've never seen before?"

Carmina rubbed at goosebumps on her arms. "That would be weird."

"That's what it's like. I never understood math before, and now I can speak it fluently. And I could never see it before, and now I can see it all around me." He turned in a slow circle, looking at the buildings around them. "All of the angles. All of the equations. I never even saw it before."

Others were getting up and heading out as well. Some went the same direction as Carmina and Toto, and others went in other directions. Some stayed behind, not getting up yet. Carmina imagined the men who had been up drinking late into the night would likely not be getting up for breakfast, but would sleep in until late.

"Do you always go to the kitchen for breakfast?" Carmina asked Toto.

"No, not always. I'm not always hungry that early. Smoking tends to take away my appetite too."

"Then why do you smoke?"

He shrugged. "It's something to do. Things can get pretty boring out here. No electronics. No entertainment. Just you and your own thoughts. It's a bit too much, sometimes."

Carmina frowned and looked at him. "And smoking fixes that?"

"Well… it all depends on what you're smoking."

At her expression, he laughed. "No, seriously, I don't do meth or anything. And pot makes you hungry, it doesn't take your appetite away. I dunno. Smoking gives me something to do with my hands. Helps me to relax."

"It's not good for you, you know."

"Really?" his voice rose to a falsetto. "I never knew that before, KC! Why didn't anybody ever tell me it was bad for me?"

Carmina covered her eyes when others of the homeless who heard Toto's squeaky falsetto turned around to look at them.

He laughed. "I'm not naive, you know. I'm a lot more experienced than you are."

Carmina didn't make any comment. You couldn't measure all experience by how old you were. And he wasn't much older than she was.

"Why don't you lead the way?" Toto suggested. "You need to learn your way around."

"Oh." Carmina looked around for landmarks. "Is it this way?"

"No. The river is that way."

"And it's… upriver, right?" Carmina tried to visualize her surroundings. She envisioned a big satellite map of the area, filling in the details she could remember. She closed her eyes, trying to make it clearer. Then she opened them again. "That way."

"Right. Not bad. Go ahead, you lead."

Carmina did. She got most of the way there by herself, only needing to be corrected once, about a street that didn't go all the way through the way they wanted, but terminated in a dead end.

They got there much earlier than Carmina had the day before with Reenie. The people who were outside this time were not full and chatty, but grumbly and impatient to get in and get something to eat. There were a number of young families just like at the park, and Carmina started to get worried, even though she knew there had still been food left over after breakfast officially closed the day before.

"Is there enough?" she asked Toto, grabbing at his arm. "What if they run out?"

"No, they won't run out. There's always lots. Even with people who stuff their pockets with sausages."

"Really?"

"Yeah. I wouldn't recommend it. They start to stink after a couple of hours."

Carmina giggled.

"You hungry?" Toto asked.

"Yeah."

She felt like her stomach was a great gaping hole right now. It was so hungry it hurt. But not the cramps and nausea that would send her home to her bed. A different kind of ache, that urgently needed to be filled. She took a few deep breaths.

"You're kind of pale. Are you okay?"

Carmina nodded. "I just really need something to eat."

"Do you get, like, low blood sugar when you don't eat? I had a grandma once like that."

"No, it's not that." Carmina rubbed her stomach painfully. "I just… when I get hungry, I don't feel very good."

"Okay." He nodded. "So maybe you *should* put a few sausages in your pockets."

Carmina shook her head. People were jostling now, pushing, trying to get closer to the door. She imagined that if she was wearing a watch, she would find it was a minute or two until opening. People knew and were getting impatient, wanting to be the first ones in the door. She resisted the people who were pushing behind her, trying to hold her ground and not be pushed over.

"One more minute," Toto confirmed to her. "If they open on time. Usually they're pretty exact."

"Can you tell the time that accurately? Down to the minute?"

"Well… it's harder when it's cloudy. And I lose track of myself, just like anyone, when I'm doing something and not paying attention to the time. But one look around, and I can tell you pretty closely. If I can see the sun or the shadows." He reflected. "I guess if I was in another city, I might be thrown off a bit. Because the sun angle is different, depending on your location… but I don't know, maybe my brain would automatically adjust."

The doors opened, and the crowd pressed in frantically. Carmina was swept in with everyone else. The forward motion ceased at the long tables, and Carmina picked up a plate, waiting for everyone to move forward so she could dish up. She recognized Bern, the man she had met the day before, and he helped to serve. He nodded and smiled.

"Hey, Bern," Toto said. "Have you met my friend KC?"

"She's got a name today. Nice to meet you, Casey."

"Thanks," she acknowledged.

He put a big spoonful of scrambled eggs on Carmina's plate. She moved on down the line, acquiring sausages and toast. She and Toto sat down together. Carmina dug in immediately. She shook the salt shaker over the eggs and continued. After a few minutes, she noticed Toto watching her.

"You were hungry, all right."

Carmina shrugged. "Mm-hmm."

She didn't try to carry on any conversation while they ate. When they were full, both sat back, relaxing.

"Do you want to come over to the university?" Toto asked.

"I dunno… why?"

"Thought you might be interested. I guess you probably don't want to sit in on calculus… but you could go around to the art department or something."

"What could I do? I don't have money to take courses."

"They'll usually let you sit in. And they probably have showings you can view. You can talk to the professors, they like to encourage young students."

"I don't know." Carmina was reluctant to show up where she didn't belong.

"Okay. Maybe another time."

TOTO SAID goodbye to Carmina and left the kitchen, heading off to the university. She watched him disappear around the corner, and looked around, trying to decide what to do. She turned away, thinking she would head back to the park with the fountain, but as she walked the other way, she got a hollow, breathless feeling. She wasn't hungry, she had just eaten, but she suddenly realized being with Toto had helped to fill the void being away from her parents had left. And since he had walked away from her, she was afraid of being alone again.

Carmina felt like she was floating above the ground. She felt disconnected. Like she was dissolving from existence. She turned back and ran down the sidewalk, looking for Toto. She pushed through the other homeless who were still standing on the sidewalk in front of the kitchen. She ran down to where she had seen Toto turn off, and searched the street for him. She couldn't see him. She turned around.

"Do you—can you tell me where the university is?" she asked the people standing at the bus stop.

One of the businesswomen pointed. Carmina ran on. She was getting frantic, sure she wasn't going to be able to find Toto again. She was alone. All alone again.

Turning a corner, she just about ran into Toto.

"Whoa! Hey, KC. I thought you didn't want to come."

Carmina stopped and bent over, hands on her knees, trying to catch her breath. Toto looked at her for a minute and then reached over and rubbed her back.

"Hey. Are you okay?"

"I can't run," Carmina gasped.

"I think you just did."

Carmina was seeing black blotches in front of her eyes. Her head spun.

"Do you need to sit down?" Toto suggested. He moved her a couple of steps to the side, and helped to lower her to the curb. "Put your head between your knees."

It took a few minutes before Carmina's breathing started to slow back down. She relaxed, feeling his warm hand on her back, calming her. Like Esther did when Carmina wasn't feeling well. He touched her head, stroking her long dark hair. She opened her eyes and looked at him, and he withdrew his hand.

"Okay now?"

Carmina nodded and cleared her throat, congested from running.

"You got asthma?"

"No… it's this other thing."

"You changed your mind about the university?"

"Yeah."

"Well, let's get going, then. I might not be a real student, but I still don't want to walk in late."

Carmina nodded. Toto helped her to her feet, and they walked together down the sidewalk.

"What's your real name?" she asked Toto after they'd been walking for a while.

"What's yours?"

Carmina sighed, realizing that was something she couldn't share with him. And he probably had reasons for keeping his real name private too.

"Is the government trying to find you?" she asked instead.

Toto looked over at her and raised his brows. Carmina felt a little embarrassed, but persisted. "Is that why you're on the street? Is that who's looking for you?"

Toto shook his head, his eyes on some mark in the distance. "They're not looking for me… nobody's looking for me, KC."

"I thought maybe because of your math… maybe you knew things they don't want you to know."

"I'm not a code cracker or something. Well, I suppose I probably could crack some cyphers… but I've never had access to any important information or anything. I'm just… on my own. That's all. I'm on the street because that's the only place I can get along."

Carmina thought it must be a comfortable feeling, knowing no one was looking for him. Not having to look over his shoulder all the time. To worry they were spying on him, or on his tail trying to track him down. While she didn't like the feeling of being non-existent, it might be nice if the feds didn't know she existed. To be confident she could go ahead and continue to live her life without their interference. But Julius had warned her. He had told her they would come one day, and she would have to run. He'd known it all along. Carmina had laughed sometimes at his paranoia. Rolled her eyes at Esther when Julius wasn't looking. She had thought he just worried too much. Until she saw the flashing lights in front of her house, and saw her parents walked out to the waiting cars in handcuffs. Then it had all become way, way too real.

~

CARMINA DIDN'T WANT to go to the math class with Toto, but she walked with him to the door of the classroom so that she would know where he was, and didn't have to feel lost without him. She could just go back there and check on him if she started feeling alone. Once he went in, she went back out on the lawn, and crossed the commons to find the art department. Toto was right, there were plenty of things for her to look at. The walls of the corridors in the art building were covered with paintings, sculptures, and other installations. There were several rooms set up as museums or galleries she wandered through at a leisurely pace, studying and analyzing the various pieces.

"I don't think I've seen you here before."

Carmina startled. She turned and looked at an older woman, her hair pulled back in a sort of French braid. A professor.

"Oh. Hi. Is it okay? I just was waiting for a friend…"

"Sure. We're glad to have the public viewing this work."

Carmina nodded. She pushed her rather messy hair behind her ear.

"What are you working on right now?" the Professor asked.

"Who, me?"

The woman caught Carmina's hand and looked down at it. Carmina looked at the graphite smudged on her little finger and the heel of her hand. She laughed at the mark of her work.

"Oh, yeah. Just sketching today. I don't have any real projects right now."

"Looking for inspiration?"

"Yeah, maybe…"

"What are you thinking of?"

"Some kind of public art. My teacher…" she paused, wishing she had said mentor or professor instead. "He thought I should work on social change."

"That can be challenging. Any thoughts?"

TOTO LOOKED Carmina over as they walked away from his classroom together. "You're practically glowing. You must have had a good time."

It had been such a relief to do something normal and familiar again; talking with a teacher about art projects and discussing some of the works in the gallery. It had taken her mind off of the current problems. For a while, she had just been herself again, instead of homeless and on the run.

"It was nice," she agreed.

"You're glad I suggested it, then? That you decided to come along?"

"Yeah, for sure." Carmina let out a long, satisfied sigh.

As they walked along, she noticed an odd hitch in Toto's stride. Not a limp, exactly, but sort of a stiffness or a twist or something.

"How about your class? Learn anything?"

He laughed. "I don't know if I *learned* anything, but I saw a lot of sweet functions."

Carmina frowned at him, her eyebrows pressing down. "That's just… weird."

He nodded his agreement. "I know it is, but I can't help it. That's just the way my brain works these days." At her grimace, he shrugged. "You looked at your art, I looked at mine."

Carmina's stomach was rumbling. She looked at the sun high in the sky.

"So what time do your Spidey senses tell you it is? I'm guessing it's way too late to get to the fountain for sandwiches."

"You would be right," he agreed. "By the time we got there, the truck would be gone. You want to go to the commissary?"

"What's that?"

"School cafeteria."

Carmina shook her head. "No…"

"Come on. Lots of food there. Have I ever led you wrong?"

"I've only known you a couple of days."

"And have I let you starve in those two days? Come on. I'll show you."

She was hesitant to go, not wanting to have to pay for a meal. But she was hungry, and needed to get something in her belly. So Carmina followed Toto's lead. The commissary was buzzing with activity, wall-to-wall students. Though they were better-behaved than the kids at the high school. She felt awkward and out of place there, sure everyone's eyes were on her and would know she didn't belong. They would call the police and have her taken away like her parents.

"Toto…"

"Chill, it's okay. Just blend in."

She didn't know how she was supposed to blend in when she felt like she had a spotlight shining on her. The kids around her didn't look much older than she was. Some of them hardly looked old enough to be out of junior high. And like her, they all shouldered backpacks, toting around their schoolbooks. Toto started to head toward the line-up for the food, and Carmina resisted, falling back. He looked back at her.

"Come on."

Carmina shook her head.

"Seriously. It's okay. Come on."

"No. I can't."

He stared at her for a minute. "Fine. Why don't you go sit over there; get us a couple of seats? Close to the garbage can. Just sit down and look like you're studying, or something."

Carmina let out her breath. "Okay."

That was something she could manage. She wandered over in the direction Toto had pointed, and found a couple of seats. She sat down on one, putting her bag down on the other so no one would take it. She pulled her graphic arts text out of her bag and opened it on the table in front of her. She looked over at the line-up to see what Toto was up to. He dished up food onto a tray, and when he got to the check-out till, went through a pantomime of having lost his money or whatever payment card the students on a meal plan used. The conversation lasted for a few minutes, with the students behind him growing increasingly impatient. Then a girl moved forward and offered her card to be scanned. Toto spoke to her, first objecting to having her use one of her meals on him, Carmina supposed, and then thanking her, his hand on her arm and his smile brilliant.

He walked over to Carmina's table and she removed her bag from his seat.

"We could have gotten more if you had come up," Toto pointed out. His tray was full, but split between them, it wouldn't be a huge meal. Carmina couldn't afford to be picky. "But we'll have enough," he assured her. "Keep an eye on that garbage can, and if anyone is going to throw out something you want, just say 'you're not going to eat that?' They're not going to throw it out if you want it."

"I can't do that," Carmina objected.

Toto rolled his eyes. "You'll learn."

They started divvying up the food on Toto's tray. He motioned to the soft drink. "Help yourself to a drink, too."

Carmina shook her head. "Pop isn't good for me."

"Well, it's not good for anyone. But it helps keep you hydrated and get enough calories when you're on the streets."

"Can't."

He pursed his lips, looking at her. "Okay… you want me to get you a coffee or water or something?"

"No."

"You don't want anything to drink?"

Carmina shook her head again. "No. Thanks."

He raised an eyebrow, but left her alone, not pursuing it any further. A girl chatting on her phone came over with half a plate of spaghetti to dispose of.

"You're not going to eat that?" Toto questioned, putting out his hand for her to stop. She looked at him, and without even pausing in her phone conversation, put it on the table next to him and continued to walk away. Carmina looked at Toto.

"You want some spaghetti?" he questioned.

"Yeah, sure."

He divided it between the two of them. Carmina worked through the lunch, her anxiety over being too visible gradually fading. Nobody paid them any attention. Toto licked his lips and wiped his mouth with a napkin. Carmina eyed a half-package of chips that was approaching the garbage. She glanced at Toto to see if he was going to ask for it, but he seemed to be satisfied, not interested in the salty snack.

"Are you—you're not going to eat that?" Carmina fumbled through the words, her face getting hot.

The studious-looking boy in the glasses who was headed for the garbage looked at her. "Hi," he greeted. "You want them?"

"Sure. Thanks." Carmina took the bag from him.

"Enjoy."

He gave her a friendly smile, and then moved on. Carmina slid her fingers into the bag and pulled out a few chips, which she crunched through happily.

"You sure you don't want a drink with that?" Toto asked.

She shook her head. "Thanks, this was good. I didn't think we'd be able to get anything."

"You just gotta learn the ropes. Don't be afraid to ask for stuff."

"Yeah, I guess."

"It helps that you look like you belong here," he observed. He used his napkin to dab the corner of his mouth. "You keep neat and clean so you don't look homeless, and people are a lot more accommodating."

Carmina pushed her hair back over her ears self-consciously. "I should wash up somewhere. I've been in these clothes for three days, and haven't washed anything except my face and hands."

"If you got a couple of bucks, you can use the showers at the Y or the pool. Otherwise you're stuck with sinks in public restrooms. It hasn't been too hot… you have any other clothes?"

"No."

"Well, I guess that's where we need to go next."

"I don't have the money," Carmina protested. Her heart started pounding faster because of the lie, and she was afraid Toto would be able to tell by looking at her.

He nodded. "It's okay. There's Salvation Army and other places. You have to poke through a lot of stuff to find what you want. But what else are you gonna do?"

"Oh. Okay."

"You done? Ready to go?"

Carmina got up, picking up her backpack and taking the chips with her. They emptied their trash into the garbage can and Toto led the way out.

She noticed when they got down to the sidewalk that Toto's odd gait was getting more pronounced.

"Did you hurt your leg?"

Toto made a strange, twisted grimace. "No. Why?"

"You just look… like you're limping or something."

"I'm just fine." His tone was abrupt. Carmina glanced at his face, worried she had insulted him or something. His eyebrow was twitching. Carmina looked around uneasily.

"Okay…"

"Let's go back to the bridge. I'm getting a headache."

Carmina didn't want to argue it. He was looking paler than usual. And the limp and the twitch worried her. Licking his lips, Toto pulled out a cigarette and put it in his mouth. He had a lighter, but couldn't seem to get it to work. He swore.

"Here, can you…? My hands are shaking too much."

Carmina took the lighter from him, a knot in her stomach. She flicked it experimentally.

"Maybe now would be a good time to quit," she suggested.

Toto growled angrily. "Turn the dial and push down the thingie. A five-year-old could do it."

"Well, *you* can't!" Carmina retorted, hurt by his sudden pique.

He swore again, pressing his hand to his head. "Will you just do it?" he pleaded. "Sometimes the nicotine will head these off."

Carmina tried flicking the lighter again. The flame disappeared. "I thought nicotine was bad for headaches."

"Are you a doctor? You gotta hold the thing down."

Carmina got it to stay lit, and held it tentatively toward Toto's cigarette. He inhaled a few times and got the cigarette going. Carmina handed the lighter back to him and he shoved it in his pocket. They walked along in silence. Toto's limp was now very pronounced, his whole body twisting and rolling as he walked. She wondered whether she should hang onto him, to make sure he didn't fall down. He didn't speak, and she didn't dare ask anything. After a little while, he put out the cigarette on his jeans, groaning and stabbing it out clumsily, and he put the half-used cigarette into the big pocket of his hoodie. Carmina wasn't sure they were going to make it to the bridge before he collapsed completely, but eventually she saw it looming about a block away.

"Just about there," she encouraged Toto.

He nodded wordlessly, his face white and pinched, twisted in pain. Staggering, he made it to the shelter of the bridge and collapsed, curling up in a ball. Carmina looked around for help, but most of the others had left to pursue their daytime pursuits, or else were similarly occupied, lying asleep or unconscious in untidy lumps here and there. She knelt down by Toto, brushing debris aside so she wouldn't cut her knees on broken glass or a sharp rock.

"Toto? Are you okay? Do you need me to do something?"

He just groaned.

"Do you have medicine? Is there something in your bag? Should I get help?"

"No, just sleep. Shut up."

"Are you sure?" Carmina's voice was choked up. She fought to keep tears from escaping her eyes. She hardly even knew this boy. Why would she cry over his problems?

"Shh."

"Okay," Carmina whispered.

His lips puckered to shush her once more, but no sound came out. She knelt there watching him hold his head in agony. The scars on his scalp were red instead of white now, and he continually clutched at them, groaning miserably. Carmina touched his arm, trying to calm and soothe him, but he shook her off with a snort of protest. All she could do was kneel there, or as her knees felt bruised and tired, sit there, and watch him fight the pain. Occasionally, he would stop and lay completely still, eyes closed, and Carmina would think it was over. But after a few minutes it would start again.

As it got later in the day and the sky started to darken and get overcast, a few more people started to arrive, getting ready to settle for the night. Carmina's stomach growled. But she couldn't leave Toto. She opened another granola bar from her emergency kit, and chewed on it while she watched Toto.

"He havin' another attack?"

Carmina looked up. It was the same tall, black man who had offered his help when Toto had gotten into her stuff. Most of the others seemed like they didn't want to get involved in what was going on.

"I guess. He said he was getting a headache… but he didn't want me to do anything. Does he get them like this a lot?"

"Sometimes," the man said unhelpfully. "I guess it's 'cause of getting hit in the head like he was. Looks like he was pretty bad beat up, that boy."

Carmina nodded.

"Just shut-up," Toto groaned.

The black man gave Carmina a shrug, and moved away.

She leaned over Toto once more. "Do you want water or something?" she asked. "Is there anything I could get you?"

"No."

Carmina got out her sketch pad and started to draw. Even though the light was fading, she needed something to distract herself. She drew while she still could.

∽

IT HAD GOTTEN dark enough that Carmina had given up and put away her sketchpad when the police showed up to roust them. At first, Carmina just heard the shouting. The noise came from the other side of the bridge, and she thought some of the others had gotten into a fight. But then she could see the sweeping beams of the bright flashlights, and people started running past her to escape.

Carmina's first instinct was to grab her bag and go. That's what Julius would have told her to do. Every man for himself. Get out of there while she still could. But she looked down at Toto. He couldn't run. He couldn't even stand. She couldn't just leave him behind, and run away to save herself. No matter what she had been taught.

She sat by Toto, protecting him with her body, watching the dark figures work their way through the homeless who were too feeble or too drunk to make a break for it. Some of them fought back. Most of them were just dragged away without protest.

"Come on, get up. Get out of here," one of the cops told Carmina, getting close enough to give her a kick to get her started on her way.

"My friend is sick," Carmina protested. "He can't go anywhere."

"Well, whether he's too drunk or not, you don't look like you are. Get out of here and find a shelter. There's no sleeping in public."

"I'm not sleeping."

"Don't get fresh with me."

He kicked her again, harder this time. Carmina winced at the blast of pain in her hip. She moved away from him, still staying close by to help Toto. Since she was out of his way, the cop kicked Toto, raising a loud groan from him.

"He's sick! Don't kick him! He needs help."

"I'll help him out, all right." The cop kicked him a couple more times. Each time, Toto jerked away and cried out.

"Stop kicking him!" Carmina screamed. "He's sick! Help! Somebody help me! He's beating on my friend!"

Her screams gave the cop pause, as he looked around at the other officers bent on clearing them out. "Will you just shut up and get out of here?"

"No! Help me! Somebody help!"

A couple more dark forms drifted over toward them. It was creepy how quiet their shoes were in the dark. They moved like shadows.

"What's going on? You need a hand?" one of them questioned the first cop.

"This one won't shut up. You want to put some cuffs on her and get her out of my way?"

"No!" Carmina shouted again. "Help my friend! Don't let him beat on my friend! He's sick!"

She could see the face of the nearest one as he peered through the dark at her. He shone his flashlight in her face, assaulting her eyes and making everything pitch black with red afterimages after he moved it away. He played it over Toto.

"Just how much did you friend drink?" he questioned, his voice heavy with irony.

"He's not drunk. He's sick."

"I'm giving you one chance to get out of here instead of getting arrested. You want to take him with you, you've got two minutes to get him on his feet and get out of here."

Carmina looked down at Toto. She knew there was no way she was going to be able to do it, but she had to try. She crouched down beside him.

"Toto," she begged in a low voice. "Come on. It's the cops. You want to go to jail? He's just going to keep kicking you until you get up. So get up now, for me. I'll help you up. Come on."

He didn't open his eyes or make any attempt to get up. Carmina grabbed his arm and tried to pull him up by force. He wrenched his right arm away from her, and when she caught his left arm instead, it was mushy and limp and he only stirred weakly.

"There's something wrong with him," Carmina insisted. "Can't you help? He's sick!"

The new cop, who had said he would let her and Toto go, if she could get him up, leaned in close. She expected him to take Toto's pulse, or look at his eyes. But instead, he started punching the helpless boy in the chest and stomach. Toto's body clenched and writhed with every punch, and he started crying out in protest.

"No! No!" Carmina tried to insert herself between the new danger and Toto. "Please! *Please!*"

"This is a waste of time," announced the third officer who had been quiet until now. "Just grab both arms and get him up. Put him in a van. And I'll take her."

They grabbed an arm each and started to drag him along the ground, scraping his back through the dirt and rocks. His pants started to come off, hanging down below his hips, showing tattered blue jockeys underneath. Carmina closed her eyes and looked away. Her face was wet. The remaining cop pulled her around by the shoulder.

"You have any weapons, needles, or anything sharp?"

"No."

"Lace your fingers behind your head."

Carmina did what she was told as he groped and patted. Then he took both her hands behind her and handcuffed them together.

"Please bring my bags," Carmina said, looking at her backpack and Toto's.

"Why should I? Maybe next time you won't come here to sleep."

She just stood there. She had no idea what to say to him. He grabbed both bags anyway, and holding onto the short chain between her handcuffs, steered her back to one of the waiting police vans. Toto was lying on the pavement. Someone had pulled up his pants. Several cops were standing around looking down at him, talking to each other or on their phones or radios.

"I told you, he's *sick*," she insisted to the cop escorting her.

"Sick with what?"

"His head. I don't know. A migraine or something. Just look at his head. You can see how he was injured before."

"In you go." He tried to lever her into the van.

Carmina resisted. "Are you calling an ambulance?" she shouted at the little clutch of cops. "He's sick, you need to take him to the hospital."

One of the policemen, she wasn't sure if he was one of the ones who had been hurting Toto or not, walked over and looked at her with hard eyes. "Your boyfriend will be fine."

"He's just… a friend. But he's sick. You have to help him. You can't just ignore how sick he is. He's not drunk. He's sick."

He cocked his head, his eyes moving back and forth as he looked at her, as if he were reading a book. "We called for an ambulance."

"Oh." Carmina let out a shuddering breath. "Oh, thank you."

"What do you know about the shape he's in? Were you there when he got sick?"

Carmina nodded. "He just said he was getting a headache. But it's been really bad. He just lays there and moans." Carmina tried to see past him to Toto. "It's really bad. I'm afraid he's having a stroke or something."

"You can talk to the paramedics, tell them what you know."

He looked at the cop who was holding onto Carmina. "Put her in my car." He pointed. "She can wait here for now."

Carmina gratefully let him lead her to the police car in question.

SEVEN

Carmina was so relieved they had stopped beating up on Toto, that it didn't occur to her to be worried about being arrested herself. She sat in the police car and watched for the ambulance to arrive, watched the EMT's approach and check Toto over. One of them was brought over by the cop who seemed to be the boss, and Carmina answered the best she could, which was not that much more than to say that he had scars on his head, as they could see, that he had a headache, which they could see, and that she didn't know any of his medical history or if he'd ever been on any meds to help control the headaches. The EMT thanked her anyway and went back over to Toto. The two medics put Toto on a stretcher and loaded him into the ambulance. Then they left.

She sat there watching the comings and goings of the police officers, a tightness growing in her stomach and chest. Most of the other police vehicles pulled out before the cop in charge came to talk to her again. He opened the door and looked down at her.

"What's your name?"

Carmina kept her mouth shut. This was what Julius had always warned her about. This was the test of whether she had learned. The cop looked at her, eyebrows raised.

"Your name," he repeated.

Carmina shook her head.

"Look, kid, you don't give me your name, I just take you in, run your fingerprints, and the computer spits out your name. So let's save the runaround and just tell me your name."

She said nothing. He opened the front door of the car and held up her backpack.

"This is yours?"

"Yes."

"You don't mind if I look inside, do you?" he unzipped it.

"No, you can't," Carmina snapped.

He looked at her, pausing. "Well, lucky for me, when I arrest you, I'm allowed to search your bag."

"You need a warrant."

"No, I don't. Not when you're under arrest."

"Am I?"

He fixed her with a stare. "You're under arrest."

"What for?"

"Vagrancy."

Carmina didn't have an answer. The cop finished unzipping the backpack and checked inside. He pushed things around, frowning. "You have a wallet?"

"No."

"ID?"

"No."

"You don't have a wallet or any kind of ID?"

"No," Carmina agreed.

"Why not?"

She looked down, her arms still folded across her chest, saying nothing. The cop sighed noisily.

"Fine. We'll print you at the station."

IF SHE THOUGHT Officer Mikkelson was ticked off when she wouldn't tell him her name, it was nothing compared to how angry he was when her fingerprints didn't pop up a name on their computer system. He slammed his hand down on the table.

"You've never been arrested before?"

Carmina shook her head.

"Just tell me your name!"

She swallowed. She wanted to tell him. Even if it was just to give him her new street name, KC. She was afraid that somehow he would still unwind it to find her real identity. She stared steadily at the floor while he stared at her. The long minutes of silence drew out.

Eventually, he picked up her backpack and dumped it. Carmina watched him, her heart thumping hard and fast, afraid and angry, and he pawed through each item, inspecting it for something to identify her. He looked at Cynthia with a sneer on his face, fingered everything in her emergency kit, even opened her pencil case. He inspected her graphic arts text for a name on the inside, touching the torn page and looking back at her. Carmina was glad she had ripped it out.

Mikkelson left everything lying scattered on the table, and escorted her out of the interrogation room. He took her to a woman cop. "Finish booking her as a Jane Doe."

The woman cop nodded, and took Carmina by the arm. "Let's go, hon'."

Carmina's breathing was fast. She felt like she couldn't get enough air. "What's going to happen?"

"You'll need to be searched and changed into a uniform. You'll be put in a cell for the night. At least you'll have a bed."

She sounded sympathetic. Carmina glanced at her face.

"How long have you been on your own?" the woman questioned.

Carmina was tempted to answer. She pressed her lips closed and clenched her teeth, refusing to talk. The cop sighed and shook her head. "Never mind."

She was given a uniform and taken to a room where she was told to change. Carmina lifted up her shirt, her face flushing immediately. The cop frowned.

"What's that?"

Carmina looked down, figuring she meant Carmina's scars, but she had seen the money belt. Carmina swallowed.

"My money."

"Your money! How much money?"

Carmina didn't answer. The cop approached her, and pulled back the zipper. She looked at the wad of bills and didn't take it out. She pulled the zipper closed again.

"Keep your shirt on."

Carmina stood there, wondering what was going on now. They reversed their previous course, back down the halls, to where Officer Mikkelson had transferred custody to the woman. Mikkelson was sitting with Carmina's possessions in front of him, filling out an inventory form.

He looked up at their approach, scowling, his eyes tired. "Is there a problem?"

"Well, yes sir, there is."

"What?"

"Can't process her for vagrancy. She's carrying cash."

"Cash?" he repeated in disbelief. "How much cash?"

"More than twenty."

"Her pockets were already checked."

"She's wearing a money belt."

Mikkelson looked at Carmina in consternation. "You're just full of mysteries, aren't you? I suppose next I'm going to find out you're a millionaire. Or forty years old. Or a man."

Carmina couldn't help but giggle. She looked from one officer to the other. "Does that mean I can go?"

Mikkelson chewed on his lip, thinking about it. "I could try for loitering, but the judge would throw it out when they heard the story of you taking care of your friend. So I suppose you may as well go. It will at least keep me from having to fill out this stupid inventory form."

He crumpled the paper into a ball, and started gathering her items together.

"I should just let you re-pack it. My wife says I can't pack worth a darn. I'd put it all back wrong."

Carmina moved closer so she could take care of her belongings properly, glad she didn't have to watch Mikkelson handle them anymore. She started packing everything away.

"That's a cute doll," the woman cop commented.

Carmina glanced at her. The woman reached for Cynthia, and Carmina swiftly pulled her out of reach.

"That's Cynthia," she explained.

"It looks like you've had Cynthia for a long time."

Carmina carefully tucked Cynthia into the bag. "Cynthia has a secret."

"Two young ladies with secrets," Mikkelson teased. "What, have you got diamonds sewn into her clothes?"

Carmina stroked Cynthia's curly yarn hair, and didn't explain. She tucked her other items in around Cynthia.

"I suppose I should drop you off somewhere," Mikkelson said.

"No. It's okay."

"You know where you're going?"

Carmina didn't answer.

EIGHT

Neil walked down the sidewalk, examining the waiting figures. His search of the previous day had produced no fruit. But he was still convinced he could find her. The homeless were often referred to as being invisible, but Neil knew there were only so many places for them to go. If they wanted to be safe and to eat, sleep, and shower, there were certain places they had to show up sooner or later. And if he could make contact with someone who had seen her, talk to the people who administered or volunteered at those facilities, he would eventually find her. Even though Fisher and his men were already on the case and out there in force, trying to find some sign of where Carmina was or where she had been, Neil felt like he had a better chance of finding her. And just because he had not had any success making contact with anyone who had seen her yesterday, that didn't mean he wouldn't be able to find her today. If he talked to enough people, he would track her down.

The only trouble was his feet. They were still sore from the amount of walking he had done the previous day. He had hoped that by walking around a bit, they would loosen up and the pain would go away, but he'd obviously done way too much. So he limped along looking at the crowd waiting for the soup kitchen to open for breakfast, hoping to catch a glimpse of Carmina. There were a number of teenagers, but he had no luck in picking her face out from amongst them. Pretty soon, he would have to sit down and get the weight off of his feet.

The doors to the kitchen were opened, and the crowd surged in, eager to fill their bellies. The greasy smell of smoky bacon hung in the air, making Neil's stomach writhe uncomfortably. He waited until most of the crowd had pressed into the big common room, and the line was down to a single-file queue, before trying to get in the door.

Inside, things were moving along quickly. There were a lot of people to be fed. Once more, Neil scanned the faces, looking for Carmina. He was pretty confident now that she wasn't there. She had gone to another facility for breakfast, or had food with her or given to her already, or like him, she had no interest in food first thing in the morning. Neil joined the line at the serving tables, and showed Carmina's picture to each of the servers.

"I'm looking for this girl. Anyone seen her around?"

Most of them shrugged, barely glancing at the picture. Neil supposed she would look quite different by now. She wasn't neat and clean and posing for a school picture anymore. Now she'd been on the street, without friend or family, for several days. She was probably dirty and worn and desperate. You'd have to look very closely at the photo now to be able to tie her to her previous existence.

One of the servers lingered on the picture for a moment, then shook his head as everyone else had done.

"You've seen her?" Neil questioned, studying the man's expression. "Maybe? Not sure?"

"I'm not interested in getting anyone in trouble," the big man said gruffly. "I'm here to help people out, not make trouble for them."

"I'm not here to make trouble for her either. I'm here to help her. She's gone through a pretty rough few days, and I'd like to help her get back on her feet again. She doesn't need to be living on the street. We can help her."

"Turning someone over to the cops doesn't help them. Sorry."

Neil moved onto the next server, thinking about it. The man had seen her. He was sure of that. He hadn't denied it. And if he'd seen her before, chances were she would come back here. Maybe not for breakfast. Maybe for supper. Or maybe to the nearby shelter to sleep. He was getting close.

After showing her picture to each of the servers, Neil started to work his way through the tables of homeless, showing them Carmina's picture. Most didn't even make a pretense of looking at it.

A sudden cramp seized Neil, and he grabbed the table for support, hunching over in pain. The world moved in and out of focus, and he felt for the empty seat he had seen a moment earlier and lowered himself into it, rubbing his lower belly tenderly, waiting for the pain to work itself through.

"You okay?" a man's voice.

He nodded. "Yeah. Just gotta take a break for a minute," he breathed.

"Have you had something to eat? Do you want me to get you something?"

Neil wondered if he looked so ragged that his good Samaritan thought he was homeless himself, or if it was an offer to anyone he would have made sitting at the table holding his stomach.

"No. Thank you." He tried to force himself to move. He felt for his clipboard and opened it up to slide Carmina's photo back in place. He'd have to come back again. Maybe when there was a different crowd. Carmina had been there. Someone would know something.

"What's that?" the voice inquired.

"Girl I'm trying to help out."

"What's her name?"

"Carmina. Knight."

A grunt of acknowledgement. No recognition. "Can I look at those pictures?"

Neil had Esther's sketches in the clipboard as well. He had thought at first that they might help. More personal than a photograph. Not the type of thing people were used to looking at when a cop came around looking for someone. Maybe they would build trust. Or intrigue people enough to persuade them to stop and look.

With his fingers shaking, Neil unclipped the sketches from the clipboard and slid them in the direction of the voice.

"These are good. Did you draw them?"

"No." Neil laughed, and wiped at the corner of his eye, which was leaking a bit from the pain he battled. "No. Her mother."

"Her mom is looking for her?"

Neil considered. It wasn't precisely accurate, but close enough to the truth. "Yes."

"They have a fight, or what?"

"It's a long story. But no, no fight. Something else scared the girl. Made her run. I'm trying to find her." He breathed a few times. "To help her."

"She's pretty."

"Yes, she is." The cramp started to ease. Neil continued to rub the sore spot. Breathing got easier, and the world came gradually back into focus. The man to his left stacked and straightened the pictures, and put them back into the clipboard.

"Is she in trouble?"

"No… though she might think she is."

Neil rubbed his face. He'd missed a spot shaving. It was a good thing he had a razor at the office, he could touch it up when he got there, before Mandy saw him. Neil took a quick sideways look at the man. Tall. Black. Graying.

"Have you seen her?" Neil asked.

The man stared straight down at his food. "Are you sure you don't want something to eat? You look like you haven't had a good meal in a long time."

"No, no. I'm not big on breakfast. My system's not ready for anything but coffee at this time of the morning."

"Breakfast is good for you. Most important meal of the day. That's what they say."

"Yeah. Just don't try telling my stomach that. Where did you see her?"

"I'm not aiming to get anyone in trouble."

"I told you she's not in trouble. She doesn't need to be out on the street. There's no reason for her to be running. It's all just a misunderstanding."

"So you say."

Neil shook his head helplessly.

"Someone who's not in trouble doesn't get the feds out looking for her," the black man commented.

Neil wondered what it was that labeled him a federal agent so clearly. He hadn't said or done anything that should have given him away. It might have been obvious he was some kind of cop, and not a private detective or worried father, but how did the man pin him so quickly as a fed?

"She's part of a case I'm working. But she's not in trouble. She hasn't done anything wrong."

The man considered this for a few minutes, then shrugged. "I'm not looking to get anyone in trouble," he repeated. And that was his final word. His tone clearly indicated he was done. He went back to eating his breakfast. A few people around them threw glances in Neil's direction, and it became obvious he was disturbing their breakfast. He nodded and got up to leave them in peace.

"If you see her. If she needs a hand. Have her call me." He put his business card down on the table. No one picked it up. Neil walked away.

~

TOTO STIRRED, and Carmina sat up in the uncomfortable hospital chair to look at him. His face was a better color today, pink again instead of white or gray. He moved around a bit before he opened his eyes. His eyes went over to her.

"KC. What are you doing here?"

"Checkin' on you."

He stretched and let out a loud, straining yawn. "Man. I don't know what they put in that IV, but I gotta get some of that."

"Probably morphine."

"How long have I been asleep?"

"I dunno. Since I got here last night."

"What night? What day is it?"

"Can't you tell by the position of the sun?" Carmina teased.

Toto looked at the window. "It's still today? I mean, I've only been here one day?"

"Yeah. Just last night."

"And they already let you go?"

Carmina shrugged. Toto looked her over, suspicion in his eyes.

"What?" Carmina demanded.

"Are you a spy? I mean, undercover or something? You shouldn't be out yet."

"They decided to drop the charges."

"Since when?"

She didn't fill him in on the details. Tell him she had money? She didn't want anyone to know she had money. She was just like any of them. Living hand-to-mouth, one day to the next. Except she had an emergency stash in case something unexpected happened. She knew the money wasn't enough to set her up—to get an apartment, or a car, or anything that would let her live a normal life, instead of sleeping rough—but it was enough to cover food or clothes or a taxi in an emergency. And she intended to start padding it out as soon as possible.

"Did I miss breakfast?" Toto questioned, his mind turning to more immediate concerns.

"No, they're coming around soon."

"What about you? You need something too."

"You're not sharing?"

He opened his mouth, looking for the words before stammering out: "They don't give you a lot here. There's not that much to share!"

Carmina grinned. "I'm just kidding. I'll go down to the cafeteria. See what I can get."

"Ah, she's learning."

Carmina's stomach was already complaining. She really hoped the breakfast trays would arrive soon. Everything at hospital seemed to happen in slow motion. 'A few minutes' could well mean an hour or two. And she couldn't wait that long.

"You can go ahead," Toto said. Carmina looked back at him. She hadn't realized she'd been looking at the empty doorway, willing them to bring in Toto's food.

"Sorry."

"No, seriously. Go ahead. It will take you longer to get what you need. I don't need to be babysat."

"Okay. I'll be back in a while."

"After I've eaten, I'll get out of here."

"Shouldn't you stay and let them run tests? To figure out why…?"

"I already know why, KC. Because I got my head bashed in. All the tests in the world aren't going to change that."

"But maybe they could give you something."

"They're not going to give me a prescription for narcotics. And that's what I need."

"Why won't they?"

"You really are naive, you know that?" Toto said. "They don't give homeless people narcotics. It's like giving them booze. Even if I come into the ER with a migraine, they won't give me anything. They say I'm drug-seeking."

"But that's not fair!"

He shrugged.

"Life ain't fair, KC. Get used to it."

IT HAD BEEN a few days since Neil had seen Julius. Julius still looked just as angry. Just as tired out. If he was that paranoid, that concerned about a conspiracy against him and his family all day long, it must be exhausting. They hadn't been able to get much insight on his personal life from his clients, but they had confirmed the suggestion he was always available to them, any time night or day. Esther, on the other hand, had a very regimented schedule. She worked on certain pieces of art, in certain lighting, every day. Meals and bedtime were the same time every day. She would rarely leave the house for a social event or a showing, and if she did, would put on only the briefest appearance. The two were as different as night and day.

"You again," Julius growled, on seeing Neil.

"I am the agent in charge of this case. So you are going to see me now and then."

"Like I told the rest of them, I don't have anything to say. You may as well not waste your time."

"Yes, that's what I hear."

Julius sat back in his chair, arms folded across his chest. "Then why are you here again?"

"For the same reason as the last time."

Julius looked at him and gave no sign as to whether he understood or not.

"We are still trying to locate your daughter. I'm getting closer."

Julius' eyes widened slightly. He did not like the suggestion. Last time, Neil hadn't known why Julius didn't want him to find Carmina, why he insisted Neil leave her alone. This time, Neil understood it a little better. Yes, Julius loved his daughter. He wanted her to be safe, away from the grasp of government agents.

"She's a smart girl, isn't she?" Neil went on. "She knew she had to disappear. Didn't stick around to ask any questions. She ditched anything that might identify her. Cut up all of her ID cards and tossed her phone in the pond."

Julius' facial features started to relax a little. Hearing that Carmina was doing all of the right things soothed his anxiety.

"But all of those things can't keep her safe. And it makes her harder to identify if something happens, and she ends up in the hospital or at the morgue."

"She's a smart girl. She knows what to do," Julius echoed Neil's own words.

"She's still pretty young. And even someone like you, who knows all of the dangers, can still get caught. I still figured out what you were up to. All of your precautions didn't keep that from happening."

Julius said nothing.

"I'm getting closer. I talked to a couple of people who have seen her today. I just need to get their trust, and they'll help me to find her. A pretty girl like her doesn't go unnoticed."

"She's got her mother's beauty," Julius growled, with an impatient head-shake. "I couldn't do anything about that."

"She's darker, like you. I don't think she particularly takes after Esther… in fact, I don't think she takes much after either of you. But she has her own kind of beauty."

"She's *my* daughter," Julius shouted, suddenly rising out of his chair. "You just leave her alone. Quit trying to find her. You've got me. You've got Esther. Carmina can't help you. Just leave her alone!"

Neil didn't move from his seat. No guards burst in. Everything remained quiet. Eventually, Julius backed off and just sat back down. Neil didn't bother pointing out that the reason they wanted Carmina was not to question her about the forgery business, but simply to find her a safe place to live. If Esther didn't know about the business, what were the chances Carmina would?

"Your wife… Esther is a bit… eccentric, as you put it."

"It's her artistic temperament."

"I'm not sure that's all it is. Have they told you she's having problems at the prison?"

Julius' scowl deepened. "I would guess so. She likes to be home. To work on her art. To follow her routine."

"She has stopped speaking. She's very upset about this whole affair."

"Then let her go home. You think she's a danger? A flight risk?" His nostrils flared. "The woman couldn't be less of a flight risk. She couldn't be more innocent. She's like a child."

"Is that why you chose her? Made her a party to this crime?"

"I made her my *wife* because I knew she would never be a danger to me. She's not capable of deception."

That, Neil could believe. He took a sip of his lukewarm coffee while he thought about it. As different as the two were, they were strangely suited to each other. Though paranoid, Julius recognized Esther's innocence, her lack of guile. She would never do anything to harm or deceive him. And in turn, she needed someone who was strong. Someone who would provide for her and look after her, and provide an environment where she could just do her art; just drift from one project to the next all day, every day. Her artistic genius and his brilliant, twisted mind provided the perfect combination needed for a successful forgery scam. One that would last much longer than a few paintings, but for years, even decades, without detection. Until the right investigator came along and started to put the pieces of the puzzle together.

"What is Carmina like? Is she like her mother?"

"No," Julius shook his head, bushy eyebrows burrowing down over his eyes. "No one is like Esther. Carmina… is her own person. She's not like either of us."

"She doesn't make friends well? Everyone says she spent all her time at home. Never over with friends."

"She didn't need friends. She had her family."

Neil considered this, and let Julius sit and stew for a bit. Julius shifted in his seat, his eyes moving around the room restlessly.

"When she was a little child, she was sick," Julius said. "Away from school a lot. So she was an outsider, not accepted into their little groups."

"And she didn't develop friendships as she got older?"

"Some," Julius allowed. "But she had us. Family is more important."

"Except now that she really needs them, her family won't help her," Neil pointed out.

"I have always helped her."

❧

NEIL GOT BACK to his desk and sat down. Agnes was trying to signal something to him. She'd have to either come over or call him on the phone. He started going through the piles of paper that had accumulated in his in box. There was an envelope with one of his business cards taped to the front of it, and he slit the flap and pulled out the single sheet of paper inside.

"I was trying to tell you about that," Agnes said, suddenly leaning over his shoulder and making him jump.

It was one of Esther's pictures, her style and the subject matter immediately recognizable. Neil's eyes traveled over it, picking out the details. You couldn't see Carmina's face, only her profile, a back view. There were long, striped shadows falling across her. The corners of the page were dark, with animal eyes shining in the dark again.

"What is it?" Agnes said.

"It's Carmina."

"In jail?"

Neil looked again at the striped shadows. Jail? They could be the bars of a prison or cage. Carmina hadn't gone to the kitchen for breakfast today, even though one of the servers clearly knew her. Neil picked up the phone to call the city police. He identified himself.

"I'm trying to find out if you have a Carmina Knight in custody."

He listened to the tap of keyboard keys as the operator checked.

"No, no one with that name or any similar."

"Is there any possibility she was arrested but has already been released?"

"No, I don't have that name in my system."

"What about a Jane Doe?"

The operator's sigh carried down the line. "Jane Doe? Can you give me a description, agent?"

"Girl, mid-teens, dark hair and eyes. Caucasian."

"Let me run it…"

Neil waited. Agnes raised her eyebrows at him, and he shrugged. It was a while before the woman's voice on the phone responded.

"No, sorry. No one answering that description."

"Anyone busted for vagrancy or loitering last night?"

She laughed and didn't touch her keyboard. "Every night, agent."

"Can you check?"

With a grunt of protest, she tapped her search into her computer.

"A few individuals, and two larger groups," she observed. "Both sweeps made downtown. You think one of those nets scooped her up?"

"Maybe. Or maybe they just scared her off. No teenagers in those lots?"

She tapped through them. "Not many. They're usually pretty quick and get away. No one with your girl's description."

"Okay. Thanks."

He hung up. "It was worth a try."

"How would her mother know if she was in jail?" Agnes pointed out.

"Sometimes mothers can get a feeling. Maybe it's just what she's afraid of."

NINE

Neil walked down the dark alley, looking behind bins and boxes for any sign of Carmina. The light from the street barely made it to the alley, and combined with a tiny bit of light from the moon, made it just possible to discern general shapes around him. He wasn't sure how he could know Carmina was here, but he knew it in his gut. Somehow, she was here, afraid and alone, and he needed to find her. To bring her home.

His breathing was faster and shallower than usual. He tightened his grip on his gun and tried to slow his breathing down to a slower pace. Tried to normalize all of his body's functions. He was focused. Hyper-alert.

"Carmina…? Carmina, are you here…?" he searched the darkness. "Don't be afraid, hon'. I'm not going to hurt you. We just need to talk."

There was a furtive movement further down the long alley. He hadn't realized it was so long and winding when he entered it. It doubled back on itself, going on forever.

"Carmina?"

For a brief moment, he caught a glimpse of a figure. Too tall to be the girl. Too menacing. The gun was slippery in his hand. Neil swallowed. His breathing was choked. Too loud to his own ears.

"Hands up!" he croaked. Way too quiet. Way too tentative.

There was a flash of light, and a blasting pain in his middle.

NEIL AWOKE WITH A VIOLENT JERK. He was flat on his back, soaked in sweat, his guts on fire. But he wasn't in a back alley. He hadn't been shot again. He was on his own bed, where he'd actually fallen asleep.

Catching his breath, he rolled onto his side and tenderly massaged his belly. He had to start being more careful about what he ate. He had been off of the recommended diet for someone with a shortened bowel for too long, and if he was going to make it through this case without a trip to the hospital, he was going to have to get back on track.

After a few minutes, his gut had settled down enough for him to crawl to the bathroom. If he was lucky, then by the time the sun came up, he'd be recovered enough to get to the office.

CARMINA HAD BEEN awake for a long time, sitting up drawing and watching Toto sleep. Even though she hadn't gotten a good night's sleep since she had run away, she'd awoken early in the grey light of morning, unable to settle her brain down enough to go back to sleep again. Finally, she gave up and got out her drawing materials.

It was very quiet. She felt strangely removed, like someone else was sitting there drawing, and maybe she was back home in her room, just waiting to wake up and go to school. That was where she really existed. Out here, it was more like a dream. She kept waiting to wake up and go back to her old life again.

Toto snorted and rolled over, slapping his hand over his face to block out the growing light. He moved around restlessly, and eventually pulled his hand away and opened his eyes, looking around.

"What are you doing up already?"

"Couldn't sleep."

"You gotta sleep while you can. Stay sharp. You get too tired, you get sloppy and maybe get hurt."

It was something Julius would have told her. In spite of the fact that he never slept. How many times had she woken up at two or three in the morning, to see or hear him pacing up and down, up and down. Seeing his bloodshot and baggy eyes in the morning, she worried over him…

"I try. I'm just not sleeping very well."

"Uh-huh."

Toto sat up, rubbing his eyes and clearing his throat.

"Is it time for breakfast?" Carmina questioned.

He smiled. "Not yet. You're going to have to wait for a while longer."

He shuffled over to her so he could see what she had been drawing. The page was filled with the faces of various of the other homeless that slept there or that she had seen. So many different people, old and young, male and female, dirty and clean.

"You're really good with faces," Toto observed. "You know what you should do? Out where there's busking, like at the park, sometimes you see artists doing people's faces. Not so real, like these, but those funny, cartoony ones…"

"Caricatures?"

"Yeah, that's it. How long would it take you to do one of those? Five or ten minutes, and the person pays you twenty bucks or something for it. You could get some cash that way."

Carmina thought about it. "I'd have to get some board to mount them on or something. So they could be framed."

Toto shrugged. "But you could do it, right?"

"Sure," Carmina agreed. "Might be a good way to get some money. For clothes and stuff."

She looked down at her new t-shirt and shorts. They were passable, but there hadn't been a lot she liked at the clothing place Toto had taken her to when he checked himself out of hospital. There was a lot of old, stained, or crappy stuff. But not a lot of stuff she liked.

"Maybe enough to get a room at one of those subsidized places. So you don't have to sleep rough."

Carmina shrugged and didn't comment. She wasn't sure she wanted to be cooped up inside somewhere. If people got to know her, that could lead to the federal agents finding her. And that could lead to jail or some other kind of detention.

Toto reached over and took her hand. Carmina was startled, and had to brace herself not to pull away from him with a jerk. Talking with Toto was grounding, it helped her to feel real and present again. She pictured his hand keeping her anchored, keeping her from floating away on the wind. He was a nice guy in spite of his shortcomings.

"How are you feeling today?" she asked him. She studied his face, looking for any of the paleness she had seen there before his migraine. There were no twitches, no grimace of pain. When he had walked with her home from the hospital, the odd gait had completely disappeared.

"I'm fine. In the pink."

"Do you know when you're going to get a headache like that? Is there anything you can do if you sense one coming?"

"I can usually figure it out a few minutes before… but there's not really anything I can do. They just come."

"Does something trigger them? Was it the math class? Like, concentrating too hard?"

"No. I don't think there's anything that causes them… just the effects of the head injury. Nothing I can do about that."

"Yeah. That sucks. How often do you get them?"

He didn't answer, and she looked at his face. He stared off into the distance.

"Not too often," he said. But his voice was flat and helpless, and she knew that even 'not too often' was too much. She couldn't imagine facing that kind of pain, completely randomly, never knowing when or where it was going to hit.

Her gut gave a twist that made her grunt, reminding her she had issues of her own to deal with. Everybody had their own challenges. There was no point in trying to fix Toto's, when she had her own body to think about. Toto's eyes focused on her.

"You okay?" he questioned, giving her hand a squeeze.

"Yeah. Okay."

"You sure?"

She shifted around, trying to find a position that would ease the pressure she felt building inside. "Yeah. I think… I'm gonna go for a walk."

"Nothing is open yet."

"I don't want anything. Just a walk."

"Do you want some company? It can be dangerous, wandering around all by yourself."

"Umm—no. Not this time. I just need some fresh air."

He was kind enough not to point out they were already sitting in the fresh air. They had slept in the fresh air. There was really no escaping the fresh air. Carmina pulled her hand out of Toto's comforting grip. She put her art work back in her bag and got up.

"I'll see you later. Are you going to be at the kitchen for breakfast?"

"Yeah, probably."

"Okay. I'll meet up with you there."

With raised eyebrows, he watched her walk away.

SHE ENDED up being late getting to the kitchen. Not too late to get something to eat, but late enough she wasn't part of the initial rush to get in. After getting her plate, she looked around for a seat, and eventually found one across from the tall black man that slept close to them, who Carmina had now learned was called Snake. A dangerous-sounding name for a man who seemed to be nothing but caring and compassionate toward his fellow sufferers.

"Hi," Carmina greeted him, sitting down.

"Hi, Casey."

She started to shovel food into her mouth, looking around for Toto. She was surprised not to see him as soon as she got there. Looking back at Snake, she found his eyes still on her. She raised an eyebrow questioningly.

"Someone was looking for you yesterday. Different name, though. Not Casey."

Carmina chewed her eggs slowly. Her heart beat fast. "Yeah," she agreed.

Snake looked away from her and cut his sausage into tiny triangular slivers.

"You didn't tell him anything," Carmina said.

"No, of course not."

"Good."

Carmina continued to eat. She had a sudden stabbing pain in her side, and tried to ignore it.

"He said your mother was looking for you."

Carmina drew in a swift breath. She shook her head. "He's lying. My mother's not looking for me. She's in jail."

Snake considered this, his brows drawing down. "Maybe she got out."

Carmina's hopes rose at first, but she pushed them down, stuffed them away. It was a lie, meant to draw her out. They wouldn't let either of her parents out that quickly. There was no hope of that.

"She's an artist too," Snake said. "He had pictures she'd drawn of you. Beautiful work."

Elbow on the table, Carmina rested her forehead in her hand and closed her eyes. Esther loved to draw pictures of Carmina. For as long as she could remember, she had been Esther's favorite subject for her original work. 'My muse,' Esther would say, and kiss her in the middle of the forehead. Would she still be able to draw in prison? Would she continue to draw Carmina, or choose a new subject? What if some bully ripped up her pictures? Destroyed them?

Carmina's eyes burned and she rubbed them, trying to prevent herself from breaking down. You had to be tough on the streets. You couldn't let yourself get sentimental. She might never see her mother again. There was no point in imagining what might happen to her, in making a tragedy of the whole thing. She cleared her throat and swallowed a few times, trying to relax the lump that strangled her breathing.

"Hey, KC," Toto greeted cheerfully. "You didn't save me a seat?"

Carmina rubbed her eyes and looked up at him. The old woman to Carmina's right stood up, picking up her empty plate. "I'm done. Take mine."

"Oh, you don't have to…" Toto protested unconvincingly. She ignored him and just walked away. Toto shrugged his shoulders, and sat down in the vacated chair. He looked at Carmina and then across the table at Snake. "What's up? Something wrong?"

Carmina shook her head. "Nothing." She forced a smile she didn't feel. "Just wondering where you were. I thought *I* was late!"

"I lost track of time." He got a little pink.

"You? I thought you always knew what time it was, with your brain thing."

"I can still get distracted." He started to eat. "I went by this art supply store, so I can show you where it is later."

"It wouldn't be open yet."

"No. But they had these pictures in the window. You remember that old toy, like from the eighties? Spirograph?"

Carmina knew exactly what he was talking about. "With the different sized gears, and you could make all of those patterns?"

He nodded, smiling broadly. "Wow." His face shone, euphoric. "Those are beautiful."

Carmina laughed, and shook her head. "You're crazy, Toto."

"Not crazy," he protested. "Just brain-damaged."

TOTO HAD TAKEN Carmina to the art shop, and she had to admit the Spirograph pictures—which Toto breathlessly informed her were made of hypotrochoid and epitrochoid curves—were beautiful. She left Toto standing outside looking at them while she went inside to buy the supplies she would need if she was going to attempt to draw caricatures for money. She was anxious about the dent the purchase made in her little stash, and hoped the money she earned from the drawings would quickly fill the hole. When she exited, Toto was still staring at the pictures.

"I'm all set," she announced, holding up her bag. "Let's go."

He had to tear himself away from the window, and dragged his feet for the first couple of blocks, looking frequently back over his shoulder to try to catch another glimpse of the mesmerizing spirals of color. Finally, he turned his attention back to Carmina.

"How did you get all that stuff?" he demanded, frowning at her. "You said you didn't have money."

Carmina was silent, considering her answer. She didn't want to admit she had lied to him. And she didn't want to lie to him again. But she couldn't tell him she had cash. It might be too much of a temptation for him. And she couldn't say she had stolen them, when she walked out with a store shopping bag full of goods.

"We… worked something out," she said finally, deciding to leave it vague. He could assume she had agreed to do some work for the owner. Or trade something. Or draw something for his window display. But that apparently wasn't where Toto's mind went.

"You didn't agree to sleep with him, did you?"

Carmina was shocked. "No! I wouldn't do that!"

After studying her expression, he seemed satisfied her reaction was an honest one. "Lots of people down on their luck barter with sex…" He struggled for words, forming the beginning of a sentence and then failing to carry it through. Finally, he sighed. "It never turns out well."

"I'm not going to do that. I'm… I've… got other talents."

Toto snickered.

TOTO AND CARMINA cut across one of the little patches of grass to get to the fountain in the park. The fountain seemed to be the place where most people ended up, sooner or later.

Toto stopped short, and Carmina just about ran into him. She looked around. "What's wrong?"

Toto pointed to a sign. Carmina looked at the familiar red 'do not' circle and slash symbol, and read the words without taking them in at first.

'Please do not feed the homeless'

There was a by-law referenced and a monetary fine if you got caught. Carmina shook her head in dismay.

"Do they think we're monkeys at the zoo?" Toto demanded. "Don't feed people who have no home, and maybe they'll go back into the woods? What —?" He couldn't even put his thoughts into words. His face was getting red and his voice louder. People were turning to look at him.

"Shh," Carmina tried to quiet him. "They won't give me money for pictures either, if you're noisy about it."

Toto drew back his leg, and kicked the sign, sending it flying several feet away. Carmina took a quick look around for any trouble.

"Okay, come on," she ordered. She grabbed Toto by the arm and tugged him toward the fountain. Muttering under his breath and shaking his head, Toto wandered through the nearby paved paths to work off steam or scope out a place to set up.

He stopped, staring at one of the park benches. Carmina walked over to him.

"Oh, they got new benches. Those are nice."

They looked like brushed chrome and wood, and had a modernist design. Toto turned to look at her, scowling.

"Don't you get it, KC? Even after seeing the sign?"

Carmina looked down at the bench again, looking for another sign, or for something that would explain Toto's ire.

"Why do you think it has bars across it?" Toto asked, motioning to the bars between each seat of the bench. They looked sort of like arm rests, but were too short to rest an arm on.

"I don't know. So your butt doesn't bump into the next person's when you sit down."

Toto snorted. "You are so naive, KC!" He shook his head. "Look at it. They're designed to keep people from sleeping on them. Because you can't lay across the bars. Duh!"

"Oh. Yeah, I guess…"

"I guess the homeless don't need to eat or sleep."

"We can still sleep," Carmina said, taking his hand to try to calm him. "Under the bridge, like always."

"You know what they're doing? They're starting to put spikes in the cement in some places. Like the spikes to keep pigeons off of signs and ledges. So you can't even sleep in sheltered places. So nobody can sleep anywhere."

"Then where do they expect people to sleep?"

"Nowhere. They don't want any homeless sleeping anywhere."

Carmina couldn't think of what to say. She gave Toto's hand a comforting squeeze, and walked away.

THERE WERE a few other buskers around. Not a lot, because the work day had started, and most people were in their office cubicles, stuck on the endless treadmill of their daily grind. With the sun shining on her face, Carmina felt a little giddy, excited about the opportunity to put her craft to practical use.

Toto helped to pick out a location, and Carmina had him sit on the edge of the fountain, where the light was good, and she stood there and with a couple of colored pens, sketched a quick cartoonish picture of him, exaggerating the shape of his nose and dark eyebrows. When she was done, she showed it to Toto.

"That's great! I don't know how you do that."

Carmina ducked her head, a little embarrassed.

"Just practice."

She walked around, drawing caricatures of some of the other people in the park, busking or watching, or sleeping on the grass. When she had done a few pictures, she propped them up along a bench for display, and she and Toto sat down on the edge of the fountain to watch people's reactions. Whenever anyone stopped or paused to look, Toto immediately jumped up and approached them.

"Would you like one? The artist is right here. She can do one of you. Or from a picture, if you want her to do someone else."

A few people agreed, and Carmina sold her first original works of art. It was odd, she thought as she watched people browse through the park, Julius had never offered to sell any of Carmina's work, even though some of them were really good. And he rarely sold any of Esther's original work, unless it had been specifically commissioned. Mostly, he just sold the reproductions, making money off of the old masters, rather than speculating on anything new. Carmina had just assumed Esther didn't want to part with any of her work. She did become quite attached to some of her pieces. But it was odd Julius had never pushed to her to sell more. Much of her work just waited, carefully preserved, in storage. Carmina didn't really want her mother to sell a bunch of pictures of her, but she did wonder why it had never been an issue.

"KC. Earth to KC!"

Carmina snapped back to reality. "What?"

"Customers. You know. The people who are going to pay you."

"Sorry."

Carmina looked at the young couple.

"Can you draw us together?" the woman asked.

"Of course," Carmina agreed instantly. She gave them directions and fussily changed their positions before finally settling down and starting in on the drawing.

TEN

You did really well today," Toto observed. He'd been watching with eagle-eyes every time Carmina was paid and tucked the money carefully out of sight. She was sure he'd kept a tally, even if he hadn't tried to. His math brain wouldn't have let that go unnoticed. She felt a little nervous of his attention to the money. This was the same boy who not long ago had taken her backpack while she was sleeping to rifle through the contents.

"Yeah, it turned out well," she said.

"You should celebrate! Go out somewhere for real food tonight, instead of soup-kitchen crap. Hey?"

Carmina narrowed her eyes at him. "I like the food at the soup kitchen."

"Yeah, 'cause you haven't been eating there for weeks and months. After a while, it gets pretty blah. So come on. Go somewhere special."

Carmina calculated what her net was going to be, after having spent money for art supplies, and now having to spring for supper too. She would barely squeak by with a profit.

"Fine. Where do you want to go?"

"Are you offering to take me?" he asked with overdramatic surprise.

"Well, since it was your idea, and you've been helping out all day. Why not?"

"Hmm…" Toto licked his lips, thinking about it, his eyes rolling up to the sky in contemplation. "You know what I would like?"

"Are you going to tell me?"

"Pancakes. Let's go to the pancake house."

"Pancakes," Carmina repeated, dismayed.

Toto looked at her in surprise. "You don't like pancakes?"

"Well… yes, I like them, but…"

"But what? Let's go for it! It's been ages since I had real pancakes."

"Didn't you have some at breakfast this morning?" Carmina thought back to the kitchen's breakfast, and tried to visualize his plate. She was sure he'd had two or three pancakes, along with his eggs and sausages.

"Well, yeah, but I said *real* pancakes. Not those industrial mix things. They're like cardboard. Real, tender, buttery pancakes made from scratch."

Carmina almost groaned aloud. She packed away her unsold display drawings carefully, so the edges wouldn't get banged up in her bag. She zipped it up and turned back to face Toto.

"Do you really hate pancakes that much?" Toto questioned, studying her face with sad puppy-dog eyes.

"I said okay."

"But if you really don't want to…"

"It's fine."

"You're sure? You're not mad? We can go somewhere else, if you really don't want the pancake house."

"No," Carmina sighed. "Lead the way."

"All right!" Toto fist-pumped like a little kid. "Pancakes!"

Carmina laughed at him and followed. It took about twenty minutes to walk there. When the waitress came out to seat them, she looked at their backpacks disapprovingly. "We're really not supposed to allow backpacks in here."

"We can pay," Toto promised. "We'll put the bags under the table and no one will see them."

She hesitated, pursing her lips and looking from one to the other. Carmina straightened her posture, not liking the way the girl seemed to be looking down at her.

"You don't want our money?" she asked archly.

"Well… come in, I guess. I'll put you in a booth."

Toto looked at Carmina to make sure she was going to come. "Yeah? Okay?"

"Fine. But if she's going to keep being all stuck-up…"

"You're going to have to learn to deal with it. She's not the last one you're going to run into. At least she's letting us in."

"We're clean. We've got money. Why shouldn't we get in?"

"I know we should," he agreed in a low growl. "But you don't get how people act…"

"Hmmph. I'm starting to."

The waitress seated them, and gave them each a menu. "Your server will be with you shortly."

She turned and walked away.

"Good," Carmina observed. "We won't have to deal with *her*, at least."

"Forget about her. Let's enjoy ourselves. This is a celebration."

"Right."

Carmina glanced at the menu, and looked at the others in the restaurant who already had their meals. Everything looked and smelled so good. She hadn't even noticed the pervasive smell of grease at the soup kitchen, until she smelled food without it. It smelled clean and fresh. It called to her, tempting and enticing her.

"Oh, that smells good."

"I told you."

"Yeah. What else do they have? Just pancakes?"

"Waffles, crepes… or they've got stuff like omelets and hash browns too. But the pancakes are the best."

She couldn't deny how irresistible they smelled. Carmina breathed the sweet scent deeply, as if she could drink it. She knew she should go with the eggs and hash browns. Maybe some bacon and sausages too. But the pancakes and waffles smelled so inviting.

"Excuse me a minute," she told Toto, and made a beeline for the restroom across the dining room. Once there, she relocated the money in her pockets, smoothing out the bills and putting them into the money belt. She left enough in her pockets for the bill and a generous tip, then went back out to see Toto.

"I ordered you a drink," he told her. "The waitress was by while you were in there. I know you said you shouldn't have pop, so I got you juice."

He smiled proudly, expecting praise.

"Uh… thanks. That's great."

The waitress returned a few minutes later with their drinks, while Carmina browsed through the menu.

"WAS I RIGHT?" Toto asked. "Good stuff, huh? Their pancakes are nothing like the stuff at the soup kitchen." He patted his happy tummy, and hooked his thumb around his waistband to pull it out slightly. "Woof. I'm stuffed."

Carmina shifted uncomfortably. While her mouth had been in heaven for every bite, her digestive tract was objecting every inch of the way. Already, she was bloating up and there was a bubbling, fermenting feeling in her gut. She burped and reached to take another drink, then realized she had already drained her glass. All of that orange juice. She had downed it all. She wasn't used to the syrupy waffles, and had tried to cut the sweetness with the juice. Until it was all gone.

"You want me to get you another drink?"

Carmina looked at the hovering waitress. "No. Thanks. Just the bill."

"Sure, hon'."

Carmina leaned back, massaging her side and lower abdomen.

"Are you okay?" Toto questioned. "You're not looking so good."

Carmina slapped her money down on the table. "Take care of the bill. I gotta—" she lurched for the restroom without finishing her sentence.

SHE SAT ON THE TOILET, trying to suppress a moan of pain. Her irritated gut was pushing everything through at lightning speed, and there was nothing she could do about it now. She knew better. She knew to avoid pancakes and waffles and their sweet, syrupy toppings. And juice. The sugar and the acid were a brutal combination that shot through her system like fire. Tears of pain and resentment ran down her cheeks. She whispered swears and curses under her breath. Like anyone would hear them. Like they would help.

"Miss? Are you okay?"

Someone, the waitress Carmina thought from the voice, had come to check up on her. That was how long she'd been in there already. Everybody was wondering what was going on.

"I'm just... not feeling so good," she said, her face getting hot with embarrassment. "Just tell my friend… tell him to go home, I'll catch up with him later."

"Is there anything I can do for you? Do you need… an ambulance or anything?"

"No, no. Nothing. Just leave me alone. He paid, didn't he? He didn't just take off?"

Carmina felt the money belt, prepared to take more money out if Toto had cut and run with what was supposed to be the payment for their meals.

"Oh yes, he paid. That's not a problem. And he's waiting for you. He's just worried you're… not feeling well."

"Well, I'm not. I'll be out when I can… but he should just go. I don't know how long it will be…"

"It's not food poisoning," the woman said emphatically, in a low voice, as if Carmina had made an accusation. "No one else is sick. It's too fast for food poisoning."

"No. It's not food poisoning. Really. It just… didn't agree with me. That's all. Nothing was bad."

The woman hovered for another moment, looking for some other way to be of help. Then she finally started to walk away. "Let me know if you need something… I'll come back in a while, I guess. Make sure you're okay."

"You don't need to. I'll be fine."

The waitress gave a snort, and walked back out of the fetid bathroom.

WHEN HER INTESTINES finally stopped writhing and cramping, Carmina felt wrung out and empty, as if she had lost more than she had originally put into her system. She was weak and shaky and very sore. She knew better. She knew not to eat the things she had. She could have just ordered eggs and breakfast meats. She might even have been able to have a waffle without any toppings. But to eat like she had was to invite certain illness.

She washed her hands well, and sponged off her ghostly pale face with a wet paper towel. There were dark circle under her eyes. They already looked sunken and skeletal. Carmina wasn't sure how much fluid she had lost, but it was obviously too much. Julius would have insisted on an IV for rehydration. But she wasn't going to the hospital, and no doctor was making a house call when there was no house.

When Carmina finally walked out the restroom door, Toto was sitting there at the table closest the restrooms, both backpacks at his feet, and he jumped up the moment he saw her.

"KC. Are you okay? Seriously… you look like hell. Is it food poisoning? If you threaten to sue—"

"I'm not threatening to sue anyone. It's not food poisoning. It's my own stupidity. Just come on. Didn't I tell you to go home?" she snapped.

"I couldn't!"

The waitress came over. "Are you okay, miss? Can I get you anything? A drink, maybe?"

Carmina shook her head. "No way. I'm fine, just let me be."

"She's just trying to help, KC."

"I'm saying I don't want help. Let's just go, please."

Toto nodded and picked up both backpacks. "Okay. Come on."

She followed him out the door. They went about half a block before she spoke again. "I can carry my bag."

"Not right now, you can't. You just take care of yourself."

"You carried your bag when you were sick."

"I didn't look like you."

Carmina laughed, even though neither of them really thought it was funny. She stopped walking for a minute, needing to catch her breath and work up the energy to walk further.

"Why didn't you want a drink?" Toto said. "You really look like you need one."

"Electrolytes. More juice or water is just gonna make it worse."

"Electrolytes. Like in a sports drink?"

"Yeah."

"Let's get you one, then."

Carmina nodded her agreement. "Drugstore. Need some other stuff too."

They started walking again, slowly.

"What else do you need?"

She looked at him sideways. "None of your business."

"Oh…" he reddened a little. "Okay. Sorry."

He obligingly led her to the nearest corner drugstore, still insisting on carrying her bag.

"You stay here," Carmina told him at the door.

"I'll help you—"

"Stay here," she insisted.

"But… okay. Fine. Okay."

She looked at him for a moment to make sure he wasn't going to just follow her in anyway, and went into the store. She quickly gathered the items she needed and took them to the cashier, looking down with her face flaming hot as he rang them up and bagged them.

Outside, she took one of the electrolyte drinks out of the bag and opened it. She took a few swallows with Toto watching over her anxiously.

"Okay… let's go home."

ELEVEN

It was the second time Carmina had overslept Toto. Usually, she was awake at first light, or even earlier. But the sedating effects of the medications she had bought, and being exhausted from pain had apparently done the trick, and she slept until what seemed like late in the morning.

"Hey, you okay this morning?" The words were whispered close to her ear, and Toto stroked her hair gently to wake her. Carmina yawned and forced her eyes open, looking around.

"Yeah, I'm good. What time is it?"

"We should probably be moving on, before anyone shows up to roust us."

Rather than sleeping under the bridge, as usual, Carmina had chosen a spot in the park, close to the public restrooms that stayed unlocked throughout the night. Toto had warned they might not get a lot of sleep. The police might wake them in the night, and certainly early in the morning before joggers and commuters started to travel the pathways.

Carmina stretched and sat up. "Okay. Let's go for a walk."

They each picked up their bags—Toto had apparently decided she was strong enough to pull her own weight again—and started walking. The park was pretty in the early light of dawn. Dew sparkled on the grass and leaves. Like one of Esther's paintings.

"Where are you today?" Carmina murmured under her breath.

"What?" Toto looked at her.

"No, nothing. Just talking to myself. Just thinking…"

"What about?"

"Just… someone from my old life."

They walked on in silence for a while.

"You know why I'm on the street," Toto said. "Are you going to tell me any of your story?"

She shook her head. "Too dangerous."

"I can already guess some of it."

She glanced at him, wondering how much she could have given away.

"You come from a good family. Well-off, I mean. Used to having everything done for you. Probably had a falling-out with your dad, or step-dad. Usually what happens when a girl like you ends up out here. Maybe he tried to mess with you and it was the only way to escape."

He looked at her expectantly. Carmina shook her head.

"All wrong?" Toto demanded. "I know it's not *all* wrong. Maybe he didn't mess with you. Maybe he was hitting you. Or just too strict."

Carmina didn't look at him or give anything away. Toto growled in frustration. "Fine," he said. "Why don't you tell me, then?"

"No."

"I can guess anyway. Most teenagers on the street, it's drugs or abuse, or else they got kicked out for something. Religion or sexual orientation. Are you…?" he trailed off. He looked at her and shook his head, changing his mind about asking his original question. "Maybe you let in the Mormon or Seventh Day Adventist missionaries or something."

Carmina laughed at his expression. "Yeah, that was it."

He looked thoroughly dissatisfied with her response. They continued to walk. Toto put his hand around hers, and after due consideration, Carmina decided to leave it there. She never had a boyfriend at school. Hardly any friends at all, if she was to admit the truth. So even though Toto's hand felt strange and foreign in hers, a little uncomfortable, she let it stay there. She remembered her vision of Toto's hand anchoring her to the ground.

They got to the edge of the park, and Carmina stopped walking. She stared at the old brick building that abutted the green.

"What?" Toto asked.

"I'm thinking."

He was quiet as she stared at the wall. It was covered with graffiti, but underneath all of the defacing paint, she liked its bones. The location could be seen from the park or the street. The morning sun lit it up like a stage.

"What are you thinking?" Toto prompted finally.

"I'm thinking… I found my project."

"Your project?"

"This is my wall."

He was looking at her like she was completely nuts.

"I can't explain," Carmina told him. "But… I'm going to need some supplies. That wall is going to take a lot of paint."

"You're going to paint it."

"Yeah."

"Why?"

"Because it's there."

"You want to know what's going to happen if you paint it? You're going to get arrested. You can't deface property."

"I'm not going to deface it. That was done a long time ago."

"You're crazy."

Carmina nodded. "Maybe," she agreed.

IT TOOK a while for the caricature business to bring in enough money for Carmina to buy all of the paint and other supplies, including a ladder, that she would need. Storage was an issue, but with a big chain and padlock, she locked it all together and hoped no one would want the pile of equipment enough to try to take it.

She had the plan in her head. Hadn't written it up like she would have for her design class. But it was just as clear to her as if she had. She was excited to start. Jittery over it, her hands shaking. She set up the ladder and made sure it was stable, then started to paint.

It was late in the day when the cop showed up. He stood there looking at Carmina. She took a deep breath and stepped down the ladder to talk to him.

"What's all this?" the cop questioned.

"School project. Public art."

"You have permission for this?"

"You prefer the graffiti?" Carmina asked, looking at the wall. One-third of it was now a neutral gray. The rest was still covered with layers of graffiti.

"Of course not. It's an eyesore. But you can't just paint over it because you feel like it."

Carmina went over to her backpack and pulled out a piece of paper. She handed it to him. He looked it over for a moment, then handed it back.

"Okay. You're making good progress. What's it going to be?"

Carmina raised an eyebrow at him, and climbed the ladder again. He stood around for another minute or two, and then continued his beat.

NEIL LOOKED over the faces of the crowd, but no Carmina. He watched them getting their plates and sitting down with them. People visited, but for the most part, they just ate. A few watched him covertly, knowing he didn't belong. Neil looked for the big man, the server who had recognized her picture last time.

"You scared her off," the server said when Neil approached, without Neil saying a word or showing her picture again.

"What?"

"She hasn't been coming around here for breakfast anymore. Someone must have told her about you; or else something happened to her. Haven't seen her in a while."

Neil tried to swallow the acid that burned in his chest. "You think something happened to her? Has anyone said anything?"

"I haven't heard anything. But I probably wouldn't. People come and go. You never can tell why."

"But you think it's because I spooked her."

"The timing seems right."

Neil swore. He looked around. "Who would know? Is there someone who knows her?"

There was the black man, but Neil couldn't spot him in the sea of faces.

"You want to make things worse? Why don't you just leave her alone?"

He was startled to hear Julius' repeated refrain. But he couldn't just leave Carmina to her fate on the street. He'd seen what happened to kids like that. She was so young and naive, a loner, no street smarts. The time that she'd been missing was stretching out, taut as a rubber band, and he felt it was only a matter of time before it snapped, and she turned up dead or the victim of a violent crime.

"I can't leave her to get hurt or killed," he told the server. "If you're around these people every day, you know what I'm talking about. It's not an easy life. I want to help her."

"Sometimes you just have to leave people alone. She doesn't want your help."

"She doesn't know what her options are. She's running because that's the only path she knows, not because it's the best thing."

The server chewed on his lip for a minute. "Sometimes," he said slowly, "the cops don't know the whole story. You think running away from home is more dangerous than staying. But you don't know what she might have faced at home. Most of these kids don't leave home over a misunderstanding. There's abuse. Some pretty serious situations."

"I know why she left home. And it wasn't over abuse. She has a good relationship with her parents."

"So *they* say."

Neil hadn't really considered the alternative. He was so caught up in the forgery case and in getting Carmina back that he hadn't really stopped to wonder whether things went any deeper. Were there other reasons Carmina had run away? Had the arrests of Julius and Esther just provided her with the opportunity to run that she'd already been looking for? Julius could certainly have been a strict or unreasonable father. Esther would be easy to push around, or to keep in the dark. Julius had already kept her in the dark about so much else. If Julius was abusing Carmina, or was even just smothering her with his rules and paranoia, would Esther even be aware of it? Neil had speculated the wolf in Esther's pictures of Carmina was Julius. Was it? Did Esther subconsciously see him as dark and predatory, even if it wasn't something she could put into words?

Neil breathed out a long sigh. "If she comes here again, would you tell her I'm not going to force her into anything? I'm not going to do anything that will hurt her. She knows she can't go back to her parents anyway."

"Anything I tell her is just going to spook her worse."

"Then what would you suggest?" Neil snapped.

"Just leave her alone."

Neil knew he wasn't going to be able to do that.

~

CARMINA WAS WALKING with Toto down the back alley, lost in thought. He seemed to sense she wasn't in the mood to talk, and just walked with her in silence, kicking rocks and scuffing his feet as he went. Toto stopped abruptly and pressed his face up against a chain-link fence that enclosed a small work or storage area. Carmina waited for him to move on, but he didn't.

"What is it?" Carmina questioned.

He took off his jacket and threw it up across the barbed wire strands at the top of the fence. Carmina's stomach gurgled, and she pressed her hand to it.

"What are you doing?"

It only took Toto a few seconds to scale the fence and drop to the other side.

"Toto!" Carmina protested in a whisper.

"Shh!"

"What are you doing?"

He grabbed what looked like a big spool, and started to climb the fence again with it under his arm. He didn't get all the way up, and stopped to juggle it.

"Catch this!" he ordered in a whisper.

"No!"

From his awkward position on the fence, Toto swung the spool up and over the top of the fence. Carmina stayed out of the way, and it crashed to the ground. Toto finished climbing up and over.

"I told you to catch it!"

"No! You're stealing, I'm not going to help!"

Toto put his jacket back on and picked up the spool, marching on. Carmina jumped to keep up with him. "What's your problem all of the sudden?" Toto demanded. "You've never had a problem before."

"With stealing?"

"With… taking what's been left behind. You've got no trouble raiding dumpsters."

"For things people have thrown out. That's not the same."

"They just left it out. They're not using it anymore. What's the difference? Put it in a dumpster or put it behind a fence. It's there, why shouldn't we take it?"

"You," Carmina corrected. "I didn't take it."

"It's a spool of wire," Toto pointed out, showing it to Carmina. "You think they care? Next time they need it, they won't even remember it was there. They'll just go out and buy a new one anyway."

"What are you going to do with it?"

"Sell it. Just like fishing balls out of the water trap at the golf course. You do the work and sell it to the next guy." He gave a dramatic shrug. "Everybody benefits."

"Except the guy you stole it from."

"He doesn't care. He probably won't even go looking for it again. You do him a favor by getting it out of his way so he has more storage space." Toto laughed at this.

Carmina didn't think it was funny. "I don't steal," she maintained.

"Well, good for Miss Goody-Two-Shoes! You have all of this art talent anyway, you're bringing in plenty of money. I don't have anything like that. So I get by how I can."

Carmina didn't argue it any further, walking next to him in silence.

THE PAINTING PROJECT had taken a long time. Carmina was ready to finish it, but everything had to be just right.

"Why do you want to go to the park?" Toto questioned. "We can't get a good sleep there. We'll have to be up too early."

"I'm not going to be sleeping," Carmina laughed.

"What do you mean, you're not going to be sleeping? You're just going to sit in the park, awake, all night?"

"No. I'm working on my wall."

"At night."

She said nothing.

"In the dark."

"Yeah."

"You can't paint in the dark!"

"I have a flashlight."

"And you think the cops won't arrest you the second you turn it on?"

"Not if they don't see."

"They'll see your flashlight."

"Not if I have a lookout to warn me when the patrol is coming."

He took a breath, and then stopped. "So I'm not going to get any sleep either?"

"Not if you're going to watch for cops."

"Seriously, KC? Come on. Do your painting during the day. Like you have been."

They both looked at the wall. The basics were done. The main structure of the picture. And she had very carefully marked the positions of the rest of the lines during the day, so she'd be able to add them by flashlight during the night. Toto's eyes went over the painting. The lower half of a couple of barn doors. Bare beams inside the barn that the open half of the doors revealed. All very boring and vague. Nothing to garner anyone's interest. Carmina knew Toto was disappointed in it. He'd expected something exciting. Something brilliant. Instead he got open barn doors and an empty barn. She'd failed him.

"The rest has to be done at night," she said. "So nobody sees the finished product until morning."

"Why?"

"For full effect."

"KC... this is dumb. You can't paint at night. You're going to get caught. You won't be able to see well enough. Honestly."

She shrugged. He could stay and help her, or choose not to. She wasn't his boss.

But she knew he would stay.

CARMINA HAD KNOWN she would be tired when she climbed down the ladder for the final time. But she had really had no idea how exhausted she would be. She'd stayed up late before. Even had nights where her stomach had kept her up all night. But lying in bed with a stomachache was nowhere near as tiring as going up and down the ladder every time Toto heard or saw someone coming, constantly moving back and forth across the mural, reaching, and carrying heavy paint cans, and all the rest of the physical work she had done.

But now it was done. The sun would be coming up soon; she knew that even without Toto's magical mathematical brain. He had fallen asleep on watch, no longer able to keep his eyes open. But that was okay. That was all built into the plan. She quietly put her equipment away, around the other side of the building where it was out of sight, and she left Toto there at the base of the painting while she completed the final step of her project.

TWELVE

Neil was breakfasting—actually eating a breakfast that was not composed of coffee—when his phone rang. His stomach instantly clenched. Early morning calls were rarely good news. He picked it up and looked at the caller ID, but didn't recognize the name. He answered it anyway.

"Crowther."

"Do you watch the morning show?" a male voice demanded without introduction.

"No." Neil reached for the remote to turn on the television. "Who is this?"

"Stan. Stan Burpeau."

He tried to place the name.

"Which morning show?"

"The one with Rivers."

He changed channels.

"Okay. What am I looking for?"

His brain was grinding away rustily, still trying to place Burpeau's name.

"Arts and lifestyle. They recycle the stories about every twenty minutes so it should be on again soon."

Neil took a bite of toast and watched the screen. He had the volume off and didn't have to listen to the inane chatter of the hosts. He never could understand how people could actually want to listen to that patter first thing in the morning. The 'up next' banner at the bottom of the screen announced the upcoming arts and lifestyle segment, something about a mysterious painting. He waited until the screen blacked between segments to unmute the sound.

"Okay, it's coming on now…"

The chipper female anchor came on-screen, standing in front and to the right of a huge painted mural. Neil frowned, sorting out the images and trying to make sense out of it, and why it should be important to him. It was a barn with the top half of its doors standing open. Across the open top-section was a gorgeously rendered spider web. Drops of dew decorated it like jewels. The spider itself peeked in from the top corner. Woven into the spiderweb, like the messages in *Charlotte's Web*, was the word 'human'.

There was, in fact, a real human sleeping at the base of the picture. A young man in a gray hoodie. His arms clasped around a beaten-up backpack.

The sun was just coming up, and lit up the side of the building that the mural was painted on like a billboard.

"It's one of hers," the man on the phone said. "I'm sure of it. I'd recognize her style anywhere."

Suddenly Neil placed the voice and the name. Mr. Burpeau. Carmina's art teacher. Then this painting was Carmina's? How could it be? Neil tried to tune into the anchorwoman's voice, cranking the volume up.

"…Painted overnight… apparently a social statement on homelessness… the artist is, as yet, unknown…"

"You think Carmina painted that," he said.

"I know she did. The instant I saw it, I recognized her composition."

Neil watched as the anchorwoman had the nerve to go up to the boy sleeping at the base of the mural. She crouched down and spoke, wakening him. His face showed confusion, and he looked around, taking in the daylight, the anchorwoman, and her camera crew. He rubbed his eyes blearily and stumbled to his feet.

"Where did she go?"

At some word from the anchorwoman, he turned and looked up at the mural.

"Did she finish it? Oh, she did." He laughed. "She put Fibonacci in there!"

"She put what…?"

"On the spiderweb, that's a Fibonacci spiral. I guess she wasn't up to hypotrochoid and epitrochoid curves!"

The anchorwoman looked at him like he was a lunatic. "Can you tell us about the artist?"

"Well, she… I guess she took off. She's kind of a nut about privacy. She wouldn't want me to talk about her."

"Did you know what she was doing?"

The boy stretched his back and his shoulder muscles, yawning loudly. "I knew she was working on a project. I didn't know what it was going to be." He looked at the painted silhouette of a sleeping man, which he'd been blocking when he slept there. "And I didn't know I was going to be part of it."

"Human," the anchorwoman observed, reading the glistening web. "My guess is that was not one of the words Charlotte wove into her web to describe Wilbur the pig. Humble, I think, was the closest."

The boy shook his head. "At least K— at least she knew not to put humble over my head." He snickered.

"What can you tell us about her?"

"I think I'd better keep quiet. She has a mean right jab."

"Is she an old woman? Young?"

There was a glimmer of amusement in the boy's expression. "Let's just say she's old. Old bag lady goes all militant with her message…" He laughed.

The anchorwoman didn't know how to take this suggestion. She faced her cameraman seriously, and signed off.

The station switched back to commentary in the studio, and Neil turned the television off.

"Thank you for letting me know, Mr. Burpeau. This is very helpful."

"I hope so," Burpeau said. "I hate to think of Carmina out there, all alone. She's so vulnerable. She's not the kind of kid you would think of as tough and street-smart, able to manage on the streets…"

"Well, she's done remarkably well so far. And it doesn't look like she's quite as alone as all of that."

"The boy, you mean? Do you think he's helping her?"

Neil cleared his throat. "Hopefully he's helping her, and not taking advantage of her."

"I'd really like to see her again. I guess she won't be back in my class again, but at least with this project, I can give her a final grade."

"You think she did this as a school project?"

"I think Carmina's going to create art wherever she goes, whether she's in school or not. But this is the kind of thing she talked about doing for her final project. A public art installation. I asked her to consider social messaging."

"I guess she did that."

He could hear Mr. Burpeau's pleased smile even over the phone line. "Did she ever."

NEIL WASN'T the only one to watch the morning show, and by the time he got into the office, the police department had already identified the officers who walked the beat by the park and might have some information as to the identity of the mural artist. After identifying himself, Neil was directed to the public relations department for further information.

"Officer Bartlett remembers talking to the artist. Let me get you his information, and you can talk to him directly."

"Yeah, thanks."

He waited for a minute while she got the information and then politely offered to transfer him. Neil introduced himself again to Officer Bartlett, who seemed a little puzzled by the inquiry.

"Why do the feds care about the identity of the artist?"

"I believe she's a runaway connected with a case that I'm working."

"Oh. Well… she is a young girl, not an old bag lady, like the boy said."

"I don't think anyone really believed that line."

"She's pretty young. I certainly didn't expect anything so… sophisticated from her."

"Can you describe her?"

"Fourteen or fifteen. Straight hair, brown. Green or brown eyes. Caucasian, I think. Mostly. "

"You didn't get a name?"

"No. Sorry."

"Was she homeless?"

"No. That is, not that I noticed. But you can't always tell."

"You haven't seen her around anywhere else? Sleeping rough? Soup kitchen? That kind of thing?"

"She didn't stand out to me. I thought she was young... must be doing it for a school project... that's all."

"She was painting at night, and you thought it was for a school project?"

"No, I never saw her paint at night. Only during the day. The last week or two."

"They said this painting sprang up overnight."

"No way. Lots of hours went into it. She did the last part overnight, maybe, but covering up the graffiti with a base coat, and the barn doors and all, she did that during the day."

Neil nodded to himself. That made a lot more sense.

"So you talked to her?"

"Yeah. Made sure that she had her paperwork. Permit and owner's permission and everything."

"And she did?"

"Everything was in order. Would have had to kick her out otherwise."

"Who is the owner of the building?"

The police officer didn't answer right away. When he did, his tone was hesitant. "Well, I don't really know. I mean, I saw the letter, but I didn't really pay much attention. The address looked right, and it said she had permission... I don't remember any details."

"You don't check those details?"

"No. We don't have information on who owns the building. That would be the job for by-law enforcement. I was just... making sure that she wasn't defacing property..."

"But you wouldn't know that, unless you knew that she had permission of the owner."

"She appeared to."

"Okay... I'll look into it. Will you give me a call if you happen to see her around the neighborhood? I really need to talk to her."

"Okay, sure. Give me your details, and if I happen to see her..."

Neil did so, and hung up. He rubbed his tired eyes and phoned Agnes. She picked up.

"Hey, boss. You look ready for bed already."

He looked across the room at her, and shook his head. He closed his eyes and spoke into the phone.

"I need you to track down some information. Ownership of that building that Carmina painted the mural on. How to get a hold of them."

"No problem. Have it to you in a few minutes."

"Thanks."

He hung back up and worked his way through the next few items in his in box. Agnes left her desk to bring him the information instead of e-mailing it to him.

"Here you go. Looks like they haven't been very responsive to inquiries in the past. Outstanding fines for not cleaning up graffiti. I've got numbers, but I don't know if they're good."

"I'll give them a try anyway. But how would Carmina have gotten in contact with them?"

"I don't know… maybe there's a sign in the window or something?"

"Yeah, maybe. Thanks."

Agnes knew her stuff, and in a few minutes, Neil was talking to a harassed-sounding property manager.

"I don't know why you would be asking," he said, "but I'll tell you the same thing as I keep telling all of the reporters. Nobody had permission to paint a mural on the side of that building. Nobody contacted us about it, and nobody was given permission."

"You're absolutely sure of that."

"How could I not be sure? Yes. She is no better than a gang-banger tagging the walls in his territory. It's just graffiti."

"Have you seen it?" Neil asked, surprised.

"I saw what they showed on TV, yes. Do you know I've had calls from as far away as Hong Kong? It's gone viral. It's all over the place. Huge mural pops up miraculously overnight, big message from above, everybody's talking about it. And calling me."

"Well, sorry to add any more stress to the situation. Maybe this will actually help you to sell the building. Get it out of your hands."

There was silence on the line as the manager considered this, then grudgingly admitted: "That certainly wouldn't hurt my feelings any. If that's all, officer…"

"Thank you for your help."

The man hung up. Neil put his receiver back down and sat there staring at it. He had an uneasy, slightly nauseated feeling in the pit of his stomach.

"What's up?" Mandy questioned. She was walking by, but stopped when she saw Neil's face.

"I told you that I doubted if Carmina has any more idea about the forgery business than her mother."

"Yes...? Did you find out that Esther really did know a bit more than she let on?"

"I found out that Carmina had permit papers to paint that mural."

"Yes. So?"

"The building owner never gave permission. And I'm pretty sure if I call the City, the development department and parks department won't have any record of approving a public art installation at that location."

"But you said she had the permit papers. Who told you that?"

"The beat cop who checked them."

She stared at him for a moment with a frown. Then she got it. "So unless the cop is lying, and he has no reason to..."

"Carmina's papers were forged."

"The apple doesn't fall far from the tree."

"Apparently. Now I'm wondering if she had a hand in the family forgery business."

"Even if she did..." Mandy shook her head. "She's a juvenile. And a young one, at that. We're not going to charge her with forgery. If she was involved, it was due to her father's coercion. She wouldn't have been doing it without him."

"And Esther?"

"You didn't think that she knew about it. She wouldn't have been the one to get Carmina into it."

"But if Esther didn't know about it, then why are we still pursuing charges against her? You've talked to her. You know that she's as innocent as any child, no matter what she was involved in."

Mandy considered him for a long moment. "If you want to drop the charges against Esther, you're going to have to prove that she couldn't form intent. And that's going to take a lot more than anecdotal evidence about her breaking down under questioning. You need some kind of a diagnosed disorder. And her lawyer will have to agree to it."

"Her lawyer is a hack."

"But he's still a lawyer. Persuade him that it's in his client's best interest..."

Neil sighed. "Yeah."

WITH ESTHER still on his mind, Neil signed for a courier delivery. He looked down at the tidy, handwritten address. His name. But he had no idea whose writing that was. Until he opened the envelope. Agnes came over with another stack of reports to be processed.

"Oh. Another picture from the mom?"

Neil nodded, looking down at the detailed pencil sketch. Obviously one of Esther's. There was no attached note from either Esther or the prison.

"Looks like someone else saw the morning show today," he observed.

"Are they allowed to watch TV at the prison?"

"I'll give you three guesses."

Agnes laughed.

The picture was of Carmina's painting. It was a side view, and her face was half in shadow, but she was recognizable. She was painting a brick wall. There was a spiderweb above her. Not a pretty, spiral-shaped orb-weaver web like the one that Carmina had painted. It looked huge and strong, poised like a net over Carmina's head, ready to drop on her. And behind her, lurking in the darkness, was a monstrous spider, like Shelob out of Tolkien, sneaking up behind her.

"I don't like it," Agnes said, with a shudder.

"No. It looks like she's in danger… but then, Esther would see *us* as a danger to Carmina, wouldn't she? Julius would, anyway. Maybe it's a statement about us getting closer to finding Carmina."

"I don't think so," Agnes pushed her hair back over her ear and glowered down at the drawing. "If she thought that you were a danger to Carmina, why would she keep sending you pictures? She's trying to help you. She knows you want to help Carmina."

Neil stared at the picture, trying to glean every last tidbit of insight that it could offer him. If only Esther was in a position where she could really help him. He was so close to being able to find Carmina, to talk to her face-to-face. But she kept flitting just out of his reach.

NEIL COULDN'T WAIT for a prison transport to bring Julius to the office, so he decided to mix things up a little, and interview Julius at the prison instead. It might have an effect on Julius, being confronted in what was now his own home. For Neil to trespass on his territory.

When Julius walked in, he looked surprised and perplexed to see Neil there. "What's this?" he demanded. "I thought you and I were done. I'm not talking to you."

The prison guard paid no attention to the protest, leading Julius to the table and running the chain that connected to Julius's wrist chain through the anchor on the table, securing him in place. Despite Julius' words, he sat down, and studied Neil from beneath his glowering eyebrows.

"I'm not talking to you," he repeated.

Neil put a large photograph on the table. A good full-color shot of Carmina's mural.

"What's this?" Julius picked it up and frowned at it.

Neil watched his face closely. Julius' expression changed as he studied the picture, and by the time he laid it down on the table again, Neil was sure that Julius had recognized it as his daughter's work. If it had been that apparent to her art teacher, it must have been obvious to the man that had watched Carmina's talent develop as she grew up. A master of forgery would recognize that 'certain something' that was as good as a signature on her work.

"I'm guessing that when you were teaching her how to stay below the radar, you never had a discussion about refraining from painting huge murals in public that would attract the attention of media all over the world."

"What makes you think this is Carmina's painting? There's no signature."

"Her art teacher recognized it. And so did your wife."

"They're seeing what they want to. This is just painted by some... poor... nobody."

"This mural leads me to wonder just what part Carmina might have had in your forgery business."

Julius' eyes went wide. His lids were always so heavy, the bags under them always so puffy, that Neil hadn't thought that they could open that far.

"What business would Carmina have in... forgery?"

"Your wife forged paintings. You forged documents. It looks like Carmina took after both of you."

"This is original work," Julius tapped the photo. "What are you talking about?"

"How does someone go about painting something like that?"

Julius shrugged, and Neil could see the confusion still plain on his face.

"Sure you have to start by getting the materials that you need. Paint, rollers, brushes… but how long is it going to be before Officer Goody-Two-Shoes comes by and kicks you out? To do something like this, you need papers. Permits. Permissions."

Light dawned in Julius' eyes. "So you say."

"Maybe you've never had to get those, if you've never done a project like this. But Carmina planned it for her school art project. And her teacher would have talked to her about all of those kinds of preparatory steps."

"Her teacher. That's nothing to do with me."

"She forged the paperwork. Everything she needed. She didn't just pull that talent out of thin air."

"Any kid with a computer can do the same thing."

"Carmina seems to have done a particularly good job of it. Like maybe she's had a little training. A little background in how to pull it all together."

"You have these 'forged' papers?" Julius' eyes glittered as he studied Neil's face, reading the answer there. "You don't look like you do. So how would you know anything about her talents or experience? Officer Goody-Two-Shoes probably has no idea what the proper papers would look like."

"I'm thinking it's a pretty big coincidence. Daddy's arrested for forgery, and then Carmina shows up with forged documents. Maybe we'll have to prosecute her after all."

"You wouldn't dare."

Neil just sat there, looking at Julius and letting him stew over it for a few minutes.

"Maybe if I got a little cooperation from Daddy, I would know I didn't need to go after her." Neil picked up the photo and looked at it. "But you can see how close we are to bringing down the boom. It won't be long now. If Carmina thinks that sleeping outdoors is rough, wait until she tries sleeping in a jail cell. And has to defend herself against older offenders. Then she'll redefine *rough*."

Julius stood up, blood suffusing his face in fury. He was chained to the table, so he couldn't actually do anything about Neil's threats. Neil just sat there looking at him, waiting.

"You come here pretending to care about my daughter. You say you just want to protect her. You just want to make sure that she has a safe home. But as soon as you see your opportunity to twist the screws, you show your true colors. Threatening my daughter? No one threatens my daughter!"

"I don't see anyone here who's going to stop me." Neil looked around. "It's not like you're organized crime, Mr. Knight. You may be a white-color criminal, you may have a high-class lifestyle, but you don't have a syndicate behind you that you can threaten me with. You are here. You're all by yourself. Your daughter is out there. She's at my mercy. So instead of threatening, maybe you should reconsider your position. Maybe you would like to negotiate a plea at this point. To ensure that we're both happy. You and I both. Knowing that Carmina is safe."

Julius slammed his fists down on the table. It was obvious that he would have preferred to launch himself into Neil instead, beating him to a pulp for even voicing such a threat. Neil honestly wasn't too thrilled with it himself.

"If I cooperate with you, you'll leave Carmina out of this?" Julius' voice was tight with rage.

"If you cooperate, we won't charge her."

"*And* her mother?"

Neil was surprised to see Julius play that card too. Until now, Julius had acted like it didn't matter what happened to his wife. He proclaimed her innocence, but did nothing to try to protect her.

"I can't make any promises there. My boss tells me that there is not enough evidence of your wife's innocence at this point. Maybe that's something that you could provide. It really is all up to you. If your wife was really not involved in the forgery business, and was just duped by you, then provide us with the evidence to prove it… and we'll be able to let her go too."

Julius sat there, glowering at Neil. Neil waited, watching him simmer.

THIRTEEN

Toto tracked Carmina down on one of her favorite benches in the park. Close enough to see her painting and the activity going on around it, but far enough away not to be noticed by the media.

"You kind of dumped that one on me, didn't you?"

She raised an eyebrow. "You're the one who fell asleep on guard duty."

Toto opened his mouth, looking for a retort. "You didn't get caught," he said lamely.

"You got on TV."

He sat down next to her. "Did I ever tell you I wanted to be on TV?"

"Mmmm… no. Did you really mind? I thought you'd get a kick out of it."

"No, I didn't really mind."

"Good."

"I like the Fibonacci."

Carmina smiled. "I had to throw some math in there for you, didn't I?"

"It's very cool," Toto said, looking across the park at the painting. "Everybody likes it."

Carmina put her feet up on the bench. It had turned out well. And the unveiling had been perfect. The cameras had shown up just as the sun started to light up the wall. Toto hadn't even stirred until the reporter had decided to wake him up. They would have lots of footage of him lying at the base of the picture, in the perfect position, just as she had imagined it. Her stomach was gurgling and cramping.

Toto must have heard it. He glanced at her, amused. "Ready for some breakfast?"

"Yeah."

"Are you still avoiding the kitchen?"

Carmina nodded. "Too dangerous."

"I really don't think there's any federal agents after you."

"Snake says there was a fed asking after me."

"Cops investigate. But that was ages ago. You don't think he's going to go back there every day? Even if some do-good cop is looking for you, he'll pop back one or twice, ask some questions, and give up. You can go back to the kitchen."

Carmina shook her head. "No."

"Even if some cop does come after you, he can't do anything. He can't arrest you for running away or being homeless. You haven't done anything against the law. He can try to talk you into going back to your mommy and step-dad, but he can't make you."

Carmina readjusted her position, easing a cramp in her side. "They could take me away. Lock me up. Torture me."

He stared into her eyes and shook his head. "No, KC. They can't. You've been watching too much TV. None of that stuff is true."

"They just have to say I'm a danger to myself, and they can lock me up."

"Not for long. Just for eval. And the doctors would say that you weren't a danger, and release you."

"They could… say I'm a terrorist."

Toto shook his head. "Come on, KC. Think. They can't. Nobody would believe it. You're a kid. Not a terrorist."

"They train kids to be soldiers in the Middle East. Train them to be suicide bombers."

"But not here. They are not going to say you're a terrorist."

"They could say I can't take care of myself and have to be in a foster home or orphanage."

"Orphanage? KC. They put you in a foster home. You just run away again."

"They could… declare me incorrigible and put me in juvie."

"For running away? I'm telling you, nothing is going to happen to you,

KC. Maybe this cop shows up again, maybe he doesn't. If he does, you just tell him that you don't need any help, that you're not going back home, and that he can go jump in a lake."

She looked at him. He sounded like he knew what he was talking about. But Carmina had listened to Julius for years, and he'd always warned her about what could happen. Had told her about all of the ploys they would use to lock her up and torture her. Carmina had mostly believed him. But she felt herself floating away from him. He no longer grounded her. Esther was no longer there to anchor her. They had been the center of her world for as long as she could remember. But now she only had Toto. He was the one thing keeping her feet on the ground now.

"Maybe tomorrow," she said.

"You'll go to the kitchen?"

"Yeah. Maybe. Tomorrow."

He gave her a little smile, the corners of his eyes crinkling up. "That's progress, anyway. So where do you want to go today?"

Carmina didn't want to go far. She was already pretty hungry and she'd been working all night. "That Chinatown place. They were pretty good."

"Sure." Toto glanced back at the television cameras and reporters. "We'd better cut around the long way. If they see me walking with you, they might guess the identity of the painter…"

"Yeah."

They started walking.

"Why don't you want them to know you painted the wall?"

"I don't want them to find me."

"People saw you painting it."

"I was invisible then. Now… it's been on TV."

"Who called the TV stations?"

Carmina looked at him sideways. She knew by the twinkle in his eye that he had already guessed the answer. "I did."

"Why?"

"Because the whole point is social change. That means people have to see. Lots of people. They have to see it to understand."

They were quiet as they took the long way around to the alley behind the Chinese restaurant.

"What do you think you're going to change?" Toto questioned.

After taking a look up and down the alley, they both quickly scaled the garbage bin.

"I dunno," Carmina said. "Getting people to see the homeless… to see that they're people, not just animals."

They pawed through the food and containers at the top of the bin. Carmina looked up at Toto as they both used their hands to scoop noodles into their mouths. Carmina chewed and swallowed.

"We're not animals," she repeated.

Toto snorted, and took another big bite.

THE TELEVISION SPOT and the photos did not do the mural justice. Neil stood in front of it, gazing up at the huge spider that hung over the web, and at the delicate lines of the spider web. He'd looked up Fibonacci spiral after watching the morning show, and could see it now; in place of the usual concentric circles of an orb web, there was a carefully proportioned Fibonacci spiral. Neil wasn't sure what the significance of it was. But it had meant something to the boy who had been sleeping at the base of the wall, the boy who knew Carmina. He had also reviewed an outline of Charlotte's Web to remind himself of the details. Charlotte had been trying to save Wilbur, the pig. Carmina was, apparently, trying to save the homeless young man, or to bring attention to the plight of the homeless. Charlotte's web had described Wilbur as 'some pig,' 'terrific,' 'radiant,' and 'humble'. In choosing just one word for her web, Carmina had chosen 'human.' Charlotte's Web was about compassion for an animal. Carmina's mural was about compassion for a human. Recognizing humanity in the homeless.

The dew drops on the spider's web were perfect. They reminded him of the droplets of water in Esther's picture, the one where Carmina was a naiad.

There were a lot of people gathered around to look at the mural. Speculation was rampant about the artist, about what the message of the picture was. Neil stared at the sleeping silhouette at the bottom of the painting. Where the boy had been sleeping at the beginning of the television show. He was key. She had painted this picture for him. Like Wilbur the pig, destined for slaughter, Carmina wanted to protect him, to save him from the life he had chosen on the streets.

Neil stepped back, and turned a slow circle, looking over the faces of the observers, scanning the rest of the park that was in sight, looking for some sign of Carmina. She had been here. If he had come here instead of to the soup kitchen, he would have seen her. The mural might have been finished overnight, but she'd been painting it for days. If he'd just come here, he would have seen her. She might still return, to look at her picture and listen to people's reactions.

NEIL WAS WALKING AIMLESSLY, which wasn't such a good idea with his PF. His feet were aching, and he wasn't sure how far he was from his car. It wouldn't do to have to call someone to rescue him. There was a small, inner city park up ahead. Nothing like the big green space where Carmina had painted her picture, but it looked like there were place to sit. He'd rest his feet for a little while, and then be able to make his way back to the car.

There was a lot of concrete and water. Little pools, planters full of ragged flowers and greens, places to rest and look at it all. A lone skate-boarder cut through one of the concrete paths.

It was certainly not lonely. He had expected it would be pretty quiet at this time of day, when people were still at the office. But there were plenty of people strolling through, sitting looking at the water, eating a late lunch, sleeping in the small patches of grass beneath the trees. And buskers. A young man with a guitar. A girl doing acrobatics, her body twisting into unbelievable shapes. An older man, a human statue. It was a relaxed atmosphere. Cheerful. He wasn't sure whether any of the street performers were homeless, or if they just enjoyed the fresh air, the chance to put their talents on display, like Carmina had done in the mural.

He sat down, picking a place in the sun. The concrete was warm with the afternoon heat. Neil watched the comings and goings. Businessmen taking a shortcut. A pair of lovers hand-in-hand. A mother with a stroller and a couple of young, excited children. They hurried on ahead to paddle their fingers in the water.

"I want to go to the fountain," the little boy squealed. "Can we throw pennies in the fountain, mommy?"

Neil followed them with his eyes. Once they were out of sight, he followed after them. It was not hard to keep up with them, and after a couple of turns, he could see the fountain in the center of the park. It was strikingly similar to the one Esther had drawn the naiad in. Perhaps Carmina had come here sometime with Esther. Maybe for a family picnic, or to throw pennies in the fountain as the little children were doing. Neil circled the fountain and sat down on the other side, resting his feet again. He flexed and rolled them, trying to loosen up the painfully tight tissues.

"I want to see the drawing lady."

Neil looked across the fountain at the little boy.

"I don't see her here today," the mother said, taking a look around.

"I want her to draw my picture!"

"We don't have the money for that. If we see her, you can watch her draw. But we can't pay for a picture of you."

The little boy threw a penny into the fountain, just about hitting Neil with it.

"Sorry!" the harried mother apologized.

"It's okay," Neil walked gingerly over to her. "What was your son saying? There's a lady that comes here to draw?"

The woman pushed her hair out of her eyes. "Yes. A young woman… she sells caricatures. Little ink portraits."

"Young? Like a teenager? Shoulder length dark hair?"

She nodded. "Yes. You know her?"

"Sure. Is she usually here?"

"Lots of days. Usually in the afternoon."

CARMINA WAS DOZING in the warm sunlight when Toto shook her awake. She squinted at him, not wanting to open her eyes and wake up.

"What?"

"Are you going to sleep all day? We should move on before the cops show up."

"I didn't sleep last night."

"Not my fault."

"Well, *you* went to sleep. You were supposed to be on guard."

"You didn't get busted last night. And if you don't want to get busted today, you'd better get up before the afternoon patrol rolls through."

Carmina groaned. It was so warm in the sun. The grass was springy and smelled sweet. With the murmured buzz of conversation around her, she knew she was safe. Lost in the midst of the crowd. Invisible. But with Toto there to keep her grounded.

"Now?"

"They'll be around before long. Before the office rats get out of the race."

"For sure?"

"Unless they got a call somewhere else."

Carmina considered this, frowning at Toto.

"What?" he asked, spreading his hands apart.

"Why don't *you* call them somewhere else? So I can keep sleeping."

He stared at her. "Really? You want me to send the cops on a false call?"

Carmina sighed. As much as she wanted to sleep, she wasn't a trouble-maker. She was a law-abiding citizen. Getting the police called away to a false alarm might hurt someone who was really in danger. She sat up, rubbing her eyes and pushing her hair out of her face.

"Okay, I'm up."

FOURTEEN

Neil saw the boy before he saw Carmina. He was actively funneling passers-by toward Carmina, promoting her drawing skills. His eyes paused for a minute on Neil, narrowing suspiciously. Neil gave him a vague smile, walking by without comment. The boy's head swiveled, following him. He made a movement toward Carmina to give her some kind of warning, but then stopped.

Neil stopped and watched Carmina at work. She had the same serene, tranquil expression as Esther did when she was at work, immersed in a picture. Other than that, there was no resemblance between mother and daughter. Carmina's hair was darker, her face rounder than Esther's, her eyes as focused as Esther's were vague. She wasn't heavy, but she wasn't slim and lithe like Esther.

He looked at the row of pictures leaning against the bench. It was amazing how she could make a few lines convey so much. The pictures were spare, a few colored lines, but were vibrant, full of movement and emotion. Humor.

When he looked back at Carmina, she had looked up from her drawing, and she met his eyes, startled. He saw her eyes quickly scan their surroundings, looking for avenues of escape. Then she went calmly back to her drawing, looking at her subject and then back at the paper as she put her finishing touches on the picture, as if she hadn't seen him. Neil saw her sign with KC, the same as on the display pictures. She turned the picture around to show it to her customer.

"That's amazing!" the woman marveled. She looked at Neil. "Don't you think it's incredible how she does that?"

Neil nodded. "She's very talented."

She handed a bill to Carmina, which Carmina immediately tucked into her pocket. She slid the picture into a protective wrapper, and handed it over. "Thank you, ma'am. Have a nice day."

"You too!" the customer trilled happily, walking away with her purchase.

Carmina's eyes turned to Neil. "You want your picture done?" she questioned, raising her eyebrows.

"I think you know who I am," Neil said.

She didn't flinch. "You want your picture done?"

Neil decided it would be worth it to spend twenty dollars to have her full attention for a few minutes, and to start to build a relationship with her. "Yeah, sure."

"Stand over here."

Neil shifted. "Actually, could I sit?"

She looked him over, and nodded. "Right here. Turn your face to the left… look up a bit…" She held her hand up in a 'stop' motion. "Good. Right there. Try to stay still."

She pulled out a new mounted drawing page and started to sketch him.

"My name is Neil."

"Yeah. You need to stay still. Don't talk."

So much for ten minutes of her attention and building a relationship. Neil sat frozen and silent as she worked on the picture.

"I'm done with your face. You can talk."

"I'm Neil."

"So you said."

"Since you're signing KC, I assume you're not going by Carmina."

"No." She sounded as if her teeth were clenched. "Just KC."

"Your parents have been very worried about you. A lot of us have been very worried about you. Anything could have happened."

"I'm fine. So you can stop looking."

"Are you staying at a shelter? How are you getting on?"

"Not really your business."

"Carmina."

She looked up from her drawing. "What?"

"I'd like to talk with you."

"You are."

"I can help you. You don't need to be all on your own. We can get you a home. A foster family or a halfway house. You don't need to face this all alone."

"I don't want anyone else."

"Your parents wouldn't want you to be alone. They would feel much better knowing someone was looking after you. Giving you the support you need."

"Do I look like I need help?"

He had to admit, she'd adapted remarkably well to her circumstances. She looked tidy and professional. Not homeless. She had already started up her own business, and twenty dollars for a ten minute sketch—less whatever her materials cost—wasn't a bad start. She obviously had friends, at least in the boy, who was hovering anxiously nearby. And the people he had talked to at the soup kitchen. She wasn't bruised or thin, hadn't been forced to take up prostitution.

"I'm sure there are some things you could use," he said tentatively. "At least an apartment with a bed."

"I'm fine without any help."

He sat still, trying to think through the situation and come up with something that would persuade her to abandon her situation and agree to come back with him. Nothing was coming to him immediately. Carmina continued to work in silence. Eventually, he saw her pen her initials into the bottom corner of the page, and she turned it around.

There Neil was, with a star-shaped sheriff badge, six-shooter, and bowed legs. He grinned. Being a caricature, the hollowness of his cheeks and worry lines across his forehead had been exaggerated, but it was certainly recognizable.

"That's brilliant," he said, chuckling.

"Two bills," she said, sliding the picture into a protective sleeve.

Neil dug a twenty out of his wallet and gave it to her.

"You wouldn't like to see your mother?" he asked.

She handed the picture over, her face freezing into a mask. "Is she out of jail?"

"No. But she's allowed visitors."

Carmina looked around for her next customer. "I dunno. I'm not… keen on going anywhere near there."

"Well, you certainly could. I'm sure she'd be very happy to see you. Julius too. He's been quite concerned for your welfare."

"He would tell me to stay away."

"Well… he might. He's an interesting character… I'm curious whether he's always been so paranoid. And whether he's ever been medicated for it."

Carmina shot a frown in his direction, and motioned to a woman with a baby stroller standing nearby.

"Are you next? Did you want a picture? They're twenty dollars."

"No… I'm just watching. I don't have the money."

Carmina looked at the baby sleeping in the stroller. There was apparently no one else waiting to have their picture done. She looked in her partner's direction, and he again started working the crowd for her. Carmina went to her backpack and dug out a small sketch pad. Opening it up, she drew a quick pencil sketch of the sleeping baby. Not a caricature this time, just a few lines representing his fat cheeks, closed eyes, and pursed lips. Signing KC, she then tore the page off and handed it to the mother.

"No cost. Keep it flat in a book until you can afford a frame."

The woman looked stunned. "Thank you! You're so good! It's beautiful." She carefully tucked it away in her purse.

"That was very nice of you," Neil said.

Carmina looked at him as if she had forgotten he was there. She shrugged. "She couldn't afford it. She still deserves to have a nice picture of her baby."

"I wonder what Julius would think of that."

She wrinkled her nose.

"I'll bet your mother would approve, though."

"Probably."

"Esther could really use a visit from you. It's been very… difficult for her, being away from home. And finding out about the way Julius has been selling the paintings. She's having a hard time. Very uncommunicative."

Carmina opened her mouth to ask something, and then snapped it shut again. Neil waited, expecting that given the chance, she still might.

"I'm not going anywhere."

"And I'm not going to force you to."

"Oh." Her voice was soft. Surprised. She'd been expecting pressure.

Maybe even coercion. Julius would certainly have filled her head with all kinds of frightening scenarios. The feds arresting, kidnapping, even torturing the entire family. They would do whatever it took to get Julius' secrets. To access his wealth. Then they would throw them in a dark hole somewhere. Maybe dead, maybe alive. But certainly no one would ever see them again.

Carmina contemplated him in silence. Her eyes went to the boy working the bystanders. There was a lull at the moment, not a lot of people around.

"It didn't take you long to pick up a boyfriend. Or did you two know each other before this?"

"He's not my boyfriend… not really… just a friend."

"What's his name?"

"I don't know his real name. Toto."

"Like the dog in Wizard of Oz?"

Her eyes were on the boy. Soft. Thoughtful. "No. Not like that."

"You went with Charlotte's Web rather than Wizard of Oz in your mural."

Her eyes went to Neil briefly, then back to Toto. "You saw that."

"Everybody saw that. You did a good job of it. I saw it on TV, but up close and personal, it's even more stunning."

"What makes you think it's mine?"

"There are a number of people who recognized your style. Mr. Burpeau. Your mother. Your father, too. For someone so young, you have quite a talent."

"Will the painting change anything?"

Neil thought about it. He sighed. "I don't know. I wish I could tell you yes, but there's no telling. How would you change things for him, if you could?"

"I don't know. Make things easier. Somehow."

Toto noticed Carmina's gaze, and walked over to them. "You got your picture, dude. Don't you think it's time you were moving on?"

Neil shifted. "Yes. I suppose I should. KC…? Anything you need?"

She shook her head. "No."

He didn't feel right, leaving her there like that. Knowing she was going to be sleeping on the street again. Her mother lying awake in prison wondering what had happened to her, her dreams, when she fell asleep, filled with dark nightmares of wolves and other predators. He took out his wallet and removed the rest of the cash.

"Will you take that and stay at a hotel tonight? So I can tell your mother you're safe?"

Carmina took the money from him.

Neil studied her face. "You're not going to do it, though, are you?"

She looked at Toto, and shook her head.

"Maybe you could at least go somewhere to eat. Somewhere good. The two of you."

Carmina grimaced, and Toto stared down at the ground as if he'd been caught doing something wrong. Neil wasn't sure of what look passed between them. Would she use the money to buy drugs for him? Support some other habit? Was Neil wrong in his assessment that Carmina hadn't been forced into anything illicit?

"Will you be safe tonight?"

"Sure."

Neil looked at Toto for a minute, then back at Carmina. "I'd like to talk to you some more. Like I said, I won't try to force you into anything. Can I find you here? Count on you not running away?"

She looked at Toto, clearly anxious. Neil wasn't sure what message Toto was sending back to her with his gaze. He took her hand. Carmina rocked forward and back a little, like Esther did when she was upset. Toto pulled her into a one-armed hug, and looked down at her face.

"He can't make you do anything, KC. I told you that, didn't I? He's not going to take you away." Toto looked Neil in the eye. "He can't do anything to hurt you."

"They do, though. Sometimes police or feds do…" Carmina protested.

"He's not going to. Are you, mister?"

"If I did something to harm you, it wouldn't look good for my case," Neil told Carmina.

Relief showed on her face, and her shoulders dipped. An ulterior motive, she could believe. She might not be ready to believe yet that Julius had filled her head with paranoid delusions, but she could understand Neil trying to protect his case.

She nodded in response to his previous question. Toto gave Neil a warning glare. A look that said that in spite of his comforting words to

Carmina, he was appointing himself her guardian, and he didn't trust Neil one hundred percent. Neil gave him a slight nod of understanding.

"Maybe tomorrow, then. I'll see you again."

NEIL SAT down at his desk with a satisfied sigh. As sore as his feet were, it had been a successful day and he was happy. Carmina might still be on the street, but he had made contact. She was okay today. And he had started to build a relationship with her.

There were a series of phone message alerts in his e-mail box. He got back to his feet and went down the hall to Mandy's office. Mandy looked up from her work.

"Well, you look like the cat that swallowed the canary," she said, with a note of surprise in her voice. "What did you do?"

"I made contact with Carmina."

Mandy gave him an approving smile. "You did! Where is she now?"

"She's still on the street. Didn't want to come in from the cold. But it's the first step."

Mandy nodded in agreement. "That's big news. I'm glad to hear it. Really glad she's okay."

He nodded. "So, what were the messages about?"

"Well… they were about Carmina."

"Leads?"

"No. A new roadblock."

Neil sank into Mandy's visitor's chair without invitation. He wiggled his toes, wishing he could take his shoes off. He rolled his ankles stiffly.

"Oh, sorry." Mandy waved a hand at him. "Yes, please, sit down. Always." She shuffled through the papers on her desk. "We got a blip on the missing persons report that was filed for Carmina."

"A blip?"

"An alert that some of the information on it might be incorrect."

Neil considered this, frowning. "Something like what?"

"There was a problem with the birth certificate number on the form." She said it slowly and precisely, like it was important.

"Oh. Did I transpose a number or something?"

"The birth certificate number that you entered on the form was for an Alicia Allen."

"I must have reversed a number…"

"Nope. We checked it against the number the school had on file. Same one."

"And Alicia Allen is…?"

"Deceased. Died as an infant."

Neil blew his breath out. They had needed a birth certificate with no established identity. So they used a deceased infant. An old trick.

"It was a forged birth certificate."

"That's what it looks like."

"Julius just couldn't do anything the honest way, could he?" Neil felt the anger and frustration rising inside him. "Need a piece of paper? Just create it yourself!" All of the trouble he had caused for his wife and his daughter, because he wanted to make money the easy way. "So why did they need a forged birth certificate? What are they hiding?"

"Carmina is adopted."

Neil frowned, thinking back. "I don't think that's something that turned up during the investigation."

"We've made some initial inquiries. It looks like she was adopted sometime between the ages of two and four."

"That's a pretty broad range."

"We're trying to pin it down more precisely, but the Knights don't have a lot of close family friends, and people are having difficulty remembering the details."

"They don't remember whether she was two or four when she came into the home? That's a pretty big difference."

"She was small. Apparently had some health problems that may have caused delays too."

"Right." That aligned with what Neil knew from the investigation. "So she might have appeared much younger than she was… But why the fake birth certificate?"

"Something hinky about the adoption."

"Black market?"

"That's what it looks like."

"Why? They've got the money, the means. Why not do it above-board? Especially if they weren't concerned with adopting an infant?"

"That is going to be an important question to answer in sorting this mess out."

"Does… does Carmina know she is adopted?"

"I don't know."

Neil pondered the added difficulties trying to bring Carmina in after revealing to her that her parents weren't even her legal parents.

"So where did she come from? Who are her real parents?"

Mandy just looked at him.

NEIL WALKED BACK to his desk, and didn't sit down. He no longer felt like sitting down and gloating over making contact with Carmina. He walked over to Agnes' desk. "Did Mandy tell you about Carmina's birth certificate?"

Agnes nodded. "I'm on it. We'll review the public records. See what we can find. Missing persons, kidnappings, anything odd. She had to come from somewhere."

"I found her."

Agnes took her hands off of her keyboard and swiveled to look at him directly. "You found her?"

Neil nodded. "Only first contact. She doesn't trust me yet." He didn't want her to get too excited by it.

"She will."

"I hope so…" Neil pulled the picture Carmina had drawn out of the sheaf of papers in his hand, and put it on Agnes' desk. "She drew that."

Agnes looked at the sheriff and laughed. "She drew you! Look at that! It's great!" She picked it up and took off her glasses, grinning at it. "Are you going to keep it? If you're not, I want it."

"I think I will."

"Good. You should. But if you don't, I want it."

"Okay."

"She really is good, isn't she?"

"That was drawn by a fifteen-year-old." Neil stared at it and nodded. "She is very good."

HE HADN'T YET SEEN Esther in prison. He hadn't seen her in person since the day she had drawn the picture of Carmina as a werewolf. But he wanted to let her know Carmina was okay. If he asked for Esther to be transported from the prison, she wouldn't be available until the next day. But he wanted her to know Carmina was safe as soon as possible.

"I don't see that there's much point in you talking with her," warned the warden who came to see Julius in the reception area, when he had explained who he wanted. "She won't talk to anyone. The doctor is calling it selective mutism, says there's nothing we can do to compel her. It's like a sickness."

"I really don't need her to answer any questions. I want to talk *to* her."

The warden shook his head, frowning. "Some prisoners are just a pain in the neck. She shouldn't be here, you know. Just causes trouble."

"She causes trouble?" Neil repeated. "She doesn't seem like a trouble-maker to me. She's not starting fights or something, is she?"

The warden rolled his eyes and snorted. "Of course not. But she attracts abuse. Has to be watched any time she's not in her cell, and can't manage a cellmate. We have rules, and she doesn't care. You can't negotiate with her. She just lives in her own world and won't adjust."

Neil nodded. "Ah. Yeah, I get it."

"You're sure you want her? Because it's a pain to move her, and if you just make her more upset, she's going to have to be put in an observation cell. And she *hates* the observation cell."

"I'm hoping it will actually help her to calm down and relax. Take my card to her. If she knows it's me, maybe she'll come see me without any trouble." He handed his card to the warden.

The man examined it. "Oh, you're that one. She's sent a couple of pictures to you."

"Yes. I appreciate you getting them to me."

"Only way to settle her down," he grumbled.

"I think this will help. Honestly. I'll do my best not to upset her any more. I won't take long."

"Fine."

"If you let her have a paper and pencil, she'll be easier…"

"You think we haven't figured that out yet?"

Neil's face warmed. He supposed it was an obvious, patronizing thing to have said.

"Come with me, then." The warden led the way to a small meeting room.

It wasn't as bare and clinical as the one he had met Julius in. There were no anchors to chain prisoners to. The furniture was white and the walls painted a calming green. When Esther was brought in, she wasn't manacled in full arm, leg, and waist restraints, as Julius had been—the so-called 'four piece suit'—but simply in handcuffs, chained with her hands in front of her. Even the ugly orange jumpsuit could not take away from the slim blond's natural beauty. She didn't look at Neil as the guard who brought her in unlocked her wrists and sat her down. Esther reached immediately for the paper and pencils in the middle of the table. Neil reached out.

"I have a picture for you to look at this time, Mrs. Knight."

She froze, her hand on the paper, and shot a look at him. Neil took out the caricature Carmina had drawn, and laid it carefully on the table in front of her.

Esther stared down at the picture. Neil watched her face smooth. She looked up at his face, perhaps comparing it to the caricature, understanding Carmina had seen Neil face-to-face for her to draw the picture. Neil gave her a reassuring smile.

"I saw and talked with Carmina today. She's okay. She's doing well."

Her eyes held his face. She didn't pick up the blank paper and start drawing, she just looked at him and waited.

"She doesn't trust me yet, and didn't want me to help her. But I will help her whenever she asks. She's drawing caricatures in the park for money. She seems to be safe for now."

Neil thought he could see tears in the corners of Esther's eyes. She looked away, picking up the blank paper and pulling it to her, starting to draw. Neil tried to think of what else she would ask him about Carmina if she wasn't mute.

"She's made friends. People that help her out. There's one young man in particular who seems to be helping her out, protecting her."

Her first rough strokes skated across the paper. Esther's face was intent on what she was doing, and Neil would have thought she was lost in her own world, as the warden had said; but he knew this was her way of connecting the two worlds. This was the only language she had right now. He could see Carmina's face form at the center of the picture. Gradually, her face was framed by long spiral curls and a jaunty cowboy hat. But her face was not a happy, cheerful cowgirl. Her expression was a dramatic cry of distress. As Neil watched, Esther bound her in cords around the middle, like the tragic victim in an old silent-movie-era Western. The heroine needed to be saved from an onrushing train. Neil supposed the picture was meant to be paired with Carmina's picture of him. He was the sheriff, the one who was supposed to save her from danger.

"I'm going to do my best to help her," he said. "But she has to let me. I can't do anything unless she agrees. I'll be going down there again tomorrow or the next day."

Esther was drawing something in the upper corner of the page. A lurking shape, dark and lithe, stalking the bound girl.

"I know there's danger. She knows there's danger. But so far, she's been careful. She's in good shape. She's not alone."

Esther darkened the wolf shadow.

"I don't think the boy is a danger to her. He's more experienced. He's teaching her the ropes."

Esther's pencil rested for a moment. She looked at him, her eyes questing.

"She really is okay," Neil reassured. "I gave her money for a hotel tonight, but I don't think she's willing to sleep indoors. She still has it, if she needs it. And money from her art."

Esther darkened shadows on Carmina's face, making her look thinner, gaunt.

"She looks healthy. I don't think she's going hungry. When I first found someone who recognized her, it was at the soup kitchen. She's getting regular meals. Other people are showing her where to go."

Esther looked up at him, then back down at the picture. She continued to work on the details, but Neil couldn't identify anything else she might want to know from him. She didn't add any new elements to the picture.

"Mrs. Knight…?"

She looked up at him.

"Carmina was adopted?"

She stopped and stared down at the picture she had been drawing. Neil waited for some sort of response. Eventually, she picked up another sheet of blank paper, and started drawing. This one was different. No darkness. No wolves. A basket or wicker cradle with a sleeping child in it. Not quite a baby anymore, but a toddler, face serene in sleep. Neil remembered her words back when he had questioned her after the arrest.

'I always wanted a little girl. Carmina was a dream come true.'

Esther had wanted a little girl, and Julius obligingly obtained one for her. Through whatever channels suited him. Neil only hoped Julius hadn't kidnapped her or committed some kind of violence against her parents.

"She was a beautiful little girl," Neil observed.

She worked on details of the child's nightgown and the basket, a faint smile on her face. Neil opened his mouth to ask her about the forged birth certificate. To question the legality of the adoption. Then he stopped.

The last time he'd presented her with evidence of forged documents, it had crushed her. She hadn't yet recovered from that setback. Then she had only been confronted with the reality that her work was being sold as something it wasn't. How would she react if she found out that her beloved daughter was not really hers? Witnesses had said the two were like sisters or best friends.

Neil had promised the warden he wouldn't upset Esther any further. He had reassured Esther that Carmina was safe. He wouldn't tell her the adoption was fake until they either brought Carmina in or had run into dead ends in their investigation and could no longer avoid it.

"I'll do everything I can to bring her in and find her somewhere safe to live."

When he stood up to leave, Esther was lightly shading the figure of a woman standing near the child's cradle.

FIFTEEN

Carmina was trying to ignore the noises that had woken her up, and to go back to sleep. Suddenly Toto was beside her, shaking her by the shoulder.

"KC, get up! Come with me!"

"What's—"

He didn't let her finish, wouldn't let her roll her sleeping bag back up after she slithered out of it and felt for the edges.

"Leave it. Come!"

He dragged on her hand, pulling her along behind him. Carmina grabbed her backpack, turning around to try to see what was going on, to try to identify the noises and sort out the shadows moving across the camp. Toto pulled harder.

"Gotta get out of sight," he insisted. "Move it."

Carmina stopped trying to see, and hurried after him. In a few minutes, they were away from the bridge, and stopped for shelter in an alley.

"What happened? What's wrong?" Carmina asked. She was breathing hard. Toto wasn't out of breath, but still, his voice sounded strained.

"Sometimes people come by… looking for trouble."

"Trying to start a fight?"

"No. Looking for someone to beat down. Or… kill."

Carmina clutched at Toto's arm. "What? We should go back. Or call the police."

"Got your phone with you?"

Carmina didn't say anything.

"That's what I thought. Someone will call the cops. But it will be too late. By the time they get there, whatever is going to happen will have happened."

"But we can't just let them! What if… what if it's someone we know?"

"It will be. But I don't want it to be you."

She held onto his arms, trying to come up with something they could do. There had to be a way to stop whatever was happening. They couldn't just run away. Toto pulled her to him, hugging her close. She could feel his heart thudding away. Not as fast as hers, but hard and quick. He was scared and worried too. But they were powerless to do anything. Carmina pressed her cheek to his chest.

"How many were there?"

"Five. Six. I didn't stop to be sure."

"Did they have… weapons…?"

"Baseball bats."

Carmina closed her eyes, the horror creeping over her. "What if they hurt—"

"Shh." He didn't let her finish.

Carmina swallowed the rest. There were so many who were vulnerable. Old, weak, or crippled. They wouldn't be able to get up quickly and escape, like she had. Carmina was getting to know them, to recognize them and learn their names and their quirks. To appreciate the small kindnesses, dry humor, and long patience of the others who slept near them. Half a dozen men with baseball bats could do a lot of damage. A tear leaked out of Carmina's eye.

"Why? Why would they do that, Toto?"

"Some people just like to hurt others."

She hugged him more tightly. She was glad they were far enough away not to hear the thumps of the baseball bats. The shouting and the crying out. It was ten minutes or more before they heard the approaching sirens. Toto was right. Whatever was going to happen had happened. Ten minutes with a blunt weapon and plenty of potential victims was more than enough time. She tried to keep from sobbing, but a couple gasps still escaped her.

Toto's shirt was soaked with her tears. He rubbed the back of her head and back.

"It's okay, KC. It's over."

"They won't catch anyone."

"No."

She sniffled and looked over her shoulder, toward the sirens. "Should we go back?"

"No. Not tonight."

Too many questions by the cops. Too much pain. Too many friends hurt or killed. She and Toto would wait until it was quiet and cleaned up, and not ask anyone any questions.

"Can we walk?"

"Yeah. We can go to the strip, where it's still light. But you have to stick with me."

AGNES STARED at Neil in consternation. She took off her glasses, and pushed back her hair on one side.

"You're going to be a magician," she said, in a tone of disbelief.

"I already am a magician. You just didn't know it."

"Are you serious? Do a trick for me."

"Well, I don't have any of my gear with me." Neil reached into his pockets, jingling his keys, then leaned forward and pulled a quarter from Agnes' ear. "Good thing you brought that with you," he teased.

Agnes looked at him, frown lines between her eyes, looking thoroughly baffled. "You know magic," she repeated.

Neil played with the quarter, making it disappear and reappear for her. "Sleight of hand. I do."

"When did you learn that?"

"I picked some of it up as a teenager. That's when I got interested. Then I've just added a few tricks here and there…"

"So you're like a professional magician."

"I don't usually do paid gigs, no. It's mostly just a hobby. But I've used it for cover a few times before."

Agnes pushed her glasses back into place, and cocked her head to the side. "How?"

"It's just another way to be invisible. People are used to buskers, homeless, civil servants, all of those types are on the street all the time, but they're invisible. Nobody really pays attention. Undercover often masquerades as homeless or civil servants, even moms pushing carriages, but it's pretty rare to see one busking, especially with a specialized skill like magic. So that makes you far less suspicious."

"And you get to wear a costume." Agnes smirked.

"Who wouldn't want to wear a hat and cape?" Neil spread his hands in a shrug.

"But you're not going undercover now. Carmina has already seen you and knows you're an investigator."

"Yes… well…" Neil tried to put it into words. "I want to start building a relationship with her. So she will get to know me better and trust me. And you have to be able to at least get close to someone. And to have something in common."

"So you think that this way… you can hang out with her."

Neil shrugged slightly. "Something like that. There's no way she's going to stand for having an investigator hang around for no reason. But if I'm there as a magician, doing my act, she can't really argue with that. I'm just doing like she is, showing my talent and earning a little cash with it."

"And you think she'll relax, and let you talk to her that way."

"That's the hope. That's what psychology tells us."

"What does Mandy think of all of this?"

Neil raised his eyebrows and rolled his eyes. "Well… she's willing to give it a try. She says if it works, she doesn't care how silly I might make the department look."

"Well, that's loaded."

Neil perched on the corner of Agnes' desk. "As long as it all works out, it will be fine."

CARMINA HAD BEEN DOING her drawings for about an hour when the agent named Neil showed up. At first she didn't really see him. He was dressed differently, for one thing. When he had appeared before, to talk to her the first time, he had looked every bit a federal agent. She and Toto had both made him immediately. But showing up on a Saturday in full magician's get-up was a whole different story. At first, she didn't even look at him as he set down his big black box and started to prepare for a show. She'd seen street performers with all kinds of different skills and angles. It was best to pay no attention and focus on your own thing.

It was Toto who had drifted over and nudged her. "Did you see the magician?"

Carmina shrugged as she worked on a sketch.

"Did you see who it is?"

She looked up, and watched the magician for a moment before she recognized him. "What's *he* doing here?"

"How do I know? He said he might come back, but…"

"Does he think he's fooling us? That we can't see him?"

As they both stood glaring at him, the magician caught their gazes, and gave them a cocky smile and thumbs-up. It certainly didn't look like he was trying to stay undercover.

"Just ignore him," Toto advised. "Pretend he's not even there."

It was difficult advice to follow. If it had just been another busker, maybe another homeless person, she would have been able to tune them out just fine. But knowing that it was the agent on her parents' case, that he was set up there in order to keep an eye on her, made it impossible to ignore him. He wasn't bad at what he did. To begin with, his skills were a little rusty, and he muffed a couple of early tricks before he got into the groove. But he got more confident in his patter, played to the audience in a way Carmina felt showed he really was enjoying himself.

But she also noticed, as she had before, that there was something wrong with his feet. She'd drawn him like bow-legged sheriff, but he wasn't really bow-legged. It was something else. His movements were a little stiff when he was on his feet. He didn't move quickly. He had brought a stool with him, which he incorporated into several acts, and he spent much of his time sitting on it, both between and during sets.

She watched him a little during a lull, when she didn't have anyone to draw for. She even tossed a few quarters into his cup, earning her a grin and a wink.

When the lunch van rolled around, Carmina moved in quickly to get herself a sandwich. When she broke free of the crowd again, she saw Neil sitting on his stool, with a sandwich of his own, apparently brought from home.

"A la peanut butter sandwiches?" Carmina said to him.

Neil chuckled. "A fan of the Amazing Mumford?"

Toto raised his eyebrows at both of them as if they were crazy. "What?"

"He was on Sesame Street," Carmina said. "That magician on Sesame Street."

"Oh." Toto shrugged. He unwrapped his sandwich and took a big bite. "The kid's show, right?"

"You never watched it?" Carmina asked.

"I dunno. Probably. I don't remember."

"Is that… because of… you know?" Carmina glanced at Neil, not knowing how much Toto would want revealed about his past.

"Getting my head smashed in?" Toto supplied for her.

She shrugged, embarrassed.

"I don't know. I can remember lots of stuff from before that. But I don't remember a lot from when I was really little. How much do you remember from when you were little?"

Carmina thought about it, chewing her sandwich—tunafish, not peanut butter—slowly. She tried to ignore the fact that Neil's eyes were intent on her as well. Avid. Listening in.

"I don't know. I remember a little bit from kindergarten, like… not a lot before then."

"Anything at all before that?" Neil questioned.

Carmina looked at him.

He looked away. "Just asking," he said. "You don't have to say anything."

"I remember some things from further back," Carmina said slowly. "My mom sitting up with me when I was sick. This doll I had. I dunno. Just impressions. Sitting in the car. Waiting at the doctor's office."

"Was that Cynthia?" Neil asked. "Your mom said you had a doll when you were little, called Cynthia."

Carmina looked at him. There was more to his question than he would have her believe. He knew something. She looked warningly at Toto, not wanting him to give away the fact that she had Cynthia with her in the backpack. Toto looked back at her blandly, as if he'd never seen the doll.

"Yeah. Cynthia. She was a… special doll I had back then. When I was little."

Neil nodded. "She was your comfort object?" Neil questioned.

Carmina frowned at him. "What?"

"Like a security blanket or teddy bear. Something that helped you emotionally when you were feeling lonely or had to be away from your parents."

"Oh. Yeah. She was my comfort object."

"Were you sick a lot when you were little?"

Carmina was uneasy with his questions. She wrapped back up the second half of her sandwich, and went back over to pick up a fresh drawing board, ending the conversation.

"What's wrong with your feet?" Toto asked Neil.

Neil flexed and rotated his feet slowly. "I have this condition… it's called plantar fasciitis. If it won't heal on its own, I might have to get surgery on them."

"I've heard of that." Toto nodded. "It's like warts, huh? You freeze them off."

Neil smiled slightly and shook his head. "No. Not like plantar warts. They're both on the bottom of the foot, that's all. No other similarity."

"Oh. Well, I'm brain-damaged, so what do I know?"

Neil spread his hands out in a shrug. "How would you know if you don't ask?"

Carmina saw a big goth girl eyeing her, and approached her. "Do you want a picture? Twenty bucks."

"Yeah, I saw the sign."

"Come over here."

TOTO AND NEIL both watched Carmina settle into drawing another picture. Some of the tension went out of Toto, and he looked at Neil.

"So, a g-man with bad feet. Means you can't exactly go out and chase the bad guys, can you?"

"No. Not until they heal up, one way or another. But I'm still able to do a lot of other stuff. Not just desk work." He gestured at Carmina by way of example. "I… well, there's the magic tricks," he said, looking down at his trick box.

Toto grinned. "I've never seen a g-man do magic."

"Well, now you have."

"I guess it's just another kind of confidence trick."

Neil found himself frowning. "Yes, I suppose so," he said. "Except you know it's just a trick."

Toto threw another glance in Carmina's direction. "She's pretty… paranoid, you know. Still thinks you're going to grab her or something."

"Well, hopefully she'll see I'm just trying to help. It may take a while. She's been… taught to be suspicious."

Toto's eyes were curious. "I wondered… she doesn't act crazy, you know, like the dudes in the tinfoil hats. But the ideas she comes up with sometimes… I mean, I'm a suspicious guy, but I don't think you're gonna kidnap me and take me to some unclaimed island to torture me or something…"

Neil nodded. "She's not crazy. Like I say. She was taught."

NEIL SAT on the edge of the fountain, watching Carmina draw. She was getting more accustomed to his occasional visits while she was working.

He found that waiting about thirty minutes between sets helped him to get a better audience, with the ones who had already seen his act wandering on, giving a fresh lot a chance to see what was going on. So in between, he had time to walk around or chat with Carmina.

Carmina finished with the picture she was working on and collected her fee.

"You know," Neil said, "you never asked me what your parents were arrested for."

Carmina looked at him, and looked at Toto across the fountain. She looked back at Neil. "What does it matter what you call it? He always said you'd come sooner or later. Wanting his money and my mom's art."

Neil considered this perspective. It had surprised him that she hadn't demanded to know why he had taken them away. He had thought she should argue with him about the charges, try to persuade him of their innocence and that he ought to let them go. It hadn't occurred to him that the charges would be inconsequential to her. That the charges were just part of a larger plot she had no hope of overcoming.

"You think that's what this is about? Money?"

"Isn't it?"

"It's about the illegal sale of forgeries."

A shadow passed over her expression, but she kept her face frozen, and simply shrugged. "Like I said, money."

"I thought you would care about art fraud. I was under the impression you cared something about art."

"Of course I do."

"Then why don't you care about this?"

"Because it's not true. It's a set-up."

"You don't believe your father and mother were selling forgeries?"

"No."

"What if I showed you proof?"

"I wouldn't believe it."

"What if your mother told you it was true?"

Carmina frowned at this. She took out her sketch pad and started to sketch the fountain. Without Neil sitting on the edge.

"When I showed your mother what Julius had been doing, she was very upset. She knew he'd lied to her."

"Then why didn't you let her go?"

"She's still responsible for her part in the scam. He could not have sold forgeries if she hadn't produced them."

Carmina just shook her head and kept drawing.

"I wish you would agree to go see your mother. I think it would be good for her."

"Why?" Carmina raised her eyes over the sketch pad for a moment. "What's wrong?"

"I told you she was uncommunicative. In fact, she's been mute almost from the beginning."

Her eyes glistened with tears. She looked back down at her work, not blinking, not letting them fall. "It's too dangerous."

"I'm not going to lock you up. We haven't charged you with anything. Although… I gather you tried *your* hand at a little forgery as well…"

Her eyes snapped up, and for an instant he was afraid he'd pushed it too far, and she was going to run. He held up his hands.

"We're not charging you. I only meant to tease."

Toto was there, having seen some sort of sign or signal from Carmina. "What's going on?"

"It's fine," Neil said. "A stupid joke."

"KC? You okay?"

She nodded, wiping at the corner of her eye. She glared at Neil. "Why don't you go home now?"

"I think I'll do one more set."

She went back to her sketch. There weren't a lot of people around for the moment, so she didn't have anyone to draw, and he didn't have anyone to perform for.

"I'm sorry," Neil said. "I'm sure you didn't realize, when you made up fake permission papers for your mural, about how that was illegal. You're a kid, and didn't really think about the potential consequences. That's all I meant. Like I said, you're not in trouble."

Carmina breathed out and shook her head.

SIXTEEN

Carmina scanned for customers, and saw the familiar tall magician setting up his props. Although she rolled her eyes at him hanging around yet again, she was getting used to him being there, part of the scenery. She was still wary of him, but not so scared as she had been. He nodded at her across the compound, and she gave a brief wave.

"Mumford is here again," Toto observed.

"Yeah."

Toto lit up a cigarette, and moved around to Carmina's other side so that the smoke wouldn't be drifting into her face. She got out her samples and started setting them up. Toto circulated around the park, watching for anything out of place and for potential customers. Carmina stood and watched him, frowning.

"Something wrong?" Neil questioned, coming over to talk to her.

Carmina shook her head. "No… just looks like he's limping…"

Neil watched for a minute. "Yeah. Maybe he turned his ankle or something."

As Toto circled back around, he smiled at her. "What's wrong, Case'?"

"Are you okay?"

"Sure. Why?"

"You just… look like you're limping or something."

He looked down at his feet and grimaced, his face twisting. Carmina swallowed. She looked at Neil. His brow wrinkled, not understanding what she was worried about. Carmina tried to go back to her drawing as if everything was normal.

Neil went back to his props. Toto continued to walk around. Carmina kept an eye on him. When she saw his facial twitch return, she finished off the picture she was drawing and collected her fee. She motioned to the studded man who was waiting.

"I don't think I'm going to be able to do you today," she said.

He frowned at her and tried to question her, but she waved him off. Carmina approached Toto, and waved for him to come closer. Toto blinked when he got close to her, gazing at her as if his vision was too blurred to see her.

"KC…?"

"Are you getting a headache?"

He nodded, canting to the side a little. Carmina put her hand on his arm to keep him steady. "Do you want to sit down? Lie down?"

He brought his hand up to his temple, squinting at Carmina. "I gotta… I gotta go, Case'…"

"I know. Sit down for a minute, let me pack my stuff up."

She guided him to sit on the edge of the fountain. Neil came over, cutting his skit short. "What's wrong, KC?"

"Toto. He's having… he gets these spells… headaches, and he has problems…"

Neil removed his magician hat and put it to the side. "Hey, Toto. Are you okay?" he questioned, leaning in to get a closer look.

Toto shook his head, groaning. "Gotta get out of here. Gotta get home."

"Let Neil look at you," Carmina said.

Neil looked in each of Toto's eyes, his forehead wrinkled in worry. "Does this happen often?"

Carmina held Toto's left hand, but it was limp and she didn't know whether he could feel her hand. "We should go to the hospital," she suggested. "But I don't know if they'll help him. He said they won't give him painkillers, because he's homeless."

"I'll call for an ambulance, if you think he needs it."

She nodded.

Neil continued to monitor Toto's pulse and look at his face. "He looks like he could be having a stroke or something."

"Yeah, I know."

Neil pulled out his phone and called emergency. Carmina touched Toto's hair, trying to comfort him, but he pulled away from her touch, moaning. He tried to lie down, but there was no space to lay on the edge of the fountain, and all they could do was guide him down to the pavement, trying to keep him from hurting himself. Toto's body clenched into a ball.

"Go home," he groaned again.

"I can't get you home," Carmina said. "I'm sorry. We're going to get you help."

People were starting to gather around, trying to see what was happening. Neil tried to keep them back. "There's an ambulance coming. He's taken care of. Please just move on."

There was the distant whine of a siren, and Carmina looked at Neil in relief. It wasn't an ambulance, but a police car that pulled up on the street, and a couple of policemen came over.

"EMT's been dispatched, what seems to be the problem?"

"He's having some sort of attack—" Neil started.

"Oh, I've seen this one before," one of the cops growled, and he kicked Toto in the leg. "Get up, there! He's drug-seeking. There's nothing the matter with him."

Neil reached out to prevent him.

"No, he's sick!" Carmina protested. "Don't kick him!"

"He's got you snowed. There's nothing wrong with him." He bent over, grabbing Toto's arm and shaking him roughly. "Come on, get up. No sleeping in the park. You need to move on."

Toto just moaned. The policeman tried to haul him to his feet, and when that didn't work, kicked him in the back, making him cry out.

Carmina tried to push him back. "No, leave him alone!"

The cop grabbed her, his grip tight, digging into her flesh. "Look here, sweetie—"

Neil was up in the cop's face in an instant. "Excuse me, officer," his voice was low and dangerous. "You are crossing the line. This is not the way you treat citizens."

The cop spluttered, trying to protest. His partner's hand went to his holster, and Neil shot him a warning look.

"Agent Neil Crowther," he said to the first. "And if you kick that boy

again, or don't let her go this second, I will be calling your superior personally to discuss your immediate and long-term future."

Both cops took a quick step back. The one dropped Carmina's arm as if
he'd been burned. "What's your business here?" he asked defensively.

"The boy is sick. I called for an ambulance."

Neither of them dared suggest Toto was merely faking it now. They were
all quiet. Carmina knelt down next to Toto, but didn't touch him. Before
the ambulance got there, Toto started convulsing, his whole body shaking in
a full-blown seizure. Neil crouched down, pushing Carmina gently aside.

"Give him some space."

He did his best to move Toto away from the side of the fountain, to
keep from smashing his head against the concrete.

"You see? He's been drinking or taking drugs," the cop said. "He's over-
dosed on something—or he's in withdrawal. Ask the girl what he's taking."

"I've been watching him." Neil's voice was calm and flat. "The most he's
had is a cigarette. Is he epileptic?" he addressed the question to Carmina.

"No… his head is just messed up."

The seizure gradually slowed and stopped. Neil grasped Toto's wrist to
take his pulse, and watched his breathing. "He's okay."

They finally heard the approaching siren of the ambulance. Carmina
turned and watched it approach. The EMT's got out and approached. Neil
moved out of the way.

"He had a seizure while we were waiting for you. Before that he had a
headache, and… KC, what did you see?"

Carmina wiped her nose. "He starts walking funny, and gets a tic in his
face, and when it gets bad, he can't move and doesn't want anyone to touch
him or make noise… his left arm gets all limp."

They checked Toto over. He was conscious again, groaning and pushing
away their hands in protest.

"He had a head injury," Carmina pointed out. "He got beaten on the
head."

"What's his name?"

"Toto."

"Toto, we're here to help you. Let us take care of you."

They spoke to each other in low voices, murmuring back and forth
words that Carmina couldn't understand. In a few minutes, they retrieved
the gurney from the ambulance, and carefully loaded Toto onto it.

"Can I go with him?"

"I'll take you to the hospital," Neil said.

They looked at the cops. Neil looked pointedly at their name badges. "Thank you for your assistance, officers. I'm sure we'll be talking again."

They took it as their dismissal, and with scowls pasted on their faces, they walked away. Carmina sniffled. "Thank you."

"Do you think I would stand by and let them abuse you and Toto?"

"When he had the last one…" she wiped at her nose and picked up her backpack. "We got rousted by cops, and they kicked him and kicked him." She swallowed hard. "And they punched him in the stomach and chest. They kept saying he was drunk, but he wasn't drunk."

Neil had headed over to pack up his props, but he stopped and looked back at her. "There's no excuse for that," he said.

Carmina nodded her agreement. "That's why… that's why I painted the mural. To show homeless people are human too… you have to treat them like humans."

He stood there looking at her, his expression sympathetic. "You're right, KC. We should treat everyone like they're human."

Carmina swallowed. She walked over and helped Neil to pack his magic props away in silence. He hefted up the box, and started to walk toward his car. She knew his feet were bad and wondered if she should offer to carry it for him. But it was still fairly early in the day, and he wasn't limping yet.

Carmina hadn't seen Neil's car before. He always just showed up at the park on foot. But she knew with the box of magic tricks that he must have one nearby. It was parked in a pay lot. A big, dark four-door. She was no expert in cars, but this one looked old and comfortable. Neil loaded his box into the trunk, and unlocked Carmina's door for her.

"Hop in, KC."

Carmina slid into the seat, and she reached across to unlock the driver's door while Neil walked around the car. He got in and put his key in the ignition.

"You can call me Carmina when there's no one else around," she said.

He looked at her, and at first she thought he hadn't heard her quiet voice over the growl of the engine starting. Then he gave her a slight smile. "You kind of miss not hearing it, huh?"

Carmina shrugged.

"Carmina. It's a pretty name. Did your mother pick it out?"

"Yes… I guess so. I never really asked. I doubt if my dad had much to do with it."

Neil backed the car out of the parking stall and navigated to the entrance of the lot, where he inserted his parking ticket and then his credit card.

"What is your dad like?" he questioned, when they were on the road once more, heading for the hospital.

Carmina glanced over at Neil, assessing his expression and the question. "He's nice," she said. "I know he can come across as kind of gruff and abrupt sometimes. But he just… shows his love differently. When I said he probably wasn't the one that named me, I didn't mean he didn't care about me… just that he wouldn't have been fussed about names, he'd let my mom take care of that."

"I do think he loves you," Neil assured her. "I've talked to him about you, and while he wasn't helpful, I know he was concerned for your welfare. He wanted you to be safe."

There was a lump in Carmina's throat, and she didn't speak for a while, just looking out the window.

"I don't know what to think," she said finally. "You seem like a nice guy, but he's always taught me…"

"That the feds are just out to get his money."

Carmina shrugged. "Among other things… Toto says I'm paranoid. That the things I worry about aren't going to happen."

"Toto seems like he's been on his own for a while. Like he's had some experience living on the streets."

"Yeah."

"So he probably knows what things are real dangers, and what things are just unwarranted fears."

"But my dad's older than Toto. He has more experience."

"With…?"

Carmina thought about it. All of her life, they'd lived in the mansion. They'd been sheltered. It wasn't like living on the street, where you had to be suspicious of everyone. She knew some of Julius' history, but not all of it.

"His dad was a prisoner of war in Vietnam," she explained. "He was tortured."

Neil glanced over at her, raising his eyebrows. "Well, I can see how that would be traumatic for a child."

"He doesn't remember it. But he remembers his dad… afterward. And his mom too. He says Vietnam is still holding prisoners of war. There are lots of soldiers whose bodies were never recovered, and they're still prisoners of war."

"Do you think that's true?" Neil questioned, without looking at her.

"I… don't know… I know his dad was tortured. That's real."

"Yes."

"And you arrest terrorists and torture them. I've seen that on TV."

"*I* do?" Neil repeated.

"Well, you guys… FBI, CIA, Homeland Security… other secret agencies no one has even heard of."

Neil's mouth thinned and he didn't comment.

"I've seen it on TV," Carmina repeated. "You're allowed to torture terrorists. Water-boarding and everything."

"How would that affect you?" Neil questioned.

"If you can torture terrorists, you can torture anyone, if you think they might be a terrorist. My dad's dark… but you don't even have to be dark to be a terrorist. You could think that *I* was."

Neil looked away from the road and met her eyes briefly. "I don't think you're a terrorist."

Carmina felt her face flush. She looked out the side window, a mixture of embarrassment and relief swirling around her brain in a confused muddle.

"Has Julius always been paranoid?" Neil questioned after some time had passed.

"I don't know. He worries… a lot… but he's only paranoid if… it's not true? Right?"

"Well… fair question… I'm not a psychiatrist. I don't know where worrying and fear cross the line and become paranoia. Why don't I change the question? Has he always been so worried about things?"

"I think so. Sometimes it's worse than others. If he's stressed about something… if there's a story on the news that worries him…"

"And how about your mom? How does she function?"

Carmina shifted uncomfortably. He made it sound as if both of her parents were incompetent. Julius and Esther were good parents, they loved her and had always given her everything she needed. They have never neglected her or hit her. She'd always felt safe with them, lost without them.

"She's a good mom. She's always been there for me," she told Neil.

"I'm glad to hear that… she seemed a little… fragile."

Carmina watched a homeless man walking through traffic with a sign while the cars were stopped at a red light. Few people rolled down their windows to give him anything. Some of them honked or made rude gestures.

"No. She's tougher than you'd think. She's just… different."

"Julius says she has an artistic temperament. But I think it's a bit more than that."

They pulled into the hospital parking lot, and Carmina breathed a sigh of relief. Neil found a space, and they walked into emergency together. Neil explained who they were looking for at the reception desk, and the nurse motioned for them to sit down.

"Can't I go sit with him?" Carmina protested. "He's all by himself."

"The paramedics are with him now, until the doctor sees him. Go sit down. You'll be paged when you can see him."

Neil didn't pull rank, but gestured Carmina toward the chairs in the waiting area. Carmina dragged her feet and flopped into a chair.

Neil looked over at her. "Do you still want to talk? Or do you want me to leave you alone?"

She folded her arms and just sat there in silence to begin with. She was angry about not being able to get in to see Toto. But then she started feeling guilty. It wasn't Neil's fault, and she was pouting like a two-year-old. "We can still talk."

Neil glanced over at her. "If you want…"

"Yeah. Sorry. I know I'm being a baby."

"No," Neil shook his head. "You've had to be very grown up, the last few weeks. You're worried about your parents. You're worried about your friend. I don't think you're behaving like a baby at all."

Carmina let out a long sigh. She glanced around. "Maybe we should get something to eat while we're waiting. It will probably be a couple of hours."

"Cafeteria's downstairs. I can get you something."

She nodded, and they got up and followed the blue line all the way down to the big, bright, basement cafeteria.

"What do you want?" Neil questioned. "Donut?"

"No… how about fries? Or a sandwich?"

Neil nodded. He grinned. "I shouldn't be eating donuts anyway." He patted his stomach. Looking at the menus, he bought them each a burger meal, though Carmina asked for water instead of pop, and he did the same. Carmina looked at his tray as they sat down.

"You didn't have to get the same as me," she ventured. "I wouldn't care."

"We just have similar tastes."

He watched her salt her fries. Carmina rolled her eyes. "I like salt."

"I use a lot too."

"You don't have to watch your sodium intake?" she teased.

"Well, not exactly. I have to…" he trailed off, and gave her a little frown. "Never mind. You were going to tell me about your mom, before."

Carmina took a big bite of her hamburger. She hadn't exactly been about to tell him anything. As she chewed, she scratched the back of her neck, thinking about it.

"When Toto got beaten up, it messed up his brain."

Neil nodded slowly, as if not sure where she was going with this.

"It messed things up, but it kind of rewired his brain in a way that… he's like, a math genius now. And he wasn't before."

"Really? That's unusual."

"Yeah. He says it was like waking up and being able to speak a different language, and to see colors he hadn't been able to see before. Because he never saw all of the math around him before, or never understood how it worked."

"Okay…" His eyes were intent on her, trying to anticipate where she was going next, to make the connections.

"Well, my mom is sort of like that. It's kind of like… she speaks a different language."

Neil blinked a few times. "Art," he suggested.

Carmina nodded. "Yeah. Like she speaks art… and that isn't the same as talking about art. She can talk about art, in English, like everybody else. But it's like… like English is her second language. It's harder for her, not natural."

"And sometimes she can't speak English at all."

"I don't know if she can't… or won't… or what. But you can't push her." Carmina dabbled a few fries in a puddle of ketchup. "So I kind of grew up, with art as one of my native languages. And it's natural for me to talk to her that way."

"How… specific is this language? Can you communicate complex thoughts? Or just general ideas?"

"A picture's worth a thousand words," Carmina offered with a laugh.

"Right. But… really… she hasn't spoken at all in a couple of weeks. I get some ideas from what she draws, but it's not like a conversation, really. I can't get anything exact. I don't know if I'm getting what she intended. Or if she intended anything."

Carmina took another bite of her burger and chewed it slowly. She thought back over all of the times she and Esther had drawn or painted, side by side, or even on the same piece, communing with each other on a level Carmina could never have related to Julius. Or when she was a little girl, sick in bed, feeling lonely and discouraged, and Esther would sit beside her and begin to draw a picture of Fairy Carmina and her animal consorts, or Princess Carmina and her subjects, or a dozen other worlds or ideas that would comfort Carmina and make her laugh, and she would go to sleep with dreams full of fantastic creatures and happenings instead of fear or pain. Bedtimes stories with Esther were mostly pictures, and very few words, if any at all.

Carmina had been surrounded by a rich imaginary world, full of magic and color and a language that was almost impossible to describe to Neil.

"It's not… linear…" she tried. "It's not so logical and sequential as spoken language. It's not really… questions and answers."

Neil nodded, almost as if that was the answer he had been expecting. He took a small sip of his water. "I showed her the caricature you drew of me, as an old west sheriff. And she drew you, as the heroine tied up by the villain, in danger."

"She's worried about me."

"Yes. I reassured her the best I could. But there was a wolf in the picture, lurking nearer."

Carmina pushed away her discomfort at the thought. She was safe. She had found a safe place to sleep and to ply her trade. She had made friends. Toto helped to protect her. Even Neil seemed more intent on protecting her than hurting her.

"The big, bad wolf," Carmina said lightly. "What would a fairy tale be without a villain?"

"Well, I'm hoping not to have to actually tangle with a real wolf on this case."

Carmina snorted, his words hitting her funny bone. "Have you had to fight with wolves on other cases?"

"No, not real ones."

THEY HAD BEEN SITTING BACK in the chairs again, waiting for permission to go and see Toto, when a nurse walking by spotted Neil and stopped to talk to him.

"Agent Neil Crowther," she said in delight. "How are you doing? You're not here for yourself, are you?" she looked at him critically.

"No, for a friend."

The nurse's eyes went questioningly to Carmina, but Carmina shook her head. "Not me either. We're just waiting until we can go in."

"Oh, well that's good. I hope it's nothing serious. I didn't remember you having a daughter…" she addressed Neil again.

"No, she's not mine! Just a friend."

"Oh, I see." She lingered, obviously in no hurry to leave. "How are you? Everything… working properly?"

"As much as can be expected," Neil agreed pleasantly. But he glanced aside at Carmina, his face getting a little red.

"I'm so glad. Well… sure nice to see you again. You take care of yourself, okay?"

Neil nodded. "Yeah, I will. Thanks."

She sketched a little wave, and then walked on. Carmina stared studiously down at her knees and did not ask any personal questions.

"I was injured," Neil explained. "In the line of duty. I was in hospital for a few months while they fixed me up and waited for me to heal."

"Really?" Carmina couldn't resist asking for more details. "What happened? Did you get shot?"

"Actually, yes. I did."

Carmina was surprised. She had been sure he would come back with something less dramatic. Breaking a leg in a traffic accident. The problem with his feet. Something like that.

"Really? Who shot you? Did he get away, or did you put him in prison?"

"It's sort of complicated… I did get shot. And it was in the middle of a big operation."

Carmina nodded, wondering what part was complicated. Neil stared at the blank wall, reviewing it in his mind. "My partner made a mistake, and I ended up getting shot."

"What mistake did he make?" Carmina asked.

Neil didn't answer right away. He stared at the wall. Carmina looked down at her hands, trying to envision what it might have been. His partner had cleared a room, but there was still a shooter there? He had searched someone, and not found the second gun? He had distracted Neil, or been distracted by something himself? It must have been a pretty blatant mistake for Neil to still blame him for it.

"He shot me," Neil said finally.

Carmina looked at him, blinking, wondering if she had heard correctly. "Your partner shot you?"

Neil nodded. "Yes."

"Dang! How did he do that?"

"Bad judgment… I don't remember all the details."

"Wow. Did he get suspended, or kicked out or anything?"

"No. It was just a mistake. These things happen. Didn't make me too happy, though."

"I guess not! Where did he get you?"

Neil rested his hand over his stomach. "Right in the gut."

Carmina winced, inadvertently covering her own belly too. "That's bad. I mean… it's good he didn't get you in the chest or in the head, I guess. But in the stomach, that's really bad. There's so many different organs he could injure, and you could bleed out right there."

Neil looked at her thoughtfully. "You're right," he agreed.

"What did he hit? You said you were in hospital for a long time, so he must have got something."

"Mostly intestine," Neil explained. "And that causes lots of problems, because you get bacteria in your abdominal cavity, and things can get badly infected."

"Is that what happened?"

"They didn't manage to find all of the holes the first time they did surgery, the way it folds back on itself. So things got a lot worse. They had to go back in, and infection had already set in."

"That's really bad," Carmina repeated, rubbing her own stomach.

"They had to remove quite a length of intestine, and sew it back together, so it's much shorter now than it used to be, and that causes me problems."

"You can't absorb all your nutrients," Carmina filled in. She looked at his hollowed cheeks. "That's why you're so thin."

He looked surprised at her comment. "I should be used to it by now. My doctor gets after me for not taking care of myself properly. But it's such a change to have to focus on getting high-calorie, lower fiber foods, but still staying away from sweets, because they cause issues. And making sure I'm getting enough sodium so… well, you asked if I have to watch my sodium intake, and I do, but not because of hypertension. Because I have to make sure I get enough."

Carmina nodded. "You'd better learn," she pointed out. "You don't want to be sick."

Neil agreed.

Carmina opened her mouth to speak, and a nurse spoke over the public address system. "Friends or family of… Toto please come to curtain four."

There were a couple of giggles from the waiting chairs, and Neil and Carmina got up immediately to go see how Toto was doing.

SEVENTEEN

Y ou *should* go see your mom," Toto told Carmina.
She was glad he had waited until Neil was gone to express his opinion.

"You don't know anything about it."

"Just what I've overheard between the two of you. He said you could go see her, so why don't you?"

"It's too dangerous."

Toto shook his head. "You're doing it again."

She rubbed her forehead. "No, I'm not."

"How is it dangerous? You think if you go to the prison, they're going to lock you up?"

Carmina shrugged. She looked down, knowing he was going to tell her she was being paranoid.

"If Mumford had something to arrest you for, he would have done it already. He's had plenty of opportunities. He doesn't have to get you inside the prison to do it."

"But…"

"You should go see her, KC."

"You don't know anything about it," Carmina told him again.

Toto was silent. After a few minutes, Carmina looked up at him.

"I need a smoke," he said. "Why don't we get out of here?"

"You're not ready to leave already, are you?"

"Sure. I got enough drugs on board."

Carmina looked Toto over uncertainly. He was still pale, and should probably get some more sleep while he had the opportunity of a soft bed and clean sheets. And at least one hospital meal. His smile at her was a little wan.

"I just want to go home, Case'. Whenever I get one of these… I just want to be back… where I belong."

She moved from the visitor chair to sit on the side of the bed, and held his hand. "Where's home?"

"You know where home is," he laughed. "Under the bridge."

"You don't have anywhere else?" she questioned. "Somewhere… with a mom or dad?"

He squeezed her hand. "No. That life was never in the cards for me."

"You never had a mom or dad?"

"I've had plenty. Moms, dads, grandmas and grandpas, aunts and uncles, everything you can think of. For about five minutes, and then I get shipped off to the next one."

"Foster homes?"

"Some of them. But not anywhere permanent… I've been under that bridge longer than any other home."

"That sucks," Carmina observed.

"Yeah. And if I had a chance to go see my mom, even if she was in prison and I was scared, I'd still go and see her."

Carmina pulled away from Toto's hand. "Why don't you get your clothes on?" She picked up his neatly folded clothes and threw them onto his legs. "I'll see you in a minute."

She flounced out of the hospital room, pulling the door shut behind her.

NEIL WAS WORKING through the pile of papers in his in box. He got through a few more reports and, sighing, put them aside and went over to see Agnes. He sat on the corner of her desk.

"How are we doing on identifying where Carmina came from? Who she really is?"

"Not turning up a lot of leads," Agnes admitted, pushing her glasses up onto her forehead and rolling her neck. "No kidnapping cases match up, as far as I can tell."

"Well, that's good. I'm glad she wasn't stolen away from anyone. But that means she was sold. Much harder to trace, because likely no one ever reported her disappearance."

"If she had some distinctive feature, a birthmark or something…"

"I can't even get proper dental records," Neil contributed. "Julius refuses to let her get x-rays. Too much radiation. Government conspiracies."

Agnes nodded. "It certainly doesn't make it easy."

"What about her medical records? She was sick when they got her. With what?"

Agnes put her glasses back over her eyes and punched a few keys on her computer. "I wish I could say they were helpful. There's no medical history. Her family history and medical history prior to the adoption are listed as unknown."

"What was she hospitalized for?"

"Various admittances for cramps, diarrhea, dehydration…"

"Flu? Parents a little too quick to take her in?"

"It looks like it was serious enough for medical care in most cases. She wasn't usually discharged the same day."

"So…" Neil considered the facts. "She was small and had intestinal issues… could be failure to thrive and she was taken out of a negligent home… she could be from a foreign country, even, not used to the food, parasites…"

"She's caucasian, or appears to be."

"There are other countries that offer caucasian children for adoption."

Agnes groaned. She tapped a few more words into her computer, and she looked at him over the top of her glasses. "Or, it could be Munchhausen by proxy," she suggested. "One of them could be making her sick intentionally."

Neil considered the suggestion. "I don't think either of them fits the profile."

"Then I think medical records are a dead end."

The phone started ringing, and Agnes glanced at it. "That's your line."

Neil looked at the number upside-down. It wasn't familiar, and he hesitated before answering. Finally he reached over and picked up the receiver before it could go to voicemail. "Crowther."

"Is this… Neil…?"

Neil slipped from his position perched on Agnes' desk, and jumped to his feet. Agnes looked alarmed.

"Carmina?" Neil asked.

Agnes' eyes widened, and she watched him intently, trying to listen in on the conversation.

"Yes." Carmina's voice was small and hesitant.

"What's wrong? Is Toto okay?"

"Yeah, he's fine. I just wondered…"

He realized why she had called before she could get it out. "Did you want to go see your mom?"

"Yeah," her voice rose a little when she answered, surprised he had guessed. Neil gave Agnes a silent but emphatic fist-pump, and she responded with a big smile. "Do you think we could do that?"

"I'd be happy to take you," Neil agreed. He left a few moments of silence, careful not to sound too eager. "When would you like to go? Do you want me to pick you up?"

"Is it too late for today?"

"No. Not at all. Where do you want me to pick you up?"

They agreed on a place, and Neil hung up.

"That's excellent!" Agnes cheered. "Looks like you do know some magic after all!"

"I think it was dealing with those two cops and getting Toto to hospital that did it." He didn't mention their discussion of his accident with Agnes. He had a feeling Carmina seeing his vulnerability had been part of her change of heart as well.

"Well, however you did it, good job! Maybe this will be the break we need."

"I don't know if we'll learn anything new or not, but those two need to see each other. Esther needs to see Carmina is okay, and maybe if Carmina sees Esther is okay… she'll be more willing to cooperate with us. And come in off of the streets."

$\sim$

CARMINA PACED UP and down waiting for Neil. She felt visible and vulnerable. She wanted to go back and lie down with Toto, and just pretend she hadn't made that phone call. Neil would understand if she changed her mind. She just couldn't get in the car with him.

But she already had gotten in the car with him. In the aftermath of Toto's attack, she hadn't even thought of the danger. Neil said he'd drive her to the hospital, and she had simply jumped in without thinking of the possible risks. But now that she was thinking about it, climbing into a car with a near-stranger didn't seem like such a good idea. There were so many things that could happen to her.

She knew she couldn't trust him. He was Government. He was a Fed. One of the people who had arrested her mother and her father. The one in charge of arresting them. He'd tracked her down and forced his way into her life, showing up repeatedly at the park to worm his way into her trust. She had no real reason to trust him. She had just gotten used to him. And the story about getting shot; that was probably all made up. What were the chances it had really happened? That he really had a shortened bowel from being shot by his own partner? It was just a story, designed to gain her sympathy and trust.

She paced back along the street, the cramps in her belly building. If she stopped moving, she started to shake. Why had she done something so stupid? Julius would be horrified. Calling a fed? Agreeing to cooperate with him? How could she do something like that?

Neil's car pulled up, and she bent down to look at him. He opened the door for her to get in. "Hi, Carmina. Hop in."

She just stood there. She looked at the interior of his car. She had sat there already. And she'd been safe. He hadn't done anything to hurt her, and he hadn't arrested her. He had only taken her where she wanted to go. She looked at him. Still the same Neil. The Neil she had seen performing magic tricks for children. That she had seen perching on his stool to give his sore feet a break. The same Neil who had confided in her about being shot and the difficulty in eating properly and keeping weight on. But that had to have been a story. It couldn't really be true.

Neil waited. She expected him to get impatient with her, snapping at her to get in or trying to reason with her. But he just shifted the car into 'park' and turned on the radio. He flipped through a couple of stations.

"What do you like to listen to?"

It was a bit ridiculous, with her still standing on the sidewalk, frozen, too terrified to get in. She swallowed, focusing in on the station the radio was currently on. "I'm not big on popular stuff. I'm more into oldies. Classic rock."

He flipped stations again. "The radio in your art classroom had some kind of opera or instrumental playing. You listen to that?"

"Everybody gets a say. We listen to different things on different days."

He paused on one station that sounded promising. "Do you want to put your bag in the trunk, or do you want to hold onto it?"

Carmina shifted her back pack off of her shoulder, and hugged it to her. "Hold onto it."

He nodded acquiescence. Carmina took a steadying breath, and slid into the passenger seat. A fiery pain stabbed at her lower belly, and she tried to breathe through it and not betray it to Neil. It was a few minutes before she could bring herself to close the door, but he didn't push her. Carmina pulled it shut with an ominous-sounding thump. Her hands were shaking violently.

"Okay?" Neil asked.

"Yeah." Carmina's voice was tiny and cracked.

Neil nodded, and slowly and smoothly put the car into gear, and they were on their way.

NEIL FELT BAD FOR CARMINA. She sat rigidly next to him, her face a deathly white, hugging her backpack to her for dear life. He had been beginning to wonder if she would even be able to get into the car. But she had mastered her fear and was now sitting next to him. For a while he just let the radio play and hoped the music would help to calm her.

"How's Toto?" he asked eventually.

"He's okay. I wish he'd stayed in hospital a bit longer. Got a bit more rest. I wish… I wish they'd figure out how to fix him up. So that doesn't keep happening. Sometimes I think he's going to die."

"He looked pretty bad," Neil acknowledged. "I certainly wouldn't want to look forward to having that sort of random attack. But… there may be nothing that can be done about it. Just looking at the scars on the outside of his head… imagine the damage that must be inside the brain. You can't exactly stitch it up or graft new tissue."

"Yeah."

"He's lucky to have a friend looking out for him."

Carmina gave him a surprised look. "I don't take care of him, he looks after me."

"The way I see it, it goes both directions. You look out for him when he has an attack. He helps you to get along in a new environment."

Carmina frowned, considering it. Neither of them spoke for a while.

"What's going to happen?" Carmina asked.

Neil glanced over at her for further information.

"When I go see my Mom?" she clarified.

"Oh. Well, we'll get to the prison and get you checked in. They're going to want you to walk through a metal detector, like at the airport. They may want to do a pat-down too, and if they do, you just stand still and stay calm. You won't be able to take your bag into the room, so you might want to leave it in the car. They'll take you into a meeting room, and you sit down, and then they'll bring Esther in. She'll be in handcuffs, but they'll take them off." Neil thought through anything else Carmina might want to know. "It's not bad as prisons go. The room I have seen her in has green walls and white table and chairs, but I don't know if they all do. She'll be in a prison jumper. The guard won't stay in the room. At least I don't think so; maybe they do with minors."

"Are you coming in?"

"I'll help you get checked in. I'll let you visit with Esther by yourself."

He didn't tell her he would be watching and listening from the monitoring room.

"Do I need… identification?"

Neil couldn't repress a smile at the question. "Do you have anything you didn't cut up?"

"Um, no…" She ended with a little giggle.

"Well, I'll be with you and take responsibility for you. Technically, you're a ward of the state now, and I should have a social worker sign off everything, but the prison is fine with me signing you in."

"I don't want any social worker…"

"Not yet. I understand. I'm not going to push you into anything."

She looked away from him, back out the window again. "I've never been to the airport."

"Hmm?"

"You said they have metal detectors at the airport. I've never been there."

"You've never flown?"

"Not commercially. Only little planes, on private landing fields."

Neil tucked this nugget away for future reference.

"Well, it's nothing scary. You just walk through this special doorway. You empty your pockets and take off your watch or anything first, so you don't have any metal on your body. Then you walk through. If it squeals, they might wave a wand around you to see if you have metal snaps on your clothing or something like that. Or they might want to pat you down."

She nodded. "Okay."

"You don't have any piercings or implants or anything?"

"Not even pierced ears." She pulled her hair back to show him.

"Wow. That's unusual these days. You okay, then?"

Carmina breathed in and out slowly. "Yeah. I guess so."

"We're just about there."

NEIL HAD DONE A PRETTY good job describing what Carmina would go through once they got to the prison. He talked and joked with the guard, keeping the atmosphere casual and light. There were no beeps when she went through the metal detector, and they didn't ask to pat her down. It all went remarkably smoothly, and it was only a few minutes before she was sitting in the little meeting room with green walls and white furniture, like Neil had described. He hadn't mentioned there was an observation mirror along one wall, and a camera hanging down from the corner nearest the door. She felt anxious and exposed.

There was a pile of paper and a few pencils in the middle of the table, and Carmina wondered if that was for lawyers to make notes on. Her fingers itched to pick them up and start drawing, but she kept her hands in her lap.

She breathed out nervously and rubbed her aching stomach. She wanted to get up and walk around, loosen up a bit, but she stayed in the chair, waiting.

The door made a loud noise when the handle turned, making Carmina jump. Then the door swung open, and Esther was escorted in. Carmina drank her in hungrily. As Esther waited for her wrists to be released, her eyes were on the paper on the table, not looking at Carmina. Then her eyes moved to explore the rest of the room and she saw her daughter.

The guard was just unlocking the second bracelet of the handcuffs when Esther focused on Carmina, and Esther pulled away from him with a jerk, making him drop the handcuffs on the floor. He tensed and reached for his weapon, instinctively protecting himself. But Esther had eyes for no one but Carmina.

"Carmina," she whispered, as she took a couple of steps closer and they reached for each other. "Oh, Carmina, Carmina, Carmina," she said rapidly, pulling Carmina to her and holding her tightly.

Carmina hugged her back in relief. So relieved to be back in her mother's arms. She had been lost ever since she had started to run. Even with Toto anchoring her to the ground, she had still been directionless. Part of her was blank and missing. Now Esther filled that space, holding onto her, crooning to her in a low voice no one could understand. She kissed Carmina's hair, and rocked her back and forth slightly. "My baby. Oh, my baby!"

Carmina realized she was crying. Not just a stoic tear or two, but her cheeks were flooded with tears. Her nose was running, and tears and mucus drained from her sinuses down her throat, making her gulp between the sobs, trying to get herself under control.

It was a long time before Esther released her tight grip, letting Carmina breathe more freely, and she held Carmina by the shoulders at arm's length, looking her over. Carmina pulled her damp hair from her face, trying to wind it behind her ears and shoulders.

"I'm okay," she assured her mother. "Really. Everything's fine."

Esther wiped at Carmina's tears with the sleeve of her uniform, trying to gently mop them up. "It's okay, baby."

"I know. I'm just glad to see you."

"Me too." Esther stroked Carmina's hair back, examining her expression intently. "I was worried."

"Why don't you ladies sit down now?" the guard said. He cleared his throat and motioned them toward the chairs. "I'm not actually supposed to let you touch during a visit."

"Oh." Carmina withdrew from Esther, and looked back at the chair she had been sitting in. "Sorry. I didn't know."

Carmina sat down, and with obvious reluctance, Esther sat down in the chair opposite.

"How have you been?" Carmina questioned. "Are they treating you okay?"

She noticed now that Esther had a small cut next to the corner of her mouth, and a shadow under one eye.

"I miss my house," Esther said. "All my art projects. Here... all I can do..." she picked up one of the pieces of paper and a pencil. She closed her eyes briefly, envisioning what she wanted, and then started to draw. She rocked back and forth slightly, moving toward and away from the picture, but her movement didn't affect the drawing in the slightest.

The guard quietly exited the room, leaving them alone together. Carmina reached out. "Can I draw too, do you think?"

Esther nodded. Carmina helped herself and started to draw, her eyes moving between her own picture and Esther's as they each drew their own thoughts. Esther's quickly took shape, two faces close together, Carmina's and Esther's. Subtly changed to make them like sisters or even twins. Still recognizable, but Esther's cheeks fuller to match Carmina's, Carmina's hair mimicking Esther's flowing style, something different about the shapes of the mouths. In the space behind them was the mansion. Darkened, looking cold and empty.

Carmina concentrated on her own picture. She'd been almost automatically drawing the scene that kept replaying in her mind. Toto lying on the ground, his face twisted in agony. Neil crouched over him, fingers over his pulse. She stopped, regretting her choice of subject. It made her feel more anxious, and would make her mother worry. Esther looked over at Carmina's picture. Her hand found Carmina's and gave it a quick squeeze. Esther pulled back away again quickly, and Carmina knew it was because touching was against the rules. She didn't want the guard to come back again, maybe even taking Esther away, back to her cell. They both looked at Carmina's picture.

"Toto," Carmina explained. "He's a guy... he helps me out. He's my friend." She touched her pencil to Toto's face, fixing a slight flaw. "But he gets sick. His brain is messed up, from being beaten." She darkened one of the twisting scar lines on his head.

Esther looked at Carmina's picture for several long minutes. Then she picked up a fresh piece of paper, and started a new picture. This time it was Carmina and Toto together. Toto was smiling. Sometimes in real life, he gave her a smile, but it was brief and fleeting. Most of the time he looked serious or sad. Carmina was smiling in the picture too. Their images were reflected in their eyes. Carmina laughed as Esther stretched out Toto's ears, bringing them each to a point.

"I don't think Toto has elf ears."

Esther always teased Carmina about whether she had pointed ears hidden under her dark hair. Carmina pulled her hair back behind her ear to show it to Esther as Esther sketched pointed ears onto Carmina in the picture. Esther decked the boy and girl elves out with laurel crowns and glimmering jewels. She had somehow made Carmina and Toto look alike too, but Carmina couldn't figure out how, what Esther had changed on them.

"I like it," Carmina said.

Her hands had found another piece of paper, and she was drawing. A scene she hadn't dared to draw in the last few weeks, even though it had played through her mind over and over again. Julius in the black car, his dark face grim and glowering. Esther being escorted out of the house; distressed, frantic, trying to pull away from the agents that held her on either side. Tears started to run down Carmina's face again. She sniffled, trying to keep herself calm, keep herself from breaking down into sobs again.

She had to be strong. Just like her mother was. Esther could have cried about being locked up, about how she was being treated there. She'd obviously been hit by someone. But she was calm and serene, lost in her drawing. Carmina watched her painstakingly adding a gleam to each jewel. Esther looked over at Carmina's picture, and she stopped drawing. She looked up at Carmina's face, and then down at the picture again. Her fingers hovered over it. Not touching, because she wouldn't let the oils from her fingers transfer to the page, but so close there could only be a hair's breadth between her skin and the paper.

"I'm sorry... I didn't know you were there..." she said. "I didn't even look for you..."

"I wasn't feeling well," Carmina explained. Though she knew her mother probably already figured that part out. She knew why Carmina would be home early. Carmina swallowed. "I was so scared," she whispered.

Esther nodded, looking at her own face in the picture, twisted up like she was in pain. "So was I."

~

NEIL COULDN'T SEE the pictures very clearly from the observation room, but the tech zoomed the camera in as close as he could, and Neil could see them well enough to get the gist. He could tell Carmina's latest picture was a graphic portrayal of her parents' arrests.

"I guess that answers the question of whether she saw anything when she got to the house," Neil muttered to no one in particular.

"Mom…?" Carmina started, her voice barely audible.

The tech adjusted the volume level, as they both leaned in. Esther looked at her daughter.

"What should I do?" Carmina asked.

Neil held his breath, waiting for Esther's reply. Any other mother, he was sure would tell her to come back, to get off of the street and cooperate with the agency. Esther's eyes went to Carmina's pictures. Her lips parted slightly.

"Did you ask Julius?" she said finally.

"No!" Neil groaned, smacking his forehead with the heel of his hand. "No, Esther! No!"

Carmina shook her head in response to her mother's question. They all knew what Julius would say. Run and hide. Trust no one. Not even Neil. Especially not Neil. Stay as far under cover as possible.

Esther was looking at Carmina's picture of Toto and Neil. Carmina followed her gaze.

"What?"

"They help you?"

Carmina nodded. "Yeah."

"He is… kind…"

"Toto?" Carmina asked.

Esther shook her head.

"Neil? Yeah… he is." Carmina added some minuscule detail to the picture. "You wouldn't think that, about a fed."

Esther frowned at the other picture, of her arrest.

"He wouldn't…" Carmina started. She stopped and tried again. "He wouldn't hurt anyone. Would he?"

Esther shook her head.

"He's not like the guys that Dad talked about," Carmina agreed.

There was no answer from Esther. Carmina studied the picture of Neil and Toto with a frown.

EIGHTEEN

Carmina sat in the car, hugging her backpack to her and pressing her face into it, trying to keep from crying. Having to leave her mother behind, in prison, overwhelmed her. Her parents were her whole world. Esther was the only person who understood her, who could read her and comfort her.

Neil didn't speak to her at first, and Carmina was grateful for his tact. Steeling herself, she opened her backpack to place the pictures carefully in a protective envelope. With a furtive glance in Neil's direction, Carmina pulled Cynthia out. She held the doll against her cheek, breathed in her familiar scent. She closed her eyes and tried to go back. Back to cuddling on the bed with Esther. To Julius holding her against his shoulder, pacing back and forth waiting for her cramps to subside so she could sleep. Playing tea with Cynthia while Esther drew their pictures, giving them both crowns, and Cynthia a human face. All the years of Esther putting Cynthia in Carmina's backpack, promising her Cynthia would keep her company until Carmina was home again. Cynthia was her one connection with home. The one identifier she could never give up, no matter what Julius would have said.

"Is there anywhere you want to go before I take you back downtown?" Neil asked.

Carmina swallowed and looked up, resting her chin on top of Cynthia's yarn hair. She could go by the school to talk to her friends. Or to Mr. Burpeau. She could go by the house to pick up supplies. Maybe get her computer. She sniffled and shook her head.

"No. Thanks."

"You know I can help you, if you want," Neil said. "You can trust me."

"I know."

"Okay. There are lots of possibilities. A relative, foster care, group home… you don't have to be on the street."

"Yeah."

Neil's hand hovered over the knob of the radio to turn it on, and then he changed his mind. "Did you ask your mom about the forgeries? About whether she knew what was going on?"

"You were listening," Carmina pointed out. "You know what we said."

"Is the reason you didn't ask that you didn't want to hear her answer?"

Carmina closed her eyes again.

"Or you didn't want me to hear her answer?" Neil persisted.

Both were true. Carmina hadn't really thought it through like that. She hadn't thought it through consciously. But she knew in her heart it was true. She didn't want to know whether Esther knew about Julius selling her reproductions as the real thing. Maybe Julius had involved her, had told her what he was doing. Maybe he hadn't, but Esther had eventually sorted it out or come across the evidence herself. Maybe some happy purchaser had blown it at an event Esther have been persuaded to attend, blissfully telling Esther how happy she was with an art purchase Julius had brokered for her. There were a lot of ways Esther could have found out. It had been going on for years. There had been a lot of opportunities for her to find out.

Julius hadn't exactly hidden what it was he was doing. Many times Carmina had wandered into his study to find him laboring over some document, magnifying glass or microscope or some other tools of the trade on hand. Esther's routine was pretty rigid; she wouldn't leave her projects to wander the house at random like Carmina, but there were times when she would be pulled away by some interruption or household event. If Carmina was sick, Esther would take care of her, and frequently prevailed upon Julius to help, getting overly anxious about Carmina's condition. Perhaps she had realized he wasn't just studying provenance documents, but also crafting them.

"Esther was quite upset when I showed her some of the forged documents," Neil said. "She has been mute since then. Today was the first time she has spoken since then, as far as I know."

"You don't think she knew before that?" Carmina asked, turning her head and opening her eyes to look at him.

"I think… she must have had some suspicion, sometime over the years. I just can't see all of this going on right under her nose without her getting some whiff of it. But I think she intentionally looked the other way, because she didn't want to see." He looked over at Carmina, then back at the road again. "What do you think?"

Carmina swallowed a lump in her throat. She so much wanted to talk about it. To have someone she could confide in, and who could help her sort out the truth from the lies. She had never thought her parents lied to her. She thought they always told her the truth. It rocked her world, wondering how much they had lied to her.

"Some people can live… in their own world… and not have to see what they don't want to," she offered.

Neil nodded in agreement. "Esther certainly has issues dealing with the real world. She's been very comfortable, living in the world Julius constructed for her. This has really shaken her up."

Carmina stroked Cynthia's hair, straightening out the tangled strands. She thought about the picture she had drawn of their arrest. She hadn't realized how clearly she had seen her mother's expression until she got it down on paper. She had tried to block it out, to minimize it to herself. Her own way of not dealing with the real world. Her mother's agony over the arrest had not been embarrassment, or guilt, or even concern over Carmina's fate. It had been the pain of being ripped out of her world, pulled away from her routines and projects and everything she knew and thrown into the unknown. The cruel, unpredictable outside world.

"You should let her go home. She's being hurt at the prison. You saw her bruises."

"That's one of the hazards of prison. They're watching her and protecting her the best they can. We can't let people go just because they are targeted by other prisoners."

Carmina sniffled.

Neil let out a deep sigh, as if burdened with a heavy load. "Even if they determined your mother is not guilty of anything criminal, and let her go, there's still a problem with going back to her."

Carmina shifted her position, trying to relieve the cramps that started up again. She knew Neil had been holding something back. "Don't tell me."

"It's time you knew. I can't keep it from you, it's not fair."

"No."

He was silent for a time, and she thought maybe he had changed his mind. "Did you know you're adopted?"

Images flooded Carmina's thoughts. The disruption of those early years. Holding tightly to Cynthia, the only constant in her life. Long stays at the hospital. So many different people coming and going. She knew, but the subject was taboo. They never spoke of it. Never mentioned it in passing. Never said a word about it to strangers.

"Yes."

Neil looked away from the road at her for a moment, his eyebrows up in surprise. "Do you remember it?"

"I don't remember a lot... it's all jumbled. I don't know when it actually happened... but I remember my mom and dad... weren't always my parents."

"Do you remember your birthmom?"

"No, I don't think so... maybe... a foster mom."

"What do you remember about her? Do you remember what your name was before the adoption?"

Carmina studied Neil, hearing the urgency behind his questions. Why did this matter? Lots of people were adopted. It didn't change anything.

"Carmina... it wasn't a legal adoption. We're trying to find out who you really are."

Carmina clutched Cynthia more tightly. She felt like she was caught in a swirling whirlpool. They had promised her they would never leave her. They would be her parents forever. Already, they had been taken away from her. Now Neil was saying they weren't even her parents at all. They never had been. She pressed her face down, into Cynthia, into her backpack in her lap, putting her hands over the back of her head, burying herself.

"No..."

"I'm sorry. I'm sorry to have to tell you like this. I don't know how I could make it any easier. If I could, I would tell you what happened, where you came from, who your birthmom was. But I haven't been able to trace where you came from."

"No!"

"I'm going to need your help to find out what we can."

"No. No, why?"

"Because somewhere out there, you have another mom. Another family. We don't know if she consented to the adoption or if she was tricked or you were taken away from her. She might have been pressured. She might… want to know you."

Carmina looked out the window. She couldn't sit there in the car with him any longer. She couldn't bear to hear his suggestions and questions.

"Let me out."

"You're nowhere near home yet."

"Here. Just let me out here! I don't care."

Neil slowed the car, looking at her in concern. "Carmina…"

She unbuckled her seatbelt and pulled on the door handle. "I'm getting out."

Neil stomped on the brake before Carmina jumped out. There were car horns honking behind them. Carmina stumbled a little as she hurried away from the car.

Neil was leaning toward the open door. "Carmina! KC! Please, come back. We can talk!"

She shook her head and kept going, intent on leaving him behind as quickly as possible.

NEIL REACHED for the passenger door and pulled it shut with a thump, watching Carmina scurry out of sight.

That had not turned out well.

He had hoped Carmina was ready. That having seen her mother, and having had to leave her behind again, she would understand her situation more clearly now. Esther had suggested Carmina could trust Neil. That he would help her. Carmina couldn't actually want to live on the streets as she had been. If she knew she might still have a family, somewhere to go to, maybe she could stand to think of another choice.

But like Esther, Carmina had decided to block out the real world. To ignore the fact she might have another family. She had never even hinted to him she knew she was adopted, that she had come from somewhere else. That blew him away. Was it possible she might remember something that would help to identify her? A name? Hers or a foster family's? If she had been closer to four than to two, she might remember something significant.

But she'd run again, and that wasn't a good sign.

He headed back to the office with a heavy heart.

IT WAS late before Carmina got back home. She knew that she shouldn't have run away from Neil. She should have just let him take her back home. But she just couldn't have stayed in the car with him a second longer.

Her body had reacted to the stress. She felt like her guts were being ripped right out of her. She had sheltered in a gas station restroom, ignoring the increasingly vehement requests that she leave. It wasn't like she could have left if she wanted to. And she hadn't wanted to. She wished she could just drown herself in the toilet and flush herself away.

It was all too hard. She really couldn't handle it. It was too much.

Weak and wrung out, she stopped at a convenience store for a sports recovery drink, and started the long walk home. By the time she reached the bridge, it was dark. Toto's voice had an impatient edge to it when he saw her.

"Where have you been? I thought you must have decided to let him take you somewhere, and you weren't coming back! You shouldn't be out wandering around this late! Do you want to get hurt?"

Carmina just stood and looked at him.

Toto's expression changed. "Are you okay?"

When she didn't answer, he grasped her arms.

"Did someone hurt you? KC? What happened?"

She shook her head. She stepped closer to him, right up against his shoulder, and Toto put his arms around her and held her close.

"Come on, Case'. Tell me what's wrong. Was it really bad? Seeing your mom? Neil shouldn't have brought you back here so late!"

Carmina shook her head.

"He didn't? Where have you been? Why are you out so late?"

Carmina sniffled, cuddling in his arms, seeking his warmth. "I was sick."

He swore. "Come sit down. Rest. I'm not mad at you. I'm sorry. I was just worried. I thought you'd be back hours ago. And then I thought you decided not to come back at all."

He led her over to his sleeping bag, and sat her down. Sitting with her, he continued to hold her, rocking slightly.

"Is it bad? Did you get some medicine?"

"No."

He drew back to look at her face, studying her closely in the dark, touching the hollows under her eyes.

"You need more to drink. You're still dehydrated."

"I know. Just hold me."

"Sure."

He stopped talking and asking her questions, and just held onto her, making a low humming in the back of his throat, stroking her hair and rocking her. Carmina didn't know how long they stayed there like that, before the anxiety and pain finally started to ease, and she started to calm down and feel sleepy. Toto stroked her hair and gave her a brief peck on the cheek.

"You okay now?"

Carmina nodded.

"What happened? Seeing your mom was really hard, huh?"

"Leaving her again," Carmina said, her voice cracking slightly.

"Yeah. I'm sorry. I shouldn't have told you to go. It just made things worse."

"No… things were already worse."

He rubbed her back soothingly. "What was?"

Carmina opened her backpack and felt for her folder. Toto had a tiny flashlight from a dollar store in his pocket, and he shone it as she pulled the papers out. Carmina held out the one of her parents' arrest, and Toto studied it, shining the light on their faces.

"Oh, Case'… I'm so sorry…" he stroked her hair again. "Your mom's beautiful."

Even by flashlight, even with the anguished expression on her face, Esther was still beautiful. Carmina pulled out the one that Esther had drawn of the two of them, their faces together, matched like twins. Toto frowned and shook his head.

"That's wrong. Did you draw this? It's…?"

"My mom's."

"But she's drawn it all wrong." He looked from the picture to Carmina's face and back again. "The proportions are all wrong. Why?"

"To make us look alike," Carmina looked at the picture. "Like we were really family."

"But…" he looked into her eyes. "You *are* family."

Carmina shook her head. Tears prickled in her eyes. "No. I'm not really."

"What does that mean?"

"I was adopted…"

"Oh." His voice registered relief. "So that's why you don't look alike. But you're still *family*."

"It… wasn't real. It was a fake adoption. Nobody… nobody really knows who I am."

He swore again, and gaped at her. "A fake adoption? How do they do that?"

"I don't know."

"Did they kidnap you? Can't the feds find out?"

She shrugged and shook her head, helpless to explain. "I… I ran away again. From Neil. I just couldn't… I couldn't hear about it."

"Well, it's not like he doesn't know how to find you again," Toto said, humor in his glittering eyes.

He shone the light in her face briefly, then turned it off.

"You've still got me," he promised. "We can be family. Just you and me." He gave her a gentle hug. "Now why don't you lie down? I'll go get you some more to drink."

"Let's just go to sleep."

"No. You'll just get sicker if you don't get more fluids. Stay here. I won't be long."

He flitted away before she could protest any more. Exhausted physically and mentally, Carmina just lay there on Toto's sleeping bag. She didn't even have the energy to get out her own. She closed her eyes and waited for his return.

NINETEEN

Neil scanned the park, but for the third day in a row, didn't see Carmina or Toto there. He would stay for a while, but if they didn't show up, he'd pack up his gear and check a few other places. Someone must know where they were.

His digestion was a mess after three days. Three days of stress and guilt over Carmina running again. He'd barely been able to choke a thing down, and he swore he could track every bite on its process through his gut, irritated and painful. His feet weren't doing too badly, as he wasn't spending as long busking in the park. But his anxiety over Carmina and whether she was still okay weighed him down heavily.

He started his magic show, but kept tripping over the patter, and fumbling with his illusions. Not a good way to impress the crowd. Not that he was really concerned about pleasing the crowds today. He wasn't after money, he needed to know Carmina was okay.

After a couple of failed shows, with people rolling their eyes and walking away from him, Neil gave up and packed his stuff away. He'd check out a couple of other places Carmina or Toto might be hanging out, and if he still didn't see them, would come back at noon to see if they showed up for the sandwich van. As he dealt with his own cranky gut, he couldn't help wondering whether Carmina's mysterious illness was acting up as well. He knew how closely stress and an over-sensitive body could be tied together.

At the park where Carmina had painted her mural—which was still up and hadn't been painted over by either the building owners or graffiti artists —his heart rose, when he saw someone sitting at the bottom of the painting. As he got closer he was sure it was Toto, a hat out inviting spare change, relying on the draw of Carmina's painting to get him some sympathy. Toto noticed Neil's approach, and looked around, considering escape routes. But he stayed put and didn't run. Neil tossed a couple of quarters he'd received as pity offerings into Toto's hat.

"Miss you guys. I've been getting concerned."

"You kind of freaked her out. Telling her she was adopted right after seeing her mom might have been pushing it a bit."

"She already knew she was adopted."

"Well then, telling her she wasn't adopted," Toto amended, with a wry smile.

Neil sat down without invitation, and made himself comfortable on the rather rocky turf.

"It might have been bad timing," he admitted. "But she had to know. I thought if she realized she might have another family out there, that she had options..." Neil trailed off, shaking his head. "I thought it might help. And... we need help figuring out where she came from. We can't pick up the trail."

Toto pulled out a cigarette and put it in his mouth. "Do you mind?"

"Go ahead."

Toto said nothing for a few minutes, lighting his cigarette and smoking, eyes distant.

"Is she doing okay?" Neil questioned. "I'm worried about her."

"She's okay... but not very good, if you know what I mean."

"I don't. Is there anything I can do? I can talk to her, if you think it might help. I can bring her something if she needs it... just ask, I'll do whatever I can."

"Well..." Toto puffed out a breath of smoke. "Unless you can turn back time..."

"Is it physical or emotional? I mean, I know it's probably both. But what you're most worried about..."

"She's been pretty sick. But I've been taking care of her. Mostly... it's crying about her mom. She's... really close to her mom."

"She can still see Esther. Anytime she wants to go, I'll take her up there again. She doesn't have to stop seeing her, just because… Esther's not legally her mom."

Toto shrugged. "But in her mind… you can tell her that, but she feels like you've taken her mom away. Twice now."

Neil groaned. "That wasn't my intention at all. Of course she can still see Esther. The woman raised her. It just means… there might be someone else who is willing to help her out. There might be another family she can lean on for support."

"I'll tell her. But she's not too… reasonable right now."

"I understand that. The heart isn't logical."

Toto blew smoke away in a stream. "Exactly."

"Could I see her? Explain it myself?"

"No, not right now, man. She needs time."

Neil sighed. "Of course. I feel like it's urgent, because we're not making any progress in identifying her. But of course… it won't help to sort it out any faster, if she's not willing to hear it."

Toto stubbed out the cigarette, and put the butt carefully in his pocket. "She just needs time."

"Whenever she's ready."

Neither said anything for a while.

"I'll tell her," Toto promised.

Neil took it as his dismissal, and got to his feet. "You'll tell me if there's anything she needs? Food, medicine, anything I can do for her?"

"I'm looking after her. She doesn't need anything else."

CARMINA TOSSED AND TURNED. She drifted in and out of sleep, sick and uncomfortable, her mind a feverish mash of worries. She kept waking up and looking for Toto, but he wasn't there. She tried to remember if he had told her where he was going. Had he just gone to get her another drink, or some solid food? It grew dark, and the stars came out, and she knew it was very late. Forcing herself to her feet, she picked up her backpack, and wandered through the other homeless who were settling in for sleep.

"Feeling better?" Snake questioned, smiling at her.

Carmina shook her head. "I can't find Toto. Do you know where he went?"

"No. Haven't seen him since this morning."

"I don't know where he is. Something might have happened. What if he had another attack? And I wasn't there to help him?"

"Somebody would call an ambulance. He'd be okay."

"But what if he wasn't?" Carmina persisted, a lump in her throat making her voice crack. "What if he wasn't where someone would see him? A back alley or dumpster or something? And what if it was worse, and he died?"

"There's time between his attacks. He just had one a few days ago. He won't have another one for a few weeks."

"He might! Where is he?"

"I don't know, KC. Wait until morning, he'll likely show up. Just stay calm about it. Go lay back down and rest up."

NEIL WAS TRYING to ignore the light filtering in through his window. The alarm hadn't gone off yet. It wasn't time to get up. He'd had a long, restless night, and was feeling more exhausted than when he had gone to sleep. He wasn't ready to get out of bed, but he knew it wasn't going to get any better.

His phone started vibrating on the dresser, and Neil jolted. His heart raced. It was far too early for a routine call. Something had to be wrong. Something was happening. He picked up the phone, and didn't give the caller ID more than a glance. Not someone in his contacts list, that was all he knew.

"Hello, Crowther."

"It's KC. Carmina."

"Carmina? Are you okay? What's wrong?"

Carmina snuffled. Her voice was rough, wavering between high and low notes. "Toto's gone. I don't know where he is. He didn't come back yesterday."

He knew she'd be worried about Toto's health. "He probably just got picked up for loitering or something. Why don't I call around and see if I can track him down?"

"He could be sick. Or dead!"

"I can check with the hospitals. Do you want me to come pick you up?"

There was a long silence. "Yes."

"No problem. Same place as last time? Or is there somewhere else?"

"By the fountain. There won't be anyone else there yet."

"Will you be okay by yourself? All alone at this time of day?"

"It's daylight. It will be okay."

"Okay. See you soon."

He waited until he was sure she had hung up before putting down his phone and starting to pull clothes on. Looking at the time, he knew it was too early to call Agnes. She wouldn't be in to the office for a couple more hours. She would be able to track Toto down in minutes. Neil was going to have to do it the hard way.

NEIL PUT DOWN HIS PEN. "Well, Toto's not at any of the hospitals," he reassured Carmina.

She just looked at him. "He could be sick or dead in an alley somewhere."

"I don't think so. I'm sure he's dropped out of sight plenty of times before. It will just take us a little while to track him down. Just like finding *you*, when you disappear."

"I didn't run away from Toto. And he didn't run away from me."

"I'm not saying he did. Just that it takes time to pick up someone's trail. But we'll do it." He yawned and stretched. "I could do with a coffee. You?"

Carmina rested her head upon her folded arms on top of Neil's desk. "No. Coffee always messes me up."

"Oh, sorry. Something else? Some kind of herbal tea, or juice, or something?"

"Just water."

"Toto said you had been sick lately. Are you sure you don't need some-thing more than that?"

"I'll need food… but we have to find him first."

"It might take time. What can I get you?"

Carmina shook her head. Neil kept his mouth shut only with a great effort. Carmina didn't look good. She looked pale, and thinner than when she'd gone to see Esther. But Neil wasn't one to lecture on good eating habits and weight loss. Carmina put her face in her hands, elbows on the desk.

"Boss! What are you doing here so early? Oh! You have company!" Agnes was surprised at the sight of Carmina.

"Agnes, this is Carmina Knight."

"Good to meet you," Agnes greeted Carmina. She looked at Neil, her eyes full of questions.

"Agnes, can I prevail upon you to do something that will take you ten minutes, but would take me another two hours to do?"

"Sure." She looked businesslike. Serious. "Shoot."

"We're looking for a boy who might be missing. I've made it through the hospitals. But I need you to do your magic with the police network."

"No problem. What's his name?"

"Well, we don't know what name he might have used, or he might be a John Doe. He's a teenager, about seventeen." Neil gave the best description he could, right down to the scars, and Agnes jotted it down on a sticky note from Neil's desk.

"I'll see what I can do. You getting a coffee?"

"How did you know?"

She gave him a knowing smile. "Get me one too, okay? Gotta jolt the brain cells."

Neil agreed. When he got back from the coffee station, Carmina had disappeared from his desk, but he spotted her at Agnes' desk before panic set in. Neil handed Agnes her coffee and Carmina her water. He refrained from asking Agnes whether she'd found anything yet. He watched her. Carmina was silent. They both waited, eager to hurry the process along, but knowing it wouldn't be any help.

"I've got a John Doe who matches your description," Agnes said. "Arrested last night for theft."

"Got a picture?" Neil asked.

Agnes had already hit whatever combination of keystrokes was required, and had the booking photos up on the screen. It was Toto.

"Oh, thank goodness!" Carmina sighed in relief and swayed on her feet. Neil caught her arm, and held her steady, watching her eyes carefully to make sure she wasn't going to faint on him.

"Take it easy, there. Do you need to sit down?"

"Yeah…"

Neil walked her carefully to the nearest visitor chair and lowered her into the seat. "Now… how long since you ate?"

"I don't know." Carmina rubbed her eyes. "I've been sick."

"Let's get something into you. I saw some pastries in the kitchen. They might not be great for you, but they'll bump up your blood sugar."

Carmina shook her head. "No. I can't eat that."

"We need to get something into you."

"Are you going to get Toto out of jail? What do they think he was stealing?"

"Copper wire," Agnes contributed. "A big thing on industrial sites these days."

"Oh."

Carmina looked serious about this. Neil had a feeling she had been intending to argue that he wouldn't steal anything, but maybe she knew he scavenged copper wire from previous conversations.

"I'll look into it," he promised. "We'll see what we can do."

"Now what can we get you?" Agnes demanded. "You're looking pretty crappy right now. Just about as bad as he does," she nodded at Neil. "But at least *you* know coffee isn't a substitute for breakfast."

Carmina looked surprised, smiling slightly at Agnes' disrespectful reference to her boss. "Oh, no. Don't worry about me."

"Come on. What about muffins? I could get you a bran muffin if you don't like the sweet stuff. A drink of juice?"

The girl shook her head, eyes getting a bit wider. "No…"

"What, then?" Neil questioned. "Come on, we've inconvenienced you plenty. You can tell us what you want for breakfast."

"Well…"

"Steak and eggs? Come on. Make it something hard."

With a little smile, Carmina tilted her head slightly. "Eggs do sound good…"

"Eggs," Agnes verified. "What else? Something to go with them? Pancakes?"

"No. Sausages or a McMuffin or something."

Agnes nodded. "No problem. Boss, why don't you set her up in a meeting room so you guys have some privacy. I'll bring it in there."

～

CARMINA SPRINKLED her eggs liberally with salt, and dug in.

"Do you mind if I ask you about your childhood?" Neil asked. "About anything you might remember that could help to identify you?"

She looked at him warily.

"I'm not taking anything away from Julius and Esther," Neil said. "They raised you. You'll probably never call anyone else Mom and Dad. And it doesn't mean giving up on visiting them. But you have a past. Maybe a birthmom who doesn't know what happened to her baby girl."

She looked back down at her eggs. "I don't remember. It's jumbled. It was a long time ago."

"It doesn't matter if it's jumbled. We'll try to unravel it as we go along. Just tell me about what you remember. You could draw it, if that helps."

Carmina closed her eyes, and Neil waited. "I remember being in hospital. Lots of people… nurses, mostly… I think…"

"Do you remember meeting Julius and Esther? Do you remember them taking you home?"

She rubbed her temples, frowning. "I don't know. Yes… I remember them coming to the hospital… they brought me toys, crayons…"

"Did they bring you your doll? Umm…" he tried to remember the doll's name.

"Cynthia. No."

"Do you remember anyone else? Somebody that came to visit you regularly?"

"No… maybe… I don't know…"

"Just tell me what things you can remember. Don't force it."

She breathed deeply. "A woman. I can't picture her face. Darker."

"Darker how? Darker than Esther?"

"Yes… dark hair… dark skin… maybe."

"Do you know who she was? Not a nurse?"

"No. I think… my mom… but she couldn't be, right?"

"We don't know. Don't make any judgments, just visualize what you can remember."

She shook her head and opened her eyes. She took a few more bites of her eggs. Neil watched her for a moment, then looked away, thinking over her recollections. They were pretty vague. "When did you get Cynthia?"

Her eyes met his. Neil could see she had something to say, but she hesitated. She tried to look away, but he held her gaze. He waited, hardly daring to breathe, not wanting to spook her.

"Cynthia has a secret."

Neil stared at Carmina. Esther spoke with her pictures. Toto saw and heard math. And now the doll was keeping a secret. He wasn't about to discount anything she said.

"What is Cynthia's secret?"

Carmina searched his face. She didn't say anything. For a long time, she just sat looking at him. Then she bent over and picked up her backpack. She carefully removed the doll and cradled it in her lap, looking down at its face. Neil tried to imagine what was going through Carmina's mind. What was she seeing? What was she remembering?

Carmina put Cynthia on the table, moving her breakfast out of the way. Neil studied the doll. A hand-made rag doll. Curly yarn hair. Happy eyes. She was in good shape for a doll that had been carried everywhere for the past twelve-plus years. She had not been treated roughly or dragged through the dirt. Carmina stroked the doll gently. Neil waited.

She moved a little closer to Neil. Neil inched his chair slightly closer to her, so they were sitting close side-by-side. Carmina lifted Cynthia's dress, and pulled it up over the doll's head. Neil stared with a frown at the thick, twisted mass of red fabric attached to the doll's abdomen.

"What is *that*?"

"It's called an omphalocele."

"Om-fah-lo-seal," Neil repeated carefully. "What is it?"

"She was born with her intestines and some of her organs outside her body."

Neil's own body reacted to the idea, clenching, a cramp shooting through his side. "That sounds dangerous."

"They have to be put inside with surgery." She looked up at Neil's face to see how he was taking it. "But sometimes there's not enough space. And things can go wrong."

He nodded. "Cynthia has this… and you did too?"

Carmina swallowed. She still hesitated. Finally she answered in a tiny voice. "Yeah. Me too."

"And that's why you were given Cynthia. So you'd have a special doll just like you."

"But it's a secret. Nobody could know."

"Who couldn't know?"

"Nobody."

"Does that include Julius and Esther?"

"They don't know… about Cynthia. And I had to be fixed… have my last surgery… before I could go to them."

"Because nobody could know you had been born with one either."

Carmina pulled the doll's dress back down and smoothed it out, hiding the birth defect. "Yeah."

"Did Julius and Esther know about your omphalocele?"

"Yes. They had to know how to take care of me."

"Even after your last surgery, you still needed special care?"

"A long time ago…" she was concentrating hard, trying to give him all the details. "There was a problem. The intestine got pinched off." She put her hand over her lower abdomen, wincing.

Neil remembered the time surrounding his own surgery. "And if it got pinched off, and lost blood flow…"

"It turned all black and infected. I almost died. They had to take lots of it out, and then sew it back together."

"So it's shorter now, like mine."

She nodded. "I didn't believe you when you told me about yours," she said with a little laugh, looking away from him. "I thought you found out our secret and were trying to trick me."

"I didn't figure it out. You have kept Cynthia's secret very well all these years."

"I never told before. Not anyone."

"Who was it that told you not to tell?"

"I don't know. The dark woman."

"So, your digestive problems… are those the only after-effects you still suffer?"

"My lungs too. They're too small."

"I would never guess any of it, looking at you. You've done a good job taking care of yourself, other than your trouble the last few days."

She stood up abruptly, and Neil's first thought was that she was going to run again. That he had again said the wrong thing and scared her. Instead, she inched up her shirt. At first he only saw her money belt, but she shuffled it around to her back and lifted up the strap, so he could see the deep surgical scars across her belly. Similar to Neil's, but more extensive. She touched one deep pucker in her skin.

"I used to have a button here."

"A button?"

"That's how they fed me, into my stomach."

"You were tube fed."

"Because I had so much trouble. I had to learn how to eat, before I could go home to my family."

"You must have spent a lot of your life in the hospital, in the beginning."

She put her shirt back down, nodding.

"And did you have another family, before that?"

"I don't know. I don't remember."

"Well, we're going to find out, okay? This information will help us figure out what happened."

Carmina nodded, looking down at her feet.

TWENTY

"ow's she doing?" Agnes asked, as Neil approached her desk.

"Fell asleep with her head on the table. I don't think she got much sleep last night, worrying about Toto. And she's pretty weak from this episode."

"Do we need to get a doctor?"

"I might call mine later on, see what she suggests."

Agnes shook her head and chuckled. "What are the odds of you both having this problem?"

Neil shrugged, looking away. He scratched his head. "Uh, I don't know. So… have you made any progress?"

"Well, there isn't a centralized database, and we don't know what part of the country—or the world—she came from."

Neil's heart sank. "No way to trace kids who have had this?"

Agnes gave him a mysterious smile. She had found something, but he was going to have to pull it out of her.

"It's a rare disease," she said. "But you know what's even more rare?"

Neil studied her. Agnes' eyes danced. Neil glanced down at her desk, looking for a clue. The photo he had taken of Cynthia lay on the desk in front of her.

"The doll?"

"How many dolls do you think there are with omphaloceles?"

Neil raised his eyebrows and waited for the answer.

"They're handmade," Agnes said. "Made to order. Custom."

"Twelve to fifteen years ago. Would they still have records who they sold to?"

"Every single doll," Agnes said with a proud smile.

"Oh, you *are* good. How many names do we have to go through?"

She pointed to her scribbled notes, indicating one name. "I've been focusing on this one."

"Carmen Torres," Neil read. "Carmen, Carmina…"

"They may have kept a similar name. She was old enough to respond to it, and they might have thought it would be less confusing."

"What do we know about her so far?"

"The medical records available electronically show that Carmen Torres had giant omphalocele, which means that other organs, including her liver, were outside her body. She had a small abdominal cavity, and it took a long time to stretch it out and put everything back where it should be. She had a number of complications, including a membrane rupture and…" Agnes frowned at her notes. "An intestinal strangulation? Which is when they had to remove a length of dead intestine." She wrinkled her nose. "So that matches Carmina's story. Usually with omphaloceles, they're all fixed up within a few months of birth. Carmen's took a long time to resolve and she had a lot of ongoing complications."

"So she might have been in hospital for an extended time when she was old enough to remember some of the details."

"Right," Agnes confirmed.

"What happened to Carmen Torres?"

"The available medical records end around age three and a half. But that might just be because that's when she had surgery last or because she moved afterward to a doctor who wasn't putting his records in an electronic database yet. The specialist is going to pull his paper records back from archives, and see what handwritten notes he might have that didn't make it to the computer system."

"It might be because that's when Carmen Torres became Carmina Knight."

"Maybe."

"Do we have any information about her family? Her parents?"

"Working on it. Just one thing—it is quite a move, all the way from the west coast. I'm not sure how the Knights would have identified a child from so far away…"

"It's not a big stretch for someone with access to private jets. They might have had a mutual friend."

~

SOME TIME LATER, Neil looked up to see Mandy standing over his desk. He marked where he was reading with his finger and gave her a questioning look.

"Is that Carmina Knight sleeping in my meeting room?" Mandy demanded.

Neil wasn't fooled by her belligerent tone. He smiled. "Yes, it is. And we've had a very good talk."

She smiled her approval, abandoning the scolding expression. "Good work, agent! How is she doing?"

"Physically? Emotionally? Or on helping us with the case?"

Mandy stole a chair from the closest vacant desk and sat down. "All of the above. Fill me in."

"She called me early this morning," Neil stifled a yawn, "worried because her friend Toto was missing."

"Swept up by a tornado, no doubt."

"Caught stealing copper wiring from a construction site."

"Ah. Naughty boy."

"We're seeing if we can have some influence on his release. I don't want Carmina out there on her own. I feel much better with him looking after her."

Mandy nodded and made no objection to his interfering in a local police matter.

"So once we found him and got her some breakfast, she relaxed and we had a little chat…"

"And found… what?"

"Carmina had a rare birth defect. I'll spare you the details, but it meant multiple surgeries over several years."

"Which means we can trace her!" Mandy whooped.

"Agnes is working on it right now. The most promising lead so far is a Carmen Torres."

"They kept a similar name."

"We think so. It will take a bit of time to work through the details. But it's the first real break in identifying her."

"Well, that's excellent. I'm pleased. I don't suppose she's given you any additional insight on the forgery charges?"

"No. And I don't imagine she will. But… she didn't seem surprised by the charges."

Mandy nodded thoughtfully. "You wouldn't think it was something they would be able to keep a secret from her forever. Maybe for a few years, but once she was old enough to think for herself, look around and see how the family business was run…"

"Like with Esther, I think she might have suspected… but didn't want to know."

"Do you think he involved her in the business?"

Neil rubbed his chin, thinking. "I don't know. But if he did, I don't think she's responsible."

"No. How is she taking all of this? She's sleeping, so I assume she's calm."

"She's been sick the last few days, and I don't think she slept at all last night. So she's physically worn-out. Emotionally… I think she's relieved to tell us what she's been holding in all these years. And she's still very upset about Esther and finding out she wasn't legally adopted."

"Understandable. Any worries about her being sick? Should she be under a doctor's care?"

"I talked to a doctor." Neil neglected to specify what doctor. "Apparently, as well as the digestive issues and dehydration, she's susceptible to lung infection and could have heart problems. None of that is on her medical records as Carmina, but we should probably get her thoroughly checked out, if we can."

"You'll talk to her about it?"

"I'll do what I can."

"Good. Great progress, Neil. You did a fantastic job tracking her down and gaining her trust. Not a lot of people have that kind of skill."

Agnes hovered nearby. Mandy looked at her and smiled. "Agnes?"

Agnes looked from Mandy to Neil, not sure who to address. "Carmen Torres was in foster care from the time she was born. I've just talked to her foster mother…"

"Was she cooperative?"

Neil knew how protective and closed-mouthed some foster parents could be. A habit developed out of necessity.

"She's hopping on a plane and coming here."

Mandy and Neil both stared at her.

"What exactly did you tell her?" Neil asked.

"Not much…" Agnes gave a shrug. "Just that we had a girl we were trying to identify, and thought she might be Carmen Torres. She said she'd come right here."

A V-shaped frown line formed between Mandy's brows.

"That's an unexpected response," she said. "Not that I'm complaining!"

Neil looked at his watch. "I guess we'll have a few hours. Then we'll know more."

THE FOSTER MOM, Rosa Garcia, turned out to be a small, striking-looking woman. Mexican, was Neil's guess, maybe with some Native Indian as well. A strong face, but pleasant. Neil would put her in her fifties, but her relatively unlined face could just as easily have been forty or sixty. Agnes escorted her over to Neil, and she offered him a slim, brown hand. Her grip was firm.

"Agent Crowther. Good to meet you."

"You too, Mrs. Garcia. You can call me Neil."

"Rosa."

He nodded.

"Now, where is my little girl?"

Neil smiled at her inquiry. "We should probably sit down and have a talk first…"

"Not until I see Carmen. Then we can talk all you like."

Neil had expected to be able to bring her up to speed on what had been happening in Carmina's life and what they needed from her. But there was no real reason that couldn't wait. He gestured for Rosa to follow, and led her down the hall to the meeting room, where Carmina was no longer asleep, but was sketching to pass the time. She looked up when the door opened. Her eyes slid past Neil to the small woman next to him. She froze, riveted.

Rosa bustled into the room, not waiting for an introduction. "There she is. There's my Carmen!"

Carmina got to her feet as Rosa approached, and Rosa took her by the shoulders, and then with a hand on either of her cheeks, examining her closely.

"Yes, that's my baby," she confirmed. "Can I hug you?"

Carmina hesitated, her eyes going to Neil. He gave her no sign, not wanting to force her into anything she might be uncomfortable with. Carmina looked back at Rosa. She gave a small nod. Rosa wrapped her arms around Carmina and patted her on the back.

"You have been away for a long time, baby," she said.

Carmina pulled back and looked at her.

"You probably don't remember your Mama Rosa. It was too long ago."

Carmina nodded hesitantly. "Sort of."

"Carmina told us she remembered a dark woman who might have been her mother," Neil supplied.

Rosa patted Carmina's face. "I was your foster mother. You were very young. It was a long time ago. Now sit down. Sit! You don't look very well."

Carmina settled back into her chair. Rosa took the one next to her and patted her hand. "Is your tummy bothering you?" she asked.

"Yeah. For a few days. It's not usually so bad…"

Rosa looked at Neil. "Has she seen the doctor? You know it could be dangerous for her…"

"We'll have someone check her out, if she'll let us. I think it's just the stress."

"Stress makes it worse," Rosa agreed, stroking Carmina's hand and looking into her eyes. "You need to take care of yourself."

"Neil has a short gut too," Carmina said, nodding at him. "Because he got shot. He didn't have an omphalocele."

Rosa giggled. "I get a kick out of hearing you say that. It was so funny, when you were a wee little thing who could barely lisp my name, hearing you pronounce 'omphalocele' as plain as day." She giggled again, and wiped at the corners of her eyes. She looked at Neil. "I don't think she'd better be taking any medical advice from you, though. You don't look like you're managing your short bowel very well. Didn't they teach you about getting more calories? You can't absorb them all like you used to."

"Yes, ma'am," Neil assured her. "It's just hard to teach an old dog new tricks. I still keep going for the coffee and sweets. Carmina's been managing hers very well, up until now. Just had a little setback."

"Sometimes it hurts to eat," Carmina said. "Everything's too… squished. I get heartburn and stuff."

Rosa let her eyes roam around the room. She saw Cynthia on the table. "Oh my! Doesn't that baby doll bring back memories! Your little Cynthia. You took her with you everywhere."

"I still do," Carmina admitted, her cheeks flushing.

"We used to play a little game. Like peek-a-boo." Rosa reached over and gently picked the doll up. Carmina didn't move or object. "Cynthia has a secret…" Rosa intoned. She pulled up the dress to show the omphalocele. "There it is!"

Carmina reached for the doll, and Rosa handed it over. Carmina hunched over the doll, holding it against her face, lost in thought.

"Did you tell her she couldn't tell anybody Cynthia's secret?" Neil questioned. "When she was going to be adopted?"

"No. It was just a game we played. To pass the time or to talk about what the doctors were going to do next."

"Was Carmina's omphalocele a secret?"

"How could it be? You can't go around with a baby's guts on the outside and not have people notice. We had to keep it covered to keep the germs out, but you could still see the bandages and the lump, and she wouldn't feed properly. She spent half her life at the hospital."

"But she had to be fixed up and learn to eat before she could go to her adoptive parents."

"Why don't you tell me what's going on, now? What's this all about, and how did you not know where she came from?"

Neil looked at Carmina to give her a chance to explain. She motioned for him to go ahead, and Neil described, as broadly as possible, what had transpired. Rosa sat with her arms folded, shaking her head.

"I did not like that social worker. I knew there was something wrong right from the time she took over Carmen's case. Something smelled very fishy. I never saw her again after the adoption. Never had her on any other case. I think she moved away."

"Probably got a huge pay-off," Neil said. "Do you still foster?"

"Oh… not much anymore. Sometimes I take a medically fragile child for a day or two while they figure out what to do. But nothing full-time anymore."

"Did you ever meet Carmina's adoptive parents? How did it all come about?"

"Well, they saw her picture in one of the albums of waiting children. The mother was quite taken with her. Wouldn't consider any other child."

"Esther," Carmina said.

"Esther. Yes, that's right." Rosa's eyes slid sideways to Carmina, then over to Neil. "Never felt right about it. There was never any sign everything wasn't legal. The social worker handled it just like normal. But it never felt right to me. Esther… I couldn't believe they had passed a home study."

Neil knew as soon as she said it that Rosa was right. Esther could not have passed a home study. No social worker would have judged her competent to take care of an infant or a medically frail child. At least, not the way she was when Neil had seen her.

"You met them?"

"I wasn't supposed to… I was supposed to be out of the way whenever they came by to see Carmen. But I would see them in the hallways. Watch them from a distance in the playroom. I saw enough to make me wonder."

"They're good parents," Carmina insisted. "Esther's a good mom. I always had everything I needed, and they love me… I love them… very much."

Rosa turned her eyes back to Carmina. "Oh, you poor girl. This must all be so hard for you. Where are you living, with your mom and dad… being arrested? Do they have you in a foster home?"

"No…" Carmina squirmed a little under Neil's and Rosa's gazes. "I've been… sleeping rough… on the street."

"Oh, well that won't do. We have to do something about that," Rosa told Neil.

It was Neil's turn to squirm. "Carmina has a mind of her own. She ran away. It's taken this long to find her and persuade her to come in to see me. And I don't think she would have come in today, if it wasn't for Toto."

"Toto?"

"My friend," Carmina said. "He helps me. He's been taking care of me while I was sick, but then he didn't come back last night."

"He ran into a little legal trouble," Neil said dryly.

"Oh, you have a *boyfriend*," Rosa said.

"No!" Carmina did more than get a little pink this time, her face flushed a brilliant red. "He's not a boyfriend! Just a friend!"

"Well, you can't be sleeping on the street, with or without him. So what are we going to do?"

There was no answer from Carmina. Neil didn't have any suggestions.

"You can come home with me. You need a foster home, I'm a foster mom; presto!"

Carmina was smiling, but she shook her head. "I couldn't go without Toto."

"The boy who is *not* your boyfriend."

"He's not. But he needs me too. He's been hurt, and he gets these attacks, in his brain. I can't just leave him by himself. He could die."

Rosa studied Carmina, her face unlined. Thoughtful. "You really care for this boy."

"Not like *that*, though. He's my friend. I can't abandon him."

"Well… this is going to take some thinking."

"YOU SAID—OR maybe Agnes said—you had Carmina from the time she was born. How did that all come about?" Neil asked, after getting Rosa a coffee and settling in again.

Rosa looked at Carmina. "Carmen was a special child. They couldn't give her to just anyone."

"You'd had special needs kids before."

Rosa inclined her head. "Yes. They knew I could handle it."

"And the birth mother…?"

"She was known to Child Services. Before Carmen was born, there was a three-year-old boy who was apprehended due to neglect and abuse. They knew she was pregnant and kept a hand in, trying to make sure she got to appointments and had lots of support in place. But in an ultrasound, the doctors saw the omphalocele. When they explained to her what it was, and what it would mean, she couldn't handle it. So she relinquished custody at birth. But there are not a lot of people trying to adopt a baby with serious medical issues. Taking in a child you don't even know is going to survive…"

"That takes a special kind of person," Neil said.

She smiled at that, acknowledging the praise.

Carmina spoke. "So I lived with you from the time I was born until…?"

"Until you were between three and a half and four. And living with me didn't mean spending a lot of time in my home. You were in the hospital at least half the time. Getting another surgery, recovering from an infection, trying to get your weight up. You were very bright, but had a lot of physical delays. Kids that can't go squirming around on the floor and getting dirty don't develop the same way."

There was a lull in the conversation. Rosa looked at the pictures on the table. "These are yours?"

"Yeah."

"Can I see them?"

Carmina gathered the pictures together into a pile, and handed them over.

Rosa smiled. "You had to spend a lot of time in bed, so you really liked coloring and drawing. You always had a knack for it. So good for someone so little."

"Really?"

Rosa nodded. She looked slowly through the pictures. "Your friend-who-is-not-a-boyfriend?" she guessed, looking at a picture of Toto.

"Yeah."

"And this is your mom. I remember her."

"Uh-huh."

Rosa looked at a sweeping arch, with sky beyond it. She turned it this way and that, but couldn't quite sort out the perspective. Carmina took it and held it above her.

"It's the bottom of the bridge. Where I… sleep…"

"Oh, I see now."

She turned to the next picture.

Neil caught Rosa's quizzical glance at him. "What? Did she draw one of me?"

"Unless you have a twin who is a magician."

She held it up for Neil to see. It was a pleasant enough scene, with him performing in front of the fountain, and Toto back behind him, relaxing and smiling at something hidden from view.

"Ah, you are so good, Carmen. You have so much talent! Don't let it go to waste."

"I won't," Carmina said. She took the pictures back, and packed them carefully away.

~

CARMINA WAS tired after the long day. The woman named Agnes knocked and poked her head in the door. She smiled at everyone, then focused on Neil and spoke to him.

"The boy has been released ROR. As a courtesy. Do you want me to send a car to pick him up?"

"Toto?" Carmina questioned eagerly. "He's out of jail?" She looked around to pack her bag, but she'd already put everything away. "I have to go."

"Why don't we just have him brought over here?" Neil suggested. It was a logical, reasonable thought, but Carmina shook her head.

"I want to go see him. He won't want to come here."

"Maybe he'd like to meet your foster mom."

The idea was almost laughable. She'd heard Toto talk about his numerous foster homes and other living situations. He wouldn't care about a foster mom, even if she had taken care of Carmina for almost four years. He had urged her to go see Esther, because he saw how much she missed her, but a foster mom was different.

"I only came here so you could help me find Toto," she explained to Neil. "Now he's out, it's time for us to go home. That's where he wants to be."

"Do you want me to drop you somewhere?"

Carmina shook her head. It was getting too easy to get into his car. Too comfortable. She had to remember to stay suspicious, not to let down her guard. All of these people acted so nice, it was hard to remember, and not to let herself start trusting them, thinking of them as her friends. She felt a stab of guilt at having shared Cynthia's secret. Rosa said it was okay, but Julius would be furious with her for telling Neil about her omphalocele, and showing him her scars. She knew that was taboo. Maybe it was so they could never find out where she came from. All of this information about her past was unsettling. She felt like she was getting swept out of control, in the deep part of the river where the undertow was strong.

"No. I don't need a ride."

"Carmina… you're not strong. Are you sure you'll be okay?"

Carmina nodded impatiently. Agnes withdrew from the room. Carmina looked at Rosa, not sure what to do or say. "Bye… Mama Rosa."

"Won't you stay here with me, where you're safe?" Rosa begged, taking her hands.

"No." Carmina left her hands in Rosa's for an instant longer, remembering the feeling of those strong hands when she had been smaller, her hands too tiny to go around Rosa's. She pulled them out. "I have to go. Be with Toto."

"My baby… be careful. It's not safe out there."

"I'll be safe. Toto protects me."

TWENTY-ONE

S he could have saved herself a lot of difficulty if she had just let Neil drive her downtown. But she couldn't keep relying on him, trust him to get her from place to place. So she walked and took the bus, and her feet were sore and blistered by the time she got back home, and it was late in the day, the darkness gathering. Carmina looked around for Toto, worried at not finding him there. Had it been a lie? They hadn't really released him? Or had something happened to him on the way home? She couldn't last another night without him. But just as the panic was building, she heard Toto's call.

"Case'! KC, where have you been? I've been worried sick about you!"

They hurried to meet each other, and Carmina threw her arms around Toto and held him tight.

"You've been worried sick?" she scoffed. "You're the one who took off last night and never came back! I'm the one who was sick!" She thumped him with her fists. Not hard enough to hurt him, but hard enough to let him know he had really worried her. "And I come back and you're supposed to be here, and you're not!"

"I brought sandwiches!" Toto protested, digging into the big central pocket of his hoodie and bringing out two sub sandwiches. "I just went out to get us a couple of sammies! I thought you'd need to eat…"

She punched him once more in the arm, and took one of the sandwiches. They went over to Toto's sleeping bag, still laid out from the night before, and sat down on it to eat. Carmina unwrapped her sandwich and started to eat.

"Stealing wire is stupid," she told him.

Toto looked up at her. "Who says I was stealing wire?"

Carmina raised her eyebrows at him.

"Well… I just needed some money. It looked like an easy target."

"It's stupid."

"I don't have a talent like yours. People don't exactly line up for me to solve equations for them. I gotta look for another way to make some cash."

Carmina shook her head.

"Tell your friend Mumford thanks for springing me."

"Yeah… are you going to stay out of jail?"

"Well, it all depends on the cops. I can't help it if they decide to roust me."

She just chewed on her sandwich. She wasn't stupid enough to believe that, and neither was he. They finished their dinner in silence, the darkness closing in around them.

"How was your day?" Toto asked as Carmina rolled out her sleeping bag and they were settling in for the night.

Carmina's mind whirled as she thought about her day and tried to come up with a concise answer. "Uh… I dunno… weird."

"Yeah?" He was quiet, waiting for more information. But Carmina was so exhausted from the long day that she was asleep before she could begin to tell him about it.

CARMINA AWOKE TO VOICES, shouting. That wasn't unusual, there were often disruptions in the night; drunks, crazies, nightmares. But it was closer than usual; the voices right on top of her. She rolled, shielding her eyes from a bright light. It blinded her so she couldn't see what was going on.

"Toto?" she tried to call him, but her voice was weak and frightened. He wouldn't be able to hear her over the shouting. "What's happening?"

"Get her!" It was a low, rough bark. Before Carmina could process what it meant, hands grabbed her. Big strong hands pulled her up to her feet.

Carmina struggled, but was no match for the big man. She blinked, trying to clear the bright red afterimages from her eyes to see what was going on.

"Leave her alone!" Toto's voice screamed out of the darkness. "Don't touch her. Just leave her alone!"

"Where's the money?"

She didn't know who these men were. What it was they were after. She could only see dark shapes in the dim moonlight. Big men. Not teenagers like Toto. She didn't recognize the voices. Not any of the homeless she knew. And they weren't cops.

"Toto?" She tried to understand what was going on.

The light moved, to shine on Toto. One of the men was holding Toto. Another hit him. Carmina struggled to free herself again, even though she knew logically that there was nothing she could do to help him.

"I don't have it." Toto coughed. "I… I didn't get it. Tomorrow—give me some more time…"

"You said you'd have it today!"

"I—I know—I was supposed to… I had a little… cop problem…"

The man yelling at Toto hit him again, making him cry out and double over, and cough some more.

"Stop," Carmina protested. "Leave him alone…"

The man turned around and looked at Carmina. The light flashed into her eyes again. She squinted and turned her head aside. Leaving Toto, the thug came over to Carmina. He took her chin in his big hand.

"Pretty girl, Toto. Would be a shame, wouldn't it, for that face to get all messed up?"

"Leave her be! I'll get you the money. I promise. Just had a set-back today…"

"You said you'd have it today. You didn't show up at the drop. I gotta wonder why."

"No, I just had trouble. I'll still get it to you!" Toto's voice was frantic. "Just leave KC alone!"

"Oh, I think I found my leverage here," the man crooned. He leaned in and kissed Carmina, holding her head still and forcing his mouth over hers. She couldn't escape him. Then he let go and slapped her hard across the side of the head, making her head snap back with the force of it. Her cheek throbbed and her ear rang. The sharp taste of blood flooded her mouth and made her choke.

Toto howled. "No! No, leave her alone! I've got the money. I'll give it to you. Now!"

Carmina stared toward Toto in disbelief. He'd had the money they wanted all along? He'd let her get hit—and kissed—when he had the money all along?

"I'm waiting."

"She has it. The girl has it."

Blood was dribbling down Carmina's chin. It was down her chin or down her throat, she didn't have any other choice.

The man looked over his shoulder toward Toto with a doubtful frown.

"Her belt. She has it in a money belt."

"Toto!" Carmina couldn't believe what he was doing. She struggled to escape the hands that held her still. "No… no!"

But it was too late. Toto had already said it. Her attacker was grinning, leering at her, clearly enjoying himself immensely. He grasped both sides of her shirt and ripped them away from each other, sending the buttons raining to the ground. The money belt was exposed, and all he had to do was unzip it and pull the money out. But he didn't. He slid his fingers between the belt and Carmina's stomach, cold on her skin. She broke out in goosebumps all over. He slid them all the way around behind her back, feeling for the catch. He pulled her against him in a bear hug, forcing their bodies against each other. Carmina squirmed, but there was no escape. He continued to grin down at her, then squeezed the catch on the money belt to release it.

It felt strange to have the money belt off, after having worn it constantly for so long. She felt naked without it. The man took the opportunity to slide his hands down Carmina's bare waist. Big, rough hands. She gulped, swallowing blood. He looked at the scars on her belly, brushing the backs of his fingers over them. Weighing the money belt in his hand, he turned his attention away from her, and unzipped the pouch. Thumbing through the wad of bills, he smiled, showing his teeth.

"Nice doing business with you, Toto."

He nodded to the man holding Carmina, and he released her. With a hand motion toward Toto, he had the boy let go as well. The thugs melted away into the dark.

Toto ran to Carmina as she fell to her knees. Carmina was shaking all over. She coughed, spraying blood, spitting it to the side, trying not to get it on her sleeping bag. Toto's hand was on her shoulder.

"KC! KC, I'm sorry. I'm so sorry!"

She pulled away from him.

"KC…"

Toto tried to pull the sides of her shirt together, but there was no way to fasten them. As they fell back apart, he saw the scars on her stomach.

"What—what happened to you?"

Carmina wiped at her eyes and nose. She felt for the edges of her sleeping bag to go back to bed. "Are *you* okay?" she asked.

"What? Me? I'm fine." He coughed again, and clutched at his sore ribs. "I'm okay. But you're bleeding…"

She pushed him away. "Leave me alone."

"KC. Let me help you. He hurt you. You're going to bleed all over your bag."

"Leave me alone!" Carmina growled. She pushed his hands away again. "I'm going back to sleep. Leave me alone."

He fell back from her. Even in the moonlight, she could see how wide and worried his eyes were. She slithered into her sleeping bag and put her head down. She closed her eyes and refused to look at him or answer him again. Eventually, he went back to his own sleeping bag, and lay down, propped up on his elbow. Carmina opened her eyes and watched the glowing end of his cigarette, as he smoked through one, then a second, and then a third cigarette. Toto finally laid down properly to go to sleep. Carmina watched the rise and fall of his chest as the sky started to get lighter and he fell back asleep.

AFTER HOW BUSY the previous day had been with Carmina and Rosa, Neil had a lot of work to catch up on. So when the phone rang and he didn't recognize the number, he let it go to voicemail. If it was important, they could leave him a message and he would get back to them when it was a better time. But thirty seconds later, Agnes' number popped up on the display. He glanced over his shoulder toward her desk. She motioned impatiently for him to pick it up. He did.

"What's up?"

"I've got a young man looking for you. Teenager, by his voice. He sounds pretty… frantic."

Neil leaned back in his seat with a sigh. "What does he want?"

"He said it was life or death."

"Honestly?"

"He's desperate to talk to you."

"Fine. Put him through."

"He's on line three. It should be flashing."

Neil looked at his set. He hung up on Agnes, and pushed the flashing red button to pick up the call. "Agent Crowther."

"She's gone! I woke up this morning, and she wasn't there. I've looked everywhere. I can't find her!"

"Slow down. Is this Toto?"

"Yes. KC's gone. She ran away!"

"What happened?"

Toto's words stopped like a tap that had been shut off. The line was silent. Neil waited. Toto started to cry. Dry, racking sobs.

"Have you been drinking?" Neil asked.

"No. You have to find her… Neil. You have to."

"Why would she run away from you? Yesterday, she had every opportunity to leave, to go to a new home, and she chose to go back to you. She's the one who got you out of jail. So why would she run away?"

Toto swore, desperation making his voice strained and thin. "I was… I was supposed to pay someone back yesterday. A loan. But…" he trailed off.

"But instead you got caught stealing, and spent most of the day in police custody."

Toto choked. "They came in the night, looking for me. To get their money."

Neil's stomach twisted. He tasted sour acid in the back of his throat. "What happened?"

"They were just trying to take it out of me… they wouldn't have killed me, not if they wanted to get paid… but KC woke up, and when she tried to stop them, they saw we were friends."

"What did they do to her?"

"He hit her. And… took her money belt."

Neil swallowed, trying to keep the acid down. "How did they know about her money belt?"

Toto sobbed into the phone for some minutes before answering. "I was trying to protect her. I couldn't let him hit her!"

Neil struggled to keep his voice reasonable and his judgments to himself. "Then what happened?"

"Nothing. They got the money and left. We went back to sleep. But when I woke up this morning, she was gone. She's not in any of the usual places."

"She probably just needed some space and some time to think," Neil soothed. Inside, he was panicking. Carmina had run again, this time with no money and no Toto. Where would she go?

"I couldn't just stand there and let them hurt her," Toto said. "Hitting her… and worse."

"Of course not. You knew they'd leave her alone if they got the money."

"Uh-huh."

Neil sighed. "There's not much I can do, Toto. I'll call around to the hospitals, make sure she's not been admitted. But you already know where she's most likely to go, and if she's not there, it's because she doesn't want either one of us to find her."

"She has to be okay. I didn't mean for anything to happen to her."

CARMINA LAY CURLED up on her side on the soft bed, with smooth, clean sheets pulled around her. She had a cold compress on the side of her face, that had reduced the throbbing and some of the swelling. She could still taste blood from the big cut on the inside of her cheek, and the teeth on the injured side wiggled more than they should.

Rosa stroked her head. "What do you want to eat?"

"I don't know."

"You've been sick. You need to build your strength back up again."

Carmina didn't say anything. Rosa continued to pat her hair. "How about a hamburger? I could usually tempt you with a McDonalds Happy Meal. Even when you were just learning to take food by mouth, you didn't want any soft baby food. You wanted your 'happy food'."

Carmina shook her head. "My mouth hurts too much."

"Hmm. Well, you know we have to be careful about too many liquids. What's nice and soft that you feel like right now?"

Carmina squeezed the pillow against the uninjured side of her face. "Don't know."

"Macaroni? Eggs?"

"No. I don't know."

"Think of something, little one. You need to keep your body fed."

Carmina lifted her head to frown at Rosa. "I'm bigger than you are," she pointed out.

"But not older, nor wiser, so I'll call you little one if I like."

Carmina lay back down and rolled onto her back, grabbing the cold compress to hold it in place. "I've done pretty good, all by myself. I can be grown up."

"You came to me this morning. You still need a mama to hold your hand and check up on you."

Carmina felt safe and secure in her little cocoon, with Mama Rosa watching over her. It was the first time since the whole ordeal had begun that she felt normal and present and safe. Even the time with Esther in the prison had been stressful, and she hadn't felt quite right. With Rosa there, she felt like she could just be herself and not be so scared and anxious. She couldn't remember much about those early years with Rosa, but her voice and smell and mothering were familiar and comforting.

"I don't want to eat. I just want to sleep some more."

"You've had lots of sleep. It's time to get up and at 'em. And fed."

"Just a little more? Please, Mama Rosa?"

She snuggled down in the blankets and closed her eyes. Rosa didn't say anything.

But in spite of her lethargy, Carmina couldn't go back to sleep again. She shifted restlessly. Her body had been paying attention to the discussion about food, and her stomach started to ache and to rumble grumpily.

Carmina opened her eyes. "Maybe I will eat."

Rosa nodded. "What do you want?"

"Macaroni?" She picked the suggestion that seemed the most tempting at the moment. "Do we have to go out?"

"No, I can get room service. You just rest a while longer."

Rosa got up off of the bed, and Carmina could hear her moving around the hotel room and placing the call to room service. Rosa puttered around and tidied up the room as she waited. When the macaroni arrived, Carmina forced herself to sit up. Rosa watched her as she shoveled the pasta into her mouth.

"Slow down, baby. I swear, once you learned how to eat, you were determined to make up for all of the years of tube feeding. Your tummy will be happier if you eat slowly."

Carmina had frequently been told by Julius or Esther or others who had to watch her eat to slow down or to be polite, but she mostly ignored them. When she was hungry, she just wanted to get as much food down as fast as she could, even though it meant a stomachache by the time she was done. But she tried to slow down for Rosa.

"When you're done, you can tell me all about how you got hurt," Rosa said, her eyes on the bruise Carmina had uncovered in order to eat.

Carmina swallowed. "Somebody hit me."

"Yes, that much is obvious. Was it your friend-who-is-not-a-boyfriend?"

"No."

"I thought he was supposed to be helping you out and protecting you. Where was he when this happened?"

Carmina took another bite, swallowing hard to get it down past the lump in her throat. "He was there."

"He was there! Why didn't he do something to stop them?"

"There were too many of them."

Rosa tutted. "You should not be out there where you can get hurt. You need to be home where someone can take care of you."

Carmina nodded slightly. She continued to eat, and did not speak again until she had scraped all of the pasta and sauce possible from the white bowl. "Could I really come live with you?"

"Well, of course, my dear. I'd be delighted to have you. But you have to really think about it. I live halfway across the country, and you wouldn't be able to visit your parents or friends. Not very often, anyway."

"Do you think Neil would let me?"

"It won't be up to Agent Crowther. It will be up to Child Services." Her eyes glittered as she studied Carmina. "And I *will* get my way, you can bank on that."

"But he's a fed. He might… he might stop them. Say I have to stay here and testify or something. He can do that."

"He can try. But he won't. And they wouldn't listen to him anyway."

Carmen opened her mouth to argue, but Rosa cut her off. "I've been dealing with the foster care system for thirty years, Carmen. I know how to work it."

Carmina nodded and put her bowl down on the bedside table.

"Did you tell anybody you were coming here?" Rosa asked.

"No."

"Do you think we'd better call Agent Crowther and let him know? He can talk to Child Services to get you assigned a social worker, and we can start the process of getting you transferred."

Carmina scratched the back of her head. She rubbed at her belly where the money belt had been, which still felt naked even though she had changed out of the torn shirt so it was no longer exposed.

"Do you have a stomachache?" Rosa demanded, her eyes sharp.

"No… just thinking… Do we have to call Neil? Can we go there again instead, so he doesn't know… where I'm staying?"

Rosa's brows went up, and she chuckled. "Do you think he wouldn't be able to figure it out? Of course we can go there, it you're up to traveling. But don't think he couldn't make a few calls and track me down pretty darn quick. All I have to do is use my credit card once. And it was used to book this room."

Carmina knew this. But she wanted to keep up the illusion to herself that she was safe here, and nobody could find her, not even Neil.

TWENTY-TWO

Neil let out his breath with a big puff when he saw Carmina and Rosa being escorted into the office. He felt his shoulders dip down, and realized how tensely he'd been holding himself for the past few hours. Rosa was carrying a styrofoam coffee cup, and handed it to him when he approached them.

"Chamomile tea," she explained. "To help you to calm down."

He breathed out slowly. "Do I not look calm?" he asked, keeping his voice neutral and even.

The dark little woman gazed up into his face. "No."

"I think I'm being very calm."

"Drink your tea."

He caught a glint of humor in Carmina's eyes, but she caught his eyes on her and quickly looked away. Neil looked her over as he walked them to the meeting room they had occupied the previous day.

"Are you okay?"

"Yeah."

"Toto called today, pretty worried about you."

She shrugged and sniffed, demonstrating total unconcern for Toto's feelings. They all sat down at the conference table. Carmina squirmed around, anxious or uncomfortable in the chair. Neil took a sip of the chamomile tea. It tasted a little like how he thought a daisy might taste.

"Carmen would like to come home with me," Rosa said.

Neil had suspected as much when they came in together. "I think that's a great idea. We'll have to start the process."

"If you can give me the number for your Child Services department and the use of the phone, I will start the wheels turning."

"I'll have to make the first call to officially get Carmina put into care."

Rosa nodded. Carmina shifted again, looking uncomfortable. Though most of her face was a blank mask, he could see the panic in her eyes. Her mind was probably replaying every warning Julius had ever given her about not trusting. It couldn't be easy for her to trust a fed, and the Child Services department, and this stranger from her past. Especially when the boy she had just put her trust in for the past few weeks had just betrayed her.

"Are you sure this is what you want to do?" Neil asked. "Don't make a decision you're going to regret in a few days."

She looked away from him. "I know what I want."

"In a few days, you're not going to be as angry at Toto, and you might wish you hadn't been so quick to make a decision like this."

Her jaw was clenched. "Would you change your mind about someone who hurt you?"

Neil felt his lips tighten in spite of trying to remain impassive. This was about her, not about him. "You know Toto was just trying to protect you. He knew if those men got what they wanted, they would leave you alone. He couldn't bear to see you hurt."

"Toto was stupid. He was stupid to get mixed up with them in the first place. I'm not going to hang out with someone who does stuff like that. If I hadn't gotten him out of jail and gone back there, I wouldn't have gotten hurt. I should have just stayed out of it. He deserves what he gets. He asked for it."

"Toto was stupid," Neil agreed. Carmina's eyes turned to him, surprised. "People make stupid mistakes. You're telling me you've never made one?"

"I haven't gotten anyone beaten up lately."

"Well, I hope not, but you haven't been living on the streets for long either. People who are desperate are more likely to do stupid things."

"He's really smart with math," Carmina said. "He should be able to figure out how to make himself some money. Without stealing copper wire. He understands all of that stuff, so he should be able to make money without even thinking about it. People would pay him, wouldn't they, to solve problems for them?"

"Who would?"

"I don't know. He's really smart with that stuff."

"So are computers. And you don't have to pay their benefits. They don't get distracted, and they show up for work every day."

"He can't figure out these guys were dangerous? You don't take money from loan sharks. He can figure out how much interest they're going to charge him! He has to know he can't pay it back."

"People get desperate," Neil repeated.

"Well, I'm not desperate. I've got a family to go to now, so I'm not staying there. He hurt me, and I'm not staying with him."

Neil nodded. "I don't think you should," he agreed. "I think you should get in off the streets before you get hurt any worse. It's a dangerous place to be. I just wonder if running off across the continent is going to solve all of your problems, or if you might regret leaving before you even talk to Toto again."

"I don't need to talk to him. I don't have anything to say to him."

"Good-bye?"

"No. He doesn't even get a good-bye."

"If you don't forgive Toto for his involvement in you getting hurt, he's not the one you're punishing," Neil pointed out. "You're punishing yourself. If you're bitter over it, you're the one who suffers."

"Why should I forgive him? I'm not going to stay around to be hurt more."

"But there's a difference. You can forgive him and still not go back to live on the street with him."

Carmina raised her eyebrows at this. "Then what's forgiving?"

"Well… not having hard feelings toward him."

"But he got me hurt and my money stolen."

"You can be understanding about him making a mistake. Realize no one is perfect."

"He was stupid. I wouldn't have done something like that to him."

Carmina turned her face away from him again, and put her head down in her folded arms on the table. Neil stared at her, waiting for her to turn back around. But she was done.

Neil tried to breathe through the tightness in his chest. Why should he feel so stressed and uptight about Carmina and Toto's situation? It didn't matter to him whether they made up or not. In fact, it was better if Carmina didn't make up with Toto, so she would go to a stable home where she was being looked after properly instead of out on the streets where it was so dangerous for her.

But he couldn't help thinking it was important for Carmina to forgive Toto for making a mistake that hurt her.

NEIL WAS surprised when Kyle poked his head in the conference room door.

"Hey, partner. Foss mentioned you were around." He nodded his head at Carmina. "Hey."

Carmina nodded and looked at Neil for an introduction.

"My old partner," Neil said. "Kyle Sandler."

"Oh." She looked from one to the other. Neil could see the tumblers clicking into place as she tied Kyle to Neil's shooting. "Hey, nice to meet you."

"You too." Kyle looked back at Neil. "So I wondered if you wanted to hit the pub after work. Mary's visiting her mom, so I'm bach'ing it for a couple of days."

Neil frowned, considering it. He looked at his watch. "Yeah, I don't think that's going to work out today. I'm just kind of busy with this case."

Kyle nodded. "All right. Maybe next time. Give me a call if you can tomorrow…?"

"Sure."

Neil didn't look back up from his papers. Kyle withdrew again. The silence grew.

It was Carmina who spoke first. "Aren't you the one who told me I should forgive Toto for letting me get hurt?"

"What does that have to do with anything?"

"You haven't forgiven your partner for shooting you."

"Sure, I have." Neil narrowed his eyes at her. "I know it was just an accident."

"If you forgave him, you'd still do stuff with him."

"I told you when we were talking about Toto, that you forgiving him and going back to live with him and putting yourself in the same position again are not the same thing."

"So you think he's going to shoot you again if you go out for drinks?"

Her question gave Neil pause. He had done his best to forgive his partner, but getting together with him seemed too much of a concession. He had defended that choice to himself, saying he had to protect himself from getting hurt again, but Carmina's question made it clear to him that the justification was ridiculous.

Of course Kyle wasn't going to shoot him, or do something else that would endanger him, if they went out for a drink. Neil hadn't taken Kyle up on the invitation because Neil still hadn't forgiven him.

CARMINA WAS tired from being sick and not getting much sleep the night before. And all of the stress. Even though she hadn't been able to go back to sleep at Rosa's hotel, she still felt heavy with sleep. She needed to get in a nap. The conference room table wasn't exactly comfortable, but she'd slept there the day before. So she tried again, drifting on the edge of consciousness as she listened to Rosa making endless phone calls.

Carmina had imagined it would be easy. One quick call, explain the situation, and she'd get permission to go back home with Rosa. But there were calls to social workers, judges, and a vast array of other professionals Carmina couldn't even begin to wrap her mind around. They had to open a file for her with the local Child Services, then fill it up with every bit of information they knew about her, and do the same thing at Rosa's Child Services—except there was already a file there for her they had to pull out of storage and reactivate.

She listened distantly to Rosa describing her birth mother. Carmina remembered only the broadest highlights of the story from the day before. Her birth mother hadn't wanted her when she realized Carmina had a birth defect. That she was going to need significant medical care. But there were other parts Carmina hadn't really listened to.

"She had a three-year-old son who had already been apprehended for abuse and neglect... yes... Toby... same last name: Toby Torres..."

Carmina's brain was nearly asleep. Slow to make the connections because she was so near to dreaming. Or maybe only making the connection because she was so close to sleep and it was free of the fetters of consciousness. Toby. Toby Torres.

Carmina sat up, shaking off sleep. "What…?"

Rosa looked over at her, startled.

"What happened to him?" Carmina demanded, rubbing her eyes, trying to erase the stickiness.

But Rosa was still on the phone, and she shook her head. The call went on interminably. Dates. Names. Places she'd never heard of. Doctors, diagnoses, surgeries, piece after piece of Carmina's life, reduced to a few words on a file they were just going to close after she left the state anyway.

In spite of herself, in spite of sitting up now and not putting her head down on the table, Carmina was nodding off again for a few seconds at a time when Rosa finally put down the phone.

"What is it, my little chick?"

Carmina raised her eyebrows. "Little chick? I didn't hatch out of an egg."

"What were you asking me in the middle of that call?"

"I… nothing, I guess… I just wondered…"

"What?"

"What happened to that boy? The one who was my brother?"

"Ahh." Rosa tipped her chair back, stretching and trying to find a more comfortable position. "Well, he was taken into foster care when he was three or so."

"And then what? Did he go back? Or did he get adopted?"

"As far as I know, he stayed in foster care. He wasn't one of my kids, so I couldn't tell you very much about him."

"Can you find out?"

Rosa pursed her little lips. "Not officially. But I might be able to get a few well-placed casual questions answered."

"Can you?"

"Of course. You want to know what happened to your family. Do you want to know about your birth mother too? She's probably still around."

"No… no, just the brother."

Rosa nodded. "I'll try to find out."

"Was he my full brother? Not half or step or anything?"

"Yes, as far as I know. Of course, there's no way I could be sure who the father was, but your bio mom was still living with the man who was listed as the boy's father when you were born." The corners of her eyes crinkled. "Why? Keeping track of organ donors, just in case?"

Carmina shrugged with one shoulder. "I dunno. I just never knew I had any family except Mom and Dad."

~

NEIL STEPPED BACK into the conference room to check on Carmina and make sure Rosa didn't need anything else. Rosa was talking on the phone. Carmina was nowhere to be seen. Neil made a questioning gesture at Rosa, indicating the seat Carmina had occupied last time he had been in the room. She pointed at the door.

Uneasily, Neil stepped back out into the hall, and looked up and down the corridor. No sign of Carmina. He supposed she must have taken a break to go to the restroom, and wandered down and hung around the restroom doors for a few minutes. She could be having cramps and diarrhea again. She hadn't yet seen a doctor. If she was still unable to get her system under control, she might need some medical supervision.

Mandy came out of the restroom, and shook her head at him slightly. "Looking for someone, agent?"

"Carmina, actually. Is she in there?"

"No. It's empty." At Neil's expression, she looked concerned. "Don't tell me you've lost her again!"

"That girl's as slippery as an eel. Let me find out. Maybe she just went to the snack machine or something."

He went back into the conference room as Rosa put down the phone. "Where did Carmina go?"

"To the bathroom. I'd better check on her, she's been quite a while. She might not be feeling well."

"The restroom is empty. I already checked."

Rosa's lips parted. She looked at him, fatigue washing over her features. And she'd only been on the case for two days. "Has she bolted?"

Neil looked at the seat Carmina had been sitting in. Her bag was gone. She'd left nothing behind, not even a crumb or bit of paper. He rubbed his forehead, trying to ease the muscles sore from stress.

"It looks like it. She didn't say anything? Did something happen that upset her, or did she just have time to think about it and change her mind?"

"I don't know… I've been so busy working through these calls, trying to get things arranged."

Neil slapped his hand on the table and swore.

"I'm sorry, ma'am," he apologized immediately. "I'm sorry to lose my temper, but… dammit!" he slapped the table again. "Every time I think I'm making progress with her, it's another step backward!"

Rosa grimaced. "When you've worked with foster kids as long as I have, Neil, you realize there are almost as many steps backward as there are forward. This girl's life has been shattered. She didn't have an easy start in life, and now this has happened to her. Moving forward is difficult. Almost impossible."

"Then what do you do? How can you keep going in the face of so much… discouragement?"

She looked up at the ceiling, eyes unfocused. "I just remember when they put her in my arms the very first time. She was a beautiful baby. Scary as hell, but what a beautiful little face. I loved her the first moment I laid eyes on her. And I still do."

CARMINA DIDN'T KNOW where to find him. She knew as she went from one location to another that they could be chasing each other in circles, each on the move, looking for the other, instead of just staying put where they could be found.

She bumped into Snake at the fountain. He looked her over, noting her bruised face. "That boy got you into some trouble?" he asked. "I heard the goings-on last night, but I laid low. Didn't know what else to do."

"It's okay," Carmina said. "You couldn't have done anything. They got what they wanted."

"Toto's been looking for you."

"Where is he? I'm looking for him."

"Don't know. I imagine he might go to the soup kitchen, see if you're eating there today."

Carmina's stomach was complaining, and the shadows were growing longer. "Are you going?" she asked Snake.

"I am. Does the lady want an escort?"

Carmina smiled. He picked up his big duffle bag and put it over his shoulder. "Why don't we go get some soup, then?"

He walked slowly. Carmina was impatient, but she knew Snake would have timed it properly to get there when the soup kitchen's dinner hour opened and there was still food to be had. There was no point in getting there earlier, Toto wouldn't be there looking for her an hour before it opened. He'd look for her once they started serving. So she tried to match her steps with Snake's and not get anxious about going too slowly. Her body was fatigued; she might as well conserve energy.

When they finally got there, the doors had just opened. Carmina shuffled in with everyone else, and picked up a tray, looking around for Toto. In spite of her vigilance, he managed to startle her, coming from the wrong direction.

"KC!"

Carmina fumbled her tray and almost dumped everything. He caught it and steadied it for a moment.

"KC, are you okay? I'm so sorry. I really am. I'm so sorry I got you mixed up in all of that." He touched the bruise on her face, his expression pained. He shook his head. "I'd do anything to keep you from getting hurt. I really am sorry. And about your money. I'll… I'll pay you back."

Carmina looked around. "We need to talk."

"I know."

"I have to eat, or I'm going to pass out. But then we have to talk."

"We can talk while we eat."

"No, not about this."

"I don't care if everybody knows what a stupid moron I am. They should know. Everybody should know I just cause trouble everywhere I go. So they can stand back."

"Shh."

Toto looked at her and frowned. But he obeyed the command and shut up.

~

THEY FOUND an empty bench in front of the public library and sat down. It wasn't exactly private, with people coming and going, but nobody was stopping to listen to their conversation. Like Julius told her—hide in a crowd. Carmina watched the people for a few minutes before turning to Toto.

"You got taken away from your mom when you were just little," she said.

Toto frowned, his eyebrows drawing down. "Yeah."

"Do you remember her at all?"

"No. Not really. Some impressions, that's all."

"And what happened? You went into foster care?"

A nod. "All kinds of foster homes. Passed around to a few relatives. Nobody wanted to keep me."

"Was that here? Did you live here?"

"No… out west. I ran away and came here."

"Why?"

"They didn't want me, KC," he shook his head. "Nobody wanted me. I just wanted… a fresh start. Something that was new, just me."

"But why *here?*"

"I don't know… it just always sounded like a good place to go. Kind of… I just always knew this is where I wanted to go." He sighed. "I guess I made a royal mess of that, just like every other time."

"Did somebody tell you it was a good place to go? Who made you want to come here?"

Toto looked off into the distance, trying to form an answer. "I don't know. I've wanted to since I was eight or nine. I don't really remember why. Just because I thought it would be friendly. A good place to start fresh. Why? Where's all this coming from, KC? I thought you wanted to know about those guys, how I got involved in that…"

She cut him off. "Did you have any brothers or sisters? Biological ones?"

"No… no, I don't think so… but it was a really long time ago. I was little when I was taken away from my mom, and she could have had other kids after I left." He pondered for a few minutes. "Now that you ask about it… I think she did have another kid… a girl… but she didn't keep it."

"Was your name Toby?"

Toto's eyes widened in shock. "What? How would you know that?"

"Was your name Toby Torres? Is that where Toto comes from?"

Toby grabbed her upper arms and gave her a shake. He looked angry, his face white. "How did you know that? I never told anybody my real name. Not the cops, not the hospital, no one! How would you know that?"

"Maybe the reason you wanted to come out here was because someone told you your sister was going to be adopted by a family here. So you thought it sounded like a good place to go."

Toto just stared at her. Carmina's heart was beating so fast she was afraid it was going to burst. Or she was going to have a heart attack. Rosa had said she could have something wrong with her heart. It went along with the problem with her lungs. Carmina tried to laugh at Toto's bewildered expression.

"Come on, genius," she said. "Try to put two and two together, and you get…"

"You?" Toto demanded. "How could you…?"

"I never knew my birth name. That I had another name before I was adopted. And when they said it wasn't a real adoption, I didn't think they were ever going to be able to find out who I really was, because I didn't know it. But they did. Because of Cynthia's secret. Carmen Torres. My birth name was Carmen Torres."

He shook her again. "No! You're trying to pull one over on me! You're not."

"My birth name was Carmen Torres, and I had a brother named Toby who was taken away before I was born. When he was only three. And when I was born with a…. a birth defect… my mom didn't want to take me. Because I was sick, I didn't get adopted until I was almost four. You would have been seven. And maybe somebody told you where I was going."

"You're not my sister! I don't have any sister."

"Or maybe it's just a big coincidence we both ended up here, halfway across the country," Carmina said.

He let go of her shoulders and faced forward on the bench, no longer turned toward her. His hands grasped at the bench as if trying to keep himself from floating away. Carmina knew how that felt. She grabbed his hand and held on, trying to help to anchor him, like he'd been anchoring her.

"It's not possible," Toto said.

"No."

"Is it true? Is it really? Is it really, truly, true?"

"Was your name Toby Torres?"

He swallowed, nodding. "Yes."

"My brother's name was Toby Torres."

"It's just not possible."

TWENTY-THREE

Carmina knocked on Rosa's door, her stomach cramped with anxiety. She knew the fiery little woman was not going to be happy with her unexplained disappearance the day before. But Carmina hadn't even been able to think it through. She just knew she had to find Toto, and had to tell him. She didn't think about what was polite or what anyone would think of her.

Toto gave her shoulder a little squeeze. Rosa opened the door. She looked at the two of them standing there.

"Sorry," Carmina said, looking down at the speckled rug.

"Where have you been?"

"I had to go see Toto."

Rosa looked Toto up and down. Toto squirmed under her penetrating gaze. "I thought you were upset with him."

"I was, but…"

"You don't run away from me, chicklet. You tell me what's going on. That's what family does."

Carmina nodded. "I'm sorry."

Rosa opened the door further and motioned for them both to enter. Carmina felt like she'd been sent to the principal's office. Toto was dragging his feet, though his eyes flicked around the room with interest. Carmina gave him a warning glare. He couldn't steal from her Mama Rosa.

"So explain to me why you took off, and why you're with this boy again today, after the way he treated you."

Carmina sat down on the couch, considering her approach. Toto didn't sit down, but stayed standing there, his body tense.

"Mama Rosa… this is Toto. Toby Torres. Toto… this is my foster mom when I was a baby. Rosa."

Whatever Rosa had been expecting to hear, it was not that. She shot back up from her seat, her eyes wide with shock, mouth opening. "Toby Torres? You couldn't be! Carmen's brother?"

Rosa stared up at Toto's face, wide-eyed, and took his hands in her little brown ones. Carmina didn't say anything, watching them.

"I don't know," Toto said. "That's my name. At least, the name on my birth certificate. But I ditched everything from that life a long time ago…"

"But, how…?"

"You already told me his history," Carmina said. "You know he ran away from his last home. They said he went east."

"Yes. I told you that."

"Well, he did. Someone must have told him this is where I came, to be adopted. And he decided that was where he wanted to come when he ran away."

"I don't really remember that," Toto clarified. "I remember someone said my mom had a baby girl. But I don't remember knowing what happened to her."

Rosa blinked at him. "We'll have to get proof."

"Who needs proof?" Carmina demanded. "Look at us. Look at us together."

She pulled Toto down to the couch, and scooted up next to him, holding her face next to his.

"Look at us. You don't think we're brother and sister?"

Rosa looked at them, frowning. Toto's skin was darker than Carmina's. His hair, too. His nose and jaw were more prominent. But there was something in the shapes of their faces, especially the cheekbones and eyes. She cocked her head to the side slightly, squinting.

"There is a resemblance," she admitted.

Carmina smiled at Toto. "I told you! Remember the picture my mom drew, how we looked like… siblings?"

"I still think it's crazy," Toto said. "What are the odds we would both end up in the same city? Or that even living in the same city, we'd end up meeting each other?"

"Well, we did. But it took a few years. You're the one with the math brain. You figure out the odds."

He got a far-away look, and Carmina suspected he was doing just that.

"Well… I suppose this changes things," Rosa murmured, sitting back down again. "You're not going to want to be leaving your new brother behind."

Carmina looked at Toto. "But he could come too, couldn't he? You could take us both."

Before Rosa could say anything, Toto shook his head. "No way, KC! There's no way I'm going back to foster care! Uh-uh."

Carmina's heart sank. As soon as she'd realized Toto was her brother, she had assumed he would go with her. They were family. They would live together. They would both have a home, and Rosa would make sure Toto was taken care of too. Maybe they'd be able to figure out what to do for his head and the reoccurring migraine attacks. It would all work out happily ever-after. Carmina had lost her whole world all at once; her parents, her home, everything that was familiar to her. But now she would have a new home. A new family. A new life. A good one, not living on the street anymore. Like maybe it was all meant to be, and losing her parents was just one step in the grand plan.

Toto must have seen the disappointment in her face and he took her hand to comfort her. But he didn't say the words that would take away the pain. He didn't retract his statement. Rosa got up slowly from her seat.

"Why don't I leave you guys alone for a bit to discuss things? I'll go get some coffee…"

Carmina nodded. There was a hot lump in her throat. "Okay."

They were silent as Rosa got her handbag and jacket, and left the room. Toto squeezed Carmina's hand.

"You can't go live with her," he said, his voice low and reasonable. "You don't know what it's like in foster care. I've been there. I know!"

"She was my foster mom when I was little—" Carmina protested.

Toto's voice rose, cutting her off. "You can't remember back then! You don't remember what it's like in foster care. You can't go live with that witch! We're family, you need to stay with me!"

"You—you don't know Rosa! She's a good mom. As soon as she heard I was in trouble, she flew straight out here. She cares about me."

"And I don't?" His face was dark, scrunched up with anger. "Has she been taking care of you since you ran away? Where was she when you were sick? I've been the one helping you out, not her!"

"You're the one who got me this!" Carmina retorted, pointing to the bruise on her face.

Toto's anger dropped away. He clutched his face with both hands, groaning. Carmina's first thought was that he was having another migraine.

"What's wrong? Are you okay?"

"I just mess everything up," he moaned. "Everywhere I go, I just mess everything up! The one chance I have with a sister, and I screw it up before I even know it."

She put her hand tentatively on his back. "You don't get just one chance…"

Toto uncovered his face briefly. "Does that mean you'll stay here?"

"Do you want me to get hurt more?"

"So you are going to leave! You're going to go live with that… that foster mom, and I won't ever see you again!"

"Why not?"

His brows lowered. "Why not what?"

"Why won't we ever see each other again? I'll save money for a plane ticket to come back to visit you and my mom and dad. And we can e-mail. Or video conference. You can get a phone with a camera."

"How am I going to get that?"

Carmina slumped back into the couch. "Toto…!"

"What?"

"You gotta get a job."

Toto blinked at her as if she was speaking a foreign language. "What?"

"A job. To make money. So you can afford a place of your own and a phone, so we can talk."

"I dunno… I can't do much. You know. I don't have a talent like your drawing. I'm disabled."

"Then we have to find you something else."

He shrugged and shook his head.

CARMINA GREW restless after Toto left and it was quiet again. Rosa had returned, but was trying to give Carmina her own space. The shadows we starting to lengthen. A bad time to be trying to paint by natural light. It was the time that Carmina's thoughts automatically turned to Esther. Carmina knew Esther would normally be packing up her paints and going down to the kitchen to put supper on the table. And Carmina and Esther would talk.

"I'm going to be going away," she whispered, looking out the window. "Back with my foster mom, where I was before I came to you. She's nice. Do you remember meeting her?"

She wondered what Esther would remember from that time. Esther had drawn many pictures of Carmina as a young child. Rosa said Esther had seen Carmina's picture in a book of waiting children. Something about Carmina's face had attracted Esther's attention, and she'd been drawing Carmina ever since. Esther probably wouldn't remember Rosa, the way Rosa remembered Esther. She had only been part of the environment, and Esther's focus had been on Carmina.

"Rosa took care of me when I was sick. When I was a little baby in hospital."

"Who are you talking to?" Rosa questioned, coming back into the room, out of the shower.

"Oh." Carmina ducked her head, embarrassed. "Just… imagining talking to my mom. Esther, I mean."

"I know who you mean when you say your mom, chick."

"Yeah, I guess. It's just that… I've had three now. But I only really remember one."

"You were just a baby. It's okay that you don't remember." Rosa sat down on the couch, pulling her feet up and wrapping her robe around them. "So what are you talking to your Mom about?"

"Just about… everything. Going away."

"Are you okay with it? Knowing you're going to be away from them?"

"I'd be away from them anyway."

"I know. But you'd be able to see them more often. Whenever you wanted. Coming to live with me, you're only going to see them once or twice a year."

"Yeah… But I think… it might be easier… being away."

Rosa considered. "Starting somewhere new, without all of the memories, might be easier than focusing on everything you've lost?"

"Yeah. And seeing her every week, and saying good-bye over and over… I just can't do that. It hurts too much."

"I'm surprised you're willing to leave Toto behind."

Carmina nodded. "I'd rather he came… but I don't want to stay here anymore. I want to get to know you. Maybe see my bio mom sometime. If I live with Toto on the street, he's just going to keep getting into trouble. And getting me into trouble. I need somewhere safe."

TWENTY-FOUR

The memories were vague and distant, from long ago. Carmina hadn't been able to make sense of them before, but the information from Rosa rounded them out, helped Carmina to make sense of what had happened…

Carmen had woken up when Rosa had come in and shaken her gently by the arm.

"Hi there, baby girl," Mama Rosa greeted, giving her a big smile. "Time to wake up now."

Carmen held her arms out for a hug, and Rosa leaned over and gave her a gentle hug around the shoulders, avoiding squeezing her body.

"Are you hungry?"

"Time t'eat," Carmen responded, and she pulled up her hospital gown to uncover her belly, the latest surgical incisions neatly covered with white gauze and tape, with her feeding tube button still in place.

"No, Carmen. By mouth."

Carmen touched her button. "My button?"

"No. With your mouth. Come on, now. Let's sit up."

Rosa lifted Carmen into a sitting position and pulled her gown back down. Carmen watched her take covered dishes out of her bag, and open them up. Rosa pulled the rolling table over Carmen's lap and set one of the dishes on it. She stirred the contents of the bowl with the spoon.

"How about some peas?"

Carmen opened her mouth obediently, and Rosa put a small spoonful of mashed peas in. Carmen closed her mouth, and Rosa waited for her to swallow. Carmen spit most of it back out again.

"No, close your mouth and swallow. Come on. Another bite."

"I want—"

Carmen spoke as the next spoonful was put in her mouth, and unexpectedly inhaled part of it. She coughed, spraying the rest of the peas that hadn't gone down. Rosa patted her back as she continued to cough, and rubbed it until she managed to stop.

"Don't talk while you have food in your mouth, silly. Here we go. Try one more."

Carmen managed to swallow the next spoonful properly and she made a yuck face. "Don't like. No more."

"You have to try to eat more. You're not getting your food through your button anymore, so you need to eat more by mouth. You don't want to get sick. Your tummy says you're hungry, right?"

Carmen's stomach was rumbling and ached. She rubbed it where it wasn't covered by bandages.

"Then feed tummy," she said impatiently, tapping the button.

Rosa chuckled. "Smarty-pants. Food goes in your mouth," she touched Carmen's lips, "down your throat," she traced the path, "and into your tummy. It goes through a tube called the…"

"The 'sophagus," Carmen answered promptly.

"Right. The esophagus. All the way down to your tummy. So you won't need a button anymore. They'll be able to take it out. You can eat everything through your mouth, just like Mama Rosa."

"Mama Rosa no button?" Carmen questioned, grabbing at Rosa's shirt.

Rosa pulled up her shirt slightly to show Carmen her stomach. "No button," she agreed. Carmen poked at her bare belly.

"Another bite," Rosa offered, holding another spoonful in front of Carmen's mouth.

Carmen took the bite, and gagged.

"Shh-shh," Rosa tried to calm her down before she gagged hard enough to bring the rest of the food back up again. "Swallow. All the way down."

Carmen spit the peas back into the bowl. She pushed it away. She wiped at the thread of saliva from her mouth to the bowl, breaking the long, stretchy bridge.

"No! No more."

"Shall we try something else?" Rosa took the bowl away and put the lid back on again. She opened the next one. "Mmm, mashed potato with gravy," she noted. She dipped the small spoon in and took a bite of potato and gravy herself.

"No, me!" Carmen protested. "Mine!"

Rosa filled another spoonful and moved it toward Carmen's mouth. Carmen grabbed at the spoon.

"Me! Me do it."

Rosa relinquished the spoon and let Carmen try to feed herself. She sucked the spoon off after dumping most of the potatoes down her gown, and went back for another try. After a few tries, she ended up just stirring and splashing in the potatoes and gravy, and Rosa pulled the bowl away.

"Food is for eating, Carmen. Do you want something different? A cracker?"

"Happy food!"

"No, no Happy Meal today."

"Happy food!" Carmen insisted.

"No, baby. I have some crackers. How about you try those?"

She put a bowl of Goldfish crackers on the table. Carmen put one in her mouth. She attempted to swallow it, and coughed, sending it rocketing back out.

"Chew, Carmen. They're crunchy. Try another one."

Rosa demonstrated, putting a cracker in her mouth and chewing it. Carmen put another in her mouth and made chewing motions with her jaw, but didn't get the cracker positioned properly.

"In your teeth, Carmen. Push it between your teeth with your tongue and chew it up."

Carmen attempted to push the cracker between her moving teeth as Rosa had said, and bit down on her tongue. Startled by the sharp pain, she started to cry, spitting the slimy cracker back out again, and trying to press the owie with her fingers.

"Ow, did you bite your tongue? I'm sorry. That hurts, doesn't it?" Rosa comforted, stroking Carmen's hair and cheek soothingly. "It's okay, little one."

Carmen spent a few more minutes crying and slobbering over her fingers before the pain faded enough for her to stop. Rosa tried to get her to eat another cracker, but she pushed them away.

"No. No cracker."

"You need to eat more, chickie."

Carmen tapped her button through the hospital robe, but Rosa didn't offer to tube-feed her.

"All done eating, then?" she asked.

Carmen looked at her for a minute, then made a sweeping-away motion. "All done."

"Okay. All done."

Rosa packed the food containers back away, and cleaned up the various spills, crumbs, and Carmen's face. "Now what do you want to do? Do you want to color?"

"Yes!"

Rosa got out paper and crayons and put them on the table, and Carmen leaned forward, eager to start. On the first piece of paper, she just scribbled, and then pushed it away impatiently and started on a fresh sheet. On this one, she drew the shapes around her. Hospital bed, machines, window, Rosa, Carmen herself in the bed. When Rosa wasn't sure what a shape was, she asked about it, and Carmen promptly pointed out what in the room she was drawing.

She was deeply immersed in her drawing when the social worker got there. "Hi, Carmen. Hi, Mama Rosa. How are you guys today?" Joy greeted.

Rosa looked at her watch. "Is it time all ready? My, but time flies."

"They'll be here in about fifteen minutes. Is Carmen all ready?"

"Let's fix your hair, sweetie," Rosa told Carmen.

Carmen kept drawing, taking little notice while Rosa brushed away her bed-head and put a couple of barrettes in her hair to keep it neat.

"There we go. All pretty for your visitors. Carmen, look at Mama Rosa for a minute."

She put her hand over Carmen's to stop her from drawing. Carmen squawked in protest and looked at her.

"Carmen, your new mom and dad are going to come to visit you. So I'm going to go away for a while. I want you to be good, okay? Your new mom and dad are very excited to meet you."

Carmen tried to push Rosa's restraining hand away. "Okay," she repeated.

"Okay. I'll be back again in a while."

She headed for the door, and Carmen immediately began whining. "Mama! No go! Mama!"

Rosa turned around.

"She'll be fine, go ahead," Joy advised.

But Rosa ignored the advice and went back to Carmen's side.

"Mama Rosa won't be gone for long. Where's your Cynthia?" Carmen looked around and pulled Cynthia from under the covers. Rosa smiled. "There's Cynthia. She'll keep you company while Mama Rosa's gone. Right?"

"Secret," Carmen whispered, pushing Cynthia into Rosa's hands.

"Does Cynthia have a secret?" Rosa asked.

Carmen nodded, grinning widely.

"Cynthia has a secret?" Rosa repeated.

Carmen pulled the doll's dress up with a dramatic flourish.

"There it is!" Rosa said with delight.

Carmen chortled happily.

"What's that?" Rosa asked, pointing to the red tangle of simulated intestine.

"Cynthia omphalocele," Carmen said, the words carefully enunciated.

"That's right!" Rosa laughed.

Carmen pulled up her hospital gown, pointing at her bandages.

"Where is your omphalocele?" Rosa asked.

Carmen pointed insistently.

"I don't see it," teased her foster mother.

"It inside!" Carmen announced. "All gone!"

"Yes, it is," Rosa agreed, and she leaned down to give Carmen a hug and kiss. She pulled Carmen's hospital robe back down.

"Now, you hold Cynthia, and she will keep you company until Mama Rosa gets back. I'll be back later, after you see your new mom and dad."

Carmen clutched Cynthia to her. Her eyes were teary, but she didn't whine or cry this time.

"That's my brave girl. See you later."

Carmen sniffled. Rosa walked out. Joy, the social worker, moved to the spot Rosa had occupied.

"All ready to see your new mom and dad?" she asked.

Carmen nodded.

"Good girl."

Joy pulled the doll's dress back down firmly to cover the sewn omphalocele.

"Now Carmen, Cynthia's omphalocele is a secret," she reminded her.

Carmen nodded.

"It's a secret, so you don't show it to anyone, understand? You don't show it to your new mom and dad, or they'll take Cynthia away. It's a secret."

Carmen's eyes got big. She tugged at Cynthia's dress. "Secret."

"Yes. It's secret. You don't show anybody. And you don't show anybody yours," Joy pointed to Carmen's stomach.

Carmen frowned. "It inside. All gone."

"Yes, that's right. So your secret is inside, it's all gone now. You can't show anybody. Right?"

Carmen blinked at her.

"It's all gone," Joy said.

Carmen nodded slightly.

"And you don't show Cynthia's secret to your new mom and dad."

Carmen hugged Cynthia to herself, frowning.

TWO NEW PEOPLE came into Carmen's hospital room, and Carmen looked toward Joy, who although also unfamiliar, she'd at least seen before, for reassurance. Joy gave her a tight smile that didn't make Carmen feel better. The new man and woman moved closer. The woman looked like a princess and her smile was nothing like the social worker's. It was tentative, but friendly. She moved silently to Carmen's bedside. She reached out and touched Carmen's hair. With gentle fingers, she stroked Carmen's dark hair. After a couple of minutes patting Carmen's hair, she touched Carmen's face, her light touch making it tingle.

"Little Carmina," she whispered.

Carmen stared up at her, fascinated. She'd never seen anyone so beautiful up close. She raised her hand to touch the woman's. "Mom?"

Esther nodded. "I'm your new mom. And this is your new dad."

Carmen looked at the man, who looked a little scary. Esther took him by the arm and brought him forward to the bedside with her. She put her arm around Julius and some of her glow seemed to transfer to him. His face softened and he smiled at Carmen.

"Hello, Carmina."

Carmen pulled Esther's hand in front of her eyes, hiding her face shyly.

"It's okay," Esther whispered. She looked around and saw Carmen's drawings. "Do you like to draw?"

Carmen nodded. Esther maneuvered the rolling table and sat on the edge of the bed, so she was across the table from Carmen. She pulled out a fresh sheet of paper and picked up one of the crayons.

"Can I draw with you?"

Carmen nodded and picked up a crayon. They both sat coloring. Julius motioned to Joy, and they stepped outside the room and talked quietly. Carmen looked at Esther's picture, and her mouth dropped open. She stared with her eyes open wide. It was a picture of Carmen holding Cynthia. But she wasn't sitting in a hospital bed. She was sitting in long grass, surrounded by flowers and glowing fairies. Carmen tried to grab the page to look at it more closely.

"No," Esther reproached. "Just look with your eyes. Never touch. The oils from your fingers can ruin the paper or smear the lines." She turned the paper to allow Carmen to look at it.

"Pretty," Carmen told her.

"Thank you. Tell me about your picture."

Carmen pointed to her picture and told Esther about it. Esther sat and listened to her. Carmen's words were not always clear to someone not used to her lisp, but Esther listened intently and followed Carmen's pointing finger to learn all she could.

TWENTY-FIVE

As Neil stared at the phone, trying to work up the courage to call Kyle, he was overcome with flashbacks. He breathed, trying to hold them at bay, but they washed over him…

Neil had slid stealthily around the corner, his weapon out, eyes flicking quickly around looking for any sign of the lowlifes who had received the shipping container. It was unlikely they would leave the warehouse unguarded. He heard the soft crunch of a stealthy footstep coming toward him from the other direction. But he thought it might be Sandler's step rather than any bad guy's. He kept close to the crates just in case, ready to duck back out of sight.

A tiny scratching sound caught his attention in the other direction, and Neil glanced aside to check on it. Too low, too small. Probably just a rat. He raised his eyes again as Kyle Sandler came into sight. Neil stumbled slightly, his foot catching on a worn plywood board lying across the floor, covering some kind of hole. The red lines and arrows on it were incomprehensible to Neil but probably indicated a gas line or something. Sandler's head jerked around at the noise of Neil's toe-scuff. Neil raised his weapon to his temple to salute Sandler, maintaining their silence in case there were others nearby. Sandler whipped around and his arm came up. His hand convulsed. He'd fired his gun.

For a fraction of a second, Neil was relieved Sandler had missed him.

Then he felt the impact of the bullet, and he was on the ground. He looked at his belly where the blow had hit, trying for a couple of desperate seconds to remember if they had vested up before breaching the warehouse. But they hadn't. It had all happened so fast, they had just taken the opportunity when it presented itself. They had called for backup, but since the building appeared to be empty, with no vehicles parked nearby, they had gone on ahead to scout it out. They were going to be in major trouble now. Administrative leave, internal affairs, the works.

Blood was already bubbling out of his shirt, the stain spreading larger. Sandler was at Neil's side, his face as white as if *he'd* been shot. He pulled Neil's shirt up, out of the wound, swearing desperately.

"It's gonna be okay, Neil. It's not that bad. It's gonna be okay."

Neil had to focus hard to stay present. Sandler never called him Neil. It must be pretty bad. Sandler called for an ambulance and asked for the ETA of their backup. He held one hand ineffectively over the wound, blood seeping between his fingers.

"It's okay. Stay with me, Neil. Stay awake."

Neil wasn't sure why he should try to stay awake anymore. The pain was starting to grow in his belly and in his chest. He felt tired, incredibly fatigued. Cold. Kyle grasped his hand, still keeping one hand over the belly wound. He squeezed Neil's fingers.

"Come on. It's going to be okay."

Kyle's face was grey and unfamiliar, like it was made from pieces of Kyle cobbled together into some kind of Frankenstein's monster. Neil tried to speak, but nothing came out. He could hear the air escaping his lips. It was getting more and more difficult to drag the next breath in. It was hard to believe something that had been so automatic his whole life could now be such an impossible chore.

Kyle's hand let go of Neil's, and he felt for Neil's pulse.

"Hang in there, buddy," he encouraged. His voice was rough and pained.

There were approaching sirens, then pounding feet and voices, shouted questions. Neil recognized some of the agents who swarmed around him, all of them properly geared up. They shouted questions at Kyle, asking who the shooter was, which way he had gone. Neil tried to answer them, but he could only move his lips weakly to form Kyle's name.

NEIL TOOK a few deep breaths before picking up the phone, and dialing the number that, although he knew by heart, he hadn't dialed since he had been shot. There were a few rings, and then it was picked up.

"Sandler."

"Kyle. It's Neil."

Several long seconds, or maybe only a few heartbeats, passed before Kyle answered. "Neil? Good to hear you, partner! How the hell are you?"

Neil smiled and relaxed at the sincere welcome in Kyle's voice. "I'm… doing better, actually. I was thinking on taking you up on your offer of a drink. It's gonna have to be water, but I'll drink the expensive bottled stuff."

Kyle chuckled.

"I'd love to. Glad you called. Can you get off at a reasonable hour tomorrow? We could do five-thirty, before I go home to the family. How's that?"

"Sure, I can swing that. Do you mind if I drag a friend along? I have a new roommate who really needs to make some new friends."

"Uh… sure. No problem. I heard from somebody you took in a homeless kid or something."

"Yeah. Shall we go for the coffee shop? Old Joe's?"

"You got it," Kyle agreed. "Old Joe's tomorrow at five-thirty. With your new roomie."

THE LAST FEW hours of work dragged out. Neil punched through his paperwork, checked his e-mail, and checked up on a few projects to make sure things were going smoothly and didn't need his attention. Toto showed up a few minutes before five, and stood and chatted with Agnes, waiting for Neil to indicate he was finished. When Neil key-locked his computer and stood up, Agnes gave Toto a little wave and said good-bye.

"You should head out soon too," Neil told Agnes. "Things are pretty quiet, so take the opportunity while you can. I have a feeling the St. Ives case is going to break wide open in a day or two, and you're going to be chained to your computer."

"Sure, boss." She swept her long hair back over her shoulders. "I'll get out of here soon."

Neil and Toto walked over to the cafe, and Neil looked around for the familiar figure. Kyle stood up at the table he had claimed, waving. Neil introduced Toto and Kyle, and they shook hands and sat down.

"So," Kyle looked Toto over curiously. "When I heard you'd taken in a homeless kid, I pictured someone a little younger."

Neil shrugged. "I'm not trying to be his parent. Just a friend. Keep an eye on him and make sure he's not getting in too much trouble."

Toto rolled his eyes. "Who takes care of who?" he questioned. "Seems to me I make more meals than you do."

Neil shrugged and laughed.

"Is that why you've put on weight?" Kyle asked, his eyes dancing.

"Toto's been great to have around," he admitted. "I never was great at figuring out how to eat with this short intestine… but he was with Carmina for long enough to get a knack for it. He's always got meals and snacks around when I get home."

"Sounds like a wife," Kyle cracked.

Toto's nostrils flared. "I'm not anyone's wife. Say… personal chef, or dietician or something. I just… work for my board."

"Sorry," Kyle said, with a wave of his hand. "No offense." But he was still chuckling. "You've done a great job getting some flesh back on his skeleton. Are you going to cooking school?"

"No." It was Neil who answered. "We got him some grants so he can do university properly, get a degree, or a doctorate, or whatever. In math. His professors love him."

Toto got a little pink. He took a few gulps of his jumbo coffee and Neil took a small sip of his water.

"And Carmina, she's the Knight girl, right? She disappeared after the initial arrests?"

Neil and Toto both nodded.

"How's she doing? It must have been quite a shock to her, having them both arrested, and losing everything."

"She's okay," Neil said. "She's settled in with her foster mom, who's got Carmina's health stabilized again. And we managed to free some of her things from the evidence in the case, so she's got her computer and artwork and some personal items back."

"She'd feel even better if she would learn to have a few more smaller meals and snacks," Toto muttered. "Girl always acts like she's starving, and eats until she's stuffed. Smaller, more frequent meals work better." He looked at Neil for confirmation.

"Yeah," Neil agreed. "I've been feeling a lot better."

"You're sure looking a lot better. And happier…" Kyle raised his eyebrows. "How are the feet…? You going to be able to get back in the field again soon?"

"Still not without limitations," Neil admitted slowly. "But I'm getting to be okay with that… supervising a team has its perks. And I'm enjoying the investigative work, being able to stay with a case for the long term, instead of just moving from one bust to the next." He took a sip of water and a bite of the protein bar Toto had suggested he buy. "All in all, things are looking pretty good."

He raised his water bottle in a toast, and Kyle and Toto each tapped their coffee mugs against it.

Kyle smiled, finally looking really relaxed and pleased, like his old self.

TWENTY-SIX

"What did your mom send you this time?" Mama Rosa asked, as Carmina opened the envelope that had arrived earlier in the mail.

Carmina slid out a couple of pieces of paper, and examined the pictures. There was a short handwritten note as well, but as usual, Esther had not wasted time writing more than the customary greetings.

"She got the supplies I asked Neil to send to her," Carmina observed, carefully handling the paper the pictures were drawn on.

After a minute, she set each of the pictures on the table where Rosa could see them as well.

"She has a wonderful talent," Rosa said.

Unlike the earliest pictures, drawn with number two pencils on recycled copy paper, these pictures were drawn in full-color with art pencils on the heavier, textured, acid-free stock Carmina had recently selected. The first one was of toddler Carmina, carried in the arms of a fairy in flight, Cynthia hanging down from one chubby fist.

"She's still upset about the adoption thing," Carmina said.

"Do you think so?" Rosa studied the picture. "At least my baby's not crying this week."

Carmina nodded. The little girl looked serene as she was whisked away by the fairy, no idea of what was ahead of her.

Rosa turned her attention to the other picture. Two figures in a dark mist, slightly indistinct. A man and a woman. The woman looked vaguely like Esther, but not quite. They were dressed in some kind of armor and had stern expressions.

"Who are they? I don't think I've seen them before."

Carmina frowned. "I think those are her parents. I've only seen them once or twice…"

Rosa looked back at the picture with interest. "Oh. They were estranged?"

"Yeah. I don't know what happened, but they kind of disowned her."

"They're coming out of the darkness."

"Maybe they went to see her." Carmina gazed at the picture thoughtfully. "That would be good," she said. "I hope they did."

IRENE GOT up at the sound of the doorbell, and went to the front door. When she opened it, she just stood there, saying nothing.

"Who is it?" Raymond called.

When she didn't answer, he went out and looked past her to see who it was.

"Mama?" Esther said, and looking at him, "Papa…?"

Raymond tried to close his mouth, and then to organize his power of speech. "Esther! What are you doing here?"

Esther swept back her golden hair with one hand, looking amazingly like the schoolgirl she had been twenty years before when she had taken up with Julius. In spite of her time behind bars, she didn't show her age. The lines around her eyes and mouth were very fine, only visible if you were really looking for them.

"They let you go?" Irene finally asked. "Or are you out on bail or something?"

"Can I come home?" Esther looked past Irene and Raymond into the house. She couldn't see her own room from there, carefully preserved as it had been since the day she had left. On the chance that one day she would return.

"Are you done with that man?" Raymond demanded. They had both agreed she would never be allowed back until she had put him permanently behind her. No matter how much Irene wanted it, there could be no half-way.

Esther's eyes focused briefly on her father, back to her mother, and then at some distant, unfocused space in the atmosphere. "Julius is still in prison. For a long time."

"That doesn't answer the question." Raymond's tone was hard, unbending. "Don't avoid the question. Whether he's in prison or not, I want your word you are done with him. You're not coming home until I get your promise."

Esther was silent for a long time. She bowed her head. Irene started to close the door. Esther put her hand on it. "No—don't."

"Your word, Esther," Raymond insisted. "You promise never to contact him again."

She swallowed, and nodded. "I promise."

Irene looked over her shoulder at Raymond. Her face was pale and drawn. Raymond knew she wanted as much as he did, maybe even more, to welcome Esther back into the fold. But she would abide by his ruling, either way. Raymond nodded. It wasn't until then Irene let go of the door, and enfolded her daughter in an embrace.

"Oh, my sweet girl. Thank goodness you're back."

Esther initially went rigid at the physical contact, but then relaxed into it, squeezing Irene back, and pressing her cheek against her mother's. She reached an arm toward Raymond, and he joined them, holding his wife and daughter both to him.

Esther was finally home.

MAMA ROSA WALKED by as Carmina sat at the kitchen table drawing. Carmina's computer was open on the table in front of her, the lid was bent forward slightly. Rosa glimpsed another figure drawing. Carmina spoke to her now and then, but mostly they were quiet, turning their pictures around occasionally to display them to their respective webcams. Later on, when Carmina got up from the table and went to get a snack, Rosa smiled at her.

"Did you have a nice visit with your mom?"

"Yeah. It's weird, her being there… instead of at home."

"I imagine it's weird for her, too."

Carmina nodded. "Her mom and dad are… different. But they're helping her to get her own work shown. It's strange having her spend so much time on her own pictures, instead of reproductions."

"Forgeries, you mean."

Carmina bit her lip. "Dad might have sold forgeries. But Mom only ever painted reproductions. She never intended for them to be sold as anything but good reproductions. Not originals."

"You believe that?"

Carmina nodded. "I know my mom. She wouldn't do that."

Rosa nodded and didn't challenge it any further. "How is your dad? Did you open your letter from him?"

She had, of course, already seen it on the kitchen table next to the art work Carmina had been showing Esther. But to draw attention to the fact would be snooping.

"Yes. He's good, I guess."

"He caused a lot of problems for you and your mom. But he's going to have to pay for it. Are you going to go visit him, when you fly out?"

"I don't know." Carmina looked at the letter. "I don't know if I'll really have time. I mean, I have to visit Mom. And Toto and Neil. If I want to get to the school to see Mr. Burpeau and my friends… I just don't know if I'll have time to get out to the prison, too."

"You have time if you make it a priority. I would think it's more important to see your father than your school friends."

Carmina picked at mixed nuts in a bowl out on the counter, not answering.

"You need to forgive your father."

"Yeah."

"It must be hard. He really hurt you."

"He wasn't trying to hurt me."

"No."

Carmina chewed slowly. "It's not his fault. That he's like he is. It's because of his parents."

"He didn't have to make the choices he did. No matter what kind of issues he had, he didn't have to choose forgery as a profession, and bring your mother into it." Rosa helped herself to a couple of nuts.

"I knew," Carmina whispered. "I told Neil I didn't, but I sort of did.

Not exactly, because I didn't want to know… but I knew he was forging the provenance."

"You don't need to feel guilty for what your father did. It wasn't you. And Neil didn't need your testimony. I think he had a pretty good idea you knew about it. When Julius cut a deal, it meant they didn't have to pursue you."

Carmina nodded.

"That's probably why Julius made a deal," Rosa pointed out.

"So you think I should visit him?"

"I think you should forgive him. That's the first step."

Did you enjoy this book? Reviews and recommendations are vital to making a book successful.

Please leave a review at your favorite book store or review site and share it with your friends.

Don't miss the following bonus material:
Sign up for mailing list to get a free ebook
Read a sneak preview chapter
Other books by P.D. Workman
Learn more about the author

Sign up for my mailing list at pdworkman.com and get Gluten-Free Murder for free!

PREVIEW OF TATTOOED TEARDROPS

BOOK #1 OF THE TAMARA'S TEARDROPS SERIES

Winner of Top Fiction Award, In the Margins Committee, 2016.

ONE

(i)

T AMARA FRENCH HAS BEEN *a model inmate throughout her incarceration.*

Great reference. You could go far on that one. Tamara sat on an uncomfortable bench in the brightly-lit lobby waiting for her ride. It was strange being on the other side of the guard booth. She stared at the too-white sneakers that stuck out below her dark pant cuffs, wondering what kind of life she had to look forward to with that ringing endorsement. She jiggled her legs up and down, trying to resist picking her nails. Eventually, a tall, middle-aged woman with a bun came in and stood before her. Tamara stared at her boxy black shoes for a moment before reluctantly looking up at her.

"Tamara?" the woman said.

"Yeah."

"Ready to get out of here?"

"I guess."

"I expected a bit more enthusiasm," the social worker said with a hint of a smile in the corners of her lipsticked mouth.

"I'm sorta nervous," Tamara said.

"I guess that's understandable. Come on, let's go."

Tamara sat there for another moment, then finally stood and followed the woman out of the juvenile facility. She got in the car and buckled up, holding her bag tightly on her lap.

The social worker introduced herself, but Tamara paid no attention, completely forgetting her name the next minute. The woman attempted small talk a few times, but Tamara turned on the radio and stared out the window, freezing the social worker out. Eventually the woman got the message, and stopped trying to engage her.

(ii)

They pulled up in front of a brick house that was at least a hundred years old and needed some work. There had been an attempt made at landscaping, with some flowers and bushes bunched around the concrete steps leading up to the porch and the front door. There was peeling paint on the fence and mailbox post.

"Here we are," the social worker announced. "Let's go in."

Tamara unbuckled and got out slowly. The social worker took her in, knocking on the front door and entering without waiting for an answer.

"Hello, Marion, come on in," a woman's voice called from up above. "I'll be right down."

Tamara stood beside the social worker, waiting. She held her paper bag awkwardly at her side, wishing that she didn't have anything to hold onto. She made a show of examining the front hall and living room of the house, but in all honesty, she didn't care what it looked like. It wasn't prison. Her concern was not with the house, but what the foster parents were going to be like. The front room was fairly neat and presentable. No children's toys scattered about. A load of laundry neatly folded in the basket sitting on the couch. The TV shut behind the doors of an entertainment center so it would not be the central focus of the room. The furnishings were nice, not thrift store or destroyed. There were footsteps on the stairs, and Tamara looked up for her first glimpse of her foster mother.

Mrs. Henson had a pleasant, round face. Blond hair that had been lightly styled in an attempt to hide that it was starting to thin. She didn't look more than forty. She was overweight, but not grossly. She just looked soft and comfortable. She was wearing a sweater and pants, and inconsequential gold jewelry. She didn't look anything like Mrs. Baker, but that was no guarantee.

"Hello!" her voice rang out cheerfully.

"Gerry, this is Tamara," Marion introduced as Mrs. Henson reached the bottom of the stairs. "Tamara, Mrs. Henson."

"Hey," Tamara muttered, without meeting her eyes. "Where do you want me?"

"Your bedroom is at the top of the stairs. First door on the right," Mrs. Henson offered. Tamara made the trek up the stairs. There was a dark wooden bannister, ornately carved. Not too scarred for being in a foster home. Tamara turned at the top of the stairs and opened the door to her right.

There was a bed and a crib, and Tamara stood there, her heart speeding up, wondering if she'd been sent to the wrong room. Surely they wouldn't have given her a room with a crib in it? She could almost see Julie's still form lying on the high mattress… Mrs. Henson was there a moment later, having said a quick good-bye to Marion. She breathed a little heavily after her trip back up the stairs.

"Go on in," Mrs. Henson encouraged. "We sometimes take teen moms, to help teach them how to take care of their babies. We don't have any right now, so you get this room. That way you don't have to share."

Tamara walked into the room. The walls were a light green, freshly painted, with a white board wainscoting all the way around it. There was a pull-down blind with gauzy green curtains around the window. Tamara tossed her bag onto the bed, where it sat looking pitiful and inadequate.

"The others will be getting home soon," Mrs. Henson offered. "I'll introduce you then."

"Yes, ma'am."

"I'm happy to have you join us, Tamara. I was very impressed with your file."

Sure. It was certain to be the last place she went that anyone was impressed with her prison record. She'd wowed them all at her parole hearing. There had been tears, and not all of them hers. So many of the inmates protested their innocence and refused to take responsibility or express remorse at their parole hearings. Tamara had been working on her performance for three years, and it was good. The board's vote was unanimous. Now she was free. But to what kind of life?

Mrs. Henson stirred, making Tamara jump, startled. They both looked at each other, not knowing what to say. Mrs. Henson smiled and nodded.

"Make yourself at home," she encouraged, motioning around the room.

Tamara nodded. Mrs. Henson backed off, and left her alone. Tamara stretched out on the freshly-made bed to wait. If there was one thing she was used to doing, it was waiting.

(iii)

There were no bells that rang to mark the passage of time and the transition from one activity to another. Instead, disconcertingly, it flowed along with small shifts and gradual transitions. Tamara heard the front door open and close several times, with voices reaching her ears even through the closed bedroom door. Mrs. Henson did most of the talking and others answered her questions or made comments during the pauses. Tamara couldn't tell what any of them were saying, just the tone of voice. They all seemed to be casual and relaxed.

There was a knock on Tamara's bedroom door, and before she could get up to answer it, Mrs. Henson poked her head in.

"We're going to get dinner going," she said. "Why don't you come down and help? Then you can meet everyone."

Tamara studied her for a moment, assessing her options. Was it a choice? Was there a consequence for not complying? She was so unused to making her own decisions that she wasn't sure what to do when faced with one.

"Come on," Mrs. Henson encouraged, motioning for Tamara to come.

Tamara got up slowly and followed her foster mother down the stairs and to the kitchen. She was suddenly confronted with a whole pack of new people to meet. All bigger and older than her. Tamara made an effort to unclench her fists and not look confrontational. This wasn't juvie. She didn't have to prove herself physically here.

It hadn't occurred to Tamara when she had met Mrs. Henson that the foster children would not all be white like her. But of course, she already knew the statistics. There were more non-white children in foster care, and very few non-white parents. So they couldn't pair black children with black parents. Tamara was intimidated by all of the dark faces looking back at her. She wasn't prejudiced, but juvie had taught her to be acutely aware of race relations, and how her white-faced, blond-haired presence could be aggravating to others. They would immediately judge her as stuck-up, privileged, and ignorant.

Tamara was fifteen, and not tall. There were only four other children, Tamara realized, not the mob that she had originally perceived them as. They were all bigger than her. Most of them taller than Mrs. Henson. Studying their faces, Tamara figured that they were seventeen or eighteen. One boy seemed even too old to be eighteen.

"Everyone," Mrs. Henson said, "this is Tamara, our new foster child. I know you'll all make her feel comfortable and help her get settled in."

They all nodded, smiled, and waved. Tamara nodded back.

"Hey."

Her voice was hoarse, the greeting barely audible. Tamara wasn't sure any of them had heard her. She nodded again and didn't repeat the greeting.

"Okay, are you ready?" Mrs. Henson asked with a wide smile. "This is Nita," a Hispanic girl with long hair and perfectly plucked eyebrows, "Deshawn," the darkest face, a girl with cornrows and a brilliant white smile, "Jason," black skin, close cropped black hair, probably eighteen, "and Harry." Harry seemed a particularly non-ethnic name for a boy who appeared to be some mixture of black, Hispanic, and native. He smiled nicely for her, but his resting face was serious, contemplative. He was the one that Tamara was sure must be older than eighteen. He should have already aged out of the system.

Tamara nodded again and swallowed. Now what? Was she supposed to repeat them back? Greet each one separately? Shake hands? Tamara just stood there, lost, then looked at Mrs. Henson for direction.

"Okay, let's get started on dinner," Mrs. Henson suggested. "Nita, why don't you show Tamara where the dishes are, and she can help you set the table…" She went on, but Tamara didn't hear the rest of the instructions she gave to the remaining kids. She had her instructions. Go with Nita and set the table. She made her way across the room to Nita, and Nita smiled at her.

"Welcome," she said in a low voice that was almost a whisper. "I hope you like it here."

Tamara nodded. "Yeah. Thanks."

"Well, come on. The dishes are in this cupboard here, and the glasses, and the cutlery." Nita indicated each location.

"How many…?" Tamara asked. She cleared her throat. "Is there a Mr. Henson? Or anyone else?"

"Yeah, Jesse will be home for dinner. That's Mr. Henson. So seven altogether."

Tamara counted out the plates and trucked them over to the table, where she put them down carefully. Her hands shook slightly as she set them down, and it was an effort not to let them clatter. There was a baby's high chair, pushed against the wall. Tamara looked away from it and continued with her work, breathing shallowly. Setting the table only took a couple of minutes, and then Mrs. Henson gave them various other small tasks until everything started coming together for the dinner. She looked at her watch.

"Thanks guys. Take a break for about twenty minutes. Then everything should be done cooking, Jesse will be home, and we'll eat."

The kids dispersed. Tamara headed back up to her bedroom. Deshawn stopped ahead of Tamara, blocking her way into her bedroom.

"Do you need anything?" she asked Tamara.

Tamara shook her head.

"Sometimes… people don't come here with very much," Deshawn said. "Missus buys up extra toothbrushes and all, and we all share clothes…" She glanced over Tamara's figure. "My pants won't do you much good, but if you want a shirt, some accessories…"

Tamara stood there and contemplated the idea. For three years, she had worn nothing but an orange prison jumpsuit. Social Services had provided her with two very basic changes of clothing for her release. T-shirt, pants, socks, underthings. One pair of white tennis shoes. It was more fashion than Tamara had access to in all her time in juvie, but she was aware that it was sorely inadequate for a teenager on the outside.

Deshawn made an encouraging motion.

"Come on. Let's see if there's anything you want to borrow," she said.

Tamara followed her to one of the other bedrooms.

"Nita and I share the room," Deshawn commented. Nita was not there; maybe she had gone to watch TV or something. The room was painted sky blue. There was a utilitarian set of bunk beds, a couple of dressers cluttered with scarves, jewelry, and books, and a closet that was jammed full. The knobs on either side of the open closet door had been pressed into use to hold more hangers full of clothes. "It's mostly thrift store," Deshawn said, "but you can find some pretty good stuff if you look hard enough. Sorry, it's sort of a mess. Come on. See what you like."

Tamara went to the closet and looked over the hangers full of brightly-colored clothing. It didn't appear that either Deshawn or Nita went for anything understated.

"If you want t-shirts, they're in the dresser," Deshawn pointed, "and just grab whatever you see that you like. Just bring it back or throw it in the laundry when you're done with it."

Tamara saw herself in the mirror mounted on the back of the closet door. There hadn't been any full-length mirrors at juvie. And the only mirrors that had been there were polished metal or plastic, and you could never really see your reflection very well. Tamara had grown up a lot in juvie. She wasn't the soft, shy little farm girl she had been when she went to the Bakers. They had changed her. And juvie had changed her. The years had not been particularly kind ones. But she had developed a figure now, and was going to have to learn how to dress it up, instead of simply shrouding it in a jumpsuit. She had tattoos and piercings that she hadn't had before her incarceration. Her hair was dull and lank, like everybody else's in juvie. Tamara wound one lock around her finger, staring at the stranger reflected in the mirror.

"Why don't we do something with your hair?" Deshawn suggested. "There's not much time, but if we blow-dry, we could be done before supper."

Tamara raked her fingers through her limp blonde hair, disgusted with it.

"Yeah. Could we?"

"Mmm-hmm," Deshawn agreed with emphasis. "We'll shampoo it in the bathroom, and use leave-in conditioner…" she led the way out into the hallway, still chattering away to herself what they would do. Tamara just followed.

Tamara knelt by the tub while Deshawn used the hand-held shower attachment to quickly wet her hair down. The warm water felt so good on Tamara's scalp, she wished she could get in for a full shower, and just luxuriate in it for hours. Three years of quick, cold showers. But Deshawn turned off the water way too soon, and applied a fruity shampoo with strong, capable fingers; working it in and then rinsing it back out. She handed Tamara a towel and while Tamara rubbed her hair,

Deshawn rifled through the myriad toiletries lining the back of the counter, the medicine cabinet, and a couple of deep wicker baskets under the sink.

(iv)

"Girls! Dinner!" the impatient call came again from downstairs.

Deshawn poked her head out the door.

"Just one more minute," she called back. "We'll be right down!"

She returned her attention to Tamara.

"Okay, just sit still for one more minute, girl," she instructed.

Tamara sat frozen, while Deshawn wound sections of her hair around the fat curling iron, holding it and then releasing. There was no way that she was going to be done the whole thing in another minute. But Deshawn worked quickly, sure of herself.

"That will do it for now," she announced.

She laid the curling iron down on the counter and unplugged it from the wall. Standing Tamara up, Deshawn shuffled her over and turned her to face the mirror.

"Ta-da!"

Tamara looked with astonishment at the face in the mirror. She was amazed at what a big difference a hairstyle could make. She still didn't have on any make-up, hadn't changed her clothes or accessories, all she had done was let Deshawn clean and style her hair. Her image in the mirror was no longer so harsh and plain.

"You're gorgeous," Deshawn gushed. "You've got really good color and proportions. We can have a lot of fun glamming you up. For now, this will do."

Standing behind Tamara, Deshawn used her fingers to wind and readjust a couple of curls. She lowered her head so that it was on the same level as Tamara's, and gave her a smile.

"What do you think?"

"It's… it's really pretty. Thanks," Tamara said. She cleared her throat, realizing that she was whispering. She had learned in juvie to use a strong, confident voice, not to be soft or timid. The Henson's home was so different in atmosphere, she felt like she was in a library or something. That she needed to be quiet to avoid upsetting the peace of the place.

"Come on, we've got to get down to dinner, or Missus will not be happy!"

Tamara followed Deshawn back downstairs and to the dining room table that she and Nita had set. It was now covered with serving dishes, and everyone was seated, waiting for them. All eyes turned to Tamara as she looked at the three empty chairs, trying to decide which one she should take.

"Tamara, doesn't that look lovely," Mrs. Henson complimented. "Here, sit down. These boys will eat everything before we even get a bite, if they have to wait much longer."

She gestured toward the empty chair nearest to her, and Tamara went over and sat down. Deshawn took what appeared to be her usual seat, beside Nita, which left one empty chair at the table of eight. Tamara looked for the first time at Mr. Henson. Slim, on the tall side. Handsome boyish face. Short-cropped curly red hair. He smiled at Tamara.

"Welcome, Tamara. I'm Jesse."

Tamara nodded, looking down at her empty plate. Her stomach tightened and it was suddenly hard to breathe. The only men that she had been around for three years had been guards, doctors, and administrators. The last man she had lived with before that… her foster father, Mr. Baker… that had been a bad scene. A very bad scene. Tamara swallowed. She tried to slow her breathing, but it just made her breath louder in her own ears. She was sure everyone would be hear how loudly and quickly she was breathing.

"Dig in," Mrs. Henson said, and Harry and Jason acted like two Rottweilers just told to attack, diving into the serving dishes immediately. Conversation started up around the table, and rather than trying to follow any of it, Tamara just let it wash over her like white noise. She served up small portions of each of the dishes that passed her, and dutifully passed them on.

"So tell us about your last home, Tamara," Nita said. "Where did you come here from?"

Tamara looked at Mrs. Henson. The woman just smiled and gave her a small nod, and didn't jump in to help her out. If Tamara didn't want to answer questions, she was going to have to be assertive and speak up. The conversations around the table quieted as the others paused to listen for her answer. Tamara swallowed a very dry mouthful of potatoes. They stuck right in the middle of her chest.

"I wasn't at a home," she said finally, careful to keep her voice up, not to duck her head down. She was not vulnerable and had nothing to be ashamed of. She was strong and knew how to take care of herself. She had just as much right to be here as any of them. "I was in juvie."

There was an initial silence, and then conversations started back up again without further comment on Tamara's answer.

"Sorry," Nita said. "I didn't know."

"It's okay," Tamara said, shaking her head. "It's not a secret. That's where I was."

Nita nodded.

"Most of us have been in trouble at one time or another."

Tamara glanced around at their faces. None of them looked particularly troubled. They seemed happy and relaxed. At peace with themselves. Maybe they had been in trouble before, and maybe they hadn't. You couldn't always tell by looking at someone.

"Harry's probably spent the most time in juvie," Deshawn contributed, nodding to her brother. "How much time, Harry?"

"All together?" Harry questioned, laughing. "I don't know. Longest stint was two years. But I had plenty of shorter stays before that."

Tamara studied him more closely. He met her eyes and nodded.

"Harry's twenty," Mrs. Henson said without being asked. "So he's not officially a foster child anymore. But we told him he could stay on here while he does some more schooling and gets on his feet."

Tamara nodded, looking back down at her plate.

"That's really nice of you."

"It's to our benefit too. Harry contributes a lot to the family, and since he's working part-time, he's also paying a bit of rent to help keep us afloat. So it works both ways."

Tamara bit into some sort of casserole.

"I guess you'll learn about everyone's backgrounds gradually," Mrs. Henson said. "We try to be open with each other. Everybody's been through some pretty tough stuff. We don't judge. We just try to help."

"That's cool," Tamara said, pushing her dinner around on her plate. She wasn't hungry.

She watched everyone else chow down, and conversations flowed back away from her again. Tamara watched for the appropriate time to leave the table. There was no end-of-dinner bell anymore. She had to relearn all the social graces. How to judge the end of a conversation. When one could politely leave the dinner table. How long she could look at someone before they decided she was being too aggressive. It was like living in a foreign country. A dangerous foreign country.

"Not very hungry?" Mrs. Henson observed, as dinner conversation started to peter out.

Tamara looked down at her plate, still nearly full.

"No. I'm sorry… it's good… I just feel kind of… my stomach hurts."

"It's all right. It takes time to adjust. You can scrape it into the garbage. Nita can show you where. Everyone rinses their own plates and puts them in the dishwasher."

"Sure," Tamara agreed. She stood up, grabbing her plate, and Nita got up and led the way back into the kitchen, where they took care of their dishes. Tamara looked back at the dining table. "Do you want help with clean-up?" she asked Mrs. Henson. "Or would I be in the way?"

"Of course you can help. Usually, I'd probably tell you to go do your homework while I cleared, but you don't have any today, so why don't you and I clean up together?"

Tamara nodded, and she and Mrs. Henson bussed the serving dishes back to the kitchen, found lids for things, and put them into the fridge. Mrs. Henson turned the dishwasher on and wiped down the dining room table.

"You can watch some TV or take some 'down' time. In bed at nine, and lights out at ten."

"Okay," Tamara agreed.

She wandered around the house a bit, but wasn't comfortable sitting down with anybody else, and so she made her way back to her bedroom. As she approached, the door to the other girls' bedroom opened. Nita peeked out.

"Hey," she said. "You need anything? Do you have pajamas?"

Tamara shook her head.

"No," she admitted. "If I could borrow a t-shirt or something…"

"You bet. Come in."

Nita opened the door the rest of the way for her, and Tamara went in. Tamara looked down at Nita's feet, nails freshly painted and toes spread apart while they dried. Nita giggled and hobbled on her heels over to the dresser.

"You want to do yours?" she asked. She pulled out a handful of shirts and tossed them at Tamara.

"No. Thanks," Tamara said, fumbling with the shirts to see what her options were. "I'm going to hit the sack."

She found herself strangely unable to choose one of the shirts. There were three of them. They were all cute. Any one of them would work. All she had to do was decide which of the three she liked best. Nita was watching her, head cocked slightly.

"The blue one is a really good color for you," she suggested.

Not the blue one. Tamara looked at the other two. She didn't know which she wanted, but she had to decide before Nita made another suggestion. She had to make her own choice. Tamara tossed the blue one back to Nita, and with a knot in her stomach, tossed Nita the pink one too. Tamara looked down at the purple and blue patterned shirt in her hands.

"This one is good," she said.

She felt a little sick. Worried that she had made the wrong choice. How silly was that, to be worried that she had picked the wrong t-shirt to wear in the privacy of her own bedroom? But she was. She had an overwhelming feeling of dread.

"Have a good sleep," Nita said with a smile.

"Thanks."

Tamara went back to her room. She changed into the t-shirt, long enough to reach her mid-thighs. She lay down on the bed and stared at the ceiling. There would be no bell ringing to tell her when to go to sleep. Would her body know when it was time, without the bell? Would she be able to adjust to a new schedule? Not feeling the least bit tired, Tamara lay staring at the ceiling, twitching her foot and waiting for sleep.

TWO

(i)

TAMARA AWOKE. SHE WAS confused at first, disoriented by the sight of a bedroom around her instead of her familiar cell. Turning her head to look at the clock beside the bed, Tamara saw that it was five forty-five on the dot. The usual time for the reveille bell. Groaning, she rolled over and slid out of bed.

She didn't know what time the others usually arose, but she imagined there would probably be a bottleneck waiting for the shower. Moving as quietly as possible, Tamara tiptoed across the room and opened her door. She listened for any sounds of movement. There was a light on down the stairs, but it wasn't bright. It could just be a streetlight through a window, or a nightlight. The shower was not running, so Tamara darted into the bathroom, shut the door, and turned on the light. She started the shower running and stripped down. For the first time in three years, she stepped into a warm shower. The tantalizing sample of the night before when Deshawn had helped her wash her hair didn't even come close to the luxury of a hot, whole-body shower. Tamara took a deep breath. She could get used to this.

More out of habit than anything, Tamara very quickly soaped up and rinsed off. She forced herself to shut off the water again immediately. Even though she would have loved to have stayed in the shower for an hour, until the hot water ran out and people started banging on the door to tell her to get out, she knew she had to be considerate and leave some hot water for the others. With a family of seven, you couldn't be selfish and use it all yourself. Shivering, Tamara grabbed the closest towel and dried herself off. She realized with dismay that she hadn't brought in any clothes to change into. She only had the makeshift nightshirt she had just taken off. Tamara swallowed and steeled herself. She wrapped the worn towel around her body. It didn't cover much, and wasn't long enough to tuck it back into itself. So holding the towel with one hand, Tamara tucked her shirt under her elbow, and used the other hand to open the door.

Her room was conveniently right across the hall from the bathroom, so she only had to take three steps, and she was safe in her own room again. She heard the click of another door down the hall, and a minute later, the bathroom door closed and the water turned back on. Had whoever was in the shower now seen her in her dash from the bathroom? She hadn't dared to look for anyone. Tamara pulled on her sad little Social-Services-provided outfit and looked for a comb. She found one in the top drawer of the dresser, along with a few other necessities. As she carelessly pulled the comb through her hair to get it in order before it finished drying, Tamara's eyes sought out her reflection in the mirror over the dresser. Did she want a prison hairdo for the first day of school, or something nice, like Deshawn had done for her last night? But the curling iron was in the currently-occupied bathroom.

Trying to breathe calmly through her anxiety, Tamara crossed the hall to the bathroom door. The shower was still running. She knocked on the door and opened it up a couple of inches.

"Can I just get the curling iron?" she asked.

She didn't look toward the shower or the foggy mirror. She just kept her eyes down, waiting for a response.

"Sure, go ahead," a male voice answered. The voice was deep, probably Harry, but Tamara wasn't sure.

She opened the door far enough to rifle through the contents of the vanity and the baskets underneath, and found the curling iron, a brush, and some hairspray. Tamara retreated from the warm, misty bathroom and hurried back to her own room.

(ii)

Breakfast at juvie was served promptly at six and was over at six thirty, so by the time Tamara was finished styling her hair, she was starving. She went down to the kitchen to see what she could find to eat. Mr. Henson—Jesse—was eating a bowl of cereal on the kitchen island, reading through a newspaper. Tamara stopped short. He must have heard her footsteps on the stairs, though, because he looked up at her and smiled.

"Come on in, don't be shy," he invited.

Tamara approached cautiously, not getting too close. She knew foster dads. She'd dealt with a foster dad. But she'd learned how to protect herself in juvie. How to be careful and not leave herself open.

"You're an early riser," Jesse observed, dropping his eyes back down to his newspaper and taking another bite of cereal.

Tamara watched him for any change in attitude, any extra watchfulness. He glanced up again, then back down at his paper.

"There's juice in the fridge. Cereal and bread in the cupboard," he pointed. "Coffee's fresh."

"Thanks," Tamara said.

She kept an eye on him while she opened a couple of cupboards to locate the mugs, and poured herself a cup of coffee. Tamara inhaled the soothing aroma while she waited for it to cool down a bit. Perhaps Jesse could feel her gaze, because he looked up at her expectantly, eyebrows up. Tamara looked away.

"Sorry," she said. "I'm a bit dopey. Still getting the engine started."

He chuckled.

"Did you sleep well?"

"Well... okay, I guess. The bed is really comfy and everything. It's just..."

"Somewhere new," Jesse finished for her, nodding. "That's perfectly understandable. It will take a while before it feels natural. Like home."

"Yeah."

Tamara wondered if she would ever feel like this was home. She had been warned that parole wouldn't be easy. She knew inmates who had been back within a week of being released. Some had intended to follow the rules, and slipped. Some had never intended to follow any rules. She remembered when Mitchell had come back. Tamara had thought that she would make it. Mitchell was tough, one of the few who had managed to survive juvie without getting in with one of the gangs. She was strong-willed, and made it known that once she got out, she wasn't going to be back. She would do whatever it took to stay on the right side of the law and make a life for herself. A straight, honest life.

On her return, Mitchell's dark eyes were underscored by shadows. She looked almost haunted.

"I just couldn't do it," she told Tamara, as they both stood at the sinks in the restroom. "I felt so… exposed. I didn't belong out there."

She had held up a convenience store at knife point. With no mask. In full view of the security cameras. Not because she needed money, but because she wanted to go back. Back where she belonged.

Tamara sipped her coffee. She considered what else she might want for breakfast. Her stomach was still growling. She wasn't going to be able to make it to lunch on a cup of coffee. She was used to a full breakfast at juvie.

With another careful look at Jesse, she went over to the cupboard that he had pointed out, and got herself Cheerios and a slice of bread, which she threw into the bright red toaster on the counter. She prepared the cereal and started to eat, leaning against the counter and waiting for the toast to pop.

"You can eat at the table," Jesse said. "You don't have to eat standing up just because I am."

Tamara didn't move. He didn't pursue it. She and Jesse continued to eat in silence. Mrs. Henson joined them as Tamara moved on to her toast, searching the fridge for some jam.

"You're up early," Mrs. Henson observed. "Couldn't sleep?"

Tamara nodded. She moved to the dining table as Mrs. Henson entered the kitchen, feeling crowded, anxious at both foster parents being in such close proximity. Mrs. Henson gave her a smile and got herself a cup of coffee. Tamara took a few quick bites of her toast and then laid the remainder down.

"Sorry, I took too much," she said. She dumped the toast in the garbage and slotted the plate away in the dishwasher. Then she retreated to her room.

As Tamara got upstairs, Deshawn was knocking on the bathroom door.

"Come on, Jason! Time's up! There's a line-up out here."

She smiled widely at Tamara as she waited for a response.

"Hey, girl," she greeted. "Go on in." She gestured toward her own bedroom. "Help yourself to whatever you need. Nita's awake, she's just playing possum."

Tamara hesitated.

"Go ahead," Deshawn pressed. "You going to go to school without putting your face on?"

Tamara had no experience with makeup, but she knew most of the other girls at school would probably be wearing it, and she didn't want to look any more different than she had to. So she nodded and went into the bedroom, tapping lightly on the door before she went in.

Nita didn't play possum, but propped herself up on her elbow, yawning.

"Mornin' sunshine."

"Hey. Deshawn said…"

"Yeah, of course. Help yourself to whatever you see. Except that orange scarf over there," Nita nodded at it. "That one's calling to me this morning."

"I'm kind of sick of wearing orange," Tamara said.

Nita snorted. "You don't say," she said with a giggle.

Tamara looked over the clutter of accessories on top of the dresser. She tried on a couple of necklaces before settling on one with a large, brassy sun-and-moon medal on it. She put in chunky earrings. She looked at the makeup and didn't know what to do with any of it.

"You want some help?" Nita offered.

Tamara hesitated, not wanting to owe Nita anything. She felt vulnerable letting anyone help her. Nita sat up and swung her feet over the side of the bed. She stretched and stood up.

"Why don't you sit?" she suggested, motioning to the chair in front of the small mirror and pile of makeup.

Tamara sat down. Nita started pawing through the makeup, sorting out what she wanted to use. Without further discussion, she started by applying some moisturizing cream. Then she brushed on some blush.

"Is everyone always so nice and perfect around here?" Tamara asked, watching Nita's actions in the mirror.

Nita laughed.

"We're far from perfect. We still have our fights and rough spots. But…" She paused while she moved onto selecting a shade of eye shadow. "We've all been there. Moving into a new home. Starting over again. Trying to figure out your place. First day of school. It works better if you're nice to newcomers rather than getting all territorial. A lot less grief."

"Oh."

As if to underscore her words about not being perfect, Deshawn pounded on the bathroom door, yelling at Jason again to quit being inconsiderate and get his bony butt out of the bathroom. Tamara and Nita laughed.

"And luckily, Deshawn and I both love having sisters to share with. Neither of us grew up with much family."

Tamara was going to nod, but thought better of moving while Nita worked on her.

"Me neither," she agreed.

"Yeah? Well, there you go. Now you've got two sisters who are going to love dressing you up and showing you how to do your makeup."

Tamara studied Nita's face in the mirror. Nita was beautiful. The lines of her face were almost perfect. Her smile was bright and even and could have been an advertisement for a dentist. There was the tiniest shift to the lines of her nose that made Tamara wonder if it had been broken at some point. Without thinking, Tamara touched the bump in her own nose. Nita stopped for a moment and pushed Tamara's hand away.

"Don't you worry about that," she said. "It's not obvious unless you're looking for it."

Tamara put her hand back down again. Nita handed her a tube of lipstick.

"I think you can do this part," she said.

Tamara screwed the lipstick out, and applied it to her lips. She looked at her face, at the overall effect of the makeup. It still looked like her. There was nothing too obvious or stark about the makeup. But her face was softened, more feminine. Framed by the silky blond waves, she could almost be pretty.

Nita was over at the closet, pushing clothes around. She was wearing a long Minnie Mouse nightshirt that reached her calves. She pulled out a couple of button-up shirts.

"Now how about one of these layered over your t-shirt?" she suggested. "I think that would be really cute."

Tamara took one of the shirts from her and pulled it on, then shook her head and took it back off.

"Not really my style," she said.

Nita shrugged.

"You want anything else? Don't be shy, just try on whatever you like."

Tamara joined Nita at the closet, and looked through the offerings. She pulled out a black jacket with silver hardware, and tried it on. Nita looked her over and nodded.

"You like it?" she asked.

"I think so."

"It's yours."

Tamara smoothed it with both hands and nodded, smiling shyly. "Thanks."

(iii)

Neither of the other two girls went to the school that Tamara would be attending, so she was on her own. Mrs. Henson offered to make the proper introductions at the school, but Tamara shook her head.

"Just drop me off," she said. "I can find the office and they'll give me what I need."

She didn't need to look like a little girl who couldn't manage to go to school on her own. She was strong. Mrs. Henson agreed. She drove slowly, pointing out landmarks that would help Tamara to find her way around the neighborhood in the future. Tamara stared out the window, not commenting, her stomach in a tight, sick knot. She was not looking forward to school. Of course she'd gone to all of her classes in juvie—not like she had been given a choice—but public school was not something she was looking forward to.

She checked in at the office, was given a locker, schedule, map, textbooks, and a number of covert looks. She was told who her guidance counselor was and invited to set up an appointment with him any time.

Tamara went to her morning classes, and at lunch went looking for the students' illicit smoking hangout. She had a few cigarettes left over from juvie, but getting her hands on more might be difficult. It didn't take long to find a small knot of students wreathed in smoke. Tamara nodded briefly and cupped her hand around a cigarette to light it. She drew the smoke into her lungs, the tension in her stomach subsiding slightly.

"Sucks being new," one girl offered.

Tamara nodded.

"Especially halfway through the year," she agreed.

"I'm Sybil." She had dyed black hair, a post through her lip and a piercing in her nose. Her makeup was stark, but not goth.

Some of the others offered their names.

"Hi. Tamara."

"You're staying with the Hensons?"

"Yeah." Tamara shifted her feet. "You know 'em?"

"They go through a lot of kids there. Some of them go to school. Some don't."

"Uh-huh."

Since Tamara was not yet sixteen, she didn't have a choice about school attendance yet. It was mandatory. Especially if she wanted to stay out of juvie. One of the boys, slim and pale and wearing a black leather jacket, looked her over curiously.

"So being with the Hensons, does that mean you've been in trouble?" he inquired.

Sybil rolled her eyes.

"Smooth, Jason," she objected. But that didn't stop her from listening with obvious interest for the answer.

Tamara blew out smoke in a thin, white stream. It was a question bound to be on everyone's mind.

"Yeah, I've been in trouble."

"What kind of trouble?"

"I just got out of juvie. Three years. Made parole." Word would get out one way or another. It might as well come from her and at least be accurate to start with. The more she tried to hide her past, the more the rumors would fly.

Jason whistled through his teeth.

"Wow. What for?"

"Murder," Tamara said flatly. No emotion in her voice or expression. Nothing that would show weakness or vulnerability.

"You're pulling my leg. Seriously?" he demanded.

Tamara shrugged. He could interpret the gesture as he liked.

"Who'd you kill?"

"None of your business."

"Some guy who asked too many questions," Sybil teased, and cracked up.

Tamara grinned at Sybil. Jason opened his mouth to ask another question.

"Shut up, Jason," Sybil snapped.

He closed his mouth and rolled his eyes. They continued to smoke. After a few minutes, Jason stepped on his cigarette butt and left. Sybil looked at Tamara.

"You want to walk?"

"Sure."

They walked in silence for a while. Tamara tried to make her cigarette last, not knowing how hard it would be for her to get another pack. In juvie, it was surprisingly easy. Here, she was going to have to get someone who was old enough to buy them for her, once she could get her hands on some money.

"News travels fast," Tamara observed.

"The grapevine is humming away," Sybil agreed. "Some of Henson's kids have made things… interesting around here, so when word gets out that they got someone new—well, the news travels."

"Great."

"Sorry. It'll die down again. Unless you're planning on making a splash."

"I'm not looking for attention."

Sybil nodded. They continued to walk and make small talk.

"So what was it like?" Sybil asked, and at Tamara's questioning look, elaborated. "In juvie."

"Not somewhere you'd like to be."

Sybil waited for more information, but Tamara shook her head and didn't enlighten her.

(iv)

The teacher walked up to Tamara while she was doing her classwork, and put a slip of yellow paper on her desk. Tamara looked down at it, and looked up at the teacher questioningly.

"You're wanted down at the office. That's your hall pass."

Tamara looked at it for a minute, and then closed her books and stacked them up. She picked up the yellow paper and headed out of the room and down the stairs. She got turned around a couple of times, but eventually found her way to the administrative office where she had started her day.

She presented her yellow slip to the gray-haired woman at the reception desk.

"Yes. Tamara," the woman said, looking at the paper as if there was something wrong with it. "You are in conference room B."

Tamara looked around, and the receptionist pointed to a closed door behind her.

"Right there. Go on in."

Tamara wasn't sure what was going on. Was she in trouble for something already? Maybe someone had reported her for smoking. Or maybe it was something they always did at the end of the day when a student transferred mid-term. Checking up to make sure that everything had gone all right. That they had found all of their classes, hadn't had any trouble…

She put her hand on the doorknob. The receptionist had said to go right in, but she didn't feel right about it. Tamara knocked lightly on the door, and opened it, poking her head in. It was a small meeting room, four chairs around a small table. A tall black man sat in one with his long legs stretched out in front of him. He was dressed in a suit. His head was bald, maybe shaved. He smiled, but didn't show any teeth. The smile didn't reach his eyes. His face immediately fell back into a tired, grim look.

"Tamara," he greeted. "Come on in. Shut the door and have a seat."

Tamara obeyed, trying to analyze him. Not the principal. Maybe a counselor, if he'd been a cop in a previous life. He had the air of one of the guards in juvie. Not one of the day-to-day guards, but one of the supervisors or something. Higher up the food chain. More reserved, not as quick to pull out his baton or taser. Tamara sat down in the chair across from the man and waited.

"My name is Chad Collins," he introduced himself. "I'll be your parole officer."

"Oh." Tamara blew out her breath. Now it made sense. She wasn't in trouble. Not yet. This was her new shadow. The man who would be watching for her to fail. "Hi."

"I've read your file, and I think that you can make this transition successfully, if you put your mind to it."

Tamara nodded.

"It will be hard," he went on, "but you can choose to be a different person than you were before you went to juvie. Or while you were at juvie. It's a pivotal time for you. This is your chance to turn things around."

He rubbed his chin, looking down at the slim file in front of him.

"Okay," Tamara said.

"You don't want to be sent back for something stupid. It's important that you understand the terms of your parole."

Tamara nodded again.

"So what…" she started. She cleared her throat and tried to strengthen her wavering voice. "What are the rules?"

He pulled a single sheet out of the file and placed it in front of Tamara.

"Okay, let's go over it." Pointing to the top line, he started out. "I will tell you when and where our meetings are, and you'll be there. On time. Every time. You're living with the Hensons, and you're not allowed to move anywhere else without my say so. You have a nine o'clock curfew. No matter what, you're home by nine o'clock every night. Right?"

"Yes, sir," Tamara agreed.

"No weapons, no alcohol, no drugs. Not on your person, not in your room, not anywhere near you. You don't associate with anyone carrying weapons, alcohol, or drugs. You'll submit to random drug testing. Whenever I say. On the spot. You are not allowed to be around anyone who has been convicted of a felony."

"What if…"

"No one. No 'what ifs'. It doesn't matter if you knew them in juvie, before juvie, or met them since. No criminal associations."

"Okay." Tamara nodded.

"You're not allowed to be around young children. No one under six. And you'll attend mandatory counseling at least weekly."

"Yes, sir," Tamara said. "What kind of counseling?"

"Something to help to ease the transition, give you the skills that you need to stay clean outside of juvie. Anger and stress management. Addictions counseling, if you need it. Anything that I or your therapist decide that you need."

Tamara nodded and swallowed.

"Okay."

"Do you have any questions?"

"No, sir."

"What are you going to do if you think of questions? If you're not sure about something?"

She continued to stare at the paper in front of her.

"I guess I call you," she said.

"That's right." He pointed to his contact details at the bottom of the page. "Do you have a cell phone yet?"

"No."

"When you get one, you put me on your number one speed dial. I'm the person you call if you have any questions."

"Yes, sir."

"What if you slip up and break a rule, what do you do?" he demanded.

Tamara picked at the skin around her nails, hiding them under the table.

"Fix it," she suggested. "Don't do it again."

"The first thing you do is call me. You report yourself. 'Mr. Collins, someone offered me a beer and I was stupid enough to drink it.' 'Mr. Collins, I was ten minutes late for curfew.' 'Mr. Collins, a friend from juvie called me up, but I hung up on her.' Any violation, no matter how big or small. You call me. Got it?"

"Yes, sir."

"Things will be much worse if I hear it from someone else, or it shows up in a drug test or something. Tell me, and you might not get sent back to juvie."

"Okay."

Tamara had an overwhelming desire to bite her nails, and it was only with a huge exercise of will that she was able to keep her hands in her lap, hidden, away from her face, still picking at the cuticles.

"What if you have some other kind of problem?" he questioned.

Tamara looked up at his face, the slight flare of his nostrils and curl of his lip.

"Call you?" she suggested.

He nodded.

"Now you're getting it," he agreed.

Tamara mirrored his nod. Neither one of them said anything for a while, and Tamara eventually looked back up at Collins again, wondering what else she was in for.

"How was your first day?" he asked.

Tamara relaxed a little in her seat, letting out a pent-up breath.

"Okay. Not bad. The Hensons all seem really nice."

"They're a good family," Collins agreed. "They've dealt with a lot of tough cases. Everything is pretty calm there now, and I'm hoping that you won't make things too difficult for them. Give them a bit of a rest."

"I don't plan on getting in any trouble."

"Good. But it can be harder than you would think. These things are rarely planned. But temptations show up, catch you at a weak moment. You feel loyal to a friend or family member and think nobody will know, nobody will get hurt."

"I don't do drugs," Tamara said. "Or drink. I never even had a cigarette before juvie."

He studied her, eyes narrowed slightly. Tamara felt the need to defend herself further. She might not care what the kids at school or the Hensons thought, but she thought her parole officer ought to know what kind of a person she was.

"I'm not a troublemaker," she said. "You look at my juvie file. Or my school records before… before it happened. I never got in any kind of trouble. Ever."

Collins rubbed his chin, his dark eyes boring into her.

"You have admitted to the murders more than once. In court and to the parole board."

"Yes."

"What does *that* say about you?"

Tamara stared back down at the paper again. She picked at her cuticles under the table.

"It was a bad situation," she said. "I was trapped, and hurt, and the hormones… made me so foggy and emotional. I didn't know what to do. I know it doesn't make sense when you say it like that, but I was so… confused."

There was silence from Collins at first.

"This time," he said finally, "you have someone to talk to. You're not alone."

Tamara looked at him again. His voice was low, almost gentle.

"Call me," he said, tapping the piece of paper with the eraser end of his pencil. "For any reason."

"Okay. Thanks."

Tamara nodded. She felt very teary and emotional all of a sudden, and she didn't like it. She couldn't let her guard down. Couldn't make herself vulnerable. Collins' lips pressed together in a thin line for a moment, then the look vanished. Collins unfolded himself from the chair, towering over her. Tamara scrambled to get to her feet. He offered his hand, and Tamara shook it, feeling a bit awkward.

"Call me tomorrow before curfew," he instructed.

Tamara nodded.

He was still holding her hand, and looked down at it. Tamara saw that her fingers were bleeding around the nails, and pulled her hand out of his grasp, hiding it behind her back.

"I'm not the enemy, Tamara," Collins said. He sighed. "I'll get you in to see the therapist as soon as possible. Transition and stress management. You'll go."

"Yes, sir."

"Talk to you tomorrow, then."

Tamara nodded, and he left the room. The door swung shut behind him, clicking softly into place. Tamara put her hands over her face and tried to calm and compose herself. She was tough. She could manage it. She'd show Chad Collins that she wasn't like any of his other parolees. He didn't know her. She could make it.

~

TATTOOED TEARDROPS, Book #1 of the *Tamara's Teardrops* series by P.D. Workman can be purchased at pdworkman.com

ABOUT THE AUTHOR

Award-winning and USA Today bestselling author P.D. (Pamela) Workman writes riveting mystery/suspense and young adult books dealing with mental illness, addiction, abuse, and other real-life issues. For as long as she can remember, the blank page has held an incredible allure and from a very young age she was trying to write her own books.

Workman wrote her first complete novel at the age of twelve and continued to write as a hobby for many years. She started publishing in 2013. She has won several literary awards from Library Services for Youth in Custody for her young adult fiction. She currently has over 70 published titles and can be found at pdworkman.com.

Born and raised in Alberta, Workman has been married for over 25 years and has one son.

~

Please visit P.D. Workman at pdworkman.com to see what else she is working on, to join her mailing list, and to link to her social networks.

~

If you enjoyed this book, please take the time to recommend it to other purchasers with a review or star rating and share it with your friends!

facebook.com/pdworkmanauthor

twitter.com/pdworkmanauthor

instagram.com/pdworkmanauthor

amazon.com/author/pdworkman

bookbub.com/authors/p-d-workman

goodreads.com/pdworkman

linkedin.com/in/pdworkman

pinterest.com/pdworkmanauthor

youtube.com/pdworkman